Color
Me In

Color Me In

a Novel

Natasha Díaz

DELACORTE PRESS

Text copyright © 2019 by Natasha Díaz
Jacket art copyright © 2019 by Bijou Karman

All rights reserved. Published in the United States by Delacorte Press, an imprint of Random House Children's Books, a division of Penguin Random House LLC, New York.

Delacorte Press is a registered trademark and the colophon is a trademark of Penguin Random House LLC.

Visit us on the Web! GetUnderlined.com

Educators and librarians, for a variety of teaching tools, visit us at RHTeachersLibrarians.com

Library of Congress Cataloging-in-Publication Data
Names: Díaz, Natasha (Natasha E.), author.
Title: Color me in / Natasha Díaz.
Description: First edition. | New York : Delacorte Press, [2019] | Summary: Fifteen-year-old Nevaeh Levitz is torn between two worlds, passing for white while living in Harlem, being called Jewish while attending her mother's Baptist church, and experiencing first love while watching her parents' marriage crumble.
Identifiers: LCCN 20180447991 (print) | LCCN 2018052933 (ebook) | ISBN 978-0-525-57824-6 (ebook) | ISBN 978-0-525-57823-9 (trade hc)
Subjects: | CYAC: Coming of age—Fiction. | Racially mixed people—Fiction. | Prejudices—Fiction. | Jews—United States—Fiction. | African Americans—New York (State)—New York—Fiction. | Family problems—Fiction. | Harlem (New York, N.Y.)—Fiction. | New York (N.Y.)—Fiction.
Classification: LCC PZ7.1.D499 (ebook) | LCC PZ7.1.D499 Col 2019 (print) | DDC [Fic]—dc23

The text of this book is set in 11-point Bembo.
Interior design by Trish Parcell

Printed in the United States of America

10 9 8 7 6 5 4 3 2 1
First Edition

For my Vovó and Pa,

Zuleika Ivelone Vaz Andrade Santos Thomas

&

David Meserve Thomas.

Without your courage to love one another despite all the odds,

I wouldn't be,

and neither would these words.

Prologue

One. Two. Three. Four. Six. Seven.

Squirrels dart back and forth across the park, so I count them, anything to distract myself from how bad I have to pee. The line is taking forever, but I'm not going to have an accident, not when we finally made it up to the front.

"Excuse me?" a syrup-sweet voice asks my mom as we shuffle an inch closer to the tire swing. "My daughter is riding the swing alone too, and I've got to take the roast out of the slow cooker. . . . I was wondering if they could go together."

"Sure," my mom agrees.

The lady bends down to me, meeting my gaze with Cinderella-ball-gown-blue eyes.

"Well, aren't you just the prettiest thing?" she says. "How old are you?"

I look up at my mom for permission to talk to a stranger. She nods.

"Six," I say, holding up the fingers to confirm.

"Five," my mom corrects.

The woman laughs like we told the best joke in the whole wide world.

"They're such a riot at this age, aren't they?" she says.

"Sure are," my mom says, remaining friendly enough not to be rude, but monosyllabic so as not to invite further conversation.

The lady points at her daughter. "That's my Samantha," she says. I see a small, pale girl whose light yellow hair is so fine it looks like silver thread in the sun.

"They're only a year apart. Maybe I could get your number for a playdate? I so need a break sometimes. How long have you been nannying? She is so well behaved; her parents must love you."

The lady talks a mile a minute as she rummages through her bag, unearthing pacifiers and baggies filled with Cheerios.

"Aha!" She holds up an index card with crayon all over it and writes her name and number before handing it to my mom.

The line of exhausted parents waiting behind us starts to grumble; it is our turn. The woman hoists Samantha onto her shoulder like a rag doll and walks past us to put her on the tire.

My mom crumples the index card and it hits the ground like a dry leaf. She begins to walk toward the swing, but I don't move. This isn't the first time someone has said my mom is my nanny. In fact, it happens so often that I have begun to get concerned.

"Mommy, are you really my mommy?" I ask, distressed.

My voice projects much louder than I intended, and everyone in the park turns to stare, even the blue-eyed lady. Their eyes burn through my sweater like angry moths and I lose the last bit of control I had over my bladder. Hot pee trails down my legs as I shake, terrified as to what my mom's answer will be.

My mother's golden-brown skin glows, illuminated by the sun that streams through the branches of the trees overhead. When she bends down, I see her lips quiver. She cups my face and her thumbs rub my soft, whitish cheeks, as if the gentle sweeping motion is all I need to clear the pain away.

"I'm your mommy," she says.

And then she drags me out of the park before I get a chance to ride the swing.

Chapter 1

I have lived trapped in that moment ever since.
In the dreaded ambiguity
That follows me everywhere I go.
Even here,
In this grimy mirror,
and bitter fluorescent glow.

The electric hiss, like bees caught in a plastic casing, sends shock waves from the sterile lightbulbs in the bathroom of Mount Olivene Baptist Church. The sound travels over the damp off-white tiles, back to my reflection in a mirror so streaked and blurred with soap scum my skin almost blends into the walls behind me. If it weren't for the burst of brown freckles that swarm around my nose and across my cheekbones, I'd be the way I am most of the time: invisible—swallowed up whole by the imaginary bugs and the all-encompassing beige.

Cloudy Pepto-Bismol-pink gel squirts onto me like projectile vomit from the rusted soap dispenser and sends a foamy streak across my light yellow shirt. I go to grab a handful of waxy paper towels piled up on the side of the sink and bump my phone and church program, which I've covered with poetry scribbles, sending them to the ground.

"Damn it!"

My shout echoes through the empty space and I stand with my eyes pinched shut, ready for Jesus Christ to float into the ladies' room and smite me for using foul language in his house. But no one comes. The organ upstairs begins to play, accompanied by the choir. They drag these hymns out for like, twenty minutes. Four sentences that repeat over and over and over, gaining in volume and excitement and conviction with each go-around.

Take me to the water
Take me to the water
Take me to the water
There to be baptized

This is the song before closing remarks. I need to get moving before the Gray Lady Gang rushes in here for their weekly gossip session, which, for the record, is way scarier than the reincarnation of the lord and savior.

Every Sunday, the posse of eighty- to one-hundred-year-old ladies shows up in matching skirt suits and refined wigs, ready to talk shit and bully folks in the name of Christ. The whole congregation knows that they kick out anyone who dares use the bathroom during their regularly scheduled meeting with a swat of a cane and a glare so rigid that their victim is liable to cross over right here in the bathroom.

"Did you see what she had the nerve to wear today, Eveline?

She's a two-bit hussy, if you ask me. Stuffed into that getup like a breakfast sausage . . ."

Their raspy voices rush under the bathroom door with the breeze from the fans in the hallway. I'm too late.

Currently, the talk of the town is Miss Clarisse, a woman in her sixties who owns a clothing boutique that specializes in form-fitting, outlandish attire best reserved for '90s Lil' Kim videos. She is back on the prowl for love after her fling with Pastor Davis ended abruptly a few weeks ago—the Grays threatened to circulate a petition for his retirement, deeming it inappropriate for a community leader to be seen with her in public. Miss Clarisse isn't exactly helping her case, showing up to church every Sunday in outfits so tight it's a miracle when she doesn't pop right out of them.

Their murmurs move closer, so eager to dive into the juicy updates that they can't even wait to get inside the room. The pounding from their thick heels against the floor counts down to our impending faceoff. I have to save myself.

I burst through the door just before they arrive and walk past them without making eye contact as I rush to the stairs.

"Humph!" grunts the oldest and roughest GLG member, Miss Eveline. Her straight, chin-length black wig sways ever so slightly under a wide-brimmed lavender hat adorned with netting and an embroidered silver rose.

"They can't be satisfied takin' our houses, now these white folks got to come up here into our churches too?" Oretha, a light-skinned woman who is the tallest and spriteliest in the bunch, asks.

Miss Eveline smacks Oretha's hand with a guttural "Shush!"

"That there is Nevaeh, Pastor Paire's granddaughter," Miss Eveline says. "The Jewish one," I hear, before the bathroom door closes behind them with a sharp click.

7

Chapter 2

I quietly enter our row with my arms crossed over my chest to cover the gigantic wet spot. Anything to avoid attracting attention.

Stand. Clap. Praise. Sit.

Every week it's the same. I could handle the idea of church on special occasions, but every Sunday? My dad believes organized religion is for people who are weak and lazy, which is why they would rather listen to burning bushes and holy ghosts for direction than to logic. For the most part, Daddy only claims his Jewishness as an excuse to avoid spending time with my mom's religious Baptist family or to get his own mother, who goes by "Bubby," and tries to force us to go to temple all the time—sometimes under threat of death—off his back.

"It's not about being Jewish, honey. It's about being a Levitz," he says after he pulls Bubby off the proverbial ledge and sends her home in a cab. I always try to ask him, "What does that mean? How can I be a Levitz without being Jewish?" But he just shakes his head and changes the subject. After a while, it got easier to not even try to figure it out.

My phone lights up in my lap. The screensaver I set up is a slideshow of photos chosen at random. This one is from a year ago. I should have deleted it. We were barbecuing, and my dad teased my mother by waving a chicken wing in her face. (She hates them, but I can't understand why—they are so delicious.) He chased her around with it and we were all laughing.

"Ow!"

Clawlike nails plunge into the back of my arm. I put pressure on the angry half-moon indents on my pale skin, punishment for having my phone out during services. Sundays used to be fun and easy and dependable, but that's all in the past now. Since my parents' separation, nothing is the same.

Stand. Clap. Praise. Sit.

Done.

A sharp voice accosts me.

"Nevaeh, are you hungry? I *said,* are you hungry?" my auntie Anita yells, repeating herself for the power effect.

Auntie Anita is bossy. She has three kids and says if you aren't direct, nothing gets done, but I think it's just in her nature to tell people what to do. She and my mom couldn't look less like siblings if they tried. Anita's skin is darker than my mom's golden brown, and she is almost five inches taller, not to mention the half foot added by the pile of twists that sit in a perfect heap on top of her head.

"Corinne?"

The natural crevices that outline each muscle under my aunt's deep brown skin are on display as she grabs my mom's shoulder.

My mom sits beside us with her head in the clouds. She's petite, only five foot three, but regal. Her hair is pulled into a tight ballerina bun without so much as a baby hair out of place. Her eyes keep wandering down to her hand, where she fumbles with her wedding ring. I get it. I had braces for a few years, and mid-conversation my tongue would just drift over them like a magnet—there's something about that mixture of metal and rubber covered in slimy spit. It's weird, but the constant motion soothed me.

"Girl!" my aunt yells, failing to pop whatever bubble my mom is lost in.

Death would be less painful than the embarrassment from the glare of every person in the church as my aunt, irritated, sucks her teeth so loudly that the angels in the stained-glass windows join in on the judgment.

"Come on, let's get Pa out of here before these old ladies smother him to death with their questions. It's not like he's got a direct line to Jesus. Nevaeh, go find your cousins and walk back to the house. It's our turn to drive Miss Eveline home, and Lord knows we won't have room for you all with her electric wheel-chair in there." She charges through the parishioners, dragging my mom along toward Pa's shiny smooth head.

My grandfather stands out among the wide-brimmed Sunday hats and colorful silk scarves donned by the gaggle of women who listlessly wave paper fans around their faces, fighting off the deadly forces of menopause and global warming.

"Nevaeh, how you doin' this Sunday?" Miss Clarisse intercepts me in her bright red pleather pantsuit. Her unseemly character was no doubt the cause of my aunt's quick departure.

I smile and silently fight my urge to look down at her cleavage, which jiggles with each word that rumbles out of her.

"I'm fine," I whisper.

"Damn, you're quiet!" she yells through a wave of people who shake their heads as they walk by.

She takes me by the shoulder and spins me around.

"Why don't you come down to my shop? We'll get you into some fine dresses and have you look real nice for church next Sunday. Your mama's taste is a little . . . dry after living in the suburbs with all those white folks for so long. Bring her with you and we'll get you both some attention from a brotha."

She smiles, but her voice betrays her desperation. Her shop is thirty years old, and the storefronts around here are getting picked off and sold one-by-one to the H&Ms and Zaras of the world.

"All right," I say, and allow myself to get caught up in the crowd.

I've got to keep moving. My cousins, Janae, Jordan, and Jericho, always sit with the youth group on Sundays, at the farthest end of the room.

"Nevaeh!"

Jericho, who goes by Jerry, is always excited to see me, as if I didn't just move in with him a couple months ago. His mini-fro bobs along with him as he makes his way toward me to give me a hug. I squeeze his cheek. Jerry recently went through a preteen growth spurt, but it turned out to be horizontal rather than vertical.

"Jerry, can you get Jordan and Janae?" I ask. "We have to walk back."

We turn to the crowd of kids who orbit around my older fraternal-twin cousins, protecting them like keepers in a quidditch match. Jerry looks at me, terrified.

"Fine, I'll do it. Stay here," I say, irritated and anxious as I walk toward them.

Janae looks up and nods at me as I approach. She sees

everything, a skill she likely gets from Anita, although that's about it in terms of their similarities. Janae has this avant-garde vibe that makes her both intimidating and alluring at the same time. She takes after her father, with eyes so big and brown you're likely to get lost in them. Janae rarely pipes up unless she really has something to say, unlike Jordan, who has something to say at all times about everything.

"Ever heard of an iron?" Jordan says judgily, tugging on my wrinkled shirt. "You remember everyone, right?"

Her friends nod. We've done this every week—the same song and dance around Jordan and Janae having to explain to their friends why I only just started coming to church, why I'm not in youth group, why I can't tan, and why my last name sounds like a brand of matzo ball soup.

"Your mom said we have to walk back. They don't have any room in the car," I explain sheepishly.

Jordan sucks her teeth as loudly as Anita, so I back up a few steps to give her and Janae space to say bye to their friends.

Jordan is Anita's carbon copy, the younger twin by a whole fifteen minutes—a fact she will never let Janae forget (like either of them had a conscious choice in the matter when they were barreling toward the birth canal).

"How long do you think until dinner?" Jerry asks, as if he didn't have eggs and waffles a few hours ago.

No one has answered him when the youth group organizer, Darnell, guilts us into gathering the pamphlets out of the pews just as we head toward the door. Darnell is a twenty-something social activist and a Harlem celebrity, famous for being on the front lines of all local community affairs and for always wearing some sort of political accessory. Today he has a pin on his lapel with a raised black fist on a white background.

His long dreads fall down his back, tied together with a colorful scrap of fabric, and make a swishing noise as he walks. Darnell has that untouchable artistic swagger that makes every word that comes out of his mouth sound like a call for a revolution. It also doesn't hurt that he is the type of Michael B. Jordan handsome that makes me go hot and dizzy every time I look at him.

"Nevaeh, have you thought any more about joining the youth group?" he asks, walking through the aisles behind me. "It's not so much about religion as it is about community."

I know he's trying to make me feel welcome, but the last thing I need is to join a Christian youth group, no matter how inclusive it is.

"Not really," I say, rubbing my cheeks to make an excuse for the reddening caused by his smile.

Jordan looks over but returns to gathering pamphlets as soon as I catch her eye; I'd bet fifty dollars that she, along with everyone else, has a thing for Darnell.

"Well, you are always welcome, even just to sit and observe."

I smile and nod, hoping that will appease him.

"Oh, and, Nevaeh, I think you dropped this."

He hands me a program covered in my chicken scratch—I must have dropped it running away from the Grays.

I snatch it back.

"This is some powerful stuff. Let me know if you change your mind."

Writing is the only thing that has ever made sense to me. It's how I deal with all the feelings and thoughts I don't know how to talk about. But I don't share my writing, not with anyone. I mean, Stevie has basically been my only real friend since I was five, and even he hasn't seen anything I have written.

"I'm so hungry, I think I'm going to die!" Jerry whines, as if

13

he ran the length of the city carrying a boulder rather than walking within a hundred-foot radius picking up paper.

We look up to Darnell for permission to go, and he nods, so we bounce before he can think of any additional chores.

Outside, we get hit with the thick, sticky New York late-August heat. It's like when you hold something greasy and then try to wash it off, but somehow the mixture of water and soap and oil turns into this terrible paste. Except in this instance, the greasy film now covers your whole body and everywhere you turn smells like pee.

The church is only twelve blocks from the house, but nothing moves quickly in Harlem.

My cousins greet almost every person we pass on the street, accepting compliments on their attire and Pa's sermon. The passersby pinch Jerry's cheeks and smile at me awkwardly, unsure whether I expect to be addressed or just happen to be here by coincidence.

I wonder sometimes what it would have been like if I had grown up in the city and gone to church every Sunday like I have this summer. Maybe I would know the songs and clap along. Maybe I would hold hands with the other congregants and leave with a sense of purpose. Maybe I would walk through Harlem, comfortable in the loud chaos of the streets, and smile at everyone I pass rather than avoiding eye contact.

Maybe it would feel like home.

We stop at Lucia's, a Dominican-owned beauty salon a few blocks from our house, to look at the faded posters of models plastered to the window with layers of yellowing Scotch tape. Inside, women in hair rollers sit under massive hair-dryer domes that make them look like aliens. They cackle as they pass around the pastries they swiped from their church potlucks before heading to Lucia's for their weekly group therapy session. I watch Jordan and Janae scan the styles with their eyes—they have photographic memory when it comes to hair, especially Janae. Today she has thick box braids with metal cuffs placed randomly throughout, like little bursts of glitter woven into her masterpiece.

I take my hair out of the messy bun that I always wear it in and shake it out. The mop of loose brown curls spreads across my shoulders and down my back.

"Hey, Ney, how come you've got down hair?" Jerry asks.

"What's that?"

"It's just what he used to call people in shampoo commercials when he was young," Janae swoops in.

"And?" I probe.

"And white people, when they take their hair out of a ponytail or a bun . . . it falls down," Jordan says matter-of-factly.

Jerry jumps back in, irritated to have his older sisters speak for him.

"Yours does too, Nevaeh. It falls down!"

"My hair is different than yours. I can't just oscillate between styles like your sisters," I snap.

"*Aw-si* . . . ," Jerry tries to sound out the syllables.

"You don't have to use your big words to make him feel dumb, Ney. You know he didn't mean anything by it. Plus, it's true. You do have white-people hair," Jordan claps back.

Jerry stares up at me, sorry that he upset me, even if he has no clue why. He doesn't know I've gone to bed every night wishing I had hair like theirs, thick and vibrant, like a piece of art unique to their people. (My people?)

There is a poster in the salon window at my eye level, some

'90s female hip-hop group with relaxed, asymmetrical bobs—the hairstyle is terrible. I point to it.

"What about this, Jer? Do you think I could rock this?"

Jerry giggles, distracted and happy again.

"Let's keep it moving," Jordan says, so we do.

On the corner of our block we pass a group of guys. One of them, tall and sexy, calls out, "Yo, J!"

All three of my cousins look at him, but I can tell it's Jordan he's calling. She can tell too, and her smile stretches for miles.

"When you gonna introduce me to Lightskin?" he asks flirtatiously.

Jordan's face falls to her toes. I've got the only thing close to "light skin" in our family, an off-white blip amid a stunning array of deep chestnut and mahogany.

His muscles are hard to ignore. They flex as he holds his arms out in front of him to spray his face with the type of bottle that my mom uses to water plants.

Jordan storms off without answering, leaving the cute guy behind.

Janae grabs my arm to stop me from going after her. "She's just salty because she's been hoping all summer that he would ask her out."

Janae nods in the direction of the cute guy, who's still staring at me in a way that makes my intestines twist and tighten around each other. I look away. If I get stabbed by Jordan's piercing glare again, I may not survive.

We spot my aunt out on the stoop with her sunglasses on, scanning the street like she's sure something is about to go down.

"Where have you all been? We've been waiting for years!" Anita yells.

"Coming!" my cousins chirp back in unison, and hurry toward her, unfazed by the casual absurdity of her accusation.

I slow my pace and allow enough distance to grow between us.

Sounds from the small homegrown churches built in brownstone basements cascade from each corner of the block. Most of the old Harlem has already been reborn into a whiter, watereddown version of itself, but every once in a while, I stumble across a snapshot of what I imagine it used to be. Pa told me that these are some of the last churches in the city that still hold a second service on Sunday, which means it's only a matter of time before they disappear as well, but not today. Today, the choirs from these underground sanctuaries sing with such power that you wouldn't know their time is numbered.

Standing there alone, I evaporate into the music as it makes its way through the heat like a desperately needed breeze, cooling the dehydrated street with sounds of the past.

Chapter 3

My grandpa bought this brownstone fifty years ago and renovated the whole thing himself. It's been maintained in perfect condition because my uncle Ezekiel is a carpenter and can fix just about anything.

Every inch of the place is covered in photos, most of which are of my mom and Anita from their childhood. It's easy for me to get lost in the images, the only access I have to their past. Anita's white teeth shine through the huge smile that she flashes in every photo, declaring her fierceness with a proud, blinding gaze.

My mom used to wear her hair natural when she was young. She had curls so huge they looked like the spiral slides at the playground, but as she moved into her teenage years, she began to flatten her hair, straight and smooth, until it eventually ended up on top of her head in a tight, round knot that holds her together and upright. At the end of the first wall of the living room, my grandmother hugs my mom on the day of her high school graduation. My mom's scowl is half hidden under the red cap and tassel, but Grandma smiles like Anita, a cosmic blast, only bigger and brighter.

It is the only way I knew my grandmother to be: unwilling to waste a single moment of life on anything but joy. She came to America from Jamaica when she was in her twenties, wooed by my grandfather and the thrill of adventure. The void since she left the world five years ago hurts like a hole punch perforating my heart.

Images of Jerry, Janae, and Jordan continue the photo gallery. This next chapter of our history surrounds the prominently displayed photo of Barack and Michelle Obama, who watch over us with love.

I am represented as well. My photos from kindergarten to high school are lined up in chronological order on top of the smooth, recently polished china cabinet; it's a spot in the hallway that leads to the dining room from the kitchen. The space is isolated, as if there was nowhere I fit, so they decided I'd be best left on my own.

Delicious smells waft out of the kitchen, where Uncle Zeke is putting the final touches on dinner. Zeke doesn't go to church, so on Sundays, when everyone else heads to service, he cooks the family a proper supper. His parents forced him to go when he was younger, but the minute he turned eighteen, he stopped. No one is allowed to ask him why or even talk about it.

Dinner is always the same: broiled salmon steaks, green beans, mac and cheese, and biscuits.

"You all pray in the pews," Zeke says, "but I make the gospel in the kitchen."

Ezekiel is really big. Like should-have-played-football-or-become-a-bodybuilder big, and the huge platters of food he carries through the door look featherlight in his monstrous hands. All eight of us appear around the table right as the dishes touch down, summoned by the scent of familiarity and cheesy goodness. But before we can dig in, we have to engage in a carefully choreographed dance of extension cords and fan placement.

Pa has yet to enter the twenty-first century and refuses to outfit the building with air-conditioning (he claims the cold air brings sickness), so we each carry around a fan to plug in next to us wherever we end up.

An empty chair sits next to Pa. He hasn't stopped setting a place for Grandma since her passing. Secretly, I like that she still has a spot at the table, but I've heard Anita say she thinks it's unhealthy.

Once we're all settled, we bow our heads as Pa prays.

"Make us thankful for this food and bless it to the nourishment and strengthening of our bodies, in Christ's name we pray, Amen."

The hum of the fans mellows the clanking plates and scraping forks as everyone digs in. Jerry gets through his first helping so quickly that it's possible he might have just swallowed everything whole, in direct opposition to Pa, who chews each bite of food to the point of disintegration because he claims it's better for his digestion.

"Jerry, we are approaching the next stage of your manhood, eleven, your final year of primary school. What do you expect to gain from your studies?" Pa asks in his deep, gravelly voice. He enunciates each syllable with the same care he took to choose each word. Pa's parents were descendants of slaves in North Carolina who became missionaries and moved to Liberia during the Back-to-Africa movement to start a school and family in the late 1890s. Growing up, Pa learned that it was of the utmost importance that he present himself in a formal and proper manner, a belief he has maintained into his eighty-sixth year.

"I heard that the classroom has a pet and each kid gets to take it home for a weekend," Jerry answers, between shoveling food into his mouth. "I think it's an iguana."

We all roll our eyes. It'll be a cold day in hell when Anita allows a reptile into this house.

"Mama, I need you to sign the consent form for the college trip," Jordan pipes up. "I saved my half of the four hundred dollars, and it's filling up."

Jordan tries to look confident as she confronts her mother in front of an audience, but Anita stares her down with such intensity that I almost expect her to combust.

"Auntie! You went to that fancy school, didn't you?" Jordan pleads with my mother for backup.

My mom gives a barely visible nod of support.

"Tell her, Auntie! Tell her it's worth the money! It's an investment in my future!"

Nobody moves. You don't talk about money in front of other people, even family, not in this house; it's one of the rules.

"What are you looking at?" Jordan barks in my direction. "Not all of us have rich Daddy's credit card number memorized—"

"We'll discuss this later." Anita silences Jordan and points her fork at me. "So, Nevaeh, sophomore year. Do you have to decide on a foreign language? Janae and Jordan take Spanish."

My face burns with embarrassment at the unexpected spotlight, but Zeke jumps at the chance to take the stage.

"Sophomore year! I remember it like yesterday. Patrick Ewing was out with an injury after game two of the finals. Latrell Sprewell was killin' it, but he just couldn't cut it against the Spurs." He shakes his head with such disdain you would think a family member had passed away unexpectedly—such is the tragic life of a die-hard Knicks fan.

Uncle Zeke loves to talk, especially if he can throw in some vintage NBA facts, which he always finds a way to do.

"That was the year I was going to make it onto that debate team if it killed me," he recalls with fondness. "The team took a trip to Washington, DC, and that meant you got to miss half a week of school going to museums and seeing the sights. I had to go down there and let them know to get ready for Zeke Thomas!" He stops to take a sip of water.

"So you made it happen? You made it onto the team?" Janae asks.

"No," Anita interjects. "But I did."

My uncle winks at Anita and Janae laughs, unaware of how lucky she is to have parents in a loving marriage. They are so happy it's sickening—high school sweethearts, Anita and Zeke are something out of an unmade '80s Brat Pack movie with Black people.

My mom hasn't said a word or eaten much. She just moves the food around on her plate. Anita follows my line of sight and notices the same thing. She begins to say something but then stops herself. It's hard to imagine Anita in a situation she can't talk her way out of, but this seems to be one.

"Corinne, have you started looking into work? I can put a word in for you at the flower store next to my workspace if you want. You've always made the prettiest bouquets," Zeke says, cutting through the silence.

He's right. My mom used to make huge, elaborate bouquets. She would go to the flea market and find the most amazing vases and spend hours putting exotic, colorful flowers (ones you had to touch to make sure they weren't plastic) into a magnificent arrangement. My mom looks at my aunt with moist eyes, unable to speak.

"Corinne's not working at a flower shop, Zeke," Anita hisses. "She's gonna get what she deserves after twenty years with that man, and—" She stops herself and looks at me, swallowing a rage so big I can hear it move back down her esophagus. "And then she can start fresh."

Anita looks straight into my mom's eyes so she knows the words are meant for her.

"She'll open her own flower shop if she wants, but until the divorce papers are signed, she's fine right here. All she needs is family."

"God would not test her with any obstacle she cannot handle," my grandfather adds after pausing to chew and drink from the water glass beside him.

My mom pinches her eyelids closed, sending her emotions back deep, deep inside herself while the rest of us sit here and pretend not to notice.

Another one of the rules in this house is "No one leaves the table until everyone is done," which means that even though the tension is at an all-time high, we have to sit here until Pa makes his way through his plate.

Every night my cousins and I switch off who washes, who dries, and who puts stuff away (there's no dishwasher either), but I always seem to get stuck washing, which turns my hands into shriveled turnips that smell like a wet dog on the subway. Jerry jumps as Jordan stomps around the kitchen and slams every cabinet she touches, irritated that she is forced into such close proximity with me. As soon as the last dish is back in its place, she storms out, and the three of us count to twenty in our heads to avoid her wrath before we head to the stoop for the evening like we always do.

The weather has finally cooled to a comfortable seventy degrees, and the fire hydrant has been opened for the younger kids, who prance and scream like they just discovered water. A Mister Softee truck rounds the corner, drawing everyone over for ice cream and Popsicles. Jerry saunters toward the truck, jingling a handful of coins in his pocket. Sometimes I wake up in the middle of the night to pee and I swear I can hear the truck making its way through the streets. That's something I'll miss if Mom and I ever move back to the suburbs. I like the idea that Harlem is the only place in New York where you can get ice cream right outside your door, twenty-four-seven.

"I could do something cute with this, Ney," Janae says behind me, grabbing a chunk of my locks to examine. "The texture is pretty fine, but you've got a lot of hair. What about cornrows?"

"Okay."

I've never had cornrows, but I'll do anything to gain an ally. Janae gets up and goes inside to grab her hair tools. From here, it seems like the whole neighborhood is on our block, yet somehow it doesn't feel crowded. Young adults hang out on their stoops, passing around beers and jokes. Parents take photos of their toddlers as they drop ice cream on their feet and grab at it, confused as to why they can't hold it in their hands like everything else.

"Hey."

The guy who called to me earlier from the street corner now stands directly in front of me, interrupting my people watching. Up close, he's even cuter than when I saw him from halfway down the block. I look behind me; the last thing I need is for Janae to come out here and think I'm talking to him to piss her sister off.

"I'm Jesus," he says, pronouncing it "hey-sus" with an accent that seems to only come out on certain words. He takes a sip from his water bottle and licks his plump, perfect lips, and I have to pull my eyes away before he notices me staring.

"I'm . . . Nevaeh, Jordan's cousin."

I look back at the door again. Confused, he peers at the house as well, but no one is there. "You waitin' on someone?"

"Did you need something?" I manage to say. "Jordan? I don't know where she is."

I need him to get out of here, even if all I want is for him to stay and keep talking.

Some kids run by and squirt water guns in our direction, soaking my shirt and revealing my lame nude sports bra that looks like old-lady wear.

"Jesus!" I yell, shocked by the cold water. "Oh! Sorry! I—"

A car pulls up and marijuana smoke seeps through the open window. It fills the street with a funk that is more appealing than the tables of oils and incense that billow on every other corner of Harlem but still makes me wrinkle my nose.

"You got a cell phone?" he asks.

I hold my phone up and he grabs it. "Can I kiss you?" he asks.

"Um, yes," I whisper.

He leans in to take a photo of himself kissing my cheek and then puts his name and number into my contacts and texts himself.

"I'll hit you up," he says before he hops into the car with his friends and drives off.

My hand flies up to my face to touch the spot where the ChapStick impression of his lips makes my cheek tingle like the face peels I steal from my mom sometimes.

"Scoot another step down," Janae commands as she returns,

miraculously none the wiser. She sets up a mini-tripod to hold her phone. The only places she isn't allowed to record are the dinner table and church (more of Pa's rules), so after a long Sunday, I know she's dying to capture some new content.

"Just gonna catch some B-roll," she explains, checking the rig to make sure it's secure. She starts combing out my hair in strokes that feel like she's pulling my scalp clear off my head. I try to imagine that my butt is made of cement to root myself to the ground. The noise on the block stands in for conversation as she portions the section for each braid with razorlike precision, poking me with the comb every time I wiggle and mess up her straight lines.

Jerry comes back and plops down next to me, licking a swirled soft-serve cone—half chocolate, half vanilla—that's melting down his arm.

"Is it real different here from where you normally live?" he asks me as he wipes the ice cream from around his mouth, smearing the thin line on his arm into a sticky blob.

Jerry's never been to our house in White Plains. No one has, other than Grandma. Anita and my father hate each other, and before the separation, my mom hadn't seen her sister or any of the family in years. We attended relatives' birthday parties when I was little, but as time went on, the distance between my mom and Anita grew until their only communication was a few phone calls a year and birthday cards. This summer is the first real concentrated time I've spent with anyone other than Grandma on this side of the family. We are strangers—practically craigslist roommates. Except we're not. I always accepted that we didn't see my mom's family, without ever trying to figure out the real reasons why.

"Yeah, it's different," I confirm.

He thinks for a second.

"Well, that's okay. Here's where you're from too, with us," Jerry declares with such confidence that for a moment, I almost believe it could be that simple.

Uncle Zeke comes out of the house, sipping his Sunday-evening beer and ready to put on a show. He circles his arms around his head and dances to his made-up song.

"It's shower time! Wash your body, Scotty! Wash your booty, Scooty! Wash your booty, Scooty!"

Mortified by his father's childish behavior, Jerry climbs the stairs with a dramatic sigh. Zeke follows, relishing the final years of obedience and one-on-one time before Jerry outgrows the need for any parental attention at all.

Janae finishes another braid and fastens a tiny band on the end, relieving me momentarily of the pressure between my scalp and skull. In the quiet evening, I can hear each strand of hair as she pulls it tight, so I ask the first question that pops into my head.

"You excited about that college trip?"

The words sound lame once they come out of my mouth, and I feel my face flush.

"Nah," she says as she begins the final braid. "That's Jordan's ish. I'd skip it altogether if it was up to me. For most people, college is just an overpriced social experiment that leads to date rape, alcohol poisoning, and debt."

I've never even *considered* not going to college. It's just always been the goal.

"What would you do?" I ask, intrigued.

"Work!" she says, incredulous that I could even ask. "A hundred more YouTube followers on my channel and I can get my account verified for ad sales to save up and buy a real camera. Did you know Steven Spielberg started directing movies when he was thirteen? I'm trying to make a blockbuster about the almost-end-of-the-world where a Black person saves the day instead of dying in the first four minutes."

"Like *Black Panther*?"

She peers around from behind me, her eyes narrowed and one eyebrow raised in defiance.

"Smart-ass."

"So you ARE going to go to college?" I ask.

"Mama said she didn't work her fingers to the bone all these years for her kids *not* to graduate from college, but she's only paying for in-state tuition. I heard Brooklyn College has a pretty good film program. I'll apply there."

Jordan walks over from wherever she has been hanging out. In the sunset, the shadow of her hair looks like a crown.

"Great, so white girls are gonna see you and think it's okay to get cornrows outside of their annual all-inclusive Caribbean-island vacation. This isn't some fad the Kardashians started, it's our culture."

Unlike Jerry, Jordan knows exactly how deep this topic cuts.

"It's her culture too, isn't it?"

Janae's response shotputs out of her. I can tell she's trying to make a point, but it's a question I've often wondered about. Sometimes I don't know what I get to claim as my own.

"Apparently, only when she decides it's convenient," Jordan shoots back.

Jordan bends down in front of me so our eyes are perfectly parallel and our nose tips touch. Her tightly coiled jet-black curls frame her heart-shaped face and full lips. She recently underwent a bit of a transformation (at least, that's what Janae says), after being selected to attend a young Black women's leadership conference, all expenses paid, in Baltimore. Jordan returned a few days later with a new natural hair regimen, an unwavering sense of political activism, and a dream of attending an HBCU.

"Leave her alone, Jordan. It was my idea," Janae orders, tugging my head back up from where it has inadvertently tucked itself into my neck.

Jordan sucks her teeth.

"Pandering to her fragility isn't helping anyone," she says to her sister, and pushes past us, accidentally sending Janae's rig clattering off its perch.

My stomach lurches up to my mouth and I hop down to grab the tripod and phone.

"You know I like you, right, Ney?" Janae asks once she has thoroughly scanned her phone and confirmed it is undamaged.

I nod, meeting her eyes as she flicks the last bit of debris off the lens.

"But if it comes down to it, I'm always on her side. It's a twin thing."

I nod again. So much for an ally.

Chapter 4

I check out my new look in the bathroom mirror. Janae gave me five cornrows. The thickest is dead center, with the others thinning out as they move down either side of my head. Having my hair tied back so tight shows off my eyes and lips. I like it because it's the closest I've ever come to resembling my mother. But Jordan's words replay in my head, so I face the sink and don't look up again until I'm back in the hallway, free from my reflection.

My mom and I occupy the guest room on the third floor. She's in bed already, not asleep, just lying facing the fan with her back to me. My grandma made the quilt that has been pushed to the foot of the bed; she used all sorts of fabric to sew different-colored fish against a white background like they are swimming through a cloud.

"Mommy?" I whisper.

We have this floor to ourselves, but it seems like these days any little noise bothers her, so I try my best to be quiet, even in conversation.

"Hmm?" she murmurs almost inaudibly.

"See my hair? Janae did it for me."

She turns flat on her back and barely glances at me in her peripheral vision.

"Mmmm, it looks nice, baby," she says, already facing the other way again.

"Hey, Mommy?"

She doesn't respond this time, but I know she's listening. I can see her eyelashes move when she blinks from the wind of her fan.

"Why did we stop visiting the family?"

"Your dad thought you were too young for the city. It's a long story," she says with a tinge of annoyance, although I can't tell if it's because I'm preventing her from falling asleep or because I made her think about Daddy. Either way, I can't help myself; I need to know why I was never given a chance to know this side of myself.

"Didn't you miss everybody?" I ask, trying to understand how she could walk away from such a vibrant place.

She hasn't responded after a couple minutes, so I lean over to check. This time she really has drifted off to sleep.

Sharing a bed during a heat wave should be illegal.

We have two fans blowing directly on us from both sides and I'm still swimming in my own sweat. My mom is in that deep sleep where her breathing is so steady and slow, it's barely detectable. She looks peaceful, like for the first time in a while, she has been relieved of the weight of her worry and pain. Whatever happened between her and Daddy must have been really terrible, to make him want us to pick up and leave out of the blue.

Careful not to wake her, I take my time shifting my body closer to the edge of the bed and let my feet sink to the wood before I creep out the door. The crawl space on the top floor of the house is the least logical place to go to avoid the heat, but I like it up there. Zeke built the mini-attic to store Grandma's things after she died, but I now go there to be alone and write.

The small, secret hideout reminds me of the sheet tents I used to build when I was younger; I feel safest when the space around me is tight and enclosed.

So as not to give away my location, I forego the light and use my phone to maneuver my way around. There is a corner hidden behind some boxes that haven't been touched in years where I keep my stuff, a carefully assembled duffel bag holding everything I need to survive:

1. a notebook and a pen
2. beef jerky
3. sour Jelly Bellies
4. fluffy socks
5. Harry Potter books 3, 4, 5, and 6
6. seltzer

I grab a handful of jelly beans from the plastic container I keep them in and settle against the wall. My marble notebook is almost filled with my secrets, like I'm Harriet the Spy. I've had it since I was seven, but there are still a couple of blank pages left. It's hard to imagine that in my lifetime, I might fill more of these books with my thoughts and rhymes. I leaf through the pages and fall back into my memories and words like I'm in a time machine. When I look at this book, I get a warm feeling. My words are like keys that unlock untapped resources within myself. They are my lifeline.

No new words are flowing and it's almost one a.m., so I wedge today's folded church program between the pages and get up, careful to stow my stash back in the Tupperware that protects it from any rodent or bug that might find its way up here and into my secret space. My grandfather vehemently prohibits food outside the kitchen and dining room; it is perhaps his most stringent rule. He boasts to anyone he meets that in all the decades he has lived in this city, he has never had so much as a baby mouse set foot on his property. I can't be the one to muddy his track record.

My eyes have adjusted to the dim light, so I decide not to turn on my phone to guide me. A few steps in, I crash down to the floor, taking a box of books with me. I wait to hear my aunt cursing me to the high heavens for waking her and making a mess, but after ten minutes of lying flat against the cool ground, I decide it's safe to get up and turn the light on. The books are all over the place, but it's the label on the box that catches my eye: *Corinne's Things.*

The thin pen lines stop and start with blotches of stained ink that run down the cardboard. I came home one day a couple months ago and found a pile of boxes in the front yard being soaked by the automatic sprinklers before we piled them into a car to take to Harlem. I wonder how my mom knew which items she couldn't live without, even though the life she had known for so long was effectively over.

When the last book has been stuffed into the box, I tiptoe back, finally ready to go to sleep, but I notice a black book that I missed. I pick it up. It's a tattered journal with a worn, floppy spine. Inside, my mom's handwriting reads:

Corinne's Journal. STAY OUT.

Alone in the attic, the history of my family stares back at me. There's my grandmother's wedding dress, satin with a white lace veil, stowed in a clear plastic tub. She's wearing it in the many wedding photos downstairs, her deep brown skin highlighted by the soft fabric as if she is cloaked in liquid gold. There are a couple of boxes bearing my name in the same smudged writing, and a pile of suitcases covered with so much dust that I wouldn't be surprised if they haven't been touched since my grandfather's initial migration from Liberia.

The stored treasure calls to me. To open this book is to violate my mother's private thoughts and unearth her secrets, but if I don't, I risk remaining a stranger in my own skin.

"I am sorry," I whisper to the sour, dust-filled air, and open the cover.

Chapter 5

I picked you up today, a little treat to commemorate the day Raymond noticed me. I've been imagining what it would sound like if he ever said my name, and when he finally did, it was as if his tongue and lips had been created for that sole purpose.

"Yo, Corinne, you goin' to the dance?" he asked. His eyes glided down my overalls and to my pink Chuck Taylors.

"The dance on Friday?" I stalled.

I wasn't planning to go, but I couldn't tell him that. I couldn't admit that I'm eighteen years old and have never done anything social or fun.

"It'll probably be wack," he said, filling the silence between our substitute teacher's snores from the front of the room. "How come I neva' seen you outside of class?"

My heart leapt. He'd been looking for me, expecting me to be at a party or basketball game, all the places I avoid like the plague to keep from being reminded how lame I am.

"I—I have a lot of homework. I'm taking two AP classes."

"You're one of those bookworms," he declared with a wide grin, showing off his teeth. "Probably goin' to some fancy college next year, ain't you?"

"Northwestern."

"Where's that at?"

"Chicago."

"My cousin Marlow stays out in Chi-town. He says it's brick most of the year."

A breeze rushed through the open window and blew my hair around my face, casting a shadow on the wall that looked like willow branches moving through the sky at sunset. Raymond bored his almond-colored eyes into me as he backed his chair away from the desk. The ear-piercing screech made heads twist in our direction, but the teacher didn't stir. Raymond stood to leave and turned to me once more.

"Yo, can I cop your notes if homeboy decides to teach anything?" He caught me with his eyes again, and my heart banged against my chest so hard I had to remind myself to breathe.

"Oh. Yeah, okay." I looked around to make sure this wasn't a dream.

"Bet. I'll see you Friday, seven o'clock," Raymond said before he crossed the threshold into the hallway.

My cheeks swelled hot, and even the dirty looks from my jealous female classmates couldn't deaden the excitement inside me.

I am going to the last dance of the year with Raymond Morris. Me. Corinne Paire.

Mummy made me a dress for the dance, and she spent
more than she should have on shimmery purple material
that goes to my knees and flows just enough to make me
look like I'm dancing even when I'm barely moving. She
took an unnecessary amount of photos to compensate for
the dances I never attended. Anita rolled her eyes the entire
time—she's used to getting all the attention. Popularity
seems to come naturally to Anita, a gene of confidence I
was born without.

I walked the twenty blocks to school. It was early,
and I liked the feeling of the breeze on my legs. Whistles
and hisses followed me, but I kept my eyes straight ahead.
Those boys weren't worth my time. No one was, except
Raymond.

Kids stood outside the school building in clusters. Some
waited for friends and dates, while others only stuck around
long enough to convince their parents of their cover before
disappearing to a more debaucherous evening. I waited
around for Raymond but went inside when I realized I was
overdressed and attracting attention.

The gym was decorated with streamers, and strobe
lights that sent flashes of color all over the place. A guy
from my grade was behind the makeshift DJ booth, a
folding table on risers, and was spinning a playlist of almost
exclusively Tribe Called Quest, much to some of our white
teachers' distaste.

I took a seat in the bleachers, where a few other students

who had decided to make a final go at the high school experience congregated. We placed ourselves sporadically, so as not to crowd one another, leaving enough room between us to allow for a quick getaway if we needed it.

The popular girls danced, moving between mini-circles until young men eventually plucked them from the bunch and spun them around to get in better gyrating position.

Six songs played before Raymond arrived. He floated in with his boys, and everyone, male and female, watched, hoping to catch a smile or a nod. He was electric in every way. From his curly reddish-brown hair to his matching Adidas getup, jacket and shoes in the OG black with white stripes. He made the world turn.

Raymond was fifty feet away, but I had no control. My legs shot up. I stood so quickly that my dress flew directly into a beam of bright white light and sent everyone's eyes onto me. Raymond stopped and looked, not for too long or with any real sense of recognition, and then he made his way to the DJ booth.

He's just saying hi to his friends. He'll come over soon, I told myself as the music continued to play.

Or am I supposed to go to him? I asked myself as the floor began to crowd with couples.

I don't belong here. I'm a fool.

I began to descend the bleachers.

The air-conditioning in the gym hadn't worked for years, and the air was sticky as I weaved in and out of couples caressing.

"Where you goin'?"

Raymond's voice turned me to stone.

"You're gonna leave like that, without saying hi or nothin'?"

I turned around to find him closer than I expected and had to take a step back to see him. His face was flushed and dotted with perspiration.

"I—I'm not feeling great. . . ." I moved toward the door, but he stopped me.

"Yeah, it's mad hot. Here, take a sip."

He held out a bottle of ginger ale and loosened his grip the moment it touched my palm, leaving me with no choice but to grab it so it wouldn't fall to the ground. In truth, I was parched and a bit queasy, but more from anxiety and embarrassment than the steamy conditions.

The soda fizzed as I untwisted the cap, but when I took a drink, a strange liquid hit my tongue like lava and burned my throat. Raymond chuckled as I heaved, unable to speak, and took the bottle from me, draining its contents with ease.

"What was that?" I choked out.

"Whiskey ginger, the good stuff. I swiped it from my pops."

He dragged me onto the dance floor, where everyone was grinding again. Bodies rippled and made me dizzy as we walked . . . or maybe it was the walking that made me dizzy, or the astringent taste in my mouth, which made my tongue feel fat. Raymond found a spot right in the middle of the floor, as if the room had reserved and guarded this central space on his behalf.

He started to dance and I leaned into the freedom my body felt now that the burning in my throat had worn off.

Out of nowhere, another ginger-ale bottle materialized, and this time I snatched it before he could even offer. Raymond took it from me when I was done and then spun me around so his body fit perfectly behind mine.

I'm a good dancer. Better than Anita, even. I just don't need the whole world to know it the way she does. Until now, I've been content dancing around my room alone, pretending to be on *Soul Train*. But there, in front of my whole school, I kept my eyes open and rolled my hips against Raymond. I watched them watch me and I knew for the first time that I was who everyone wanted to be. He moved his arm over my chest bone and put his mouth next to my ear.

"Let's go," he whispered.

His lips tickled my lobe and sent a jolt between my legs. Outside, some kids waved to Raymond and dispersed, his status providing privacy as we cooled off. The drop in temperature sobered me slightly, enough to realize how fuzzy everything had become. It took me a few moments to get my bearings and read my watch—it was nine-thirty already, and I had to be home at ten.

"You want a ride?" he asked, reading my mind.

His car, a light brown Cadillac, was parked a couple blocks north of the school, down the street from a Chinese restaurant on a corner littered with chicken-wing bones. The front seat smelled like old cigarettes, with a hint of peppermint coming from the worn air freshener hanging from the mirror.

"I'm at One Twenty-Sixth, between Fifth and Lenox," I said, even though I didn't want the night to end.

He didn't turn the car on. Instead, he leaned over and kissed me.

It wasn't just my first kiss; it was THE kiss. The kind that changes the direction of your whole life. The type of kiss you feel on every surface of your body. It was such an all-encompassing kiss that I didn't notice that his hand was halfway up my thigh.

"Oh." I pushed it off.

Raymond frowned and ran his fingers over his lips to rub my sticky lip gloss off.

"Sorry . . . can we take it slow?" I asked.

"You didn't take it slow when everyone was watching," he snapped, and a bit of spit flew out of his mouth and landed on my bare leg.

"I'm sorry," I said as my heart fell into my lap.

Raymond's face softened, and his hand brushed through my hair and rubbed my neck, the same way my mom used to when I was little and had a cold.

"Hey, it's okay." He pulled my face toward his and wiped the tears from under my eyes. "It's just, you got me all excited, and now I want you so bad it hurts."

Before I could do or say anything, he kissed me again, the same way that made my ankles float off the floor of the car. And then I heard him undo his belt buckle.

"Raymond . . . ," I whispered, suddenly aware of the emptiness of the street around us. The only people nearby were in the Chinese restaurant half a block away. His grip on my neck tightened and he began to lower my head toward his lap.

"I want you so bad, Corinne."

Now my name on his lips began to sound like a curse. I tried to pull away, but I couldn't break free.

"Please, baby, please. I'm hurting."

Eventually, I gave in, and he lowered me all the way down to his crotch.

I stared at the suede microfiber seat the whole time. From the glare of the streetlight, I could see it was filthy, and I counted the individual stains as he guided my head up and down, holding my neck tight so I couldn't escape. I told myself that this wasn't actually sex. I told myself that he was halfway there and it was my fault; I just had to finish it and get home.

When it was over, I watched him zip his pants and willed the bronze teeth to catch his skin, but nothing happened. He handed me a tissue, but I grabbed the ginger-ale bottle to wash the taste of shame out of my mouth and finished it all in the five minutes it took to drive me home.

"People don't see you how I do, Corinne," he said as he parked outside my house. He lifted my chin with his finger. "I always knew you were special."

He spoke with such sincerity that I almost believed him. But if that's true, I asked myself, then why do I feel so terrible?

The back of my neck is sore and raw. It's been days, but I keep telling myself if I just scrub a little harder, the stink of humiliation will go away. I wish I knew how to turn back time. If I did, I wouldn't be sitting here writing sad thoughts in a notebook, wishing it had some magic power to make me feel better.

There are no windows in the attic, so I check my phone to see what time it is right as the digits turn to 4:56 a.m. Everything is dry and numb and unfathomable as I sit here, unable to move, and picture the corner just ten blocks away where this happened to my mother. The clock pushes my thoughts forward as I remain still, in disbelief: 4:57 . . . 4:58 . . . 4:59 . . .

Chapter 6

I stand outside a car, trying to open the door to protect my mother, but I am invisible and no one can hear my screams.

"STOP!"

The floor is hard beneath my head, where I startle myself awake. I check my phone: 12:30 p.m. The journal sits next to me, still open to the page where I stopped reading, unable to bear any more of my mother's pain in one sitting.

"Stop!"

The cry rings out again, and in my groggy state I realize it wasn't me yelling in a dream; it's my mother. A loud crash sends me bounding out of the attic and down the stairs. Anita crouches over my mother, who is crumpled on the third-floor bathroom tiles, rocking back and forth.

A cell phone is smashed and shattered in the hallway. Relief travels through me: that seems to be the extent of the physical damage.

"Corinne, it's okay," Anita coos as she pets her gently.

"Mommy?"

Anita looks at me with menacing eyes, pulls herself upright, and takes two giant strides out of the bathroom.

"Where have you been?" she demands.

"I was . . . reading in Pa's office, lost track of time."

She picks apart my lie in her head, skeptical, but also unable to give it the usual unbridled amateur investigation, what with her sister on the ground and the heat wave penetrating the walls like the devil himself.

"Pack a bag," she whispers to me so as not to remind my mom the cause of this breakdown. "Your father called this morning. He's back from London and wants to see you."

I sneak back upstairs, careful to remain undetected, and rush up to the attic to grab my mom's journal. Now that I have breached the privacy of this forbidden text, I can't risk anyone finding out, or worse, anything happening to it. My backpack has a hidden pocket that the journal fits in perfectly, camouflaged by the black nylon.

Anita is standing by the front door when I reach the bottom of the stairs. She holds her hand out impatiently for my bag and passes it to Zeke.

"Your mother needs to rest. You'll see her when you get back in a few days," she says before I can ask Mom's whereabouts, and pushes me toward the front door.

Outside, Uncle Zeke puts my bag in the car my dad must have sent for me.

"We'll see you on Sunday, lil' one." He hugs me. "Don't worry, we're not going anywhere."

The atmosphere outside changes once we get onto the highway, with music on the street replaced by the occasional car horn. The houses and front lawns all present themselves with an array

45

of colorful flowers, and what the newer houses lack in character they make up for in elegance. The suburbs of White Plains may be uppity and fancy, but they're familiar. It is home.

The car pulls up to the white shingled house and manicured yard that I love. A calm settles over me, and my body hair, pin-pricked in anticipation of my arrival, softens. The navy-blue window planters hold herb gardens that haven't been tended all summer. Stalks of parsley and thyme, now tortured and gray, lie shriveled in the hard soil like herbal incarnations of Ursula's poor unfortunate souls. I check the mailbox, and catalogues from CB2 and Restoration Hardware addressed to my mother spill out, along with invitations and bills and advertisements for properties going up for sale in the neighborhood.

When I was younger, I used to make a game of getting from the curb to the front door—I was the only one who could comfortably use the unusually small stepping-stones my father installed when he first bought the place, one of the few home improvements he ever attempted. I'd hop from one to the next on one foot, imagining the ground around me was lava, as my parents walked through the lawn.

Today, I trudge through the grass with my bag in one arm and the mail in the other, unbothered by the lava because all I need is to hear the click as the lock turns to feel right again.

The moment I enter the foyer, I struggle to release the air trapped in my lungs, but I can't. The room is unrecognizable.

"Well, looks like there's more than one big change around here," my father says as he runs out of the kitchen and stops to take me in, his head cocked to one side like a puppy discovering his reflection. He looks shorter than I remember, a bit thinner as well, and his wavy brown hair, while still full, is streaked with gray.

"Just don't get tattoos and join a gang on me, okay?" he whispers in my ear, patting the tight braids against my skull as if to confirm they are not an illusion.

The mail falls from my hands like the contents of a piñata as he grabs and holds me like we've been apart for years and he thought we would never see each other again.

After an eternity, he lets me go and opens his eyes and arms wide, welcoming me to this new home as though it is a new lease on life. My kindergarten paintings that my mother curated and reframed have been replaced by huge black-and-white photographs of strangers. The bright blue Moroccan rug on which I used to jump from one swirl to the next in an effort to distract myself from my parents' bickering has been replaced by some fluffy thing that looks like a polar bear skin. Two stiff black leather love seats sit where the big comfy couch used to be, and an acrylic bench is positioned on the other side of the room.

My dad looks at me with nervous glee. "So, what do you think?"

I think this is the type of interior design that makes more sense for a new age vampire family than it does for humans. I think it smells different too, and not in a good way, like fresh paint and floor soap instead of flowers.

"It, um . . . it looks . . . clean?" I say.

He deflates, saddened by such a dull response. The front door slams behind me.

"I've told you a thousand times, if you leave the door open, you let the air-conditioning out! You act like money grows on trees," says my Bubby, who appears as if by magic, already nagging.

Dad's face falls at the sight of her, draining the little color left in his cheeks. Bubby likes to stop by uninvited, an occurrence I've been trained to dread, but for once I'm relieved. Her overbearing presence casts shadows I can hide in while I adjust to this new state of being.

"Mother, what are you doing here?" he asks.

"Such a warm welcome after not seeing me for two months," Bubby chides.

Each click of her heels against the marble floor makes him wince. Eau de Vicks VapoRub clouds the room with such strength that the air tastes like the last few days of a cold by the time she reaches us. Bubby's lips are painted with blush matte lipstick, the same color she always wears and reapplies so often that it cakes as it dries, giving her mouth the unfortunate appearance of a perpetual scab.

"Nevaeh, dear. I didn't know you were going to be here."

Her nose wrinkles as her gaze drifts up to my hair. She has never been the affectionate type, unlike my other grandma, who wouldn't let five minutes pass without giving me a kiss or a playful squeeze. Bubby always keeps her distance.

"Mom!" my father whines like a child.

"I haven't died yet, dear; that's still my name." Bubby cuts him off before he has the chance to delve further into the purpose of her unexpected visit.

My dad is a litigator, a really good one, and he can usually out-talk anyone, except his mother.

"You both look hungry. I'll make some food. We'll eat together." Bubby walks past us toward the kitchen.

Dad looks at me with apologetic eyes, though it's unclear whether he feels worse that our one-on-one time has been cut short or that he has to be around Bubby for the next few hours.

We hear the clanging of pots as Bubby begins to assemble her army of copper and wood, followed by the sharp crack of shells as she sloshes eggs into a bowl.

"I wanted to order from Mina's and have a poker party," my dad whispers, sticking his bottom lip out, playing up the immature distress to get a smile out of me.

"I am starved," I admit.

The kitchen, thank God, has not been altered, and I hop onto my favorite stool at the island.

"So, it looks like you've had an interesting summer," Bubby says.

Egg goop oozes down the thin wires of the whisk she points at me, eyes squinted and lips pursed as she cocks her head the same way my father did when he first saw me. He'd hate to know how easy it is for me to find similarities between him and his mother, but it's impossible not to. They have the same marbled aquamarine eyes, equipped with laser focus and ready to cut through you to find out what's inside.

"Umm, I guess."

Bubby goes back to whisking but keeps her eyes on me; she isn't giving up her interrogation without an answer that satisfies her nosiness.

"So you *don't* like it there," she pries, leading me with far less subtlety than she realizes. "Must be a bit crowded with her sister . . ."

"Anita."

My father grunts at the utterance of his sister-in-law's name, the same way Anita does if my mother or I mention his. A sizzle sends cinnamon-sugar mist under my nose—French toast, one of Bubby's specialties. I have to swallow before I drool on the marble countertop.

When a plate slides in front of me, I automatically close my eyes for the prayer, ready to dig in.

"Honey?" my dad asks.

I open one eye to find both of them watching me with the same level of confusion I feel when considering the amount of effort to put into a "proper" selfie.

"Oh—sorry."

The French toast slices like butter under my knife, and I make sure to add the smallest bit of cheesy scrambled eggs on top, a little salty with the sweet, before I take a bite. The same dish sits steaming in front of my father, but he doesn't reach for his fork.

"Were you . . . praying?" He speaks as if saying the word transports a sea of bile into his mouth.

"No! Well, it's what they do before dinner, just a habit."

"Corinne knows you don't have to do that. Ever." My father jumps off his stool and flicks his plate toward Bubby. "You're a Levitz!" he shouts with such misplaced fury I look away in embarrassment.

Bubby's eyes, however, glisten with more hope than anyone with two shreds of morals has felt since Trump was elected president.

"That's right!" Bubby is quick not to lose the power she has over him in his vulnerable state. "Why don't you come to shul with me? Both of you! They have a mixer after services. Nevaeh could meet some kids her own age. Good wholesome Jewish kids," she adds, and pushes the plate back toward my father, baiting him with the aroma of his childhood.

The power shifts to Bubby like she's donned a coat of armor, and she takes the stance of a wolf, starved for obedience and allegiance. My dad lowers himself back onto his stool, weak and hungry and distracted by some deep-rooted pain.

"You can't make me go to temple!" I shout. "You hate temple, Dad. You said it yourself: it's about being a Levitz, not about being Jewish! That would be so . . . hypocritical!"

The words hit my grandmother like rusty nails, but I ignore her. I meet my father with acidic rage, strong enough, I hope, to burn through the despondency that has temporarily taken over him.

"See!" Bubby declares to my father. "I don't know what nonsense that woman has put into your head for all these years, but you were raised with Jewish values, and you need your community around you now more than ever. You both do. This is a chance to take your life back, set it in the right direction."

My father volleys between us, the woman to whom he owes his life and the girl he gave life to.

"Nevaeh, you do seem . . . different," he admits.

"Of course I do," I retort. "You've been gone for months. You don't know how hard it's been. You don't know anything."

There is nothing my father hates more than to be shown up. He has spent his entire career making sure he's the best at everything, but especially arguing. His jaw tightens and the veins in his neck pulsate. Alarm takes over his face: his eyes widen and his mouth forms an O, almost like the choking victims in the Heimlich-maneuver posters that hang in fast-food restaurants.

"There are a lot of single women, Sammy," Bubby goes on. "Talia Bernstein, a widow, God rest Gregory's soul—"

"Mother," my dad interrupts through clenched teeth, "it's time for you to go."

Bubby recoils, shocked by the unexpected plot twist of her dismissal. She drops a dirty mixing bowl into the sink with a clatter.

"Who is she?" Bubby asks, looking at my father.

My father turns his head so fast I brace myself in case it rolls onto the countertop.

"What?"

"Please!" Bubby holds a hand out to silence him. "You may hate me, but I still know you better than anyone, and you didn't gut renovate your entire house for the heck of it."

She walks toward the kitchen door and stops suddenly, coming to a terrible realization: "Another shiksa," Bubby says with disappointment so thick the words choke her as they come out.

I have been unable to cry since the separation, but not for lack of trying. I've gone up to my spot in the attic and thought every sad thought I could think, but nothing. Now I feel the tears move toward my eyes, traveling from wherever tears are made. The pressure builds, ready to explode in a fountain of disbelief and disdain.

"It wasn't planned, Nevaeh, but I did meet someone," Dad confesses. "I was going to tell you when the time was right. It's been hard for me too."

His plea for empathy dries the long-awaited tears I've wished for.

"I wanted you to come home first and get settled, but she's moving in, in a few weeks," he says.

He doesn't deserve my tears. He doesn't deserve anything from me. From us. Mom can barely hold a conversation and he's already moving someone in?

"I hate you."

Those three words have never left my lips, not together, and once they do, I know why. Because as I say them, a piece of me dies.

And my father says nothing. So I push my plate away, get up, and go upstairs.

Chapter 7

The door to my bedroom swings open, and the familiar jingle transports me back to when I was seven. At the time, I was obsessed with *Harriet the Spy* and decided to booby-trap my room to protect myself from the evils that lurked outside. Shortly after, my mom put a ban on any and all booby-trapping, in perpetuity, because after a variety of my attempts to build anything sustainable with strings and buckets of paint, she was sick of cleaning my carpet every other day. I refused to leave my room in protest, but eventually, hunger took over and I had to give in. When I opened the door to creep out late one night for sustenance, I found a thin red string around the doorknob with a small bell attached, the type that would normally be found on a cat's collar. There was also a Post-it stuck next to the knob that read:

Now you'll always know if there's an intruder! Love, Dad

That's the father I know. The one who encourages me to be adventurous. The dad who pretends to be a hypnotist and waves a pocket watch in front of me as a distraction when I have a splinter so my mom can pull it out. The goofy guy who thinks dessert is an appropriate meal substitute and who does terrible impersonations of celebrities for servers in restaurants. That man downstairs is a stranger. He's a cyborg, a recently acquired body snatch.

I've never prayed in my life. On these past Sundays, when the pastor gives us a moment or two of silence to reflect, I count the seconds as they pass, or think about what I should read next or what it would feel like to be kissed in the rain. Asking an unknown force I'm not sure I believe exists to grant me the unattainable feels foreign, but I suppose that's because up until now, I've never known desperation. So here, in my own personal sanctuary, with no instructions or guidelines, I ask whatever power might be listening for help. I ask for my dad to see he made a mistake and I ask for my mom to feel better and come back and fight for us. I pray for our family to be fixed. It feels childish, but I have no choice; I ask for a miracle, and then I sink into the thick down comforter on my bed and think about how things used to be until the sun sets and night comes and I drift off to sleep.

The knob on my door turns and wakes me from my deep slumber as my father peeks his head in. He looks terrible, as if he hasn't slept since I saw him in the kitchen yesterday and hasn't showered for longer than that. Before I have a chance to ask him to leave, he sits at the foot of my bed, tears streaming down his face.

His sad eyes search for a sign that he hasn't lost me for good, and I feel myself move to him, drawn by love, even though I still feel boiling hatred with each heavy breath I take. I prepare myself for a performance, an opening argument to plead his case to this jury of one. He reaches his hand out.

"I'm sorry," he says. "Can you forgive me? Can you let me make things right?"

It's not just his words; it's the conviction with which he says them. I barely want to exhale for fear of reversing the magic from whoever or whatever heard me last night and granted my wish. I squeeze his hand, temporarily swapping roles as I assume the position of protector and comforter to his sad, broken soul.

My stomach makes a noise that sounds like an alien underwater.

"You must be starving," he says. "Why don't I whip us something up?"

He hugs me before he gets up to go, and I breathe in the familiar smell of Old Spice deodorant that clings to his soft T-shirt, perhaps the one thing that will never change about this place.

My hair falls in crimped waves around my face as I take each braid out in front of the mirror. *Jerry was right,* I think, and I make a mental note to tell him as I get into the shower and let the hot water soothe my sore scalp.

Hunger pulls me downstairs, but rather than a greeting of French toast and eggs, I find my father sitting with an older white man and a young white woman in the living room.

"Hello?"

My dad jumps up as though my presence is unexpected. "Nevaeh!"

The older man nods in my direction, his eyebrow raised, a cue for my father.

"Nevaeh, this is Rabbi Avner." My dad motions to the man. "And this is Rabbi Sarah. Why don't you take her to the kitchen for a drink so Rabbi Avner and I can finish up?" he suggests.

Their eyes follow us as I lead Rabbi Sarah toward the kitchen, and they wait until we are out of earshot before resuming their hushed conversation.

"Are you hungry?" I ask as I pour two waters. She shakes her mop of frizzy dirty-blond hair no. I hand her a glass.

"So . . . when did you move into the neighborhood?" I ask her.

Rabbi Sarah walks around, mesmerized by the fancy silver appliances, touching everything with her fingertips as she goes. "We don't live here," she says with the thick, old-school New York accent usually associated with guys named Marty or Sal or Jimmy the Nose.

"Oh, sorry. I just assumed. Is your dad a client of my father?"

"Rabbi Avner isn't my father," she replies.

Rabbi Sarah sits down and drains her glass. She's probably in her late twenties. Her paper-white skin is thin and delicate in a way that makes me look really ethnic by comparison. There are about a million evil eye bracelets running up her arm and five or six piercings in one ear.

"Sorry, your . . . husband?" I mumble from inside the fridge as I search for a quick snack before I faint.

"He's not my husband either. He's my boss," Rabbi Sarah says.

I grab a handful of shriveled grapes that might already qualify as raisins and practically swallow them whole.

"So let's talk shop for a second," she goes on. "What're you thinking about schedules? This is my first time workin' solo with a student. Do you know any Hebrew, or are we starting at square one?"

I stare at her. "What do you mean, working solo?" I ask as the overly sweet and sticky fruit stops halfway down my throat.

Rabbi Sarah's face turns whiter than it already is, and a sinking feeling comes over me. The kind that starts in the bottom of your stomach and the top of your throat at the same time and travels from both directions to meet in the center of your chest, where it sits heavy and hard.

"I'm sorry," she says, unable to undo what she has done. "Maybe we should wait for your father."

"Daddy!" I shriek.

Startled, her glass falls in slow motion, shattering on the marble floor just as my father and Rabbi Avner run into the room to see what's going on.

I take back everything I said about prayer and miracles, because whoever or whatever heard me last night is evil and clearly wants me to die a terrible, horrible, painfully embarrassing death. Last night before I passed out, I was sure it had been the worst day of my life, but today has surpassed the nightmare that was yesterday and it's only eleven a.m.

"Nevaeh, Rabbi Avner and I think that with all the changes, and living between two houses, it would be good for you to have someone on this side of things to help you navigate the transition," my father says in his official lawyer voice.

"This side of things?" I ask.

The slick leather on the love seat keeps sending me sliding forward in my shiny black spandex pants. I pull myself up.

"Nevaeh," Rabbi Avner begins, "your father reached out to us because this is a fragile time in your life, and we believe that weekly sessions with Rabbi Sarah to study the Torah and prepare for a coming-of-age ceremony would do you well."

My father's sunken eyes dart between us as he hangs on the old man's every word like a drowning victim being thrown a lifeline.

"Did you say coming-of-age ceremony?" I ask through gritted teeth.

"Yes. Mr. Levitz mentioned you have not been active in the temple and that your thirteenth birthday passed without a bat mitzvah, but now we have a chance to make up for lost time," Rabbi Avner says. "This is a good way to find your footing in the religion. I have no doubt it will come naturally. After all, it's in your blood."

He makes it sound so simple. As if all I need to do is take a DNA test to feel comfortable in my own skin and resolve a lifetime's worth of confusion and guilt.

I whisper, "Please, you can't make me do this."

I have three years left of high school. Three years of walking the halls of a school I've gone to since kindergarten. Three years left to keep myself in the shadows and out of the spotlight. This is the year I turn sixteen, and I was already hoping to avoid a party for that, but this . . . this will lead to a total social collapse.

I barely know what it means to be Jewish; it's the one part of myself I never had to worry about because my father told me I didn't have to. He said he and I were Jewish by birth, but we didn't have to be religious. This bat mitzvah will be one more thing for

me to wonder whether I have a right to claim. One more thing that makes me feel foreign to myself. One more thing to remind me I am different and don't deserve a voice because how can I speak on anything when I don't know who I am or where I belong?

"Nevaeh, this is a serious time in your life, and you need direction!" My father yells at me the same exact way his mother yells at him.

I rack my brain for a different angle, because the look in my father's eyes tells me the window for any sort of rational decision-making is closing at a rapid pace, but nothing comes to me. Rabbi Sarah enters with a plastic bag filled with shards of glass.

"Sorry to interrupt. I just wasn't sure which bin to throw this in. . . . There's like five garbage cans in the kitchen."

Rabbi Avner clears his throat, silencing her in the midst of our tense negotiation.

"Rabbi, I can't thank you enough for all your help. I'll be in touch soon with Nevaeh's school schedule and we can go from there." My father rests his case.

"I'm really looking forward to working with ya, Nevaeh." Rabbi Sarah winks and smiles, but my silent glare hangs between us like an axe ready to drop from the ceiling and chop one of our heads off.

My dad gets up and walks them to the door. He returns, surprised to find me still standing there.

"I meant what I said, honey. This is all in your best interest, I promise. It doesn't seem like it now, but when you're older, you'll thank me." His paternal voice sounds forced, like he isn't sure he believes it himself.

"I bet that's what you said to Mom, and look where it got her."

I walk past him, careful not to break eye contact, and then stomp up to the second floor, where I slam my door so hard that the little bell falls off the knob and rolls away.

The giant purple beanbag chair I spent a year campaigning for slams down in front of my door as a barricade. The chair cocoons me and I settle in, adding the weight of my body to ensure no one can interrupt. I turn the pages in the book so fast they create a furious wind that makes my loose curls bounce around my shoulders until I find an empty one.

> *In this room, there are four walls and a window.*
> *From the window, I see the mailbox on the street.*
> *The street is covered in grass that browns and shrivels or*
>   *flourishes depending on the position of the clock.*
> *I watch you come and go as you please.*
> *Sometimes, you look up at me with a wave and a smile,*
> *But usually, you're too busy, fumbling with your keys.*
> *From the corners in my room, I can run back and forth.*
> *Diagonal and horizontal, one way or the other.*
> *It took a while to realize that the direction doesn't make a*
>   *difference.*
> *Some days pass without a sound,*
> *Without a bird perched on the ledge or a gust of wind sending*
>   *damp leaves onto the paned glass.*
> *I asked you once, through the window, "Why?"*
> *You replied, "To keep you safe and warm."*
> *If safe is what you wanted, why didn't you leave the walls*
>   *blank, without this*
> *Looking-glass to the sky?*

Is it that safety only exists within the confines of your own
dimensions?
Or are you too afraid to believe that I can fly?

I just have to make it a week here and then I go back to Pa's house. Who knows? Maybe this is what Mom needs to snap her out of her daze. She won't let him do this to me. I know it.

Chapter 8

At the office. L, D

The same note that my father has taped to the outside of my door every day this week is there when I wake up on Sunday morning. I clean up bags of potato chips littering my floor from my midnight snacks and grab my stuff, ready to get out of this house before another terrible reality befalls me. As I wait for an Uber in the living room, the harsh new interior melts away, revealing my home as I remember it.

The huge gray couch that I slept on for a week after I got food poisoning and where my parents took turns holding my cold, sweaty hand, sits against the back wall. The old couple in the painting my mom bought for her and Dad's tiny apartment when she was pregnant with me during Dad's law school years stares at me with their misshapen eyes. The big wooden coffee table where we played poker and Monopoly and Uno on Sundays before grilling or ordering Italian from Mina's boasts a stack of half-completed Friday *Times* crossword puzzles, ready for my father to pick up and put down after solving a clue or two.

A horn blares outside, so I leave before the mirage disappears; I let the memories stain my eyes so I don't have to look at the truth.

The car speeds all the way to the city and drops me on the corner of Fifth Avenue and 126th before the driver tears off in the same direction he came, hoping to avoid another passenger that will bring him deeper into the city. The streets are sleeping after the morning rush to church services that came and went an hour ago. Everyone else is still in bed, recovering from Saturday night in New York City, which for many didn't end until the early hours of the morning.

"Well, hey there, lil' one," Zeke says as I walk through the door. "I didn't expect you until later, but now that you're here, drop your stuff. I could use a hand at the supermarket."

Zeke walks on the outside of the sidewalk to shield me from any splashes of filthy water or any other liquid. He's just old-school like that, and I can't say I hate it.

"So how was the visit?" he asks with genuine curiosity.

"Ugh," I grunt in response.

"Come on." His powerful arm rests on my shoulders like a block of lead. "It can't have been that bad."

I roll my eyes—a language Zeke is fluent in after twenty-plus years of Anita—and he swiftly clamps his mouth shut with a smile.

The new Whole Foods on 125th Street takes up an entire city block; the high-end market looms tall in the sky. The smaller grocery stores have all but disappeared, leaving this or a food delivery service as the only options for food shopping and the latter doesn't work for Zeke; he needs to see his food before he buys it.

We weave up and down the aisles as he picks up this and that, following the same path he takes week after week. The guys behind the fish counter greet him with a friendly nod.

"What's good, boss?" A tall man with tan skin and more freckles than me winks at us when it's our turn. "The usual?"

"Yes, sir, the ones in the middle," Zeke says as he points to the salmon steaks.

We take the fish and head toward the registers to pay.

"Good morning." The cashier bats her long eyelashes at Zeke but frowns when she notices his silver wedding band. "That will be one-oh-six seventy-seven," she says in a lower, less flirtatious tone.

Zeke shakes his head and lets out a *tsk* before he hands over a credit card so new it still has the activation sticker on the front. Instinctively, I reach for my wallet, but then stop myself. I know better than to offer to pay. If Anita ever found out, she would throw it in my face that they don't need charity or help, not from anyone, especially me.

The sun outside wraps itself around our bodies like a towel at the beach, a shock to our systems after the frigid central air in the store. Zeke charges ahead, and I have to add a hop to my step to keep up. A second wave of Sunday-morning Harlemites crowd the restaurant patios in desperate need of bottomless mimosas and fried food. Zeke swerves around them with grace, as though the four grocery bags filled with enough food for eight are nothing more than thick paper and air.

"Excuse me?" A pink hand grabs my arm from behind while we wait for the light to change on the corner. Zeke drops the bags to guard me with his body, placing himself between me and what turns out to be a police officer in uniform. He looks young for a cop, mid-twenties, with silky dark brown hair that sweeps behind his ears and white teeth that bite his bottom lip.

"Sorry, Officer," Zeke says, embarrassed to have engaged with a police officer in such a manner. "My dad was on the force for forty-five years."

The policeman's shoulders are squared, his fists clenched at his sides now that Zeke moved me out of his grasp. He relaxes slightly when Zeke backs up but doesn't take his eyes off him for a second.

"Can I speak to you?" he says sternly.

"Is there a problem, Officer?" Zeke asks as politely as possible.

"Not you," he says to Zeke. "Her."

I look up at my uncle, confused.

"It's all right, lil' one," Zeke says.

The cop beckons me to follow him as he steps back a couple of feet without looking, narrowly missing a mother and her small child, who dodge him at the last second.

"Miss, is everything all right?"

I look around, still unclear why he's speaking to me. My nerves act as superglue between my lips and I nod yes. He widens his stance and bends at the knees to move his face closer to mine.

"Are you sure? Because I can help you if you're in trouble."

"I'm fine," I say.

"Is that man making you do anything you don't want to do? They sometimes target pretty girls like you, you know."

His words travel to my ears in slow motion, one at a time, so it takes me longer than normal to piece together why he has chosen to question me.

"What? No!" I shout, surprising both of us. "He's my uncle!"

The cop looks back and forth, gauging whether this is a well-crafted ruse or he has made a terrible judgment call.

"Can I go?"

He nods and turns on his heels, disappearing before I make it the three steps back to the corner. Zeke kneels by the grocery bags he dropped to protect me, where a puddle of egg yolks ooze onto the street. He pulls out some soaked pasta boxes and holds them up.

"Shit!" Zeke roars with a power that makes me hold my breath. "Sorry."

"No, no, don't apologize. Tell me what you need; I can go back to the store," I offer, sick to my stomach that this might cost him more money on top of everything else.

Zeke rests an elbow on his knee and holds his forehead with his fingertips, massaging his temples. He keeps his eyes fixed on the ground.

"Just go home, Nevaeh," he whispers with such agony it almost sounds like a prayer.

And I walk away quick so Uncle Zeke can wipe the silent tears that roll down his cheeks onto his sleeve without an audience.

I wake up in my bed damp with sweat. I forgot to plug my fan in when I got back, and the heat must have lulled me to sleep. My gut twists with guilt as I remember the events of earlier today. I should have asked for the cop's name or badge number. I should have done something.

My stomach jumps again, but this time from hunger. Based on the smells wafting through the house, it's time for dinner.

I hear shouts rising up the stairs, so I tiptoe down to the dining room to listen at the door. Anita and my mom stand on opposite sides of the table with their fingers pointed in each other's faces.

"She has to learn about her culture, Corinne. We went to J'Ouvert every year when we were young; it's time to recognize that your fairy-tale life is over. It's time to give up the act!" my aunt yells.

"How dare you!" my mom screams. "The past sixteen years wasn't an act; it was my life. I loved Samuel and he loved me, but you think it's been easy? All diamonds and champagne? All these years and those white women still stare when I walk in to their stupid brunch parties, trying to figure out whether I'm a guest or a server. I did my best. Nevaeh goes to one of the top schools in the state of New York. She's traveled, and she has—"

"What? She has what, Corinne? What does she have that's so much better when she's walking through the world not understanding who she is? You think that's worth fancy trips and clothes?" my aunt yells.

"We're not going to J'Ouvert," my mom says firmly. "Samuel would never allow it, and the last thing I need is to get him upset with everything up in the air right now."

They must not know I'm home. Zeke must have forgotten to mention it. I don't blame him; he probably willed himself to forget I existed so he could get on with his day. A creaky floorboard announces my presence as I attempt to back away.

"Hello?" Anita calls out cautiously. "Who's there?"

With no choice, I step forward and my mom drops into her seat like a balloon deflating and falling to the ground.

"Nevaeh—" My mom starts to say something, but I cut her off. I've heard enough.

"This joo-vair thing . . . Dad doesn't want me to go?" I ask, with all eyes on me.

Anita looks at my mom and then shakes her head to confirm.

"You can do what you want," I say to my mother as I take my seat. "But I'm going."

"Well, that," Anita says, pausing to wink at me with pride, "settles that." Then she gets up to make me a plate.

Chapter 9

At two a.m. the reggae music starts blasting through the house and Janae comes dancing into our room to wake us; she throws me a tank top with a Jamaican flag on it.

"Get up!"

My exhaustion is overpowered by the adrenaline of disobedience and adventure gushing through me, so I do what she says.

Downstairs, Anita has cereal and fruit laid out because despite Jerry's whining, no one is cooking at this hour. Everyone is in Jamaican pride colors: yellow, green, and black. I've never seen my aunt so . . . undressed. Her tank top has slits across the back, exposing her bra. My uncle takes immediate stock of her short shorts with raised eyebrows and pursed lips as he comes down the stairs.

Anita and Zeke have a secret language that's been developing since they were fifteen. They communicate through looks and smiles and winks, so subtle that sometimes I find myself accidentally tuning in to their silent conversations. His cut-off T-shirt reveals the tattoos on his arm, one for each of his kids. Three black lines in the shape of a triangle, symbolizing their bond for the entire world to see.

We all watch Jerry as he eats, adorable as ever, bouncing around so his belly jiggles as he gyrates his hips to the music. Anita hands me a bag filled with what looks like ketchup squeeze bottles from a diner.

"What's this for?" I ask.

"Don't worry about it," she says.

She keeps us moving, delegating last-minute tasks and cleaning up behind us. Anita, for all her brashness, never ceases to amaze me with her level of productivity, especially when multitasking.

Once everyone has eaten something, we pile into my uncle's SUV. Grandpa walks us out and waves to the neighbors, all of whom seem to be headed in the same direction we are. The summer night is crisp and dark, but I can still see Pa watching us on the stoop when we get to the corner to head downtown.

"How come Pa isn't coming?" I ask.

"This ain't his thing, lil' one," Zeke explains in the rearview mirror.

Traffic is crazy for a Monday at two-thirty a.m. The highway is packed, and my cousins are super hyped. They dance to music and wave their mini-flags out the window to honks and cheers. It takes us almost an hour to get to Brooklyn, and then we have to park a fifteen-minute walk from Eastern Parkway, which is apparently where everything goes down.

Walking through the streets, I can taste the energy. It's like Pop Rocks and electricity. Like those sparklers you get on the Fourth of July to write words that melt into the sky. People cheer, and some of them yell, "Jamaica!" at us in solidarity and recognition.

My mom walks stiffly through the crowd, the only person out of thousands wearing a simple white T-shirt and jeans.

"What is this?" I ask, motioning to the crowd around us.

"The J'Ouvert festival. It's the kickoff for the West Indian Day Parade," Zeke says, guiding me forward gently, as if this were my first ride without training wheels. "*J'Ouvert* means 'daybreak.' It's a chance for us to wake everyone up with our pride. Just enjoy it and stay close, okay?" My uncle puts his big arm around my shoulders.

> *Under the streetlights,*
> *All I see is brown on brown on tan on yellowish golden on*
>   *brown,*
> *And it is breathtaking.*
> *We flood the pavement with a confidence that screams out into*
>   *the universe:*
> *"We are powerful!"*
> *"We are beautiful!"*
> *"We deserve to be celebrated!"*
> *The air is filled with incense and sounds that I take in with*
>   *deep, full breaths.*
> *As I drink in the delight, a transformation takes over,*
> *One that is sudden and brave,*
> *Swift and loud,*
> *As if until this very moment, I have lived confined to a two-*
>   *dimensional outline*
> *Waiting for a chance to be whole.*

Together, we move through the street and descend upon the festival. The steel drums vibrate so intensely it feels like we're in a bubble and the music is bouncing off the buildings back into the center of everything.

Everyone wears their country's colors; some women even have their nails painted with tiny reproductions of their native flag on each finger. I hear my aunt beg my mom to enjoy herself, and I wonder if maybe I should just go back with her and protect everyone from her moroseness, but before I can act on anything, Janae pulls me into a dance circle.

Two women bend over, their butts competing with each other to move faster. More women crowd around and cheer them on until there are so many of us that there is no more center and we're just a clump of people, standing shoulder to shoulder. My cousins and everyone else in our makeshift clique begin to move their bodies the same way: with their eyes closed and their faces held up to the moonlit morning sky. Their movement speaks to me in a language that, until now, I was unaware I was fluent in, but I respond with twisting hips and rolling shoulders and playfully bite my lip as they challenge me to go faster or lower or slower.

By the time our parents spot us in the crowd, we are drenched in sweat.

I can't tell if we have an actual destination or if we'll all just go until we don't feel like going anymore. As we inch forward, the smells of sweet plantains, jerk spices, and coconut bread hit us. No one makes coconut bread like my grandma used to, but the smell brings her back to me.

I can see her shaking her hips and sucking her teeth playfully at the women running around in pum-pum shorts and BeDazzled bras, gyrating their way down the avenue.

The summer before she died, Grandma showed up at our house in White Plains and found me in jeans and a tank top, covered with a cardigan. It was a million degrees outside, but my dad had just had a new commercial-grade central air system installed and the house was an icebox. Confused, she led me by the hand into the nearest bathroom.

We emerged a few moments later, Grandma marching with confidence and me attempting to conceal my now-bare midriff, exposed by the four inches she'd hacked off the bottom of my shirt with rusty shears. Her aged black purse was at least two decades overdue to be replaced, but I never saw her without it. She spent her life collecting a handful of inexplicable items she stowed in that purse, certain that at any given moment, they might be required.

"Show us whatchu got in dis hot sun!" Grandma declared.

She always spoke like she had an audience, even if she was the only person in the room.

Her body was damp with sweat, but in the natural light, her brown skin glistened like a diamond. She moved me back and forth across the floor as she made a beat with her footsteps. In the huge mirror in the hallway she caught her own reflection and opened her mouth to laugh a laugh so strong it opened the sky and sent beams of magic through the windows onto us.

Grandma was the only person who ever talked to me about my Black identity. She wanted me to know I belonged. She wanted me to know I should be proud. I always smiled and listened politely, but I never believed her, and now that she's gone, I'll never get the chance to ask her "how?".

Today, I hear her all around me, in the older ladies talking and the people cheering and the streamers flapping through the air. I'm sure she's here, dancing with me, so I close my eyes to soak her in.

In my head,

I tell her that I wish we could stay here forever,
on this stretch of Eastern Parkway,
at this very moment,
where the only way to be happy
is to be ourselves.

I wait for Grandma to respond, but instead, my mom's blood-curdling scream rips through my ears. Frantic, I push through the crowd, ignoring the dirty looks hurled at me for my discourteous behavior. Zeke tries to stop me, but I rush forward, straight into a thick cloud of bright purple dust.

The powder is everywhere, drying out my eyes and mouth and nostrils. Unable to call for help, I stop being me and fuse into *us,* this mass of unstoppable force that helps me breathe without oxygen as we wait for the air to clear. Sustained by perseverance, I know suddenly why my dad never wanted us to come here: he must have realized that the strength we generate together would always act as a barrier between me and him.

And here, in this moment, I don't hate that he might have been right.

"MOM!" I reach to the back of my head, where I keep the other loud thoughts I never let out. Then I hear her again.

My eyes open to a clearer scene: my mom stands there, her white shirt covered in purple splatters as she faces my aunt, who holds one of the squeeze bottles from the bag that I forgot about until now.

"Give. It. To. Me. Anita," my mom demands.

I brace myself for something terrible, but as quickly as I've ever seen her move, my mom grabs the bottle and squirts it right back at Anita. Another cloud of purple comes out, and for the first time since we've been here, the world goes completely silent.

It's like those scenes in movies right before something big is about to happen and the only way the characters can prepare for it is for everything to move in slow motion. We float through the time gap, waiting for equilibrium to return, and when it does, the sound returns too, and the air is filled with every color imaginable as powder erupts all over, flying like shooting stars. My uncle and cousins catch up to us and my aunt throws us the bag of bottles, which we grab and squeeze, sending rainbows into the sky.

I survey the scene. Jordan is in a flirtatious color war with a guy I've seen in the neighborhood, and despite her competitive nature, she seems to be letting him win. Jerry is doing double duty, squirting pink dust with one hand and eating a beef patty with the other—one of the families cooking must have taken pity on him (despite his robust figure, he plays the starving child quite convincingly). Janae is cheering and waving the Jamaican flag from her vantage point on Zeke's shoulders, where she can keep her eyes on all of us and everyone else.

Jesus appears with his hair colored mustard yellow from the powder. He looks like one of the painted street performers who freeze like statues and then come to life if you drop money into their bucket. We float toward one another with dust-covered feet and hands and noses.

"Lightskin!" he yells above the noise.

Normally, I'd be frozen, insecure about what to say or do, but the energy here is infectious, and before I realize what I'm doing, I boldly grab a squeeze bottle and shoot it right at him as his boys cheer me on. He laughs and I laugh and the parade spins around us, a vortex that draws us closer together. Just when I think he might kiss me with those perfect lips, my mom grabs me playfully and drags me away.

To see her now, covered from head to toe in purple and green, you would never know what a basic outfit she has on. She dances, keeping up with the young people and at times one-upping them on their moves. It's more than just the colors that have altered her appearance—every time she whips her head around, her hair flies back and I see her smile. Her flawless white teeth are radiant and her smile is contagious, so I take a mental snapshot each time she comes into view, a portrait of our new world, and I join her as we both dance.

Dance.

Dance.

Chapter 10

The alarm on my phone goes off for the third time, and I try to come up with an excuse not to get out of bed. Any excuse.

When we got back to the house after the festival, I was elated. A part of me had been awakened, and I felt like I could take on the world. I just needed to sleep, and then I would sit my mom down and tell her what my dad was trying to force me to do. I would tell her that we could start over, just the two of us, and make a new life.

But the magic waned as soon as we walked through the door when Pa informed us that my father had called while we were out. He did his best to keep my father's temper at bay, but Pa couldn't lie to him—dishonesty is just not acceptable in this house. I watched my mom retreat to the third-floor bathroom to call my dad. I listened to her muffled sobs from the hallway until she emerged, fully returned to her depressed phantom form, drifting through the house, leaving a trail of gloom in her wake.

The alarm goes off for a fourth time. It's really here, the first day of sophomore year of high school.

My backpack is out next to the duffel bag of clothes I have to bring to my father's. Now that the school year has begun, so has our temporary custody arrangement, and every couple of days, I have to pick up and move.

If things were normal, I'd be sitting on a coach bus next to Stevie, being delivered to campus. But my school, which charges upwards of 40k a year tuition, can't see the use in a bus stop in Harlem, so I have to take the subway. It takes three attempts to balance my duffel bag and backpack on my person as I hobble out the front door toward morning rush hour on the 2 train.

Halfway down the steps, my duffel falls to my elbow and I throw it into the street in frustration.

"Hey! I could sue you for assault, lady."

His voice is seven octaves lower than I remember and I haven't seen him since he left for Hong Kong two months ago, but I can't stop the smile from taking over my face. Stevie stands on the sidewalk, five foot ten and a hundred and thirty pounds, with my bag at his feet. His presence makes it easier to breathe—it's that best-friend power that obliterates any negativity or tension in the surrounding area. He's the only person I can be myself with all the time because he has a way about him that lets you know he's not afraid of anything. Unlike me, he likes to stand out. Case in point: today he's wearing fitted acid-wash jeans, an oversized ★NSYNC touring T-shirt, and a '90s color-block baseball hat.

I rush down the steps, give Stevie a hug, collect my duffel bag, and begin to head to the corner.

"Where you goin', B?" (Stevie always calls me B, although the origin behind and meaning of the nickname remain undisclosed.)

"To the train . . . or did you forget to mention that you were actually spending the summer at Hogwarts to learn how to apparate?"

"Pshh!" Stevie swats the idea away like a mosquito. "I traveled all the way into the city from Westchester—we're riding in style. I'm getting us an Uber X."

Once we get off the highway, it's like a giant Wite-Out pen came down from the sky and did a once-over on everyone on the street. We head to Riverdale, a neighborhood in the Bronx that is distinctly separate from the rest of the borough, like a secret microcosm where rich suburban families in the tri-state area send their kids to school to get a top-notch education without fear of any "urban" influence.

"This is the year, B," Stevie says to me with a hunger and determination I've rarely heard in his voice. "I'm gonna get it."

The Lena Zahira Dance Initiative is a twelve-month fellowship for five high school students selected from the three major private schools in Riverdale—Fort Hilten, Fieldston, and our school, Pritchard—to study in London at a super-fancy ballet academy. Stevie has dreamt of being accepted his entire life. His mom and I were his only cheerleaders. But ever since Stevie's mom passed away a few years ago from a brain tumor the size of a tangerine that no amount of experimental surgery could remove, I am all he has. His dad is like, 24 percent present in parenthood. He claims that because he was raised in a "blue-collar Irish American household," he can't understand why his son wants to spend his time "twirling all over the place."

Today, Stevie's excitement hits a nerve, though, sending a wave of discomfort and irritation through my body. The truth is, my support for him has only been half sincere. The idea of an entire year at Pritchard without Stevie is torturous.

"Mmm," I grunt, giving him all I can at this moment.

I feel his pain. Years ago, we started to communicate telepathically because we had already spent all day telling each other everything there was to say. When you only have one real friend and no siblings, it's easy to create a language that starts with one of you and ends with the other. It never occurred to us that we might hide anything from each other, because how could we? We can read each other's minds.

"My dad says Harlem is the new 'it' neighborhood. You're getting in at the right time," Stevie says, changing the subject.

Mr. McConnell is one of the biggest real estate brokers in Manhattan, and ever since his wife died, he is incapable of talking or thinking about anything other than property trends, which is not much of a departure from his former state of being.

"Oh yeah? Let's hope the emotional toll from the domestic upheaval will prove itself a worthy investment in the future, then."

"You're so dramatic," he teases.

"Of course I'm dramatic. I'm a writer!"

"A writer who doesn't show anyone anything she writes. For all I know, you've just been making a list of body parts or dog breed mutations that you find offensive."

"There really is nothing worse than a cockapoo," I say, not wanting to admit that my life has effectively fallen apart since he left at the end of June. "So how was Hong Kong? What's the latest in the adventures of Lian Hsu?"

Stevie is biracial too, half Chinese and half white, but he's never struggled with who he is, at least not to my knowledge; he's just always been comfortable and confident by nature. He spends the summers with his mom's mother, Lian, a ninety-three-year-old retiree who refuses to slow down.

"Ya know, she's as feisty as ever. This year, my uncle told her she had to wear one of those alert button necklaces after falling in the bathroom and she threw a fit. Said she could never wear something so ugly, but he threatened to put her in a home if she didn't."

Stevie reenacts his grandmother's reaction, morphing into an elderly woman.

"But guess who won? After a day at work, my uncle's voice mail was full of complaints from the alert company's customer service. Apparently, Lian was clogging their phone lines by continuously pushing the button to request assistance going to the market for fresh scallops, so they cancelled her subscription twenty-four hours later!"

The Uber driver is so engrossed in the story as Stevie tells it that we miss the school and have to circle back.

José hands us our iced coffees and buttered rolls from his metal cart on the corner. It's been our standing order since the fifth grade, and he always has it ready for us. A steady morning coffee routine is a rite of passage for all New York kids, city or suburban; it makes no difference. The caffeine craving starts early. It's in our blood.

We join the other students lined up at Pritchard's front doors. The school incorporated a new system a few years ago to digitize our schedules and improve school functionality. There are four streams per grade, and each stream has all their classes together. You'd think it would make more sense to send us all the information about our classes and streams ahead of the first day, but I think they like to make it more dramatic for the hell of it.

"Headed back to the jungle, Nevaeh?"

Abby Jackson steps forward. Her voice is high-pitched and irritatingly sweet, like one of those talking cartoon animals on Nick Jr. that teach you numbers and letters and the occasional word in Spanish, except Abby's character would be possessed by the devil. The three of us used to be friends when we were little: Abby, Stevie, and I. There are photos somewhere of us jumping into piles of leaves as young kids, but between fifth and sixth grades, Abby made friends with this new crew who call themselves the Bomb Squad, and she never looked back.

We turn and face her. Abby's thick dark brown hair and perfectly sculpted eyebrows frame her bright snake-green eyes. Stevie takes the lead, per usual, and drops to his knees right in front of her.

"God, grant me the confidence of the mediocre white woman and the courage to thrive off doing the bare minimum!"

Some classmates around us snicker at his clap back, but not loud enough to invite the attention of the Bomb Squad.

Abby rolls her eyes at him and gestures to my duffel bag.

"Coming home from a trip? No . . . that's not it. Hmmm . . . your laundry machine broke and you need to use the one in the locker room?" She shakes her head, taunting me. "Oh, right! You're moving some stuff back into your dad's house since your parents split up."

She looks at her robotrons and pretends she's about to whisper but instead practically shouts. "I heard that Nevaeh's been living at her grandparents' house somewhere in the Hood," she boasts. "Her mom caught her dad in their bedroom with some younger woman."

I tell myself to breathe, that my dad might be acting like a completely irrational psychopath, but he wouldn't have done that. He might have moved on, but he wouldn't cheat. Abby is just an evil, miserable, beautiful monster sent here to destroy me and feed off my despair.

Stevie pulls me forward: we're next in line, and we approach a table where two new and very flustered teachers sit.

"Name?" the man says hurriedly, wiping sweat from his brow.

"McConnell," Stevie says, ignoring the look of confusion that spreads across the face of the teacher expecting a traditional East Asian surname.

"Steven McConnell. Three. Next!" the teacher calls out, looking past me to the people behind.

"Levitz," I say, and my voice makes him jump.

"Sorry, didn't see you there. Levitz, Levitz . . . Ahh, here, Ney . . . Neh . . . Nivia?"

I hear Abby laugh behind me.

"Nuh-vay-ah," I enunciate.

"Mmmm . . . ," he says, avoiding mangling my name for the second time. "Levitz, two. Next!"

Dread takes over. Stevie and I aren't in the same stream.

Abby stands with her back to us as she continues to address her minions, loudly enough for us to hear.

"We were in East Hampton at the Maidenridge Club when I heard my mom telling her friends that everyone on Nevaeh's block saw it go down. Mr. Levitz and the hot blond girlfriend had to run into the street because Nevaeh's mom chased them, throwing clothes and cups at them like they were on an episode of *Love and Hip Hop*."

I want to scream, but the more I listen to her, the more something inside tells me that this time, Abby might not just be trying to hurt me. She might actually be right.

"Don't listen to her, B. She's overcompensating for her lack of personality. Two and three still have lunch together—look!" He holds up the stream schedule.

I fake a smile. I just need to get through the day, which I can do as long as—

"Oh, here we are! Abby Jackson, two!" the nervous teacher declares.

Acid shoots up my throat so quickly that I can't stop it. I drop my bags and run to the garbage can that Abby now stands directly in front of. I wave my arms, but she doesn't move, and then it's too late. I vomit right there in the lobby of the building, in front of everyone, all over Abby and the poor sweaty new teacher behind her. Mortified, I look around for some way to escape as Principal Lackey's voice comes on the loudspeaker.

"Welcome back to Pritchard! Two thousand eighteen is going to be a great year for all of us. Seventh graders, please remember as you prepare for your bar and bat mitzvahs to keep party planning within the school doors to a minimum, and don't forget to 'hava nice-gila day!'" She cackles like an animated witch, and her high-pitched laugh is the last thing that bounces between my ears before everything goes blurry and my head hits the floor.

"Am I dead?"

No one responds, so I hope that at the very least, if I did meet my untimely demise, I ended up in the happy place rather than some terrible purgatory where the only entertainment is an audio recording of *Our Town*.

I open one eye a slit, but the lights are so bright they hurt. Aside from a massive bump on the back of my head and a nasty taste in my mouth, I think I'm okay.

But then again, the little voice inside me reasons, *death might not have been the worst conclusion to today.*

The nurse's office is pale orange, the color of my vomit earlier today, and it makes my stomach turn. From what the clock is telling me, I've been out for a few hours, so perhaps it's not too late to slip into a coma if I close my eyes again and lie completely still.

"Nevaeh, honey, you think you can sit up?" the nurse asks, with tuna salad wedged between her teeth. "You're probably going to be sore. But if you throw up again or find yourself feeling dizzy, you need to go straight to the hospital, okay? There's a slim chance you got a concussion. We called your dad and he's sending a car to pick you up."

The getaway vehicle is appreciated, but the nurse won't let me leave unless I'm wheeled out—she mumbles something about insurance under her rancid breath. Luckily, this first week of school is all half days, so everyone has already gone home.

"B, you're alive! I thought you'd left me to deal with the mutating bottom-feeders on my own!" Stevie grabs the handles of the wheelchair from the nurse, who rolls her eyes and tells him to bring it back once I'm safely in my car. Now that we're off school property, I suppose the concerns about insurance are moot.

"Yo, you should have seen the fit Abby threw after they took you away. They made her put on lost-and-found clothes because she was covered in vomit. It was priceless. Like, she's definitely going to make you pay for it big-time. Watch your back. But oh, man, it was worth it, trust me."

For the first time today, things don't feel absolutely terrible. A black car is parked at the corner, probably the one my dad sent.

"Yoo-hoo! Nevaeh!"

Walking toward me from the opposite direction of the car is

Rabbi Sarah. Her straw-colored hair bounces on her shoulders as she moves.

Not today! the little voice in my head screams. *Not after everything else!*

"Stevie, wheel me to that car and get in," I say through clenched teeth.

"B—what? I have to bring the chair back to Nurse—"

"Stevie, do it now!"

We book it to the car. Rabbi Sarah chases us, but we are closer and hop in before she reaches us. The car peels off, and she plops into the empty wheelchair, a living monument to the worst first day of school in the history of the world.

Stevie is giving me the "we've never lied to each other in ten years what the hell is going on" look.

"My dad thinks spending time in Harlem with my mom's Baptist family is a bad influence on me, so he called a temple, and now I have to have a belated bat mitzvah. That lady is a rabbi," I tell him quickly, and even though the words burn as they come out, I can't deny that I feel better after the purge. Stevie's face softens with pity and he grabs my hand, absorbing the dread I've been dealing with on my own for the months he was gone.

"Damn, B," he says, taking in the scope of this new reality. "What if we do a flash mob during the ceremony? That would piss your dad off so bad! And we'd definitely go viral." His hands move as he frames the imaginary headline. *"BuzzFeed News: Ma-Swirl Tov! You'll Die at This Biracial Coming-of-Age!"*

I laugh. The thought of him stealing the stage in some fancy temple in the middle of such a doomed affair almost makes it worth going through with it.

"I don't think Abby was lying," I say quietly. "A couple days after you left for the summer, I came home from Bubby's country club and the boxes were outside, waiting for us to leave. No warning. No nothing."

We sit in silence together as Stevie tries his best to come up with more positive spins.

"What are you going to do?" he asks finally.

Nothing, like always, the voice inside me says, but for once, I don't want to just settle and accept this as truth. I look at my phone: it's only two o'clock.

"Sir," I say, getting the driver's attention in the rearview mirror. "Change of plans. We're going to Manhattan."

Chapter 11

Say what you want about Times Square and how overrun it is by tourists; at least it has some personality. Midtown East is as bland as an unseasoned, boiled chicken breast. We get out in front of my dad's office, just a couple avenues east of Bryant Park. Men with slicked-back hair in fitted gray suits march around us. My father's office is in a forty-story building in the center of the block, sandwiched between two shorter, equally nondescript structures. The dark green marble lobby is cold and smells of chemicals, like it had been plastic-wrapped and someone accidentally broke the seal.

"Miss Levitz." Mauricio nods from behind the security desk to greet me like he has my whole life. He reaches into his navy-blue uniform pocket to present us with two Jolly Ranchers.

Levitz, Banks, and Tanner is a highly profitable boutique law firm that my father started a few years after graduating from Yale Law School. The rumble of jittery knees fills the office as sleep-deprived junior associates chug coffee and type furiously at their desks. No one so much as looks our way as we enter, so I lead Stevie through the office to the partners' corner.

The large desk where my dad's secretary, Ashleigh, usually sits is unattended. Her person is replaced with a message written in pink Sharpie stuck to the back of her chair: *Be right back!*

I roll my eyes as we walk past the desk to the large double doors and see an episode of *The Real Housewives of New York City* paused on her computer screen. I have never liked Ashleigh. There's something about how close she stands to my dad that's always rubbed me the wrong way. Plus, I think it's weird that a grown woman is obsessed with reality TV to the point that it's practically all she can ever talk about.

"Come on," I say to Stevie, pushing open the huge oak doors to his office.

My father's face is mostly obstructed by the body in front of him, but his left eye peers in the direction of the intrusion. First confused and then stricken with fear, he stands and knocks Ashleigh, who moments before was searching his mouth for leftovers with her tongue, to the ground. Pink lipstick smears his chin.

"Nevaeh!" my father exclaims.

Ashleigh quickly shifts her shirt, trying to hide the red lace peeking out from under the airy material.

Guess she's the blonde Abby was referring to.

"Why aren't you at your lesson?" Dad asks, eyebrows raised.

The phone on the desk outside his office rings. We stand there, the four of us, until my father coughs and Ashleigh gets the hint: she might be his mistress-turned-girlfriend, but for now, she is also still his secretary. She shuffles in front of him, tucking her unbuttoned top into her high-waisted spandex skirt, and answers, half bent over so her behind points suggestively in his direction.

"It's a Rabbi Sarah Edward," she says.

My stomach drops as he snatches the receiver from her. I'm screwed. It's not like I took the time to come up with a cover story.

"Yeah, mmm-hmm, she's here, actually. I was just wondering what— Oh, I see. Well, let's not let it happen again. All right, yep, you too." He hangs up the phone and glares in my direction again.

"Nevaeh—"

I brace myself.

"Rabbi Sarah sends her apologies, says she mixed up the date."

The words fall out of his mouth as I drop into one of the chairs in front of his glass desk, relieved and confused.

"Are you okay?" he asks, rushing forward. "The school called to say you fainted. How are you feeling? The nurse said you were all right." My father cups my face, but I jerk away from his touch. He sits down on the other side of the desk, facing me the way he does his clients, enduring my coldness and willing himself to push on as though he isn't bothered.

"Abby Jackson overheard her mother at their country club," I blurt out. "She said you cheated on Mom. She told the whole school today."

He sighs and glances at Ashleigh, whose ears stand alert like a Doberman's. "Nevaeh, it's . . . complicated."

His eye twitches as she walks over to me. Her slow, seductive strides drag against the carpet my mother picked out in Morocco as a gift when Dad remodeled the office last year.

"Nevaeh, I know this is a lot to process right now, but I want you to know that I love your father," Ashleigh tells me. "Over time, I hope we can get to know each other, become friends, even." Her voice is nasal and high, which makes everything that comes out of her mouth sound like a presumptuous question.

"I'm going back to Pa's tonight," I declare with my arms folded on my chest.

"Nevaeh, that's not how this works." My father's face glows red. "You're a child, and you don't know what's best for you."

"You said it the other night, honey," Ashleigh says, moving her hand from my dad's shoulder down his arm to his thigh. "This is just a cry for help." She smiles at me from behind him, a look filled with acid and cunning, one that warns me not to underestimate her.

"Let her go," I hear her whisper into his ear as I rise from my seat and pull Stevie out of the room.

And he does.

"Maybe she's a vampire? Or like, another evil being who controls minds? Your dad seemed sort of possessed," Stevie says as we round the corner to Pa's house and come face to face with Jesus.

Every time I see him, I am surprised by how easy it is to be paralyzed by his smile. Jesus is double Stevie's lean and lanky frame, so Stevie straightens up, removing a few inches from their height differential.

"You got a man, shorty?" Jesus says playfully. He casually leans in to kiss me on the cheek. I stop breathing. Next to me, Stevie stands with his mouth wide open, probably more shocked than I am at this highly public display of affection from a stranger.

"Umm, Jesus, this is my *best friend*."

Stevie sticks his hand out to introduce himself. "I'm Stevie. Damn! Are those Air Jordan Tens from the City series? They're fire!"

Jesus smiles, and Stevie's outstretched palm connects with his as they fall into some elaborate hand dance. I've never understood how guys keep up with all these handshakes; it's like they choreograph them on the spot, filled with snaps and fist bumps and sometimes, if they want to be unnecessarily extra about it, a dab, and file them away in some ever-expanding part of their brain.

"Oh, okay, you're a sneakerhead, huh? Lemme see whatchu got!"

Stevie moonwalks back, always ready to hop into the limelight.

"Not bad. Scottie Pippen Nike Air high-tops."

I have imagined Jesus for the past few weeks in moments when I'm alone with my thoughts. I lie in bed, close my eyes, and see his lips. I wonder how they might taste.

"Yo, B, you okay?"

The tightness in my chest reminds me that I've been holding my breath for a while, so I exhale and attempt to play it cool.

"Sorry, I'm a little dizzy in this heat."

"*Or* maybe it's because your dad is—"

I cut Stevie off before he can blab my business.

"Dead! My dad, he . . . um, died. Today is the anniversary." I snatch the water bottle from Stevie's hands and take a long, dramatic drink.

"I'm sorry," Jesus says.

"That's okay. Really. It happened so long ago. I barely knew him. . . ."

The lies get harder as I build on them.

"We've got to go," I choke out, and drag Stevie down the block so fast he almost twists his ankle on the uneven pavement trying to keep up.

"Sorry. I just . . . don't want him to know everything," I say, handing him the water bottle as I open the front door.

Stevie's eyes travel from the details etched into the staircase to me, searching for a sign that his best friend is still here.

"Nevaaaeeeeehhhh." Jerry sings my name from the other room, and we find him stuffing salt and vinegar chips into his mouth. Janae grabs some chips for herself and drops one on the carpet. Within seconds, Anita is standing over Stevie, waving a spoon in his face.

"I'm gonna curse your children's children if you don't mind the carpet and stop making a mess in—"

She stops midsentence when she realizes the child she is berating is not one of her own.

"Stevie's with me," I tell her. "And I wouldn't lay a curse on him if I were you. His dad would sue us for everything we've got."

Stevie nods furiously. "It's true. He'd feel like he was owed a reimbursement for the fifteen years of parenting he had to pay for!"

My aunt looks him up and down before giving me some side-eye to remind me who's in charge and walking back to the kitchen. Janae takes her headphones off.

"You gonna be okay?"

Stevie nods unconvincingly, then asks for directions to the bathroom and darts away.

"You better not sleep with that boy in this house," Janae says. "The last thing your mom needs is a grandchild, and the last thing I need is my mama thinking we're all acting a fool. She's already got X-ray vision."

I lower my voice to a whisper. "We're friends, best friends. That's it. He's *not* who I like."

The front door slams and the room fills with the smells of

onion and cilantro. Jordan is back from work. She's a hostess two days a week at Nacho Mama's, a Mexican restaurant frequented by Columbia students.

Stevie returns from the bathroom and freezes again, but this time, the look on his face mirrors Lavender's when she sets eyes on Ron after he wins a quidditch match. I've seen the expression before; he wore it all through fourth grade whenever we had social studies with Mrs. Applebaum.

"Hi, I'm Stevie."

Jordan shoos Stevie out of her way, but he remains resolute with love and motionless before her. Janae sits up taller on the couch.

"Thank God you're home," Janae calls out, unwilling to move from her preferred spot. "You missed everything. Mama almost gave this kid a heart attack. Meanwhile, I'm just trying to get my Spanish homework done in time to catch *Grey's Anatomy* and Nevaeh has some secret boyfriend."

"Jesus? Nah, he's not her boyfriend. Not yet," Stevie says, unaware that each word might as well be a shovelful of dirt on my shallow grave. "Cool dude, though."

Luckily, before Jordan murders me, Anita comes out of the kitchen.

"It's time for dinner, and I won't wait another minute." She stops and wrinkles her nose at Jordan. "Girl, you better go take that mess off before sitting down in here. You've got the whole place smelling like a chimichanga. And get Corinne while you're up there."

"It was really nice to meet you!" Stevie squeaks after Jordan as she trudges up the stairs. He turns back to us. "I should head back to the burbs to eat dinner with *America's Got Talent*. My dad is definitely still at the office."

I can tell he wants an invite to dinner here, but I'm not in the mood, not after he put me on blast for the second time tonight.

"Good idea," I snap.

"I'm officially signed up for the college trip. I borrowed the other two hundred dollars. I'll pay it back myself," Jordan announces to the table just as my mom descends the stairs.

"Borrowed from who?" Anita asks through tight lips.

"Me," Janae says.

Janae has been saving up the money she makes from the odd video-recording jobs she gets on craigslist to buy a real camera, but last week I heard Jordan crying in the bathroom because Anita said they couldn't afford to send her on the college trip, so Janae must have decided to help her sister out.

Anita's eyes bulge: overpowered by her children, two against one.

My mom walks the long way around the table and pats my head as she passes, her way of communicating without needing to speak.

"Ow!" I grab my tender skull.

My mom stops with a look of concern.

"I'm fine," I say, but Anita clears her throat and I know my answer isn't going to do. "I hit my head when I fainted this morning, but it's seriously not a big deal. The nurse said as long as I don't feel dizzy or throw up, I probably don't have a concussion."

My mom looks at me, lost, like her ears stopped working.

"Didn't the school call?" I ask with irritation.

Even my father, who has been possessed by the devil, had the wherewithal to be concerned.

"I—I," my mom stammers. "I turned my phone off. I was resting. I am so exhausted."

"Not like you would have done anything anyway," I mumble under my breath.

"Daddy, you better pray before the food gets cold," Anita says, her hands clasped and her eyes pointed at me with equal parts curiosity and disdain.

Zeke offers me a night off from dish duty to rest after my injury, but I decline once I catch Jordan's menacing glare. I live to regret it. Tonight, Jordan has appointed herself kitchen supervisor, a role only she is qualified to fill, and after a lengthy hour and a half of cleaning under her watchful eye, I drag my fan up the stairs to bed.

Anita blocks me on the second floor. She stands before me with her hair wrapped tightly in a light blue scarf.

"I don't know how things worked in your house," she says, her body shaking as she speaks to me. "But in mine, you are going to respect your elders, especially your own mother."

The tight screw that has been holding my jaw shut my entire life unhinges with a monstrous crack.

"Maybe you should take this diatribe to your sister, who, in case you haven't noticed, has given up entirely on being a parent."

Slap!

Every pore on the left side of my face throbs from the impact of Anita's open hand. The pain spreads like a grease fire, impossible to combat. Her legs buckle, and she sits on the step as her exhalations grow into deep, devastating sobs. I tower over her, stunned at how small she looks from this angle. This woman, who my grandfather often refers to as "boisterous," is now hardly audible.

"It's taken such a long time for us to be near each other again. Growing up, Corinne thought I was too cool for her, but it's not true. Your mom didn't care how many guys asked her out, or if she got the lead in the school play; she was happy to just be herself. I always admired that, how she didn't care what anyone thought. Then she went away to that fancy college with big plans. She was on fire when she met your father. But when she came back . . . it was like the light inside her had been blown out. Little by little, she disappeared until I could barely recognize her. But I can't lose her. With Mummy gone, I just . . . I can't lose her too."

Despite the ringing in my ear from her slap, my arms close around my aunt. The olive oil cream in her hair smells the same way the bathroom does after Janae or Jordan gets ready in the morning. I've never been able to share things like that with my mom. In the summer, I would run over and hold my arm against her leg every five minutes as she lounged by the pool to see if being in the sun had made me closer to her complexion. I would study her, counting the few similarities we shared to make sure they hadn't disappeared, blown away by a gust of wind. I have always been desperate to hold on to anything that brought us closer together.

It never occurred to me that Anita might have been feeling the same thing her entire life. I never knew that our hearts suffer the same ache every time a bit of my mom drifts away in front of our eyes.

Anita calms herself and regains her composure, uncomfortable in her vulnerability.

"Nevaeh—"

"You don't have to apologize."

Anita holds two fingers up to my lips, blocking my dismissal and demanding the entirety of my attention.

"I've been holding all this anger for your daddy for years, and I let it slip out onto you. We all make assumptions about each other. It doesn't matter if you're family or a stranger on the subway; we do it everywhere, even here, in our safe spaces, where we're supposed to love each other up and down.

"People are always going to want to split you into pieces so they can feel more comfortable with who you are, and I am sorry no one ever sat you down to prepare you for that. In some ways, you've got it easy, but you've got it hard too, and your hard is different—tricky. Like a piece of paper that flies out of your hand in the wind and keeps getting away just before you've closed your fingers around it."

Anita stops to take a breath. Her face is filled with so much exhaustion even her eyelashes tremble.

"One day, Nevaeh, you're going to realize that you've got magic coursing through your veins. Same as me and your mom and Jordan and Janae and your grandma. You'll know once you've found it; there's no way you won't. It feels like lightning and thunder and sunlight all at the same time. But get ready, because when you do find it, everyone around you is going to try to snatch it away. That's okay, though, 'cause once you've got that magic, you'll know no one can take it from you." She grasps me by the chin to make sure I'm really listening. "THAT is how we thrive."

Anita's eyes well up again and I look away, pained by the ever-growing reservoir behind my eyes that refuses to release. It hurts too much, so I move to leave, but she grabs me.

"What is it, Nevaeh?" Anita begs. "What happened? I can't help either of you if I don't know what's wrong."

"He cheated and she caught him and he didn't even feel bad. He just . . . moved on."

The truth falls out of me and crashes ten feet below the base of the house, deep in the earth, a tremor that causes the pipes and tunnels of the underworld to shiver, just as Anita and I do above, on the stairs, in the dark.

"Sit down," Anita commands. "And tell me everything."

Chapter 12

I can't tell if it's being up here, at the highest point in the house, that makes me feel lighter, or if it's because I've confessed the truth to Anita. I told her everything: the affair and the bat mitzvah and the hideous, sharp new furniture and Abby and the vomit. Well, almost the whole truth—I kept finding my mom's journal a secret.

The jelly beans from my backpack are warm, but that doesn't matter. I move the candies around in my mouth and coat my teeth with a sticky, fruity film as I crack open the book and fall into my mother's memories.

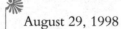

August 29, 1998

Northwestern begrudgingly let me move in a day early. The flight was cheaper on a Sunday, and the truth is, I couldn't wait to get away. Every day since the school dance has felt like the countdown clock on a bomb. My hair is falling out in clumps. Mummy said it must be the shampoo she bought at the dollar store to save money, but I can't help wondering if it's my own body attempting to escape from itself. The only way to hide the quarter-sized patches of scalp is to pull my hair up to the top of my head, tight and slicked.

My father was irritated that I chose to leave on the day of the Lord, so after services, Mummy, Anita, and I trudged back to the house to send me off without him. None of us are particularly good at goodbyes, mostly because we've never done them. I'm the first to leave for more than a day trip. Just a quick pat on the back and a promise to call once I got settled in the dorm—that was the way I started my new life. If only I could have left my stupidity behind me.

The older woman next to me on the plane asked to switch from the window seat to the aisle; she said she hated the reminder of how far away from Earth we were. I spent the whole ride with my face pressed against the cold, thick glass. The growing distance between me and New York made me feel safer, despite the forty-thousand-foot drop to the ground.

When I arrived at the dorm, the scantily clad resident advisor met me outside the building.

"No drinking in the building. If anyone dies, it's on me, and I will make your life a living hell."

She dropped a key into my hand and shot off the rest of her rapid-fire instructions.

"You're room four-oh-four. The elevator is out; stairs are to your left. Move-in starts at eight a.m. tomorrow, so be up unless you want to meet your roommate in bed."

After unpacking my two bags, I took out a calculator to

go over my budget for the millionth time. Even with the scholarship and my parents helping me out with the cost of room and board, I need spending money, which I'll make at the campus job I've been assigned in the library. As long as I keep to my plan, I'll be able to save at least $2,500 a year, almost double that if I can get myself hired as a resident advisor for the next three years. And then I might have enough to get my master's degree, the first to do so in my family, like I've always wanted.

All I used to care about was making something of myself, but now I just want to feel like my old self again. With every day that passes, that seems less feasible, so turning into someone completely different is the next best option. Anything to stop feeling the way I do: Used. Dirty. Worthless. Foolish.

The silence as I mapped out my future was calming. Normally, the mixture of sounds in my house would overwhelm me: Anita chattering away, my mom humming as she cooks, plantains popping in a cast iron skillet, but here, it was like I had moved to another planet.

When I was growing up, my father said that the devil was on the radio, so all we listened to when we were kids were the older records Mummy convinced him were acceptable. Mostly gospel, and Gloria Gaynor's single "I Will Survive." Until Walkmen were invented and allowed me to sneak a wider array of music into my repertoire, I blasted that song on repeat, drowning Anita out as she talked on the phone for hours.

Gloria came with me on the move. I put my headphones on, grabbed my Discman, and listened to the song. I danced around the twin beds that were positioned at opposite corners of the room. I danced around the walk-in closet and into the bathroom, which smelled like pine-scented cleaning supplies. I danced in front of my new windows as people walked through the streets, unaware that I was watching from a hundred feet above.

When the song finished for what must have been the eighteenth time in a row, I saw a figure behind me in the window's reflection. There's nothing like abruptly being made aware you are not alone, in a strange place, with nowhere to go. Instinct told me to grab a weapon; the closest item I could find was a pencil.

"What do you want?" I shouted, jumping around with my makeshift sword.

"Sorry to scare you. I didn't know anyone else had moved in. I'm Samuel."

His friendly demeanor and muffled laugh did little to calm me. That brash voice in my head told me not to let my guard down, not after the last time.

"I'm Corinne," I said.

"Have you eaten dinner yet? There's a great pizza place close by, if you wanna join."

The last time I'd eaten was that morning, at home. The adrenaline of the trip must have gotten me through the day, but now that food had been mentioned, the overwhelming feeling of unadulterated hunger made it impossible to understand how I had gone this long without sustenance.

"Sure, I'm starved." I was surprised to hear the words come out of my mouth.

He held the door open for me and smiled in a way that

made my whole body tingle, half from excitement and half from concern. The last person who'd smiled at me that way was Raymond.

It's just pizza, I told myself, and made sure to keep at least six inches between us as we walked the few blocks.

The only available booth at the restaurant was essentially in the kitchen, but our hunger was far more powerful than the need for comfort. A blond woman materialized before us. She bent down and whispered a halfhearted greeting as her eyes darted to her other, mostly white customers with concern that our interracial presence disrupted the space like a loud alarm in need of silencing. Samuel ordered a pepperoni pie for the two of us, and the waitress hesitated before turning the Midwestern charm up a notch and vanishing to place our order. For the first time since we'd met, I took a good long look at Samuel. His face was chiseled and sharp, the way Disney princes' always are, with green-blue eyes that played off his thick, dark, wavy hair.

The pizza, which by New York standards was not even remotely close to pizza, was delicious, but glances from other patrons kept distracting me. The waitress stopped by to check on us, and by "us," I mean Samuel. She batted her eyes and giggled, lingering until he graciously thanked her. She took the dismissal in stride and bounced away without offering me the time of day.

"So, tell me about yourself," Samuel said, oblivious to the attention we were drawing. He put another slice of pizza on his plate. "Where are you from? Why are you here early?"

"Got a good deal on the flight. New York City."

"But like, what are you? Where are you *from*, from?" he pressed.

I get this question often, mostly from white folks trying to determine whether my lighter complexion means I'm more accessible to them. Most of the time, I think they mean it as a compliment, but it always feels like a burn— like just being me will never be sufficient. I know how it feels to be dismissed, ignored, and underestimated. It's been that way my whole life. Not fun enough, not brave enough, not anything, really, until Raymond noticed me, and even then, he wasn't interested in getting to know me. Or maybe it's that once he did, he saw that I only had one thing to offer.

"My mom is from Jamaica and my dad is from Liberia."

"Aha! I knew there was something exotic about you!"

He locked eyes with me. Those irises looked like the pictures of the ocean Mummy has from when she was young, crystal clear gemstones that seduced me with their regal sparkle. His long, thick eyelashes fluttered with each blink, casting a shadow over his face that stretched all the way down to the dimple that dots his chin. His smile revealed a tiny drop of sauce at the corner of his mouth, and I had to stop myself from reaching over the table to clean it with my thumb.

"And what about you?" I responded.

"Oh, nothin' special. Just your run-of-the-mill East Coast Jewish boy. Although . . ." He stalled with a dangerous grin. "I have been known to make a French toast so delicious that it will make you wanna marry me on the spot."

"Yeah, and why are you here early?" I ask, suppressing a giggle.

"My mom is certifiable, so I had to get out of there. I've been here for a week. Convinced her I was joining the Jewish student house and we needed to get a head start on the first freshman Shabbat."

The waitress came by with the bill and left it, along with her number written on the bottom next to a smiley face. She didn't even consider that I could be competition. Samuel threw money down on the table before I even got a chance to open my wallet. So what if he wanted to know what I am? The fact is, he wants to talk to me more than he wants to talk to that waitress. I watched her look at the untouched receipt with her number, baffled as to why he hadn't taken it.

"Thank you for dinner," I said to Samuel, loud enough for her to hear.

"No problem," he said, and opened the door for me. "My pleasure."

Out of nowhere, I heard Gloria Gaynor on the radio, *"As long as I know how to love I know I'll stay alive."*

The words reverberated through the restaurant and onto the street as we left. It felt like a sign from the universe that in this new life, everything was going to be okay. But then Samuel insisted on taking me to my dorm room, even after I assured him I would be fine. My body went numb on the walk up the stairs—I'd done it again, given the wrong impression. When we got to my door, he blocked the entrance to my room, boxing me in so I couldn't move. He leaned in, so close I could smell the pizza sauce on his breath, and I resigned myself to doing what he expected, but he just kissed my cheek and stepped away.

"Good night, Corinne," he said softly. "I'm glad I found you."

And then he went to his room a few floors up, leaving me with the hope that maybe this time, everything would work out the way it does in dreams and fairy tales.

My mom and I used to dance to "I Will Survive" in the living room. I know every word, backwards and forwards. The day we moved to Harlem, we lay in our shared bed listening to the honks and cries of the city. That song was the sound of home and safety, an anthem of strength and perseverance, the first song I ever re-member hearing as a child, and I needed it, so I took my iPhone out and began to play it on speaker. My mom snatched the phone from me and turned it off so fast she almost cracked the screen with her nail. Then she grabbed my face with her velvety hands and pulled me toward her so we were eye to eye.

"You don't play that song anymore, okay, Nevaeh? I never want to hear it ever again."

My mom let her words sink in, and when she was ready, she lay back down and our new life began in complete and utter silence.

Chapter 13

It turns out that the nervous teacher who got caught in the cross-fire of my regurgitation on the first day of school is also my science teacher, Mr. Bowels (pronounced "bowls"). He's young, one of the annual crop of new teachers, fresh out of their master's program, who come in bright-eyed, bushy-tailed, and ill-prepared for the unique, privileged wickedness private school teachers face. There are bets circulating that he won't make it past the first month.

Principal Lackey greets us as we enter biology and does not look pleased to be here. Her face is set in its natural sour look, the one where her nose and eyes and lips scrunch together like she just took a giant bite of a lemon. Mr. Bowels towers over Mrs. Lackey, but he shakes in fear as he stands before us. Word must have gotten out about the class-wide wager on his tenure, which can't be good since it's only his second week on the job.

I slide into a table in the back of the room to unpack my textbook and notepad along with everyone else. The empty seat next to me makes me wonder what Stevie is doing in his first-period class, but I snap to when Lola Perkins pulls out the seat next to me and pauses for my approval before she sits down.

"You catch that rally yesterday? The cops tried to block us, but we shut down the West Side Highway for a couple hours. Got some real face time on CNN. I'm so sick of these pigs thinking they can do what they want to us and get away with it."

I heard about the Black Lives Matter rally. Jordan and Anita got into a fight about it last night when Anita just about chained herself to the door to prevent Jordan from leaving. She claimed she wasn't going to let Jordan put her life in danger to march around with a group of reckless, destructive kids all in the name of "the culture," but I'm not going to tell Lola that, so I just smile and nod.

Lola is one of the few other students of color in my class at Pritchard. She hangs out almost exclusively with members of the Black Student Union, a tightly knit crew of Black and African American kids, unified in their otherness as a way to repel the whitewashed, patriarchal culture that permeates this private school. There is an even smaller Latinx group and a larger Asian one, but none of the self-segregated crews of color ever seemed interested in welcoming Stevie or me, so we've mostly just chilled on our own. To be fair, I didn't make much of an effort to join any of the groups. I'm not a joiner by nature.

Activism isn't really a thing at Pritchard. The administration loves to believe they have created an inclusive environment, but we aren't encouraged to engage in conversation that might break up the cohesive facade Pritchard markets to wealthy families. They love the idea of diversity until they realize it means actually engaging with living, breathing Black and Brown people.

We, the chameleons,
Come with a full range of disguises.
Trained and deft in shape-shifting,
Ready to fit in with the masses at the drop of a hat.
The art of blending in becomes instinct.
Stepford wives,
conditioned and compliant,
and thus worthy to serve as ambassadors.

"Don't get comfortable!" Mrs. Lackey shouts before shoving Mr. Bowels forward and transferring the power to him.

"Thank you, Principal Lackey. Today, we're going to switch things up and begin working in two-person teams. Over the course of the year, each team will complete a series of projects together, and the team with the most successful results will get to forego the final exam. We will discuss what 'successful' means in the weeks ahead."

The entire class bangs on the tables and explodes into a chorus of joyous shouting at the prospect of forgoing the final. The ruckus sends Mr. Bowels running behind his desk.

"I've posted a team list by the Laws of Nature poster. Please check it now and reseat yourselves next to your partner," he squeaks from his crouched position.

A communal groan threatens to overwhelm his tentative control, but Principal Lackey gives Mr. Bowels a "stay strong" look of encouragement.

"Okay, one person per table, go up and report back to your table mate," Mr. Bowels suggests in an attempt to rally the troops.

"NOW!" Mrs. Lackey's voice booms.

Heavy feet march toward the list, and Lola joins them, so I

hang back to wait for my destiny. A few moments later, my chair is pulled out from behind me, sending me and my belongings clattering to the ground.

"I always sit on the left; it's my good side," Abby sneers, shoving past me as she takes my seat.

"Ahem." Mrs. Lackey stares in our direction with disapproval.

Lola gathers her things and pats my shoulder softly, a show of support, before walking toward the front of the class to join her new partner.

"Mr. Bow-ells!!" Abby raises her arm halfway so her hand hangs limp at the end of it, the way members of the British royal family often greet plebeians.

"Bowls," he mumbles under his breath as he makes his way through the class. "Yes, Abby, what can I do for you?"

"We don't have the same free periods. I have equestrian practice, and Nevaeh has . . . well, I don't know what she has, but this won't work. I need a new person."

My heart bursts out of my chest, overjoyed at the prospect that her unabashed entitlement might serve some good after all. Mr. Bowels looks at Mrs. Lackey for backup, but she raises an eyebrow. This is clearly a test.

"Well, Abby, I understand, but these teams are nonnegotiable. You will have to compromise and find some time after school to work together."

Abby flicks her wrist, dismissing him. Then she leans toward me with a smile.

"You better not bring any bedbugs to my house, because I'm sure as hell not setting foot in your neighborhood," she says loud enough for the kids at the tables on either side of us to turn and stare.

Abby raises her chin so her upturned nose faces the ceiling and pulls out her phone to take a selfie. I slide down in my chair until I am completely hidden behind the notebook in front of me.

"How can they put you together? That's like, a hate crime," Stevie gripes as we leave the building at the end of the day. "Wait, isn't that the rabbi lady?"

I look up to see Rabbi Sarah leaning against a black car.

"I'll call you later," I say to Stevie.

"What are you doing here?" I ask her after I power walk to the curb.

"Thought I'd pick you up in case you get another attack of the twinkle toes."

She opens the car door and stretches her arm out, preventing any chance of me running in the opposite direction. Abby Jackson walks by with her minions, so I hop in and slam the door before we become any more of a spectacle. The car makes its way off campus, but rather than heading toward White Plains, we get onto the highway and head straight into the city.

"Isn't the driver going the wrong way? I'm staying at my dad's tonight."

"We're taking a detour," Rabbi Sarah explains.

We pull up in front of a short building in the East Village. She jumps out of the car and ushers me into a temple, where she touches her hand to her mouth, kisses it, and then taps a small, thin rectangular object on the right side of the door frame before leading me down some stairs. Chatter and giggles crescendo until we find ourselves in a basement classroom, surrounded by kids ranging in age from about eight to twelve. A young white

113

woman with curly dark brown hair in a floor-length paisley skirt
and layered solid-colored-cotton shirts of varying sleeve lengths
waves us in.

"Nevaeh, hi! Sarah told me about you, I'm Chaya. Welcome!"
She runs over to greet me and then turns to her class. "Sheket,
b'vakasha!" she calls out.

"Hey!" all the kids respond as they take their seats with a swift
obedience that puts Mr. Bowels's classroom technique to shame.

Rabbi Sarah senses my hesitation and nudges me forward to
join the group. We take seats at a table with a boy who looks a
few years younger than Jerry but is dressed like an AARP spokes-
person. His thick linen button-down is tucked into dark blue corduroy pants, and his brown shoes look orthopedic. He passes out
sheets of paper titled *The Hebrew Alphabet.*

"I'm Mordechai," he tells me. "You are most welcome to
join us."

He takes my hand in both of his, clasping it as though he is
the leader of this small community, charged with vetting potential
new members. The teacher announces that it's time to split into
study groups. The older kids congregate in the far corner of the
room, while the younger kids come to our table, filling in the
unoccupied spaces between Mordechai and me.

"Aren't we going over there?" I say, pointing to the kids closer
to my age.

Rabbi Sarah shakes her head. "You need some lessons in the
basics first."

Mordechai gets the go-ahead. Letter by letter, we repeat the
alphabet back to him, and he stops regularly to correct my pronunciation, much to the chagrin of the other nine-year-olds,
who seem bemused by how little I know. The class ends with

a resounding rendition of the Hebrew version of the alphabet song and a blessing from Mordechai. He hands me a homemade laminated business card that reads RABBI IN TRAINING with a phone number, an email address where he is available for guidance, and the name of his YouTube channel, to which he claims to have a few hundred followers.

"So, what do you think?" Rabbi Sarah asks once the rest of the kids have been picked up by their parents.

"I think someone needs to watch Mordechai before he starts a cult," I snap. "And I think you're out of a job once my dad hears you brought me to day care for the afternoon. There is nothing he hates more than wasting his time and money."

"I have no doubt he'll be pissed that you've fallen behind, especially since you skipped out on the first lesson," she says calmly, the way a chess master might lay out an unexpected check.

"It's your word against mine, and based on your own account, you never showed up," I shoot back.

She thinks hard, but the folds on her forehead multiply as the realization sets in that she may be caught in a stalemate.

"You got me!" She waves an arm like a white flag and peacefully forfeits. She begins to head up the stairs.

The black car that picked us up is still waiting, and we walk toward it, Rabbi Sarah leading the way.

"Hey, don't worry. It's not your fault. I get that you're just doing your job." I hold out my hand as a peace offering—the last thing I want to do is taint this victory with negative karma.

"Yeah, although . . ." The look of defeat on her face melts away to reveal a devilish grin. "I'd hate for this to get circulated around your school. I hear high school kids can be brutal."

She holds up her phone and pushes play on a video. Mordechai stands at the head of a table and sings, as do I, along with the rest of the kids, who alternately sip apple juice and chant words in singsongy voices:

"א, ב, ב." *Alef, Bet, Vet.*

"ג, ד, ה." *Gimel, Dalet, Hay.*

The video ends, and Rabbi Sarah grabs the hand I extended to her minutes ago and shakes it.

"See you next week, Nevaeh."

Checkmate.

Chapter 14

"Pussycat, is that you?" My father comes out into the hallway to greet me as though we enjoy one another's company again.

I immediately drop my things and cover my mouth. The air in the house is deadly, like a fart in the shower, pungent and hot; it detonates like a bomb of nastiness over all my senses, almost sending me down for the count.

"What is that smell?" I gasp through my fingers.

"Dinner."

Ashleigh appears in an apron, carrying a bowl of cooked cabbage and broccoli, which she thrusts into my chest. The steam exfoliates my face and coats my nostrils with a vile sulfuric scent.

"It's a thirty-day regimen to clean your system of toxins. We could all use a cleansing around here, wouldn't you say?"

She looks me up and down like I'm a stray dog in desperate need of a bath.

"You can set the table." She nods in the direction of the dining room, as though I don't know my way around.

Dad and Ashleigh march in just as I place the last fork, each carrying their own steaming bowl of garbage. Ashleigh takes a seat at the head of the table.

"The sharp edge of the knife faces toward the plate and goes on the right side," she says with a sneer. "Figures your mother didn't teach you how to set a proper table."

Ashleigh lifts the knife from the left side, where it rests beside the fork, and slowly moves it to the other side of the plate, twisting it in the air so the sharp edge no longer faces out. I can't tell why it matters, but my body burns with embarrassment. Suddenly feverish, I shiver when the cold silver in my hand sends a chill up my arm as I pick up the knife before me and move it to the other side of my plate.

It is a feeling I know well, especially when in the presence of white women. I look so much like them, and yet, when it comes down to it, I am never good enough. Not for them.

> *She's one of those, she's one of them.*
> *I know because I've hid from them.*
> *Cried from them.*
> *I think I just died inside again.*

> *Fingers licked clean—a wolf that's snuck the last bite.*
> *Hands wrapped around my neck, tighter and tight.*
> *She's one of 'em.*

> *Those draped stolen gold*
> *And*
> *Diamonds bought from the severed hand of a seven-year-old.*

> *Them, an apology never uttered of their own accord.*
> *They, defined by the bar set with appropriated trends.*

Because when you have pearl teeth and glitter breath
What counts
Is how many worship you in the end.

"Nevaeh?" My dad breaks me from my thoughts, deflecting attention from Ashleigh's cruelty. "How was your first session with Rabbi Sarah?"

Rather than responding, I put a spoonful of what at some point might have been quinoa into my bowl. After a few bites, I give up—sustenance, I tell myself, is not worth the irreparable assault on my taste buds.

"You know, before Ashleigh started at the law firm, she worked in event planning," Dad says. "Maybe you could team up to plan the bat mitzvah party."

I shoot dagger eyes at Ashleigh. Jordan may hate me, but I bet she would be proud of how well I employ her torture techniques if she were here. Ashleigh, it seems, is impervious, because she jumps right in to tell me all about the party she has imagined.

A giant legal binder plops down in front of me and opens to reveal hideous swatches of pastels and shimmery fabrics that I would refuse to consider even if I were willingly participating in this extravaganza.

"I know the best dry bar to straighten your hair so it isn't all frizzy for the photos," she declares, and shows me images of celebrity socialites in an array of outfits. The only consistency is that they all look like her and nothing like me.

"I have a real vision for it: think, *My Super Sweet Sixteen* vibes." She closes the binder with pride.

"Nevaeh, honey, what do you think?" my father asks, smiling.

"I think it's super impressive!" I announce, giving him what he clearly wants. "But I'm not sure when Ashleigh could possibly find the time, what with *her busy schedule of home-wrecking.*" My lips burn as the words come out, but I don't feel bad. I feel rage.

Ashleigh zeroes in on me but allows a feigned sadness to wash over her as my dad places his hand on her shoulder, comforting her the way he used to comfort me. From where he sits to her left, he can't see the glimmer of joy in her eyes as he chooses her over me, but I can.

"I am so sorry, Ashleigh," my father says.

One of his eyes twitches, no doubt because he's tormented by his lack of control over this whole situation. He sits back down and takes Ashleigh's outstretched hand in his. "Nevaeh, what has gotten into you?"

I could ask him the same question.

The disappointment seeps out of both of us and fills the space with a funk so foul it overpowers the stench of this lukewarm meal.

Samuel Levitz does not make mistakes. Or so he thinks. That's how he planned his life. That's how he chose his wife. That's how he raised me. Except a few years ago, I found a tape with a commercial on it that surprised me.

The commercial is terrible. In it, my dad walks into the frame and leans against a desk in front of a backdrop of bookshelves. After rattling off statistics regarding his past successes, he looks directly into the camera and assures you, his future client, that there is nothing he won't do to help you. It's corny and low-budget. It never aired. Thank goodness.

My dad said that once he saw the final product, he could not in good conscience put something that looked so tawdry on a public forum, even if it was only going to run during weekly local daytime television.

Ashleigh moves behind my father to squeeze his shoulders and release the rising tension caused by his delinquent daughter. He moans in gratitude for the relief and she shoots me a devious glance, reminding me how easily she can wrap him around her tacky French tips.

Nauseated, I get up from the table to go to my room. Behind me, I hear Ashleigh's whispers poisoning my father and his judgment.

To this day, my dad says that stupid commercial was the only mistake he has ever made.

Maybe it was, the little voice in me says. *Until now.*

Chapter 15

My phone buzzes on the way to the cafeteria, and the tiny photo of Jesus kissing my face pops up on my screen:

> Hey, boo, whatchu doin' tonight? Free crib in the hood.
> Roll through wit Stevie. I wanna c u.

He has begun to text me every so often, just the occasional emoji or gif, but that doesn't stop my heart from falling down to my knees. I put my phone away and get in line for food; I may be an awkward, antisocial virgin, but even I know to give at least a five-minute lag time before responding.

Today, the menu is pad Thai, vegetable green curry, and a dim sum cart, in addition to the regular sandwich options, salad station, and the obligatory ice cream cooler. (An alumnus recently donated a huge amount of money to renovate the cafeteria, with one stipulation: that there be at least seven ice cream flavors available to students at all times.)

I balance an overloaded plate of noodles and dumplings on my tray against a bowl of raspberry chocolate chip ice cream, along with my phone, which keeps buzzing with more texts from Jesus, as I make my way into the courtyard, where Stevie waits for me by our tree.

"You in White Plains for the weekend with your prepubescent stepmom?" Stevie asks.

"I was supposed to be, but my dad had to switch weekends. Apparently, he came down with the flu."

My phone buzzes again and Stevie grabs it, annoyed to be competing with a cellular device for my attention.

"Are you serious, B? You couldn't lead with 'we got invited to a party'?" He jumps up and screams, drawing eyes from all over the quad. "Is Jordan going to be there?"

I don't have the heart to tell him that he doesn't stand a chance. His association with me puts him at the bottom of the list, even if he weren't also younger and rich, the last likely being the worse offense in her opinion than the other two combined.

"I was getting to it, jeez. Come on, let's go. I have a triple of bio." I fake a projectile vomit at the thought of the next three hours with Abby.

"You think you got problems? I only have two weeks until my preliminary audition tape is due for the Zahira fellowship, *and* I have a double of social studies. Mr. Miller sat me next to Abraham Moscowitz."

Abe has been at Pritchard with us since kindergarten. He's nice but has the absolute worst hygiene of anyone I have ever met. Every crevice around his braces is stuffed with food, and the stink is so palpable you can taste it. In the past I would have pitied anyone forced into a yearlong partnership with Abe, but considering I'm stuck with Abby, I'd trade in a second.

The first team assignment is due next week, and Abby and I have avoided doing any work. Normally, I would just do it myself and let her take half the credit to avoid the torture, but there is no way one of us could complete this assignment alone. A folded piece of paper waits for me in front of my seat.

My house, next Wednesday after school.
Do the reading, because I won't.

Mr. Bowels, who already seems to suffer from some sort of glandular disorder that leaves him perpetually drenched in sweat, also seems to be fighting allergies, making it impossible for him to finish a sentence without sneezing. Abby raises her hand.

"Mr. Bowels?" She waves her arm with urgency. "I am *not* feeling well. Like, I need to leave right now."

"Well, okay, Abby. I hope you feel bett—"

Abby stands abruptly, cutting him off, and turns to me.

"Have to get my house ready for the party I'm throwing to-night," she whispers. "Too bad you didn't make the cut." She grabs a few of my curls in her hand. "And don't even think about crashing with this nappy hair of yours and ruining it for everyone."

She saunters out of the room and a small rush of cool air hits me as the door closes behind her. Like a true ice queen, she's always leaving a trail of biting wind in her wake. I wish I had it in me to say something back, but it's easier to just settle into her absence and pretend it doesn't hurt.

"She said *what?!*" Stevie screams as I fill him in on the way to the subway.

"I just feel like natural selection should have done away with people like her by now," I go on. "Plus, she doesn't know what she's talking about. If Jordan or Janae heard her call my hair nappy, they'd laugh their asses off."

It's odd how sometimes these comments bother me, and how at other times I can't help but chuckle at the absurdity. I guess I'm just used to never being enough of anything.

"Who needs her dumbass party? We're hangin' with Jesus tonight!" I proclaim loud enough for some Hasidic women pushing strollers to turn around and give us dirty looks.

We head up the stairs to the 242nd Street station; it's the last stop on the 1 train in the Bronx, and the entire station is above-ground. There's usually a train waiting to be dispatched on the platform, which means we almost always get a seat.

Stevie practices his rusty breakdancing skills through the empty car. A man joins us and throws a dollar at Stevie's feet, which Stevie pockets before grabbing the seat next to me.

"So, what kind of party is this, B?"

"I dunno, like a regular party," I say, as if I have any real sense of what that means.

One of the consequences of having only one close friend is that you don't get to flex your social skills very often. Outside of the slew of bar and bat mitzvahs that Stevie and I were forced to attend a couple years ago, we haven't been to many parties, and I don't want to text Jesus with questions that will reveal how utterly unsocialized I actually am.

The train pushes forward—238th, 231st, 225th, 215th, 207th—and fills as we go with students and men and women ready to go home after a long day.

"WHAT TIME IS IT?"

A young man followed by three friends walk onto the car with a '90s-style boom box. They are shirtless, with sweat dripping down their flushed brown skin. I look over at the man who gave Stevie the dollar; he's about to figure out he used his cash on the wrong performer.

The guys turn the music up loud and begin to two-step and clap in unison in a semicircle.

"IT'S SHOWTIME!" the rest of the crew respond to the question before one of them hops up and climbs the center pole. He grabs onto the higher handrails on the ceiling and flips off them, landing gracefully on the ground and spinning himself around like a basketball on an NBA star's finger.

The troupe performs an array of skills: body contortion (the smallest guy puts both his arms behind his back and then dislocates both of his shoulders before pulling his arms over his head in front of him and popping both of his shoulder blades back in); breakdancing (what Stevie was trying to do just moments before their performance began, but with success); and gymnastics (the tallest guy does backflips up and down the entire subway car without stopping, defying the laws of space and dizziness).

After they finish, the little guy comes around with a worn Yankees cap for donations. I've been trying to figure out why he looks so familiar, and then it hits me: he goes to my grandfather's church. Embarrassed that I don't have cash, I hide behind my cell phone, hoping he doesn't recognize me. Luckily, Stevie gives up everything he has, including the dollar donated to his lackluster performance earlier.

The group hops onto the platform at the next stop and onto the next car, where they begin the routine all over again.

The sounds of the train amplify as we lurch forward into the darkness of the subway tunnel, encapsulating us in a dissonance of metal wheels on metal tracks. Dyckman is the last stop above-ground until 125th, and as we adjust to the shrill mechanical noise that fills our immediate space, a faint echo punctuates the inhuman shrieks as the train barrels toward 191st Street.

"WHAT TIME IS IT?" the echo asks, challenging the chorus of steel and electricity for their audience.

"IT'S SHOWTIME!"

Chapter 16

With the little information I have from Jesus about the party, Stevie becomes my default stylist, and the result is a jumbled ensemble that most closely resembles the attire of a young female with a 1990s self-titled sitcom. Essentially, I look like Stevie.

"Where do you think you're going, Thing One and Thing Two?" Anita says as she materializes by the front door just before we sneak out.

"Just to a friend's house," Stevie interjects with enough confidence that I let him go for it. "Abby Jackson. She's in our grade and she's a total witch, but if we don't show, they'll torture us, and we're already the weird, racially ambiguous kids. Honestly, Auntie," he says, placing his hand on his hips. "You'd hate it."

Stevie pats Anita's arm like an old friend.

She looks around. Janae and Jordan are out, Jerry went with Uncle Zeke to a movie, and my mom is in bed like a slug. A quiet, empty house is a rare treat for Anita, who works the front desk of an orthodontist's office nine hours a day. Her raised eyebrows relax and she taps her left foot as she makes her final decision.

"Be home by ten-thirty," she says, before cautioning, "I'll be up."

Outside, the sun has only begun to set, casting swirls of rainbow sherbet through the sky. I swear it adds a sweet taste to the air—the same sweet taste as when you are dehydrated and you finally get a few drops of water on your tongue.

The change from summer to fall in the city is drastic and sudden. One day, the temperature goes back to being manageable. The dust in the air stops floating through the humidity and returns to the ground until the rain washes it down the gutters. The women selling flavored ice on the corner trade their freezer on wheels for a cart or a table, where they sell churros or sprinkle chili powder on expertly sliced mangoes to spear with a stick. The city breathes again.

We wait until we're around the corner to put the address Jesus sent me into the map on my phone. There's no way to know how far my aunt's supernatural sight extends, and after our narrow escape, I'm not willing to take any risks. Luckily, the party is only a ten-minute walk away.

We head up Lenox Avenue. I am immediately grateful that Stevie chose my high-top sneakers as opposed to sandals or anything with a heel, because the ground is littered with shards of glass that crunch under our feet. We stop in a bodega to grab a couple sodas and some chips as an offering and then turn the corner toward the party. A group of kids stand on the stoop of a brownstone, holding brown paper bags with bottles in them. My legs stop functioning, as if Medusa just turned them to stone.

This is a mistake. I don't know how to act at a party, or how to drink. The only time Stevie and I have ever gotten drunk was in his basement last year when we were the only people in our class not invited to Abby's freshman year welcome-back party. We both ended up green and immobile, me vomiting in the sink and Stevie in the toilet, respectively.

"Nevaeh?" a familiar voice shouts as we start up the steps.

Janae and Jordan stare at me. Jordan wears a halter dress and a jean jacket, and Janae sports a crop top with high-waisted vintage denim jeans that are no doubt a hand-me-down from Anita. Both of them look beautiful yet understated, especially in contrast with Stevie's and my explosion of colors and layers.

"You look like a radiant Nubian queen," Stevie declares, lunging forward in an attempt to take Jordan's hand in his. She pivots toward the open entrance and shoots him a look of disgust usually reserved for me.

"I'll meet you inside, B!" he says, trailing her with zero shame.

"I didn't know you were here this weekend," Janae says apologetically.

"Yeah, um, no worries," I assure her as I struggle to propel my legs to follow her. "Jesus invited us."

We enter a brownstone with a layout that mirrors ours. A face I can't quite place stares back at me from a wall of portraits.

"Seventh grade—but don't judge me. I hadn't found my swagger yet."

Jesus stands behind me, the current version of the kid I knew I recognized. The photos stop in middle school, before he grew his hair out, bulked up, and had his braces removed. We walk over to a table nearby where a bunch of alcohol is set up—Heinekens and forties of Old E next to bottles of Smirnoff and Hennessy. I place my Diet Coke on the table with the rest of the mixers. Jesus hovers over the drinks, searching the bounty to refill the red Solo cup already in his hand. Surprisingly, he goes for the Diet Coke I brought.

"Can't get messy if you're hosting," he whispers. "I just stumble around a few times and no one can tell the difference."

He pours the remainder of the soda into a cup for me.

"You didn't tell me the party was at your house," I say, more confident in my ability to flirt now that the expectation of drinking has been extinguished.

"Or what, you wouldn't have come?"

We both know that is not the truth.

I follow Jesus through the house, toward the back. My grandpa's brownstone has a backyard, but it's the only part of the property that has remained untouched. As it stands now, the whole space is just a plot of overgrown weeds and trash flung over from the neighboring homes. Jesus's parents, however, have made their yard a priority, so even with twenty teenagers milling around, it looks immaculate.

A metal fence separates this yard from those on either side, with expertly manicured shrubbery that weaves between the links to create what looks like a wall of floating leaves and flowers. A path of slate stones leads to a small gazebo that rests at the far end of the yard. It's decorated with Christmas lights, each bulb glistening in the night sky like a fallen star caught in a spider's web.

Tonight, the air is crisp, and as we walk down the stairs of the deck, I see Jordan chatting with one of the guys that Jesus hangs with on the corner.

"So, Lightskin, whatchu been up to?" Jesus asks me just as we pass her.

Her disdain stings even though she hasn't so much as looked in my direction in weeks. As we move down into the garden, the air is rife with oversprayed cologne, cigarettes, and warm beer. Jesus guides me through the crowd, and people stand or nod or pat his back as he makes his way toward the gazebo. Inside, there's a bench just large enough for two people, as long as they don't mind being pressed up together. Jesus walks in first and holds his hand out, inviting me to join him.

"Have you always lived here?" I ask, awkwardly placing myself beside him.

"Yep. My dad grew up in Harlem ten blocks away, across from the Hamilton Houses." He points in the direction of the cluster of public housing buildings that tower above the short brownstones, which make up the majority of the residential buildings in Harlem. "He's never left Harlem, not even through law school."

"My mom grew up in Harlem too," I say, glad to point out something we have in common. "But she went to college in Chicago and never came back . . . until this summer."

"And your dad?" he pushes.

The lie I told about my father being dead makes me hold my breath, and I make a mental note to never take my phone out in front of Jesus. It would just take one photo or text message to pop up and reveal the depth of my deceit.

"Um. He was actually a lawyer too. My mom says that's what killed him, the stress," I lie as convincingly as possible. Jesus places his strong arm around my shoulders, protecting me from my feigned grief and I take a sip of my soda, desperate for a change in subject.

"This backyard is amazing. How did you get these lights to hang like the floating candles in the Great Hall?" I ask to deflect him.

His brow raises so high it blends in with his hairline.

"Great Hall?" he asks.

"Have you not read Harry Potter?" I ask, with the sinking realization that even Jesus is not perfect.

He reaches over and takes my face by the chin and brings it closer to his.

"Nah, ain't been to the Great Hall either, but we're both here now," he whispers, so close that I can smell the Diet Coke on his tongue.

And then he kisses me.

He kisses me so slow and soft that I don't know if this is the pace at which people usually kiss or if he's easing me in, a starter package you have to max out before graduating to the next level. Time stops as we begin to breathe in sync and pull each other closer, leaving the party and the people around us miles away. It's amazing how easy it is to forget my problems when I have the taste of Jesus and his cherry ChapStick to distract me.

The soft pink velvet
Between your lips is enough
Forever. Again.

If it weren't for
The moon's eyes, I think we could
Live here in the dark.

"How will I ever
Sleep?" I ask. "I guess to dream
Of us," you suggest.

Chin stubble rubs hot
On my soft skin, leaves me with
Scars to prove you're real.

An explosion of cheers interrupts our love swaddle, sending us back down onto the hard bench. I pull away to find a throng of partygoers clapping and taking photos. The phone flashes blind me as people document my first kiss like amateur paparazzi.

"You should probably go out there and host," I say, ready to be out of the spotlight.

"But I like it here witchu," he teases, and kisses me one more time. Then he nods at my empty cup. "You want a refill?"

Even though I am sober, a lightness has taken over my body, as though just being in Jesus's presence has the same effect as cheap, illegally purchased booze.

"I'm okay," I say with a giggle, and look around, positive it was Stevie who led the charge on the barrage of photos.

He's never going to let me live this down, I think, but I don't see him anywhere.

Inside, the gathering has mutated into a dance party three times its original size, and I have to shield my nose from the musty air. Janae seems to be on DJ duty, perched on the windowsill with a laptop sprouting wires that reach all over the room to their respective speakers.

The floor is covered in a layer of sweat and dirt at 12 percent proof, but Stevie weaves through the grime with ease, dancing with so much excitement he is practically center stage. People around him half rock, half watch as he moves the way he was meant to: with the perfect balance of grace and grit. Stevie is blind to the suggestive eyes and body rolls coming at him from all angles, because his eyes are locked on Jordan, who's dancing not too far away with the guy she was talking to outside on the steps.

The guy has greased-back hair and wears his shirt with the top two buttons undone, something out of the late-'90s Marc

Anthony videos Anita makes us watch because "that's her celebrity crush and she can do what she wants." He must be at least twenty-five, way too old to be at this party, and he looks at Jordan the same hungry way my dad looks at Ashleigh.

The music stops midsong. The silence startles me, but people just file out of the room to get drinks as Janae hops down from her perch to figure out which cord was accidentally unplugged.

I wave at Stevie, but he marches past us to the drinks table, where Marc Anthony is pouring Hennessy into Jordan's red cup. She bites her thumb and giggles at what he says, batting her eyelashes so vigorously she might give herself a migraine.

"Hi, Jordan!" Stevie says.

The creepy dude moves back as Stevie shoves himself between them.

"What do you want?" she asks through her teeth. "I'm busy."

"You think you're slick," the guy says. At what looks like six foot five, he towers over Stevie. "We was talkin'."

Stevie turns to him, his nose hitting six inches under this guy's chin.

"Well, now *we're* talking," Stevie challenges, taking a step back as the giant raises a fist.

Jesus swoops in just then and grabs the guy by the shoulders.

"Aye, Marcos, chill. Tu ta bien?"

Marcos's breathing normalizes as an evil grin spreads across his face. He brushes Jordan off with a wave of his hand.

"Yeah, bitches like her always got something to complain about anyway. I need a little cream in my coffee," Marcos says with a wink in my direction.

Jordan storms past us and slams the front door, wiping her eyes as she goes.

Stevie takes a power stance in her wake. Legs wide, elbows at perfect ninety-degree angles. From the back, he looks like Superman, if Superman lost a hundred pounds.

"What did you say?" Stevie yells, clawing at the air between him and Marcos.

Marcos takes a step forward and kicks his foot back on the floor like a bull seeing red, ready to charge.

"You better get ya man, blanquita," he says to me, spit flying out of his mouth.

Marcos easily outweighs Stevie and me combined, but Stevie is not going to back down; it's not in his DNA. Jesus throws his arm over Marcos's shoulder.

"You been out back yet? There's nutcrackers. Jeff brought a fresh batch from the bodega on Two Forty-First and Matilda."

Marcos hesitates, weighing whether Stevie can step to him without any sort of consequence with the need to refill his Solo cup.

"Those Wakefield nutties are what's up," Marcos says to Jesus, turning his back to us, enticed by the promise of alcohol more than he is by the prospect of pummeling Stevie to a bloody pulp.

Relief floods Jesus's face and he mouths the word "go" with enough urgency that I grab Stevie and drag him outside before he does something else stupid.

The lock clicks behind us and spits us onto the street, where the eau de breakfast sandwich and cigarette wafts underneath the streetlights and it's just the two of us wearing too many colors and no one we want to kiss is anywhere in sight.

"Ney!"

I turn to find Janae hanging out a window near the front door, trying to keep as much noise off the street as possible.

"You know you didn't have to do all that! I had eyes on the situation," she yells.

"No, *girl,* we obviously didn't know that!" Stevie shouts, adrenaline still pumping through his veins.

"You got moves, my guy." She nods, ignoring his rage with an even-keeled smile. "What time you supposed to be back by?"

I check my phone. It's 10:45. Shit.

"Tell her you went the wrong way toward Fifth Ave instead of Lenox and you got all turned around," Janae shouts as Stevie and I book it down the street, confident that Anita is already cursing our names from her stoop eight blocks away.

Once Stevie is safely in a car and on his way home, I go inside to find that the house is unexpectedly quiet. Anita must have passed out.

"Don't have to do more than stick your Lite-Brite toe out and guys show up ready to do your bidding, don't they?" Jordan accuses as she stops me in the hallway on the way upstairs. Her eyes are red from crying, but even in her ratty pink terry-cloth bathrobe and bare, clean face, she looks magnificent.

"I—I don't know," I stammer.

Jordan backs me into a corner of the hallway where a huge vintage mirror hangs. She turns me around so the two of us stand together. Her eyes are fixed on mine in the reflection, pleading for me to see that the solution to our tumultuous relationship is right in front of us.

"Just because you didn't choose to pass doesn't mean you don't have a choice, Nevaeh."

Jordan sighs a deep, sorrowful sigh. The type of sigh that sounds like the depletion of any lingering patience.

"I'm tired," she goes on. "Tired of people like you who think it's my job to make you feel better about your internal struggle when you barely recognize the one that rests on the surface of my skin. Tired of being seen as good enough to put my body on the line in the streets, but not worthy of affection or praise or flattery. Tired of thinking about college and how if I can't convince Mama to let me take out loans and go to an HBCU, I'll have to deal with the racist theme parties and dumb jokes and biased curriculums. Tired of people constantly ruining my joy with their foolish, fragile tears and excuses. If you wanna be with us, then you've gotta be about us, and that takes more than the blood running through your veins. You need to do the work, so do it, 'Lightskin.' Stick that toe out and take some of the load off my shoulders. Because I am tired, and I have to wake up tomorrow and face it all over again."

I raise my eyes from the ground, where they drifted in shame halfway through her monologue, and meet her gaze in the mirror. I want to tell her I think she is the definition of beautiful. I want to tell her I'm still learning how to be me. I want to tell her I am sorry and that I didn't mean to dismiss her, but I don't.

I shouldn't keep her from sleep any longer, so I clamp my mouth shut and wait until she evaporates into the night.

Chapter 17

The steps creak under my feet. I planned to spend the evening dancing alone with the butterflies in my stomach and shooting poems out
of my fingers like firecrackers, but not now. Now, as I head to the
attic, my former sanctuary, which has revealed itself to be a chamber
of consequence and retribution, there is only one thing I can do.

I have begun to crave my mom's journal entries because they
bring me back to earth. Her words drill into me, releasing the pain
my body won't allow me in tears. The hurt, I find, is a twisted
comfort. Temporary and raw and deserved, it comes from the truth,
which I tell myself means it is a pain that can lead to growth. I tell
myself that growth means there may still be hope for the future.

January 10, 1999

I was only home for two of the four weeks of winter
break. Mummy tried to convince me to stay, but I told her
I had an extra assignment that I needed to get back to in
Chicago, so I flew out a couple days later.

139

The assignment is Samuel.

We've been inseparable since the day we met. At first, I wasn't sure I could love a white man. I've always kept them at arm's length, never really interacting with them unless they're teachers or other authority figures. Anita has told me stories from being on debate team about how they treat her. She says they always talk over her, like her voice is just a piece of paper that they can crumple and throw in the trash with one clench of their fist. Samuel isn't like that.

He takes me on adventures, like breaking into the RA lounge to make French toast at two in the morning. He tells me I'm beautiful when we stop for a drink of water or stay up late to study. He makes me laugh so hard I worry I might choke on the oxygen that gets trapped between my belly and my mouth each time he impersonates our teachers or makes fun of me for being a prude. He listens to my insecurities and squashes them with unbridled confidence. He makes me feel alive again. He is nothing like Raymond.

Samuel stayed in Chicago because his mother decided to visit and spend the holidays there. He begged me to come back early, claiming he wouldn't survive that long with his mom if I wasn't there the moment she left to revive him. He literally got on his knees and started a trail of kisses from my toes to my belly button—it was so sweet and romantic.

I'll only admit this to you, but there was another reason I agreed to come back: Becky Merrill. She's this blond, volleyball-playing wench on the second floor. She has spent every waking second of this semester lusting after Samuel, and I know for a fact she stayed on campus over break because she failed our English class and needs to take a make-up course so she doesn't fall behind. The idea of her pointy nose and choppy, layered Meg-Ryan-circa-1996 hairdo anywhere near him is enough to make me scream.

So I scooped him up and promised I'd come back early, and then switched my return flight before I had even made it home.

Anita, who has a new boyfriend herself, called my bluff the first night I was back.

"You got you a man."

She threw the accusation in my direction as she handed me a plate to dry after dinner.

Our whole lives I have been waiting to have something in common with my sister so we could stay up all night talking and giggling. She told me about her boyfriend, Zeke. He tried to follow her onto the debate team and calls her every night before bed to remind her he will see her in his dreams. I told her about Samuel and how he loves to do crossword puzzles and how when he dances he makes this funny face that looks like he is blowing bubbles and how he can talk his way out of anything. I don't tell her he's white and Jewish. I know that'll be an issue—for her, not me.

We fell asleep every night next to each other in the giant bed we made by pushing our twin mattresses together, holding hands and whispering their names into our pillows like wishes on stars.

Then one night, Anita showed me a picture of Zeke. He's tall and muscular and Black. She was going to find out sooner or later, so I pulled out a strip of pictures Samuel and I had taken at a photo booth and handed it to her.

Anita's face knotted up, like she drank cold water too fast and had to wait for the brain freeze to subside.

"He's white," she observed.

"Correct. He is also nice and funny and makes my whole body tingle . . ."

"You told Mummy and Daddy yet?"

I hadn't. My parents are strict and traditional. They're immigrants who want us to have good, uncomplicated lives. Honestly, I don't know how they might react to me dating a Jewish man, or how I might respond if they don't approve. Anita read my mind as I mulled over the best way to respond.

"Well . . . ," she said, handing the photo back to me like it was a foreign object, unable to mask the skepticism in her voice, "as long as you're sure . . . Are you sure, that you are sure?"

"I love him," I said.

Usually, she wouldn't shut up for anything, but I think she could tell how much I cared and decided against further commentary. When my two weeks were up, I left New York feeling like my life had fallen into place, and when I hugged my family and told them I would miss them, I meant it more than when I'd left six months prior.

Once back in Chicago, I went straight to the dorms, frostbitten from the sub-arctic winter winds and eager to see Samuel. Before even dropping my belongings off in my room, I stopped by his and knocked on the door. No one answered. It was seven-thirty, prime dinner time, so I left a note on the dry-erase board plastered to the door and went to my room. I sat by the phone for an hour, cursing the skies that my mom hadn't given me a cell phone for

Christmas, as I had requested, and checking the cord to make sure it was plugged in correctly.

I woke up in the morning to the smell of old soup, my sad dinner from the night before. A cold Cup O' Noodles sat on my desk, near where I had passed out. I jumped up to call Samuel's room again, but he didn't answer, so I went downstairs in case he'd left a note in my mailbox. As I entered the lobby, I walked right into what looked like a morning coffee date between Samuel and an older woman.

Somehow, Samuel was more handsome than he had been two weeks before. He didn't say much as he scooted over on the couch to make room for me. We sat in an awkward silence. I introduced myself to the woman, who turned out to be Samuel's mom, Aviva. She cheerfully caught me up on all they'd been doing in Chicago, visiting museums and seeing shows, like we were old girlfriends. Samuel sat quietly.

"Where are you from, Corinne?" she asked.

"New York City."

"Oh, I love New York! You're not too far from us in Connecticut," she exclaimed, clasping her hands together as though she'd caught a firefly. "I'm glad Sam has so many friends."

Samuel's knee bounced so hard that the couch vibrated like a massage chair at a nail salon. I reached over to grab his hand, but he coughed and pulled away.

"We should get going, Mom. We don't want to be late," he said.

"*Rent.* A matinee," Aviva boasted. "Corinne, are you free this evening? It's my last night here. We can add to the reservation at Gibsons. The more, the merrier."

Flattered, I nodded, ashamed that Samuel had told his mother about me while I had kept him a secret from my parents. I turned to ask Samuel what time the reservation was when Becky's ear-piercing laugh cut through the space. Aviva waved to her ecstatically and Becky walked over, her thin lips curled in an evil grin at the sight of me.

"We'll see you at dinner, won't we, doll?" Aviva asked her.

"Wouldn't miss it!" Becky chirped, unable to keep herself from raising her cleavage a bit closer to the light.

Becky beamed, and I suddenly understood why Samuel had never called me the night before. The humiliation took over my body like a rash, spreading hot under my skin. Anxious, I rummaged through my purse to buy some time and come up with an excuse to get away.

"Oh, uh, sorry, I actually have plans tonight," I stammered, and ran off, waving goodbye before I lost control.

I cried for the rest of the day and night, disgusted with myself for being so dumb and leaving my family early to be trapped in this empty dorm for weeks before anyone I knew would be around. I cried because before Samuel, I had never felt this deep, beautiful ache that sat in my heart and exploded whenever I thought of him. Now that same ache had turned sharp and violent with every breath I took.

Around midnight there was a knock on my door. I refused to get myself out of bed, worried that if I got too close, he might intoxicate me all over again. Eventually, the knocking and the whispers stopped, and I let myself drift into a restless sleep, plagued by dreams where I fell into a deep, dark hole and couldn't claw my way out.

The next day, when I finally willed myself out of bed to get some food, I found Samuel asleep outside my door.

"Let me explain," he said, jumping up and blocking my way. "I mixed up the date you were coming back and I told my mom I was seeing someone, but Becky must have planted some sort of tracker device on me, because she appeared everywhere we went, and my mom just assumed—"

"Why didn't you correct her? Why didn't you introduce me?"

"I didn't think you'd be back in time to meet her, so I figured if she thought Becky is who I'm dating and she saw how awful she is, then when she met you—"

"Oh! You wanted to soften the blow that you're dating a Black girl by replacing me with a terrible non-Jewish white girl and have your mother be grateful I'm not her?" I screamed.

"No. No—that's n-not . . . ," he stuttered, but then straightened up like a prepared lawyer who set the prosecution up for the trap they fell right into. "So you told your family about me? You told your Baptist minister father that I'm a white Jewish guy from Connecticut?"

My hesitation answered his question and his shoulders relaxed, confident that he'd caught me in a double standard.

"I don't care what anyone thinks, because I don't see you as Black or anything other than the woman I love," he said, stepping forward. "It's just us. That's all that matters."

He kissed me, and all at once, we were one stream of breath and one slow and steady heartbeat.

Ever since Raymond, I feel so much guilt whenever I

look at myself. All I see in the mirror is a filthy, unfixable stain, and yet Samuel can't see anything but my smile and my eyes. He sees me the way I thought Raymond did. He would never hurt me, not like that. He waited outside my dorm room all night just for a chance to make things right.

"It's just us," I repeated. "That's all that matters."

My phone buzzes next to me, a text from Jesus.

**1:30 a.m. Fallin' asleep with you on my mind.
See you tomorrow?**

Thinking about him reminds me of sitting on a tire swing that has been wound up to the very top and then released so it spins like a tornado. My stomach jumps up to my throat and my hair goes electric. It feels as though I'm standing at the center of the solar system while the rest of the universe moves around and around and around.

This is how it happens, the voice in me says. *First they charm you, and then they brainwash you, until you end up like Mom, a ghost, even though her body sleeps just a hundred feet away.*

I close the text unanswered and wait for the spinning in my chest to stop. I chug some seltzer to wash the taste of Jesus away and try to convince myself that I won't make the same mistakes my mom did. I try to convince myself that I don't want him more than anything else. I can't pick a guy over who I need to become—whoever that is.

Chapter 18

"You want to get food before we go?" Stevie asks me as we walk out the front doors of the school on Monday.

My phone buzzes in my pocket. I don't have to look to know it's Jesus. He's been hitting me up ever since Friday night. So far, I've only broken down and responded twice with emojis to keep things casual: a winking smiley face and the laugh-cry cat.

"Hmm? Go where?" I ask, distracted.

"My rehearsal."

The leaves have already started to fall off the trees, coating the streets with a thin, papery layer that crackles under the feet of classmates as they flee the school grounds and head toward pizza slices and make-out sessions. Last week, Stevie cornered me and made me promise to watch his routine for the Lena Zahira dance fellowship first-round auditions, but considering everything I have going on, participating in my best friend's plan to abandon me for a year is not at the top of my list of priorities.

"I can't," I tell him, and his face falls.

I hate his rehearsals. They make me wish terrible, selfish things would happen so it'll be impossible for him to compete. I usually go because if I don't, no one else will, and best friends are supposed to be there for each other, but today I have a viable excuse.

"Sorry. Bat mitzvah practice."

"Right," he says. "No biggie." He walks away before I can remind him that he is going to be great.

Rabbi Sarah is outside when I arrive at the temple. She looks pleased that her threat of blackmail has been getting me here in a timely fashion. Rather than going downstairs, she takes a left and leads us to a waiting area outside two wooden doors. There's a small shelf to the right of the entrance holding a basket of silk caps. She takes one and places it at the very top of her head before entering.

"Grab a kippah, if you want," she says, but I keep my hands in my pockets. The idea of wearing a shared headpiece makes me want to douse my body in hand sanitizer.

The wooden doors to the dark sanctuary creak like a haunted house. Rabbi Sarah walks in, undaunted, and navigates her way to a wall, where she flicks on the lights. The room is simple, less ostentatious than my grandfather's church and many of the other temples I have been to for bar and bat mitzvahs.

Rabbi Sarah beckons me to the front of the altar, where she now wears a white scarf that she retrieved from some hidden closet. The sound of my footsteps is swallowed by the carpet beneath them. Unlike Mount Olivene Baptist Church, which seems to be constantly filled with laughter and music, this room exudes calm reflection and meditation, sort of like internal worship as opposed to loud group celebration.

Rabbi Sarah holds up her arms and the fringe at the corners of her shawl dances in the air.

"At your bat mitzvah, you'll be presented with a tallit, a shawl like this one, by family members."

Closer up, I notice that the fabric has light blue stripes running its length. She hands it to me. The silk feels like a cloud in my hands, weightless and just cold enough to remind me that it's there. It is exactly like the scarf my mom used to wrap her head in before bed. I always sat with her at night as she brushed her hair out with care, taking handfuls that she folded around her head until it made a flat crown. She'd tie the silk scarf with its splotches of purple and pink and orange and red and yellow—a rainbow explosion—to keep her hair safe throughout the night so when she woke the next morning, all she needed to do was brush it out for it to be perfect. Recently, she hasn't been doing the ritual. She has let her hair get matted and dry and uneven, unprotected from the weight of her sadness.

I hand the scarf back to Rabbi Sarah.

"In the past, the tallit has always looked like this, but recently, especially in reform communities, synagogues have begun to give the bar or bat mitzvah the freedom to bring one of his or her choosing."

Rabbi Sarah's eyes search for even the slightest bit of excitement on my part, which does nothing but send a pang of irritation up my spine as I feel my hardened heart soften toward her. She wants me to enjoy this, even though we both know that the freedom to pick out a shawl is the only choice I have with regard to this matter.

"Come on," she says, leading me back through the lobby and into a small room that looks like a repurposed, oversized closet.

The windowless walls are bare, except for one old poster thumb-tacked to the back of the door. It's from a festival the temple hosted at some point, probably a couple decades ago, judging by the thick layer of dust.

"This is your office?"

"Sure is! Whaddya think?" She beams with pride, taking a seat behind a desk littered with papers and books and mini-bags of potato chips.

"I think decorating isn't your strong suit."

Her lip twitches and I bite the inside of my cheek, embarrassed at my unwarranted cruelty.

"Well, not all of us grew up in a big house with our own room and a decorating budget," she says matter-of-factly.

The truth stings like hail against my fragile skin, the same way Jordan's words did the other night in the hallway.

"All right, we're behind schedule, so we need to come up with a game plan. Saturday, June ninth, sounds far away, but it's gonna be around the corner before you know it!" She opens a datebook and turns several pages. "I know your birthday is late March, but we had to choose from the dates we had available. Let me find your Torah portion. . . . Here it is, Parashat Acharei Mot, you will be discussing the holiest day of the year, Yom Kippur."

"June ninth," I say, and let the date that will forever be known as the worst day in the history of Nevaeh Levitz's life fall out of my mouth like a sickness.

She looks up.

"Your father didn't tell you?"

I shake my head. My father and I haven't exchanged more than a few syllables in weeks.

Rabbi Sarah's hair is covered with an oily sheen that somehow maintains a springy, spiderwebbed disarray as yellow waves sprout in every possible direction from under the silk kippah at the very top of her head. I can tell she wants to dig into my dysfunctional family life. Still, she fights the urge; we've barely gotten past the basics, and I need to start practicing the actual words if I'm ever going to learn my portion. She hands me a tattered accordion folder that weighs at least ten pounds. Inside is a thumb drive with a recording of my Torah portion and pages and pages of Hebrew text that she has written out phonetically in surprisingly neat cursive.

"You've got to listen and read along. Just familiarize yourself with the melody and the pronunciation. We can dig into the story behind the words a little longer."

"What was yours?" I ask, wondering whether it's normal to feel no connection to the words that hundreds of years of religious study claim are intrinsically tied to my person.

"My . . . ?" Rabbi Sarah turns, confused.

"Your Torah portion, for your bat mitzvah?"

She goes stiff, instantly transformed into a precise wax sculpture, making me wonder for a moment whether she was ever real in the first place.

"Rabbi Sarah?"

"I . . . um, never had one. Legally, I couldn't convert until I was eighteen because I had no guardians," she says as she comes back to herself.

"You . . . converted?" I ask.

It hits me that I know next to nothing about this woman.

"I had the option to have a bat mitzvah, but I didn't want to just pick a date. It's probably the one thing I can't stand my mother for—if she had just had me in a hospital, I'd have a birth date, or at least a certificate. Sometimes it feels like she dug a hole in me and there isn't any way to fill it, ya know?"

She shakes her head the way old ladies do when they're tired and ready to settle into a comfy chair to watch their daytime soap operas. I take the cue and leave it, selfishly grateful to know that I am not the only one walking around this city with gaping holes I can't seem to fill.

A buzz from my phone breaks the moment—it's the car my dad scheduled, waiting outside, ready to take me back to the suburbs for the night.

Traffic is gridlocked, and the sound of constant, long-winded honks begins to drive me insane. I have never been able to read or write in cars without getting nauseous, but I need something to distract myself with before I lose it. I rustle through my bag for my headphones and find that they're attached to my laptop, so I plug in the thumb drive Rabbi Sarah gave me.

She curses under her raspy breath in frustration, unaware that she already hit record, and finally, after a few minutes of muttering, she begins to sing my Torah portion a cappella.

Her singing voice is so different from her speaking voice that I have to pause and rewind to really believe it is her. Rabbi Sarah's thick New York accent is lost in this full and unexpectedly vibrant tone.

The recording plays through and starts over just as we pass my grandfather's block on the way to the FDR Drive and White Plains. Grateful for the distraction, I settle in and try not to think of my mom, seven avenues north of us, too broken to get out of bed and wrap her hair in a rainbow. Too broken to believe that when she wakes, she'll be able to start over, if only she'd decide that's what she wants.

Chapter 19

The smell of sausages wakes me from what feels like the most restful sleep I have had in ages. I sit up and look for my phone but find a note in its place.

Come downstairs when you wake up, pussycat. L, D

My eyes are so used to the darkness that the light around me almost feels like a violation, but my clock slowly becomes clear: 10:11 a.m. *"Damn!"*

The sheets tangle between my legs, sending me crashing to the floor—I'm two hours late for school. My dad bursts into my room wearing an apron and holding a pair of tongs.

"Are you okay?"

He drops the filthy metal on the ground, spraying hot grease all around him as he dives toward me and lands on top of my huge beanbag chair. I try to run to the bathroom, but he cuts me off.

"Let me go—I'm late!"

"No, you aren't. We're taking the day off!" he cries.

Before I can ask any questions, he runs back out, toward the burning smell that has suddenly overpowered the aroma that seduced me from my deep slumber just moments ago.

I drag my body downstairs after him and find the front door wide open. My dad stands over a smoking sauté pan in the front yard, pouring water from a pitcher onto the black circles that stick to it, to put out his almost-kitchen-fire disaster.

My father has never taken the day off in my entire life, which means there is only one explanation.

"Are you dying?"

A gust of wind carries my question next door, where Mrs. Robertson, perpetually in everyone else's business, pokes her head out a window to see what all the commotion is about. Mortified, my dad waves and turns to shield her from our conversation. Nevertheless, she stays dedicated to her cause and pretends to prune the plants in the window boxes, just in case another juicy tidbit heads in her direction.

"What? No!" my dad says, barely above a whisper. "I just wanted to spend time with you. I miss you."

I don't want to even smile in his presence, but it's hard not to as I take him in. His hair stands up on his head like a mad scientist's, and his apron, which falls below his knees, covers his basketball shorts, giving the impression that he is nude. I try to stifle my laugh, but it's too late. He pours the contents of the pitcher all over me, initiating a water battle, and runs into the house to refill his supply, which gives me time to dart into the garage and fill up some water balloons with the hose, preparing to annihilate him. As soon as he steps back outside, I slam him with water balloons. One after another after another, each one filled with the resentment and pain that I have not been able to express, until finally, I am out of ammunition and momentarily relieved of the tension that's been weighing me down for months.

"You win," Dad declares. He takes the full pitcher of water that he never got the chance to use and pours it over his own head, accepting his defeat. "Now that that's settled, do you want something to eat?"

The little girl inside me yearns for my dad to make me giggle and feed me French toast. She begs me to forgive him, at least long enough to go to a movie and sneak into a second one after. She pleads as loud as possible for me to give myself a break, attempting to distract me from the alarm ringing through my head warning me not to fall into the same trap my mom did, tricked by his charm and his smile and his goofiness.

My father stands before me, drenched. His focused eyes calculate the likelihood that his master plan of hooky and water fights might actually win me over long enough for me to remember that he used to be my everything.

"I want funnel cake," I declare.

A look of pure joy comes over his face, and he runs inside to change as I follow to do the same.

He'll disappoint you, the real me says to the little voice, but I hop up the stairs two at a time, humming my Torah portion to drown myself out.

On my instruction, my father and I go straight to the county fair, which stays open through October, even on weekdays. Overall, it's pretty janky as far as fairs go, and it's definitely guilty of multiple health and safety violations, but they have the best funnel cake on earth.

A chubby college-aged kid named Edgar sits at the park entrance and offers us a lackluster greeting when we walk up.

"So, uh, you planning to go on the rides?" he asks in a dull, uninviting tone, disappointed that our presence interrupts what might have been an otherwise uneventful day at the office.

"That's the plan," my father responds, asserting an unnecessary amount of passive aggression.

"Well, I gotta, like, turn them on—so do you wanna wait here or—"

"That's all right," I interject before my father goes full Johnny Cochran on Edgar. "We need to eat first."

The sugary grease soaks through four layers of napkins, the same way it always has. My dad licks powdered sugar from his fingers, careful not to lose one speck—I doubt Ashleigh's diet has allowed him anything even remotely as delicious in months. He looks at the Ferris wheel in front of us, which is motionless aside from the cars rocking back and forth in the wind.

"When I met your mom, she had never been to a fair like this. Only seen them in movies. The first time I took her, she was amazed."

He speaks as though in a trance, eyes locked on the slow, steady motion of the Ferris wheel pods.

"That was the happiest I ever saw her, until the day you were born. You were so little. You looked nothing like babies in the movies. You sort of looked like an alien, with that goop all over you."

"Dad!"

"I thought you would break if I touched you, but Corinne knew what to do from the moment she held you. She could stop you from crying before your lips even quivered by blowing cool air on your face."

He stops abruptly. He hasn't spoken about my mom since the separation. He may have convinced himself otherwise, but I know he loved her.

"Daddy, why are you making me do it? The bat mitzvah?"

The last bite of the funnel cake crunches between his teeth, and his eyes close as he savors the mouthful of fried heaven.

"At school, when I was your age, kids called me a dirty Jew every chance they got. They made me feel small and broken. They spit on my shoes. They made fun of the knish Bubby packed for my lunch while they ate ham and cheese sandwiches and green Jell-O. When it was time, I begged my parents not to make me have a bar mitzvah, but they insisted. The closest shul was almost an hour away, and on the day of the party, only two kids showed up: Edith Scheinman, the daughter of the only other Jewish family in the neighborhood, and Thomas Potts, who hadn't uttered a single word since he was in the second grade."

I'd never considered that his own rejection of his Jewishness might have been because he had been hurt when he was young. Maybe he does understand how I feel, like I was born wrong because I'm different.

"But you know what? I'm better for it. Stronger. I wanted to protect you from everything I went through, but maybe Bubby is right." He sniffles and runs his wrist beneath his nose. "This is who you are. Who *we* are; it isn't something to hide from."

A heavy panting breaks the moment as we look up to find Edgar, red-faced and sweaty, before us.

"So, like, just let me know what ride you want to go on first," he says once he catches his breath.

"Let's go!" My dad returns to his formerly enthusiastic self, and heads toward the do-si-do as Edgar trudges behind us, our begrudging chaperone on this adventure.

The lights in the house are on as we pull up stuffed to the brim with fried dough and toting a teddy bear the size of my bean-bag chair. The clock on the dashboard is broken, so I search my pockets for my phone but come up empty. I try to trace my day backward to remember when I had it last.

"Looking for your phone?" Dad asks. "I stole it from under your pillow last night so you could sleep late this morning and hid it in my office."

When we enter the house, dialogue from a cheesy dating competition show blasts out of the master bedroom, punctuated by Ashleigh's nasal laugh. I move toward the stairs to retreat to my bedroom, hoping to avoid any contact with her that might ruin this day, but a hairy arm blocks me.

In my father's hand is my cell phone, with multiple unanswered messages from Jesus.

"Who is this?" my father growls.

"A friend."

"You have a friend named Jesus who misses your cherry Chap-Stick? What in the hell is going on in that house?"

The volume at which he yells shatters whatever magical bubble has been protecting us all day. Now, with the freedom to revert to the worst versions of ourselves, the purple veins pulsating around his temples have reappeared, and the taste of disappointment floods my mouth.

"You want to criticize her parenting?" I yell back. "You just made me skip school to eat a high-cholesterol meal."

I push past him, grabbing the phone from his sweaty fingers as I go.

"I'm calling your mother. You are not to see this Jesus person again."

"Great, maybe she'll get out of bed long enough to take a shower. You trained her well—she only comes if you call."

He opens his mouth, ready to retort, but stops himself, perhaps afraid that whatever it is he wants to say is impossible to come back from. Instead, the door to his office slams so hard that the whole left side of the house shakes, leaving me with nothing to do but tell the little girl inside me *I told you so.*

Chapter 20

After spending an hour this morning rubbing my skin raw with soap and a washcloth, I was able to fade the stamp from the amusement park enough to cover it up with makeup. Stevie hands me an iced coffee and a buttered roll as we enter the school building.

"Damn, B, you said you were feeling better, but you look awful. You sure you should've come back today?"

It was easier to claim food poisoning when Stevie texted me last night to ask about my absence. I didn't have the energy to explain the amusement park. I could barely do anything except lie on my bed, wondering how everything could have gone so wrong. Eventually, the sound of raindrops falling softly on the skylight broke my daze. I used to find the sound of rain soothing; I'd watch the drops create a web of water and count the lines until I fell asleep. Last night, though, it sounded like a broken faucet of never-ending torture that kept me tossing and turning until morning.

I nod quickly, confirming to Stevie that I'm all right. The small amount of adrenaline I have left in my body is being carefully conserved for my after-school date with the devil—today is the day Abby and I are supposed to finish our first science project.

A frantic Mr. Bowels rushes past us as we head to the library with an armful of papers. We watch him lose his grip as hundreds of pages fly into the air and cover the hallway in a confetti of science quizzes. He grabs as many as possible before getting a massive paper cut and dropping them all over again. The sight is too pathetic for us not to walk over to help him, and he thanks us with a loud grunt.

The Pritchard library is massive and reminds me of the magical book room that the Beast gifts to Belle once she's proven to him that she isn't the worst type of human. Books cover the walls on the built-in floor-to-ceiling shelves. Abe Moscowitz waves in our direction as we enter, pointing to the empty seat next to him, and Stevie takes a tiny perfume sample out of his pocket and sprays it directly into each nostril.

"Stevie! What are you doing?" I ask, alarmed.

He shakes his head like he just swallowed a huge dollop of wasabi, bringing on that unique burning sensation that runs directly from your nostrils to the top of your brain like a rocket.

"I need a quick fix to survive Abe's breath. It's like he swallowed a fire-breathing lizard and every time he opens his mouth, it tries to kill me." His eyes bulge as he walks off to the seat that awaits him.

I settle into one of the comfy chairs to catch up on the reading for biology. The big chairs in this corner of the library are my favorite. They look like they've been in the building since the school first opened in the early 1900s and are so worn in that you sink into them the minute you sit down. The velvet cushions hug you back like a grandparent who brings you a warm blanket and cup of hot cocoa in the winter. The comfort makes me think of Grandma, and how she kept coming to visit us even after my mom and Anita stopped speaking. She never let my mom disappear. I wonder how different things would be if she were still here.

My bio textbook is massive and hangs over the chair. I figure the more I can get done before the end of the day, the less time I have to spend with Abby later, but the second her name crosses my mind it's like I'm a magnet that draws her to my exact location.

"I figured you'd need another day to recover," Abby says, walking by and knocking the edge of my textbook, making me lose my place.

"It was just a stomach thing. I'm fine." I will myself not to look at her in the hopes that she'll lose interest in torturing me and leave me in peace.

"Is that what they call abortions these days?" She takes a seat next to me. "I get it, girl. You don't wanna become another baby mama fighting for child support on BET," Abby hisses in a tone so evil that if I want to retain any semblance of dignity, I'm left with no choice but to confront her.

"Why are you such an intolerant jerk?" I practice quickly in my head, but when I turn, her usual piercing glare has been replaced by rapidly morphing reptilian features. As her neck lengthens and her skin begins to turn to green scales, I cower in my seat, frantic to escape and confused as to why no one else in the library seems to be even remotely concerned that a human student is effectively becoming the mutant villain of a C-level horror film.

"SSSSSILLLYYY MUTT!"

She looms over me, her mouth wide open, revealing fangs that drip poison on my head, soaking my hair. Her giant, fully transformed snake body extends toward the ceiling as her designer

162

clothes fall to the floor in shreds. I only have one chance to escape, so I use all my strength to throw my textbook at her face. Despite her size, she moves more quickly than I anticipate and whips her long tail forward to prevent the massive book from doing any meaningful harm. It smashes against the bookshelf on her left and leaves me completely defenseless and terrified.

"NAVVEAH, SSSSTOP ITT!"

Stevie shakes me hard enough to break me out of my nightmare, and I wake to find all eyes on me. Everyone is staring.

"B, you were screaming, and then you threw the book. It almost hit a group of freshmen," Stevie whispers, looking concerned. He wants me to know he's here for me. I just have to tell him what's going on. I know because I can hear him clear as day in my head. I don't know how to tell him that nothing will ever be the same, so I keep my mind blank and stay silent. After a few minutes, he gives up, resigned to the belief that the psychic power we once shared has dissipated, and heads back to his table, where Abe waits impatiently.

The sounds of books cracking open, fingers tapping on keyboards, and pencils scratching slowly fill the space. I walk the fifteen feet to my book, spread open on the floor. The risk of falling back asleep in that chair is high, so I relocate to one of the uncomfortable desks against the wall, where it will be easier for me to throw my back out than to nod off.

Abby lives in Riverdale. Her street is sort of hilly, and the houses are ginormous Georgian and Tudor mansions with yards and gates and trees, rather than the claustrophobic city-style brownstones, connected to each other by walls of brick and sweat.

From the look of it, a single developer decided to flip all the houses in the vicinity, because they all look the same, with the modern faux-stone base that turns to brick or wood a few feet up. The Jackson household, even with its indistinguishable architecture, is easy to recognize—it's the only one with a giant flagpole from which an American flag flaps in the wind.

Abby's dad was born in Kentucky or Arkansas or some Southern state. He made all of the kids invited to her eighth birthday party sing the national anthem in front of the flag before we could eat the cake. He loves America and money and big cars and the gender binary. At a recent assembly, where it was announced that the Jackson family was going to be funding the new and improved Pritchard gym, Mr. Jackson marched up to the stage in a cowboy hat and spewed his theory that the lack of patriotism in popular culture is ruining the youth of the USA.

The front door opens before I even ring the bell. Abby is dressed in a way she would never be caught dead at school: yoga pants and an oversized sweatshirt. She makes room for me to step inside, where I am greeted by the smell of pumpkin latte that has hung over our school for the past week—a particular favorite of the Bomb Squad, who always like to stay on trend.

Even though I've grown up around the wealthiest people and communities, this house takes my breath away, the same way it did when I was little. The grand double staircase in the foyer welcomes guests, each side graced with so much sunlight it looks like a ladder to heaven. I remember coming over for playdates and standing in front of different pieces of furniture with my eyes closed tight, hoping that one might come to life when I opened them again. The elegant furniture positioned perfectly on the wood and marble floors is complemented by regal paintings of

Abby, her mother, and their deceased sphynx cat, which resembled a newborn rodent more than any sort of feline.

Upstairs in Abby's room, the furniture reflects Ashleigh's terrible modern aesthetic, with sharp corners and random bubbles that prize style over comfort. I elect to sit on the floor rather than risk breaking anything or get stabbed by a loveseat. Abby joins me with her notebook and the supplies necessary to complete our experiment.

"What's the deal with you and Stevie?" she asks as she swabs her hand and places the sample on an empty petri dish, three steps ahead of me. Not that I would ever tell her, but Abby, it seems, is quite adept at science.

"What do you mean?" I ask, half paying attention so I don't mess up the control sample.

"You know, like, when we were . . ."

"Friends?" I finish her thought.

"I just thought he'd be pissed you have a boyfriend."

"Who says I have a boyfriend?" I snap.

"Please." She rolls her eyes. "The video of you dry-humping that guy the other night is all over the internet."

The video taken at Jesus's party had circulated for a few weeks, but thankfully my nonexistent social media presence made it easier to ignore. I've never seen the point in putting my every thought and facial expression on display, not that anyone would care about anything I do or say.

"Stevie and I are just friends. Why are you so interested?"

"Relax." She sighs, rolling her eyes so dramatically, I am almost impressed. "Don't flatter yourself. I'm stuck with you, so I figured I'd make small talk. Don't go all angry Black lady on me." She chuckles at her ignorant joke and scoots away from me.

An hour later the data we collected is in order and her room has been cleaned up, so I begin packing my stuff to go home and complete my half of the written assignment.

"I'll go make copies in my dad's office," she offers, holding up the notes she took during the experiment to help with the essay, and goes down the stairs.

I pace the room, looking into the world of Abby. The signed Taylor Swift poster framed on her wall, the huge glass vanity that holds more makeup than should exist anywhere other than in a Sephora store, and the bookshelf covered in photos. The photos are mostly of her and the Bomb Squad, group selfies in front of street art and fancy plates of sushi, always pursing their lips to make their cheekbones pop against their moisturized skin.

Abby returns and hands me a can of blackberry-cucumber La Croix. Her friendliness is off-putting and reminds me of the time in middle school when someone gave a substitute teacher a cup of water that had a cockroach in it. I accept the can cautiously but find to my surprise that it's untampered with and delightfully refreshing.

In the hallway, footsteps approach, accompanied by a booming voice with a distinctly non–New York twang.

"I've had about enough of this liberal nonsense. If y'all don't stop bending your will to these gutless snowflakes, I am going to consider pulling my funding for the gym—you think I won't? I don't care if it's named after my great-grandmother Dorothy, take a tip from the vermin marching in the streets and STAND YOUR GROUND."

Mr. Jackson walks past the room just as he ends his call and stops when he sees there is a visitor in his house. Abby, like everyone else, seems to be a little afraid of her father, and looks at me nervously, unsure what he might say or do.

"Well, I'll be. Is that Nadia? You haven't been around these parts in ages." He barges in, filling the doorway with the sharp stink of chewing tobacco.

"It's Nevaeh," I correct him.

Mr. Jackson contemplates whether the difference between the two names is significant enough to acknowledge.

"Well, that's one of those new-age names y'all like to make up, isn't it? I'm sure people get that mixed up with all kinds of stuff. Can't blame me, can ya?" He chuckles and gives me a quick pat on the back.

"Now, I'm sure you've been hearing all this left-wing mumbo jumbo about coed bathrooms—"

"You mean gender neutral?" I ask. No wonder Abby is so awful.

"You see! You've already been brainwashed. I'll be damned if the gym I'm paying for makes it easier for perverts to attack you young ladies when you least expect it." Mr. Jackson storms toward the door, shaking the room with each of his monstrous steps. "And you are going to tell me if anyone in that school says otherwise, you hear me?" he thunders.

Abby's porcelain face turns the same shade as the beet juice my mom used to try to convince me to drink in the morning. She gives her dad a barely visible nod as a country song bursts from the cell phone in his hand, sending him out of the room without another word.

Chapter 21

It's six o'clock when I walk into my grandfather's house.

I hang my bag on the coat closet door and walk in to find my family staring at Rabbi Sarah, who is squeezed between my mother and my aunt on the couch. My mom, despite having showered, still reminds me of a rag doll as she takes long, measured breaths that require all her remaining strength. Anita talks at both of them a mile a minute, and Rabbi Sarah flinches every time my aunt accentuates her words with swooping gestures, afraid she might get hit.

Anita jumps to her feet at the sight of me. "I thought you were at your father's toni—"

"You made it!" Rabbi Sarah interrupts. Glad to be out of the proverbial hot seat, she crosses the room, arms outstretched, and hugs me so tight I can't breathe, like she doesn't know how a hug is supposed to look or feel. She releases me after a few moments, allowing the oxygen to flow freely through my lungs.

"Anita, can I talk to you?" I say firmly.

"Excuse us," Anita says, pulling me by the elbow up the stairs.

"What is *she* doing here?" I hiss. "I told you everything in confidence. Why can't you ever leave anything alone?"

Anita's top lip curls in fury the moment the words leave my mouth. I brace myself as she begins to raise her hand, but she stops it midway and slowly points her index finger directly between my eyes.

"You done, little girl?" Now that she has my full attention, she lowers her voice. "I figured if you're spending so much time with this woman, someone should meet her and make sure she is who she says she is."

Anita grabs me close and hugs me. Unlike Rabbi Sarah, who squeezed me like a python prepping its dinner, my aunt wraps me in her arms the way only someone who has held a person they truly love more than themselves can.

"I saw something on *The View* about people who hire spies to gather information on their spouse during custody battles. If that's what's going on, I'll send her through all the damn plagues before she snitches on anyone in my house. Now, come on."

She marches back down the stairs and I follow, still annoyed, but touched that she's trying to protect me.

Anita made lasagna, a staple in this household because it's easy to make in bulk and reheats well as long as you use enough sauce the first time around. We form an assembly line, passing plates around until they are full with the pasta and veggies and garlic bread. Almost as if on command, everyone instinctively assumes the prayer position and waits for Rabbi Sarah and me to join before Pa can say grace.

"Sorry," I mouth to Rabbi Sarah, unsure if the praise of the Christian lord and savior makes her uncomfortable.

"Don't worry," she whispers with a wink. "Jesus was Jewish."

She bows her head with the rest of us as my grandfather says the prayer. Then everyone digs in, but Rabbi Sarah's fingers dance around her fork in hesitation.

"Is there meat in this?" she asks me out of the corner of her mouth.

"No."

Glee takes over her face and she closes her eyes as she puts a forkful of lasagna on her tongue. Moments pass as we watch her eat, mesmerized that the only other person on this planet who can give Pa a run for his title of Slowest Chewer on Earth has found her way to our dining table. She lets out a little moan.

"Man!" Jerry exclaims, drawing everyone to his attention. "I thought I liked food, but Rabbi Sarah got me beat."

His observation draws a laugh from all of us. Rabbi Sarah takes a long sip of water and explains, "I've only had the frozen kind, but this homemade stuff is stupid good!"

I don't even have to look over to know that Anita's "high alert" system automatically shuts off at the compliment, relieving some of the tension in the air. My mom forces a chuckle every once in a while, an act that, despite the months of practice, has yet to convince anyone she is listening to the conversations around her.

"So, this party you're helping Nevaeh with. Tell us more," Anita demands, getting down to business.

Jordan's eyebrows rise at the mention of a party, irritated that the dinner conversation is revolving around her least favorite subject: me.

"It's a comin'-of-age ceremony," Rabbi Sarah explains.

"I wouldn't do it if my dad weren't forcing me," I say, immediately turning to Rabbi Sarah to add, "No offense."

"None taken," she assures me.

After months of barely acknowledging my existence, my mom snaps to, and it seems that even the cars and street outside become muted as she breaks out in a maniacal laugh.

"You think you know him. . . . Samuel's so good at making you feel safe . . . and then . . ."

As the words come out, she looks up and frantically searches the multiple sets of eyes focused on her for mine. If she meant to say anything else, it gets lost as she begins to cry so hard I'm surprised the walls don't convulse along with her.

Jordan gathers Jerry and Janae and ushers them into the kitchen with their plates as Anita jumps up to hold her sister, who dissolves into puddles of tears and self-pity.

"Unbelievable," I mutter before pushing my chair back and running upstairs without asking to be excused.

I sit on the bed and let my feet hang off, swinging them back and forth, quicker and quicker, until I feel like I'm running on clouds.

"Are you okay?" Rabbi Sarah asks through the crack in the door.

"*No.* I am not! I wish I had never been born!"

She tiptoes over to me and clamps her palm over my mouth to shush me.

"Look, I know it's hard to be the kid and also have to be the adult, but sometimes, you gotta be the bigger person . . . because to be honest, okay is usually the best most of us can hope for, and you've got way more than okay. Trust me."

"She wasn't always like this," I say mostly to myself, but loud enough for her to hear, because for some reason, that makes it feel truer.

"They never are," she assures me.

There is a soft knock on the door, and Jerry pokes his head in.

"Nevaeh, Janae said you should come downstairs," he says with equal amounts of fear and excitement in his voice.

Oh Lord, what now?

Out on the stoop, my aunt and cousins examine the votive candles that have been placed on the steps to the house. Rabbi Sarah and I approach with caution, but luckily, my mom is nowhere to be seen.

"Do you know what this is?" Anita asks me.

I shake my head, but Janae catches my eye with a wink and positions her phone to face the street.

"Thanks for that delicious dinner, Anita, but I should, uh, probably hit the road," Rabbi Sarah says, stuffing something into my hand before running down the candlelit staircase and onto the street.

I open my palm to find a crumpled piece of paper that reads *Just in case. Sarah 718-666–6666.*

Suddenly, Beyoncé's "Single Ladies" starts to play and Stevie pops out from behind a parked car.

He's wearing a black tracksuit and begins to do a spot-on performance of the choreography from the video. The portable speaker he brought with him is pretty powerful, and neighbors start to come outside to see what the commotion is about. Stevie locks eyes with Jordan immediately, despite how utterly mortified she looks.

Janae sits on the railing of the stoop with her iPhone on its tripod, capturing the performance and blocking Jordan from running back inside the house in embarrassment. At the chorus, Stevie rips the tracksuit off to reveal a leotard exactly like the one Queen B wears in the music video, and the growing crowd goes wild.

By the last verse, there are at least forty people out here whooping every time he lands a move or adds a bit of flamboyance to his hip rolls. He pulls a bouquet out of nowhere and points to Jordan with such power that the crowd immediately parts like the Red Sea. With a cleared path, he brings it home with a forward flip, but not before flinging the flowers in Jordan's direction.

We all watch the flowers fly through the air and tumble toward her in slow motion, but just as they begin to descend, a gust of wind smashes them down directly into her face. She falls backward, but Zeke holds his hand out to catch her like a leaf in the wind. It sounds like everyone in the whole neighborhood cheers.

Janae walks over to Stevie, who hands her a wad of folded bills.

"Half up front, half when I get the edited cut? Deadline for the audition is end of next week."

Janae grabs the money and winks. "I'll have it to you by Wednesday," she says.

"How could you?" Jordan hisses, swiping at Janae's phone like a feral cat.

"You ready to pay me back for that college trip?" Janae retorts, simultaneously evading her sister's reach and shutting her down.

Stevie, who is covered in sweat and still catching his breath, walks toward Jordan.

"I'll get you more if the petals got messed up—"

Jordan shoots Stevie a steel-cutter glare that stops him in his tracks. If she could have any sort of superpower, I am one hundred percent positive she would choose to shoot fire from her eyes so she could burn a hole in his chest, rip his heart out, throw it to the ground, and stomp on it.

"Don't *ever* come near me again." Jordan's body shakes as she walks back into the house.

Stevie drops to the curb, where I plop myself down next to him and throw my arm around his shoulder.

"I've been where you are. She comes off harsh. Just give it time. Why didn't you tell me you were doing this?" I ask, salty that Janae was more in the loop with my best friend than I am.

"I tried, B, but you've been preoccupied," he says with a sadness so deep I feel it radiate into my heart.

"Do you wanna come in?" I ask in an attempt to make up for my negligence.

"You don't wanna go in there." Janae nods to the doorway, where Jordan is crying into Zeke's neck. She hands me my coat. "You're both coming with me."

Chapter 22

"I could have called us a car," Stevie whines through chattering teeth.

"Who told you to come out here without a proper jacket?" Janae asks. "You're in the city now. That means you walk or take public transportation. No more of this bougie car-app mess."

She stops in front of a building with windows that have been painted white and sport AVAILABLE FOR RENT signs.

"Where are we?" Stevie asks.

"You'll see," Janae says as she searches through her bag.

People walk past us and into the space, hurrying to avoid the chilly evening. Janae's forehead scrunches so lines appear between her full, perfectly arched brows.

"What in the hell?" She pulls out a marble-cover notebook with my name on it.

"Hey!"

I grab the notebook and look more closely at the purse—it's mine.

"Damn, relax. I must have grabbed the wrong bag trying to

get us out of there before all hell broke loose." She takes the bag off her shoulder and hands it to me with a look of annoyance as she flips the long ombre twists on her head from one shoulder to the other. "You're welcome."

Inside, a bunch of desks and tables have been pushed to the perimeter of the room, leaving rows of mismatched chairs in the center. The seats are filled with young people chatting and drinking water from small plastic cups.

Darnell, the youth pastor from church, stands by the snack table, greeting everyone.

"It's good to see you, Nevaeh." He takes my hand in his and then looks past me. "Janae," he says with a grin before he continues the welcome train.

We settle into one of the back rows so Janae can set up her tripod to film whatever this is—must be another gig she's picked up to add to her portfolio.

"Welcome!" Darnell bows to his audience. "Is there anything anyone wants to say before we get started?"

Someone stands to speak. "The courts by Marcus Garvey Park need to be repaved, and the hoops need to be replaced. My pops is holding a town hall next Friday to ask district officials to allocate necessary funds for the repairs. The white developers comin' in and buyin' up all the buildings are saying the basketball courts should be demolished—they say it's attracting drug dealers and gangs that prevent buyers—but really we're just chillin' there, cuz we can't play on it in the state it's in."

The lights are dim, but all I need to hear is his voice and my heart slams against my chest like a Ping-Pong ball. It's Jesus.

"We need y'all to come out and support us if we're going to save it. They're pushing us out and raising the rent, but this is *our* hood, and we need to show them that we're not backing down."

I slide down in my seat a little, ashamed that my appearance automatically associates me with anyone responsible for the gentrification of this neighborhood I have begun to love.

"Thank you, brother. We'll be there," Darnell says as he looks around for any other updates, but no one else raises their hand. "All right, let's open the floor. Zadie, you wanna start us off?"

Everyone settles into their seat as a singer/songwriter who looks like Zoë Kravitz and sounds like Eartha Kitt leads the group in a rousing rendition of "Lift Every Voice and Sing," the Black national anthem. I'm embarrassed that I don't know the verses, so I do my best to mouth along with the words.

A young man walks up to the stage next and hands out blindfolds to the audience. Once our eyes have been covered, he begins to do impersonations of different celebrity voices, which we yell out from the audience once we have identified them. Overall, he is pretty impressive. His Barack Obama would give Jordan Peele a run for his money, but his Chris Rock could use a little work.

After his set, a woman rushes into our row. In her haste, she steps on my foot.

"Sorry!" Jordan whispers with sincerity, until our eyes meet and she turns ice cold.

"Sit down!" someone hisses from the row behind us, so she keeps scooting in to the farthest seat from me, on the other side of the room.

After each performance, the group gives constructive feedback and encouragement. Even the young kid who stumbles over his freestyle gets a standing ovation halfway through. "You got this!" "Chin up, young blood!" they shout, encouraging him to start over and find his footing.

Finally, Darnell heads up to the mic. His blazer is open now and reveals a T-shirt that reads

SOJOURNER &
HARRIET &
IDA &
ROSA &
SHIRLEY &
CORETTA &
ANGELA &
ASSATA

Slowly, everyone in the room starts to hush, drawn to his smile and intense eyes. Just as he's got the room's attention and the last whispers are down to a murmur, he begins:

"I like them buttered and brown,
Heat-kissed without so much as a hint of smoke.
Dark, thick, and sticky,
Spilling over crevices that fold into each other.
Perfection materialized in layers too complex to accurately describe,
The taste that taught me desire.

Pancakes.

Step one: Assemble ingredients.
Reach up and take the last five dollars from the big jar that lives
*   on top of the fridge,*
Twelve quarters, nineteen dimes, and ten pennies, to be exact.
Buy Bisquick from the new supermarket that swallowed the
*   twenty-four-hour bodega*

where my mama used my birthday as lottery numbers and the
cat was an employee with benefits and OT,

Where the tabs reached back to our grandfathers' graves

And were expected to be paid with nothing more than a flash of
gracious teeth
and the change in your pocket.

Smelling like aunties and macerated sunflower-seed shells and
livery cabs and off-duty nurses.

Step two: Whisk the ingredients together, but make sure to leave
lumps in the batter,
Misshapen in their truth, because flawless doesn't actually matter—
This too is just a means to an end.

Whisk until your arm is tense,
Firm and flexed,
Sweaty and shaking,
Like your cousin who does pull-ups on the streetlight at 181st
Next to a fold-up table he chills at to play dominoes and shoot
the shit.

Then fold it together,
Raw and beige and familiar,
Smelling like the look of surprise they give me when my words
come out in the same vernacular.

Each turn of the whisk a newly aerated batter,
Until it is ready for

179

Step three: Pour a cupful onto the cast-iron skillet my mama
   smacked me with the back of her hand for cleaning with soap,
   undoing generations of seasoning.
Watch the bubbles burst on my stove top the same as yours,
Because science doesn't discriminate.

Step four: Flip it once and cook until done.
Golden and brown.
Same since the day we arrived.

Slick and crisped by heat and time.
The way your grandmother made them,
Way back in the day when a fridge was just a metal box with
   an ice cube
And nobody had nothin'

Except for hope.
Except for joy.
Except for this round, imperfect, golden-brown pancake.

Can you taste it?

Smelling like and hunger pains and Christmas mornings
And comfort that for a moment,
Our life is,
is delicious.

His command over the room slowly dissipates, freeing us all
from our stupor, and we erupt into a chorus of snapping fingers
that transforms the space into a life-size rainmaker.

I feel something I've never felt before. A longing. One that draws me up before I even realize what's happening.

"Nevaeh?"

Darnell's voice echoes from the microphone and returns me to my immediate surroundings, where I find that I am the lone person standing in the crowd.

"Come on up," Darnell says with a smile that blinds me, even in this poor lighting.

"B?" Stevie whispers with concern, but I keep moving. If I stop for even one second to think—

What are you doing? the little voice inside me asks.

I don't know, I respond, grabbing my notebook from my bag.

My stomach is in knots as I walk toward the mic, emboldened by the community and support that surround me and terrified that for the first time in my life I want to step out of the shadows and shine.

The last time I was this nervous was the fourth-grade Black History Month luncheon, when my teacher, a white lady named Cleo who claimed she was "Black on the inside," forced me and the other Black girl in our class (who was actually Indian) to recite Martin Luther King Jr.'s "I Have a Dream" speech for fifty white parents.

"Hi," I say to the crowd, but the sound of my own voice makes me grimace and I can feel Jordan's eyes burning into me. I look and see that my notebook is upside down.

"I'm Heaven," I hear myself say into the microphone.

Just breathe, the little voice inside me says.

So I turn my notebook around, open it, and exhale.

What I know, I know from my mother's lips:
That fairy tales end with abandoned ships.

181

That songs have no time or true melody,
And paintings fade with princesses left out at sea.

The day I was born, I crawled out of her legs,
A mutant or human, two sides to my head.
She sewed up her womb and limped to a mirror.
My weight was my proof, and yet, I was clear.

"You have to be strong, I can't wait for your color.
Your people will find you," said my dying mother.
She rocked me to sleep and placed me in a cave,
Asked a bird to watch over and give me a name.

It's no way to live, such a state of unknown,
To be nothing more than a cloud or shadow.
A ghost with a heart, I walk to the beat.
Food I take from a web or the cracks in the street.

There are no people of mine whose eyes search in dismay.
They look through me to others, ready to claim.
Quiet only has meaning if you've known solitude.
"You have to be strong." Her whisper hangs off the moon.

Low tides bear rock teeth, a grin harsh and jagged,
So I hop on their surface for proof I bleed red.
"The sting—may it last." I beg to the wind
That the curse will be lifted, forgiven of sin.

To wake is to breathe is to dream of my skin
And a hope that today, I will be colored in.

It isn't oxygen streaming out of my lungs anymore; it is fire. My insides turn to ashes and are reborn, exactly the way Anita said the magic would feel: lightning and thunder and sunlight all at once. The room must be able to tell, because they send snaps of rain down onto me in support.

"Who are you and what have you done to my best friend?" Stevie runs up and hugs me, excited and in shock. "That was awesome, B! How did you—"

"Lightskin! You got bars!"

Jesus interrupts the moment and my body tenses, but this time, it's not because of the butterflies. The anxiety creeps up my esophagus as I am reminded of the call to arms Jordan issued to me not so long ago.

Just because you didn't choose to pass doesn't mean you don't have a choice.

"Don't!" I shout, surprising myself and causing the crowd to turn in our direction. "Just, don't call me that, okay?"

Everyone around us is still. I feel Jordan listening, even if I have no clue where she is. Jesus tilts his head to the side and holds his chin with his pointer finger and thumb, ruminating on my outburst.

"Whatever you say, Nevaeh," he responds with a shrug. "Wanna grab something to eat?"

He takes a step in my direction, and I get dizzy from the smell of him.

"Yes!"

The excitement in my face is hard to mask, but it melts when I turn and see Stevie biting his lip, rejected now for the second time this evening.

"Stevie . . ."

"I'm out," he says, and pivots on his heel.

I tell myself that if the situation were flipped, Stevie would do the same thing. If Jordan ran into his arms, he would ditch me for a date with her. Still, I get that feeling in my gut that I've made a mistake that needs to be fixed at once, but when I turn around to explain, Stevie and his footsteps are gone.

Darnell is surrounded by a crowd of people who ask him for feedback or a photo. He winks in our direction as we leave.

"How do you know Darnell?" Jesus asks me when we step out into the cold.

"Why, you jealous?" I tease, bolder than I have ever been with each moment that passes.

He tickles my rib cage and spins me around, and just like that, his arms pull me close and we are completely intertwined from our lips down to our toes, blanketed by the streetlights and the soft music coming through windows overhead.

A loud grunt greets us from behind, and we break apart to find an older woman making her way down the street with no interest in taking the five extra steps necessary to bypass us. Her face, which seems to wear a permanent scowl, is familiar; she's one of the Gray Lady Gang from my grandfather's church.

"Good evening," I say, wiping my mouth with the back of my hand, but she pushes past us, shaking her head. If she had a giant red letter *A* in her pocket, she'd most definitely pin it to my forehead.

Jesus and I head to Wendy's, and my stomach growls as we enter. Between my outburst at dinner and Stevie's romantic flash mob gone awry, I didn't get to finish my lasagna.

"What?" I ask Jesus, who watches me intently as I line up the sauces to dip my nuggets in one by one. (Honey mustard, barbeque, ranch, and creamy sriracha—basically everything but sweet and sour, which deserves to be retired to the island of nasty condiments. Amen.)

"You eat funny," Jesus observes with a laugh that makes my insides rumble and my face turn pink.

"No I don't!"

He pulls a sauce out of the order and places it at the end, halfway through a dip cycle, messing up my rhythm.

"All right, fine!" I concede as I move the ranch back to its rightful spot in line.

He leans over to take a bite of the nugget in my hand, and his smooth teeth brush against my fingertip.

"It was about your dad, right? The poem?" he asks with caution and care.

I feel the blood drain from my face—I never expected things to go as far as they have, but now that we're here, the idea of admitting the truth makes me want to vomit, even more than the idea of doubling down on this false narrative. His eyes bore into mine with such intensity that even if I weren't such a terrible liar, it would make me look away.

"I dunno. . . ."

"All summer I watched you walkin' around, never lookin' up at anyone. Why do you act like you don't have a right to be yourself? Just cuz he died doesn't mean he's not a part of you. Don't you want to know everything about who you are?"

More than anything, the little voice inside me cries.

His hand grabs mine, warm and safe, and my knee starts to bounce, fueled by increasing anxiety and desperate for a way out of this mess.

"Maybe . . . maybe I don't know who I am yet."

"No one will unless you tell us," he says, unwilling to allow me to stay closed off. "Why'd you call yourself Heaven?"

"Nevaeh is 'heaven' spelled backward. See?"

I pull the notebook, along with a pen, out of my bag and write my name backward.

He smiles.

"What time is it?" I ask, not wanting to take my phone out in front of him to check.

His screen lights up: ten p.m.

"We should head back," I say.

Once we reach my house, I spot Anita standing by the living room window, and I can tell from her body language that she's in a mood, so I make sure we keep our distance as we say our farewells.

"So what was that tonight? Does it happen often?" I ask.

"Every month," he says.

"Cool. It's like a secret society. Dumbledore's Army," I say.

Jesus looks at me as though I've just spoken a foreign language.

"Harry Potter," I explain.

"What's the deal with Harry Potter? The guy looks like a herb to me, but my girlfriend can't stop talking about him." He gives me a giant grin.

Three sharp clinks from Anita's ring against the window send me up the stairs two at a time before she or anyone else can ruin the fireworks that go off in my chest as I take in his words and his smile and the reality that Jesus DeSantos is officially my boyfriend.

Chapter 23

News of my performance has permeated the social media air-waves, thanks to Janae's YouTube video of the evening, and everyone at Pritchard seems to have noticed. People smile at me when I enter the building and as I walk down the hallway. I'm used to gliding past without seeing so much as a glance in my direction—the constant attention is overwhelming at first, but as the weeks pass, I begin to enjoy the visibility, yearn for it, even.

The school days always go by more quickly as Thanksgiving approaches. The teachers are all irritable and in desperate need of a break, so they find excuses to show films or send us on field trips rather than preparing hourlong lesson plans. Usually, Stevie and I would use the freedom to hide in the corners of the library, but ever since the night of our unexpected performances, I've barely been able to pin him down, and it doesn't help that any free time I would normally have has now been commandeered by Jesus or Rabbi Sarah.

Today, I made sure to get to school early and have a roll and iced coffee waiting for Stevie when he arrives. Stevie hops out of a car on the corner. His neon orange headphones act as a bull's-eye among the crowd. I stand up a little taller to try to get his attention.

"Hey!" I wave to him with urgency, as though I'm injured on a road in the pitch-black dead of night.

He catches my eyes and scrunches his brow but walks over.

"Here!" I thrust the breakfast offering into his arms.

"Thanks," he says without much emotion.

"How are you?" I press.

"Nevaeh?" LaShawn Marshall, the head of the Black Student Union, stands before us and blocks the entrance to the building.

"Hi?" I say, surprised she knows my name.

"I saw your video. The BSU is cohosting an open-mic fund-raiser against police brutality. Can we sign you up to perform?" She talks a mile a minute.

My parents have never spoken to me about the cops, not the way I see Anita and Zeke do with Jerry every morning.

"Hands. Eye contact. Listen. Be calm," Anita chants to a made-up beat as she zips Jerry's jacket.

"Hands. Eye contact. Listen. Be calm," Jerry echoes.

But a sharp sickness radiates through my body every time I am forced to look at images of broken Black bodies that air on loop. My parents and I were in the kitchen, probably a year ago, eating breakfast, when the hosts of *The View* interrupted the show to share the breaking news that yet again, a cop who had killed an innocent Black child had been exonerated. The cop's month-long paid leave of absence was deemed fair retribution for the life he stole for no good reason other than that he could. I watched the screen, mesmerized, as he walked out of the courtroom smiling, likely heading to meet his family at home and celebrate his freedom.

I remember when the camera shifted to the parents of the victim, a formerly living human now reduced to a hashtag. His mother spoke with dignity and confidence, but the agony in her eyes belied the facade. She vowed on her honor that she would not stop until justice was served, before disintegrating into tears and being escorted away by a crowd of grieving loved ones.

That mother's words lingered with me long after she left . . . even after my father got up and switched the channel to his preferred CNBC, where he followed the stock ticker on the bottom of the screen like a cat following a laser pointer.

"So that's a yes?" LaShawn presses, bringing me back to the present.

"Sure, I guess."

"Great, we'll be in touch," she says before marching off.

I turn to Stevie. "Sorry."

"Was there something you wanted?" he asks.

"I just wanted to catch up."

"Well, I have to get to class," he says coldly.

"Oh, right, of course. See you at lunch?"

He shrugs and walks inside.

Are you okay?

I text Stevie on the walk home from the subway after bat mitzvah practice. He never showed for lunch, and a growing pit in my stomach is telling me that it's going to take more than coffee and a buttered roll to make up for constantly ditching him. The three dots blink but then stop, and I stare at my phone, willing a response that never comes.

The house smells of plantains, beans, and jerk chicken, which means Pa cooked dinner—a rare treat. This is Grandma's original jerk dry rub, a recipe she passed on to him before she died that he has yet to share with anyone in the family. The unusual stillness that permeates the house sets off an alarm in my head. I would be lying if I said I hadn't woken up in the middle of the night to check that my mother hadn't succumbed to her depression next to me. The image of her stiff, lifeless body makes me rush into the dining room, but to my surprise, she isn't there. Instead, the reason for the hushed energy stops me in my tracks.

"I don't know why you stay dressed like you're a dried-up piece of toast. Ain't nobody gonna give you the time of day lookin' like that," Miss Clarisse says to me in all her busty glory from the comfort of my grandmother's seat. She has taken the liberty of dragging the chair a few inches closer to my grandfather at the head of the table so they're perched on top of one another like two birds on a branch.

"I tried to tell this girl to come over to my shop and let me pick out a few things, spice it up a little," she continues. "But don't you worry, Nevaeh. I gotchu somethin'."

Per usual, Miss Clarisse's outfit is ridiculous: a purple polyester pantsuit two sizes too small and a black lace bra that protrudes from gaps between the buttons. My grandfather, usually stoic and focused on his eating and digestion, has barely touched the food on his plate. He chuckles along with Miss Clarisse's flirtation.

Despite the odd tension in the air, the two of them seem to be having a grand time. She leans toward him, her hand on his, and whispers in his ear while the rest of my family does their best to look away from the intimate date they unexpectedly crashed when they came to the dinner table.

"Nevaeh, take a seat. Your mother is at an appointment," Anita says stiffly.

Relieved that I get to avoid my mom for another night, I don't even bother to ask what sort of appointment got her out of our bed and into the world on her own.

"Not just yet!"

Miss Clarisse jumps up and stuffs a box into my hands before I sit down.

The intricate wrapping is tricky to remove, but once I get through the layers of tissue paper, I find a blue linen sheath with a classic V-neck. The color is unique, like a periwinkle with an extra splash of blue to confirm it isn't purple.

"It's really pretty. Thank you, Miss Clarisse."

"There's more in there," she says, urging me on.

I hand her the dress and continue to dig through the box. Eventually, I uncover a clear plastic sleeve flat against the bottom of the box. Miss Clarisse snatches the item from me and holds it above her head.

"The new bottom-enhancing material adds at least an inch to the cheeks," she says, proudly pointing to her butt like Vanna White indicating a vowel. "And it sucks one to two inches in on the obliques." She spins slowly, as if she's a mannequin on a life-size lazy Susan.

"You'll be the first to try my new invention: 'ScRUMPtious Gurl,' the legging that'll get more Junk in Your Trunk."

Miss Clarisse hands the package back to me but maintains her grip, posed for the blinding flash that goes off when Pa takes a photo.

"Got it!" my grandfather cheers with more enthusiasm than I have ever seen.

"Well, let's not celebrate just yet, Nevaeh. Why don't you try these on and give us a catwalk?"

My entire life flashes before my eyes at the idea of putting on a show in this getup.

"Actually," Anita butts in, "Nevaeh needs to eat and then get to work. Finals are coming up, and I don't need her daddy marching up in here to blame us for bad grades."

Anita draws me to the table with a pointed expression that challenges Miss Clarisse to push her any further. The smells wafting from the plate in front of me are so divine that I decide to dig in and ignore everything going on around me.

Grandma's jerk chicken recipe is the best. It hits your tongue with a rich earthiness, matched with the perfect amount of heat and salt, and then the tiniest hint of sweetness at the end. Even the chicken breast, a cut I usually find offensive due to its tendency toward dryness, brings me unadulterated joy as I slice it and release a river of juices onto my plate.

"We had a representative from Howard University visit school today." Jordan breaks the silence. "She said I'm a great candidate, especially if I apply early decision."

Anita, who usually orchestrates the dinner conversation with her unending list of questions and concerns, sits tight-lipped with nostrils flared. She cuts her meat with a bit more vigor than necessary at the sound of her daughter's voice breaking the unspoken vow of silence in protest of Pa's guest.

"That's a private school. You know we can't afford that," Anita snaps.

"Maybe you could afford it for her if you just let me start working after I graduate like I want, instead of wasting time at some school I don't care about," Janae chimes in, coming to her sister's defense.

Anita breathes like a bull and drops her utensils on her plate with a clang that makes Jerry jump.

"I've just about had it with both of your complaints. You don't know how lucky you are. New York city and state schools are good. That's what your father and I have saved for, and that's where you are going to apply. Corinne went to her fancy school and wasted the opportunity on that man. Meanwhile, Mummy and Pa couldn't afford to send me anywhere but a two-year associate's program, and twenty years later, all I am qualified to be is a secretary. You are both getting a four-year education, a bachelor's degree, and you are going to do it without debt. That way, when you are on your own, you'll at least have a chance. If you want to mess it up after, that's on you."

"Anita, that's enough. We have a guest." Pa's voice thunders through the house.

The front door opens and shuts behind my mom as she walks into the dining room, unaware that she is entering a lion's den.

"There she is. I got somethin' for you, Corinne! Gonna help you get over that white man!" Miss Clarisse pops up, ready to make the same presentation all over again.

Anita jumps out of her seat. She waves her arms in front of her to clear the energy or silence the room, maybe both, and storms off.

"Honey, I'm feelin' like a treat. Why don't you take me to

that new French bakery around the corner for some cake," Miss Clarisse suggests.

Pa stands to join her.

"That sounds like an excellent proposition," he says, and puts his arm on her back to escort her away from the table. For the first time, he's broken his rule and leaves before everyone has finished their meal, including his own.

Chapter 24

My mom stands in the bedroom, unclasping the pearl earrings my father gave her on their ten-year anniversary.

"Hi, sweetheart," she says with an airiness that sounds like she just woke up from a long, rejuvenating nap.

My mom is beautiful in her floor-length black skirt and deep green top. She looks like herself, or at least the version of her I have known my whole life until recently. Her skirt swooshes against the hardwood floor as she floats toward me, and I have to blink multiple times to make sure she isn't an optical illusion.

"Maybe we can do something special this week, just the two of us? I know I've been . . . unavailable—" She reaches out to caress my face, but I dodge her hand.

For months I've wished for her to snap out of her funk, but this abrupt return to the land of the living is irksome, if not downright infuriating. How am I supposed to trust that she won't disappear on me again? Maybe her breakdown the other night in front of Rabbi Sarah woke her up, but why should I be expected to adapt again to her fluctuating mental state? It's enough to give me whiplash.

"I've got homework to do," I say, and walk away.

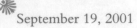

September 19, 2001

I lost you. Daddy packed a bunch of my things up during spring break last year to paint my room and never brought the boxes back. In your absence, I've been a balloon, slowly filling with thoughts I can't share with anyone. But then, an hour ago, you arrived in the mail with a note from Anita. She was searching for an old photo album in a closet and there you were. I don't know how she knew I would need you, but I am so glad she did.

I'll do my best to get you up to speed.

Last Tuesday, when the planes hit the towers, my roommate Jolie and I were out buying snacks to fill the resident advisor lounge and came back to images of melting steel. I had just returned to campus to start junior year. I was preparing for my classes and RA orientation, glad to be back where I could eat what I wanted and see Samuel freely, when all of a sudden, my world crashed to the ground.

Fear and disgust and loneliness came over me like a sickness. Hours passed as I tried to get ahold of my family. My parents had finally given in and bought me a cell phone, and I paced back and forth and dialed their number on repeat while watching the video of planes barreling into buildings. All I could think about was Tribeca coated with a thick layer of soot, now the final resting place of chipped coffee mugs and last breaths and unclaimed paychecks.

The phone finally rang at eleven p.m.

They had been home when it happened, and tried to

196

call immediately, but all the phone lines were down and had been until now. I wanted to fly back to make sure that everything I knew hadn't been obliterated with the impact, but Mummy wouldn't hear of it.

"Don't you dare," she said, ending any further discussion.

Now, days later, everything still feels different—broken. Samuel is different too.

Until now, we were moving at a slow pace in our physical relationship. He allowed me and my body to dictate the speed. But in the days that followed the tragedy, he became impatient, pushing me past my comfort zone, as if a ticking clock were counting down to our inevitable demise.

Yesterday, he appeared in my doorway looking like he had been run over by a fourteen-wheeler. Jolie made some excuse to give us some privacy, and the second she left, Samuel couldn't keep his hands off me. He started kissing my neck and unbuttoning my cardigan. I tried to calm him down, but it was like he couldn't hear anything I was saying.

A chill came over me, one that I hadn't felt in so long, not since that night after the dance with Raymond. I went into survival mode.

"Stop!" I yelled.

His whole body begged for me in a way that made me feel a stirring between my legs, but I couldn't give him what he needed.

"What is your problem?" He got up from the bed, flustered and angry.

"I'm not ready," I said.

"Well, how long do you need, Corinne? It's been over two years. I have needs, ya know. I turn girls away every day because I want to be with you, but I can't wait forever. I'm about to explode."

He walked toward the door, but I jumped up and blocked the exit. I asked him to stay and hold my hand and tell me that everything was going to be okay, but he wouldn't. He stormed out and left me alone with so much anxiety raging through my body I couldn't breathe.

I texted Samuel over and over to ask where he was, because he had left hours ago, but he didn't answer.

His phone probably died, or it was stolen and then it died. He probably lost it and then went back to the dorm and couldn't call me. Or he got into some terrible accident and was at the hospital. The worst-case scenarios kept blossoming out of each other until I went out for some fresh air.

My feet got lost in the nighttime and the hum of my classmates' bad decisions, seeping out of the dorm windows all over campus. I liked walking; it made me feel closer to New York, which I knew was drenched in the tears of mothers too afraid to put their babies to sleep, fearful that something else unimaginable might happen. After an hour of wandering, I found myself in front of Samuel's dorm. Before I could ask God for a miracle, the front door burst open and a group of freshmen ran out, wildly underdressed and singing an off-key mashup of Destiny's Child lyrics.

I crept into the building, which reeked of warm beer. His door opened with just a push. After losing his key three times last year, he taped the latch down, so it never locks.

Before even turning the lights on, I knew he wasn't there. The place felt cold and empty. I tried calling his cell again. Nothing.

It was late, so I lay on his bed. "Fifteen minutes," I told myself. I'd wait fifteen minutes, no more. Then . . .

"Corinne?" Samuel stood above me. The clock read 4:30 a.m.

I pulled him down to me and searched his face and eyes and neck. He smelled like he had showered recently, but even the perfumed body wash he used didn't hide the smell of cigarettes on his fingertips.

"Are you okay? I tried calling you all night. Why did you leave me? I didn't know what to do without you."

He yawned somewhat dramatically.

"I was upset, but I should have stayed. I actually tried to get back into your building, but no one would let me in and my phone died, so I walked around to clear my head, and on the way back I stopped at this lame house party and sort of fell asleep on the couch after drinking too much."

Something about his face seemed wrong.

"You're lying."

He sucked in his breath, pained and guilty.

"I can smell the cigarettes on you. I hate when you smoke."

"I know, baby. It's just something I do when I'm stressed. I'll stop, I promise."

The sight of him clean-shaven and recently washed made me weak, and I stood to unbutton my shirt. Samuel watched me with hunger and maybe a little ambivalence before he took my hands in his and kissed them.

"Not like this. We can wait. We should wait," he said before he wrapped his arms and legs around me and passed out almost instantly.

Samuel always says I'm all he needs to fall asleep. But nighttime has always been difficult for me. My mind races, and I get stuck dissecting details that usually mean nothing. The exhaustion from the night overpowered my thoughts, so I drifted off as I tried to ignore the smell of tobacco and convince myself he was telling me the truth.

Chapter 25

Abby sits in the seat farther from the door, the one she usually makes me walk around her to get to, and nods at me with nervous eyes when I slide into the chair. Up front, Mr. Bowels, who looks healthier and less terrified than usual, takes advantage of the unprecedented calm among his students. He begins to walk through the room, handing out vials filled with cloudy liquid. Abby's leg shakes so hard that my chair feels like it's giving me a butt massage.

"Are you okay?" I whisper, unable to ignore the anxiety emanating from her.

"I'm fine . . . Heaven," she jeers.

Abby and the Bomb Squad have begun to use my stage name to taunt me ever since my performance went viral.

Bang.

The door crashes open, sending Mr. Bowels, who has apparently not gotten his groove back, shrieking behind a desk. The uncovered vials of grayish goop fly all over the class. Our table is only sprayed lightly, but Maud, the token musical-theater-head in our class who sits to our left, gets drenched. She grasps at her hair, now hardening under the liquid, and lets out a string of incredibly creative curses. We all watch her run to the open door only to be blocked by models who have materialized out of thin air.

A shirtless blond man in tuxedo pants, suspenders, and a bow tie who might as well have walked straight out of an Abercrombie & Fitch ad flips an imaginary switch and begins to dance to music that blasts out of a device close to his crotch. The rest of the group comes to life, and the women in couture gowns catwalk down the center of the room, carrying martini glasses on trays toward the front. One woman scoops Abby up from her seat on the way and places a tiara and sash over her head, depositing her on a stool up front, while the male models remain by the door with no apparent purpose other than to guard the entrance and flex. Up front, the female models begin calling out names, and one by one, students walk up to collect their prize.

"It's your lucky day. Won't you join Abby for her sweet sixteen soiree? How sway!"

They speak in an accent that makes them sound like a cross between a valley girl and Iggy Azalea, and after each name is called, they bestow a martini glass filled with jelly beans and an invitation upon the lucky invitee. I watch as my classmates saunter up and take a selfie with the birthday queen, until the last martini glass has been given away and I'm the only student left empty-handed. The models walk back to where they first appeared, and the human Ken doll blows a kiss to the room before he ushers the models out and closes the door behind him.

The moment the door shuts, the class explodes. Jelly beans begin to fly across the room. Chatter about arrangements for stretch Hummers and speculation about who the Jacksons hired to perform as the musical act fill the air. In the classroom next door, the same techno music begins to play, indicating that our stream was not the only one lucky enough to receive the over-the-top presentation. Mrs. Lackey peers into our class. I am sure this ridiculous disruption is making her blood boil, but there won't be any sort of consequence for breaking the rules. The Jacksons practically fund this school, so Abby can do anything she wants and get away with it.

The commotion is so loud that I barely hear the bell ring, but it does, and I leave, grateful to be released from this hell.

By lunchtime, the entire school is enraptured with the prospect of Abby's sweet sixteen party, and rumors have begun to spread that the whole invitation stunt was secretly filmed for some MTV reality special coming out next fall. In the cafeteria, I weave through the animated conversations and the martini glasses that everyone clutches. The line for fresh food wraps around the room, and after five minutes I can barely stand to listen to the obtuse blather, so I grab a to-go spicy tuna rice bowl and march directly to my preferred winter lunch spot, the woodshop, where I find Stevie halfway through a burrito.

We make eye contact. He too is martini-glass-less. I take a few steps in and he lets out a roar and we both fall to the ground, crying so hard from the wood dust in the air and laughter that we'll need to find eye drops before our next class to convince our teachers we aren't high.

"Those invitations were so lame. I would rather sit through a two-day marathon of *Seinfeld* than go to that party," he says, before falling victim to another uproarious fit.

"I would rather eat dry, unseasoned chicken breast for the rest of my days!" I tell him.

"I would rather use tinfoil as a condom."

"I would rather lick the inside of Abe's belly button."

We go back and forth, distracting ourselves from the far-too-familiar humiliation and social degradation until it withers to a few hiccups and snorts. The uncomfortable silence that has existed between us for weeks takes over, and we sit in it, unsure what to do.

"Stevie . . ."

"It's fine."

"No. It isn't. I can't make it in this place without you."

"It seems like you're doing just fine, Heaven," he says with some side-eye.

"Oh my god, Stevie, are you actually so dense as to buy into this shit? *You* are the one who keeps ditching *me!*"

"I didn't ditch you when you decided to come out as *Def Poetry Jam's* newest superstar. Heaven Levitz, let me show you my struggle!" he says, and stands to do a dramatic impersonation of me.

"Oh, I see! You think it's okay to come up with a whole scheme to seduce my cousin and don't even bother to give me a heads-up? I have always supported you. You just can't stand to give up a tiny bit of the spotlight, can you? I'm sorry that I'm finally feeling comfortable in my own skin. We aren't all so lucky, Stevie."

"Oh my god, do you hear me complaining that my cousins in Hong Kong all make fun of me because I'm American and can't speak their language, or that my dad has never once acknowledged the fact that I'm mixed because ignoring it means he doesn't have to deal with it? Or that every day some stranger thinks it's funny to address me by saying *'Ni hao'* or screaming into my ear slowly because they assume I can't speak English? Newsflash: you aren't the only biracial person on planet Earth, Nevaeh."

My heart stops. Stevie has never told me any of this. How could I have been so wrapped up in my own turmoil that I didn't recognize that my best friend deals with the same exact things I do, every day?

"It's a good thing you've found your calling, though, because I'm one step closer to getting the hell out of here!"

He kicks the linoleum floor, sending wood shavings into the air like fireflies.

"What do you mean?"

"I'm sure you'll be delighted to know that I made it to the final round of the Zahira dance fellowship."

His sarcasm is overpowered by devastation from the bomb that falls out of his mouth.

This is his dream, what he has wished for his entire life. I am only now beginning to understand what makes me happy, but he has always known what he wants.

"Well, maybe I'm not," I say.

Stevie looks shocked and stung that I would be so evil as to admit this unspoken truth.

"But I'm not surprised," I say softly. "You killed it, even though I wished the whole time that you would trip and break your ankle."

"Ya know, you're turning into a real bitch," he says as a mischievous, somewhat apprehensive grin spreads across his face. "But at least you aren't afraid to say how you feel anymore."

He's right. What I didn't know was that there was a version of myself that until now, neither of us had met. The slow emergence of this new persona has been too much for me to parse and adequately acquaint myself with, let alone properly introduce to anyone else. In so many ways, nothing has changed. I live in the body I always have, but a layer has been removed, exposing my new self to the old one. The rest of the world continues to see me as I was, but not Stevie. He sees me as I am. He always has.

Stevie gets up and throws the remainder of his burrito in the trash.

"See you after school?" he asks.

I look up, surprised.

"What? You thought you were going to walk away from this without sitting through at least one rehearsal?"

I get up and follow him out into the hallway.

Neither of us says another word. We don't need to, because we're back to reading each other's minds, the way we always do. The way it's supposed to be.

Chapter 26

When I walk in, Jerry is lying across the bottom step of the staircase, but he springs up with incredible agility.

"SHE'S HERE. SHE'S BACK!"

A hoard of footsteps gallop toward me with such haste that I can barely make out who or what is headed in my direction.

"Girl, where have you been?" Jordan asks, hastily removing an apron covered in a red liquid that smells like rancid onions and overripe tomatoes.

I take the apron with my fingertips and hold it as far away from my person as possible. Anita, Jordan, Janae, Jerry, and Zeke stand waiting, as if they need me to tell them what their problem is.

Anita pulls me toward the kitchen and we clamp our hands over our nose and mouth to protect our nostrils from the thick cloud of rank funk permeating the kitchen. My eyes grow wide as I see my mother bustling about.

"She's been like this since the morning," Anita yells before pushing me farther into the kitchen and closing the door tightly behind me.

The kitchen looks like the set of *Chopped* after the first round, every drawer and cabinet ajar, along with the fridge door and the windows. My mom maneuvers around the unsteady towers of dirty mixing bowls and cutting boards that lie haphazardly on any free counter space.

Corinne Paire Levitz has never been a good cook. She did her best when I was little, locking down elementary skills to complete a handful of recipes (mostly large roasted meats that, no matter how hard she tried, always ended up underseasoned and overcooked). The unfortunate deficit was not for lack of trying. There have been multiple culinary disasters in my lifetime, all of which started out like this.

"Nevaeh!" She runs over and kisses my face. "I'm making curry for dinner! Hand me that rice. I need to add some more."

She gestures at the bag of rice with a pile of uncooked grains spilling out of it and snatches it from me to pour an unmeasured amount into an already bubbling pot of half-cooked rice.

"All right, I think it's almost ready. Go tell everyone!" she commands, and shoos me from the kitchen.

The windows in the living room have been opened, and the summer fans have been unearthed to air the place out. My family sits huddled together in their winter coats. Jerry, more distressed than he was when I first got home, has upgraded his complaints to an original soliloquy from the perspective of his own ghost, lamenting his death from lack of sustenance.

Anita perks up at my reemergence, eager for insight into what we should do, but I've got nothing to offer, so I join them on the couch in predinner purgatory.

The front door eventually opens and sends a welcome gust of freezing air into the house as Pa walks in wearing a checkered hat that only a cute old man could pull off. He hangs it on the hook by the door.

"WOO! That's a dead rat. I know that smell anywhere."

Miss Clarisse's voice slashes through the already unusual evening like a streak of lightning as she hustles in after Pa. Anita sits up as if an electric jolt shot straight up her spinal cord. She glares at Miss Clarisse, who saunters into the living room in a slinky black top that dips low in the back and barely covers her midriff above her skin-tight jeggings and thigh-high pleather boots.

"Good evening," Pa says with caution. He drapes his arm around Miss Clarisse's shivering shoulders, a move so suave and chivalrous I see a flash of him as a strapping young man. Miss Clarisse nestles her face in the warm nook between his chin and his trap muscle and lets out a little purr.

"Nuh-uh. You can buy yourself a few hours over at the Royal Orleans Hotel for all that!" Anita says, enraged by the flagrant display of public affection between her father and a woman who is not her mother.

She stands and points behind her, toward the by-the-hour motel on the corner that sports aluminum foil for window dressings and a collage of condoms on the front steps. The light purple eyesore has been on this block since the 1980s, but with the rich white people migrating past 96th Street, developers have been pushing to buy it and convert it into a luxury condo building.

"All right, let's not let this meal get cold!" my mom calls from the dining room, setting down a giant pot of bubbling orange liquid.

The congealed sludge sits like cement in our mouths and leaves a film of grease that even gulps of water won't wash down.

Jerry sits ruminating in disgust over the simultaneously over- and undercooked rice that crunches between his teeth. All of us are unmoving as my mom chatters on, failing to notice the epic gust of shade that sweeps the room every time Anita rolls her eyes.

"I gave this place a thorough cleaning, from top to bottom. Even went up to the attic," my mom says, pointing directly at me. "I started going through some things up there, and do you know what I found?"

My stomach jumps up to my throat when she mentions the attic. Her journal is wrapped in a sweater in the far corner of the room.

"I found Mummy's sewing machine. Can you believe she made all our clothes until we got to middle school, Anita?"

My mom sits in a daze, floating through a different time in her life, swaying in her seat to the memories. In the midst of it all, she jabs at a clump of unidentified protein on her plate—what the rest of us have pushed to the side—and sticks it in her mouth.

"Oh!" She gags and spits it directly back onto her plate, grabbing a napkin to rigorously scrape her tongue after several healthy dunks into the water glass in front of her.

My mother slowly puts her fork and knife down, quiet for the first time this evening. I scoop my head low, so I can see her in a better light, worried that if I don't watch her closely, she might slip away again right before my eyes.

"It wasn't that bad!" Anita jumps up and grabs my mom's plate from in front of her. "You just haven't eaten right in months. Your taste buds are tired and need to get used to food again."

Anita loves to give the types of explanations that adults give to children when they ask an awkward or unknowingly inappropriate question. We all know what she's saying is ridiculous, but the strength of her conviction is comforting and solves the issue, at least temporarily.

My mom takes a deep breath that sounds like part of the yoga routine she used to do in the living room when she had to tuck her arms and legs around her body in ways that did not seem remotely relaxing or meditative. Then she lets out a laugh so loud I can't tell if it's the breeze from the open window or the "whoop" that comes out of her that blows my hair back.

Anita joins her. And then we all get wrapped up in a fit of laughter at the absurdity of the rancid smell and the undeniable failure of my mom's dramatic reemergence.

Zeke rises from his seat and removes the giant pot of mush with a quick swipe of his hands, though even after he disappears behind the kitchen door, the awful stench lingers around us like a lost spirit.

Anita holds my mom's face in her hands, wiping tears from her eyes and laughing, reunited with the sister she lost and the friend she never got to make.

"I knew she'd come around. Must've found you a man, what with these late-night appointments," Miss Clarisse says with a wink before she picks at her teeth with a fingernail and runs her pink tongue across her gums.

"No!" My mom reaches across the table in my direction, as if I am about to slip and plummet to a rocky death. Her eye twitches and she presses her lips together tightly, protecting herself from what she actually wants to say. "It's . . . a therapist," she whispers.

Her words quell the agita that began to rush through my torso. She really is trying to get better.

"Well, therapists are men too, ain't they? And usually rich. A good man's all you need. You trust Miss Clarisse now. It's been twenty-five years since my Reggie passed, and now I got me a fine man and he gon' take care of me, ain't you?"

She leans toward Pa with her big red lips pursed and ready to suck the life out of him.

"All right, that's it, everyone up. We're going to Sylvia's," Anita announces.

Jerry rises from the dead and races to the living room to tie his shoes, praising the Lord in thanks as he goes. The rest of us get up and move toward the front door, but Anita waits, blocking Miss Clarisse's path.

"Not you."

Miss Clarisse holds her shoulders back like a show horse, unwilling to yield.

"Anita! Why must you be so contrary? Apologize to Ms. Brown at once!" Pa shouts so loud that his shiny head shakes, along with the finger he has outstretched before him.

"I'm sorry, Daddy," Anita says. "I can't do this. Not tonight."

We watch from the front door, holding our breath, as Anita's defiance causes Pa's arm to fly up above his head, ready to come down and strike her. I feel Janae tense next to me, protective of her mother, but Anita stands firm, ready to accept the consequences of her disregard.

"Daddy!" my mom screams, but Miss Clarisse stops him with a pat on his arm and a flirtatious smile.

"That's all right, baby. We'll get some takeout. You know, those spare ribs I like."

Pa hesitates for a moment before lowering his hand and escorting her to the front door without giving Anita so much as another glance.

By the time we make it back, we are food drunk after stuffing our faces with corn bread and fried catfish and smothered chicken and barbecued ribs and greens and mac and cheese and candied yams. Zeke goes up first, carrying Jerry passed out in his massive arms, before Anita and Janae and Jordan attempt to make it up the stairs three at a time, each one vying to get to the bathroom first to begin their evening beauty routine.

"I was going to tell you about the therapy after a few sessions," my mom says from the bottom of the stairs. "If you want to go speak to someone, you can. I never really understood how it works, therapy. When I was young, feelings were just another thing you pushed down inside you and ignored, but therapy helps and it's nothing to be ashamed of, okay?"

She holds eye contact until I look away, uncomfortable with this level of intimacy after such a long period of neglect and indifference.

"Okay" is the only word I can get out because the tears are building inside me, and it hurts to feel right now.

I keep my eyes down, and eventually, she slides her foot up to the next step.

"We can talk more in the morning. I'm going to turn in," she says, and heads upstairs.

"Nevaeh, is that you?"

My grandfather's unexpected voice in the dark a few minutes later sends me shrieking bloody murder into the coffee table.

"Pa! You scared me!" I scream-whisper once I've collected myself.

My grandfather stares at the messy dining table in front of him, and I go over to kiss his head like I always do. Rather than looking up and smiling at me, he just sits there, still, in the dark.

"Pa, are you okay?"

213

"When I was young, my mother told me that everything you need to know about a person is in their name. That's why she named me Nathaniel, 'the gift of God.' She died when I was a teenager, so I took a job with the consulate as soon as I was old enough to escape the pain of losing her.

"When I met your grandmother, we were both in line at the library in Kingston. I was visiting for a Baptist conference and wanted to borrow a few books for my speech. She was smart, much smarter than me, and loquacious!" He slaps his knee lightly at the memory of his wife as a young woman. "I had to keep a list of words she used in my head to look up later in the dictionary. When we got inside, I suggested we sit together, but she was meeting friends for a book club and began to walk away. I knew I couldn't delay any longer, not if I was ever going to see her again. My tongue was dry, but I heard my mother's voice in my head.

"'What's your name?' I said, holding my hand out to her, anxious to hear her response. 'I'm Nathaniel.'

"'Kaleisha,' she said.

"Her hand was light in mine, although not much smaller. I felt a thin scab on her palm that I imagined was a paper cut from turning the pages of book after book as she sipped ginger beer on the beach. The first thing I did when I walked away was look up her name. Kaleisha means 'strong, dynamic, and beautiful'; she was perfect. Two years later, we were married and moved into this house."

He looks at the empty chair beside him, and I imagine I can hear his heartbeat stutter in his chest, a hopeful delay to give her just a little more time to make it back to him.

"I miss her too, Pa. But it's good for you to make new friends." I point upstairs. "They'll come around."

He covers my wrists with one of his big, smooth hands, over-come by the memory of his first, true love.

"Go to bed, Pa. I'll clean up," I tell him as he rises, weary and up way past his bedtime.

"Your mother, she is returning to us. You just have to let her back in," he says in his wisest and most all-knowing voice.

Then he walks down the stairs to his bedroom to dream of perfect Kaleisha.

Chapter 27

Up until now, all I have known was a deep love for the holidays. They mean a break from school and the chance to snuggle between my parents on the couch, all of us still in our pajamas for the fourth day in a row, eating leftovers for breakfast, lunch, and dinner.

No more.

Now that official divorce paperwork has been filed and a judge has been appointed to the case, the only thing holding the process up is my mom. She has yet to secure a lawyer willing to go up against my father, who's representing himself. In the meantime, the judge has final say over the custody arrangement and split the holidays: Thanksgiving and Hanukkah with my dad, and Christmas and New Year's Eve with my mom.

Ashleigh went to her parents' in New Hampshire for Thanksgiving. My dad is buried under a major case that had him and two malnourished interns working overtime in his home office, so I spent the long weekend Netflix and chillin' with the hoard of beef jerky and sour Jelly Bellies I snuck into the house for sustenance.

Hanukkah, however, was a whole other ball game. We've

never actually celebrated it. The closest we've come is using the menorah Bubby sent to keep the front door open after my mom almost burned the house down trying to make chicken cordon bleu. But Samuel Levitz wasn't going to let my mom get two holidays while he got one, which means today, after I finish my biology final with Abby, I have to break my normal schedule and go to White Plains for a Hanukkah celebration.

Normally, I'd be irritated, but I have a surprise planned for the evening.

The American flag in front of the Jacksons' house flaps around like a tornado warning in the winter sky as I approach.

"Nevaeh! Is that you? I haven't seen you in ages!"

Mrs. Jackson flings the door open after one knock. She holds a full glass of wine and is dressed like she just got back from giving a speech at a country club to a bunch of Republican housewives on the current trends in Tupperware.

"How are you, honey?" she asks, showing off her newly buff-ered veneers with an uneven, tipsy smile.

"Hello, Mrs. Jackson. Nice to see you. Is Abby home?"

Mrs. Jackson peeks behind her shoulder dramatically, as if her sixteen-year-old daughter is playing hide-and-seek.

"I don't think so," she slurs, and grabs me by the shoulder, as if desperate for company not in the form of a bottle. "You are so exotic-looking! You must have a boyfriend. Does he have any friends for my Abby? Wouldn't that be great? Going on double dates, you two best friends again, just like old times!"

"Mom!" Abby screams from the top of the staircase, dressed in athleisure wear and patting her damp hair with a towel.

Mrs. Jackson whips around to meet her daughter's mortified

look, but her heel slips on the marble and she topples to the ground. I'm only a few feet away, but Abby gets to her first.

"Help me get her to the couch," she commands.

We do our best to keep Mrs. Jackson's body off the ground as we move her. She couldn't top the scale at more than a hundred pounds but might as well be a metric ton in deadweight.

Once we have her propped up on the couch, Abby instructs me to get water from the kitchen. I return with an armful of bottles with varying flavors and electrolyte percentages—her house is better stocked than my corner bodega.

"Wu happ'ned?" Mrs. Jackson mumbles.

"Mom, just lie back." Abby speaks softly into her mom's ear and snatches the basic Poland Spring bottle from me. She wets a towel to clean any nicks on her mom's head, then hands her the bottle while Mrs. Jackson groans and pets Abby's shoulder as if she were a Pomeranian. Once she finishes the water and regains enough consciousness to speak clearly, we hoist her to her feet and help her upstairs.

I wait in the hallway while Abby puts her to bed. Twenty minutes later, Abby walks past me to her room, where our next experiment has already been set up. We sit and read the directions. Her breath is heavy and measured; she's trying to keep herself together.

Each time she exhales, I almost say something.

I almost tell her I know how it feels when your mom falls apart and needs you to pick up the pieces. I almost tell her what Rabbi Sarah told me: that "okay" is usually the best we can hope for, and she's got more than that. I almost tell her I know her mom wasn't always like this—I remember Mrs. Jackson when we were little, and she was silly and bubbly—but I don't say anything.

Even though I have this new emboldened voice, now doesn't seem the appropriate time to exercise it, so I do what I've always done and keep my mouth shut.

Not five minutes into the experiment, the door creaks open and Mrs. Jackson teeters in. Her bathrobe hangs half open, and her lipstick is smeared across her mouth so she looks like the Joker. She lunges, sobbing uncontrollably and barely holding herself up. Abby caresses her. She sweeps her mother's hair to the side, whispering in her ear, and walks her to the bathroom.

"You should go," she says to me, turning to lean against the door in case her mom tries to get out and make another scene.

"Are you sure?"

"Nevaeh. I'll finish the project, all of it, I promise. But . . . please, don't tell anyone."

"What—what type of person would do that?" I ask, offended at the dig to my character.

Her eyes water and her whole body trembles, but the temperature hasn't dropped; in fact, it's actually warm in here. I realize as I answer my own question, *Abby* would do that. She's the type of person who would sing this news from the rooftops if it meant torturing one of her enemies, and she knows it.

Mrs. Jackson wails and Abby's head flies back and forth, unsure where her attention should lie.

"Take care of her," I say, nodding in the direction of the bathroom. Then I pick up my bag and leave.

My father's house smells incredible. My mouth waters and I drop my bag in the foyer, where I always used to. After the scene at Abby's, I'm almost glad to be here.

"Hello?" I call.

"Your dad said you wouldn't be back till later," Bubby says from the kitchen doorway, peering over her thick tortoiseshell glasses. "Grab an apron."

So much for being glad to be here.

Bubby is making potato latkes, and there's a brisket in the oven that I can't wait to watch Ashleigh scoff at in disgust. Bubby orders me around, complaining about her digestive issues; then she fills me in on the drama from shul. Evidently, a gentleman named Marty asked both her and her best friend, Gertie, out for coffee. Bubby declined, disgusted that he would try to pull any such nonsense, but Gertie (she found out through the Manischewitz vine) lied to her and went on the date anyway.

Listening to her go on about the way she instructed the other ladies in their crew to box Gertie out reminds me of the Gray Lady Gang at church. I wonder if all religions have these built-in mafias of the elderly wreaking havoc or if it's a coincidence that both houses of worship my families attend are run by terrifying female geriatrics.

"Your grandfather Samuel, alav ha-sholom, would never have been so classless," she says, throwing her hands in the air.

Whenever Bubby brings up my late grandfather, Daddy's eyes turn all pointy and narrow and his voice drops low as he swiftly changes the subject, but he's not here right now, so I jump at my chance.

"How did he die?"

Bubby's face turns ashen, and her voice is so unusually low and somber that I have to watch her say the words to believe another person hasn't entered the room.

"He was killed."

My heart races. Killed? How could I not know this? And what does she mean? Was he murdered? What sort of trauma was my father exposed to as a child that might have hardened him into the monster he seems to have become? The questions bubble up so quickly I can't decide which to ask first.

"Hello?" my dad calls from the front door, interrupting this monumental discovery.

"In he-eeere!" Bubby sings.

"Mom? What are you doing here?" My father walks into the room, looking disheveled.

"I thought you said Dad told you I would be home later?" I ask Bubby.

"He did. That's when he told me to come too." Bubby winks.

"What *is* that smell?" Ashleigh's voice incites the same rage in me as an early-Monday-morning garbage truck that backs down the street two hours before I need to be up.

"You must be the girlfriend," Bubby says, and pulls her fogged-up glasses down to give Ashleigh a proper once-over.

"Ashleigh," she says, and takes a step back toward my father for protection.

Bubby gives a little *tsk.*

"Well, honey, I know you said to come over to light the menorah," she says, looking at my dad, "but we can't have Hanukkah without latkes. We haven't celebrated since you were a kid, and it's Nevaeh's first proper candle lighting. A special occasion. Historic, really."

"How did you get in here?" he asks. "I had the locks changed six months ago."

"I had keys made," Bubby explains casually. "Took them out of your pocket two weeks ago. A mother needs to be able to check on her child. You look skinny, Sammy. Come have a latke, they're your favorite."

My dad is tempted by the smell. I can tell because his toes keep bouncing in the direction of the food, betraying the rest of his body, which remains next to Ashleigh.

We face one another, my grandmother and I, a highly unlikely united front against the demon who took my dad to the dark side.

Suddenly, the front door slams shut with a crash.

"Why do rich people always leave doors open? It's freezin' out there. I know some squatters who would turn that yard into a tent city before nine p.m. if they knew it came with free heat."

Rabbi Sarah walks into the room—my surprise for the evening. Between Mrs. Jackson's accident and the truth about my grandfather's untimely death, I totally forgot about her. After the way things went when she came to dinner at Pa's, I wanted her to see that there were issues on both sides of the aisle. Plus, there's nothing my dad hates more than losing control, so I'd be lying if I said I hadn't been looking forward to the deranged twitch in his eye currently on display.

With a flick of her wrist, Bubby orders Ashleigh to set the table, and while she vets Rabbi Sarah with a string of rapid-fire Jewish trivia, my father and I are instructed to set out platters of meat and potato pancakes accompanied by large bowls of applesauce and sour cream.

Ashleigh sits at the table, typing furiously on her phone.

"My nutritionist said that if I break from the plan, my chakra is going to be off," she complains to my father, who ignores her and places his platter on the table before taking a seat.

Rabbi Sarah and Bubby wander in a few moments later with a bottle of sparkling water.

"Rabbi, would you do the honors?"

222

Bubby gestures to the bronze menorah she unearthed from whatever hole my father threw it into.

"Only if Nevaeh helps," Rabbi Sarah says, a little punishment for the second surprise dinner that's been sprung on her since we began working together. "Do you remember the blessings?" she asks out of the side of her mouth.

"Sort of," I whisper back.

Rabbi Sarah begins in her big melodic voice, and I join in, less concerned about the musicality than my pronunciation. It feels good to say the words and not stumble over them the way I did in the beginning.

Barukh atah Adonai, Eloheinu, melekh ha'olam,
shehecheyanu v'kiyimanu v'higiyanu la'zman hazeh. (Amein)

Barukh atah Adonai, Eloheinu, melekh ha'olam,
she'asah nisim la'avoteinu bayamim haheim baziman hazeh.
(Amein)

Barukh atah Adonai, Eloheinu, melekh ha'olam,
asher kid'shanu b'mitzvotav v'tzivanu
l'hadlik ner shel Chanukah. (Amein)

To my surprise (and perhaps his as well), my father recites the words along with us under his breath. They are a part of him. No matter how hard he has tried to disassociate himself from his roots, he can't erase his history. Ashleigh stands with us so as not to get herself run off by her boyfriend's mother, but she holds her phone not-so-inconspicuously and jabs her thumbs at the keyboard for the duration of the ritual.

Rabbi Sarah lights the center candle, the shamash, with a

match and hands it to me to light the first of the eight candles, marking the first night of the celebration. I take it from her and let the fire ignite the next wick.

"Well, that wasn't terrible!" Rabbi Sarah cheers once we're done. "This bat mitzvah may not go to hell in a handbasket after all!"

Bubby peers at Rabbi Sarah with reemerging skepticism. "Of course Nevaeh's doing well. How could she not? She's got Jewish blood," she says with pride, sucking up to me in a way she never has before.

Rabbi Sarah winces just for a second, quick enough for me to catch it while everyone else goes about their business. By my grandmother's definition, Rabbi Sarah's identity is less valid than mine because no Jewish blood runs through her veins—a sting I know all too well. It's hard to hear people imply that you can't be who you know you are because your reality doesn't jibe with how they've been taught to see the world. It chips away at you; it sent me into the shadows to hide for the majority of my life. But despite how bad I feel for Rabbi Sarah, I can't help but enjoy hearing Bubby claim me publicly. Not just as her granddaughter, but as her people.

"I can't believe this," Ashleigh whines from behind her phone. "I'm supposed to be back in the city in two hours for a surprise birthday party and the whole West Side Highway is blocked off because of one of those dumb Black Lives Matter rallies. What in the hell does delaying traffic for hours have to do with anything?"

"You are so dense," I snap. "Did you really just say that?"

"Nevaeh," my father cautions. "Now is not the time."

"Actually, it's always the time. In fact, I'm performing an original poem at a fund-raiser against police brutality in a few

224

months because, in case you haven't noticed, your kid is one of those dumb Black lives."

I can't tell if he and Bubby are more taken aback by hearing that I'm performing or because they've never heard me refer to myself as Black. This is the first time I've ever said it out loud. I've never felt comfortable enough in myself before now. In truth, I had no idea that this could be my new normal.

"I think that is awesome!" Rabbi Sarah says proudly as she piles more brisket onto her plate, oblivious to the tension rising in the air.

"Dad, how could you not tell me that Grandpa was killed?" I casually change the topic of conversation, throwing him back into the hot seat.

"What?" He turns so fast I hear a ripple of cracks down his vertebrae. "He died of a stroke. Went to take a shower and never came back."

He looks over at his mother, who dabs the corners of her mouth and sniffles.

"It was a broken heart," Bubby explains. "I left in a huff because he forgot to pick up the dry-cleaning, and I forgot to say 'I love you' and the guilt, it was too much. He was a very sensitive soul, my Samuel, alav ha-sholom," she says, throwing her arms up to honor her late husband.

My father buries his face in his hands, shaking his head in response to his mother's theatrics and, I bet, regretting his decision to get us together for this whole celebration in the first place.

Chapter 28

As on most mornings these days, my mom is downstairs before anyone else, chugging along on her latest endeavor behind Grandma's sewing machine. Uncle Zeke and Pa set up a crafting corner in the living room for her. Over time, she has progressed from lumpy quadrilateral shapes in the form of throw pillows to shirts with sleeves too narrow for three fingers to fit through, let alone an arm. The stack of misshapen apparel has grown so large that Zeke has begun to steal a few items from the bottom every week to throw in a public garbage bin near his job.

"Have fun!" she calls out to me behind the whir of the machine, but the horrible crunch of needle and pin unintentionally colliding cuts her off.

"Mitzvah" means "good deed," and one of the bat mitzvah requirements is to complete a charitable project. So on New Year's Eve, I decided to join my cousins and the youth group as they serve food at Mount Olivene's soup kitchen. We stop to grab a bite to eat on the way, since we won't have time to feed ourselves.

The bodega on the corner by my grandfather's church is

packed with people grabbing their daily snack, which varies from lollipops in the shape of watermelon slices to breakfast sandwiches. I order my regular: a chicken cutlet with bacon, lettuce, tomato, red onion, cheddar, honey mustard, and a tiny bit of mayo on a roll.

Bodega chefs are the unsung heroes of the New York culinary scene. They make four sandwiches at a time, never mess up an order, and find a way to be a friend and a father and an uncle to every customer who walks through their tagged-up door.

I've watched them add a few extra sandwiches, at no extra charge, to the order of a homeless father of a family of five whose daily earnings only cover two. I've seen young gay men being harassed on the street run inside to seek refuge, same as women and young girls, where they are offered a seat on the stool that invariably exists in the corner—a safe spot to wait until they feel ready to go back out into the cruel world. Children come in droves to show off their test scores and receive a Fla-Vor-Ice stick and a fatherly pat on the shoulder, along with an encouraging reminder to keep up with their schoolwork.

During the six months that I've lived here, everyone who works at this bodega knows to start my sandwich as soon as I walk in, and they often add salt and vinegar chips on the side for free.

"Just in case you're still hungry, my friend," Asahd says, placing the chips in the bag before moving on to his next customer with an equal amount of kindness.

Darnell stands at the top of the church steps, hands on his hips, as he surveys his community. The line of hungry people curls around the block, men and women bundled in layers of jackets and blankets, many with supermarket carts brimming with their belongings and waiting patiently for a warm meal and a smile.

"Happy holidays!" Darnell yells to us with a huge wave.

We are the last to arrive and are assigned to the industrial kitchen under the church, where we fill bags with nonperishable foods for the people upstairs to take with them when they leave. Jordan sets up an assembly line of chips and cookies and pretzels, and Janae plugs in her portable speaker, which she attaches to her phone to play her "chill playlist," the one she probably listens to when she's creating entire other worlds in her head.

Solange and SZA and Frank Ocean croon, giving us life through their silky voices.

"So what's your school like?" Jordan asks, rolling up the top of a brown sandwich bag with a satisfying crunch. "Like, on the bougie scale, are we talking *Cruel Intentions* or Hogwarts?"

"Maybe somewhere in the middle? I definitely wouldn't be surprised if there's a hidden tunnel that leads to some dark underworld where talking serpents live, but it's mostly filled with stereotypical cheerleaders and football players and—"

"Dang, you all have a football team?" Janae interjects.

"Umm, yeah . . . don't you?" I say, unaware that that isn't typical—Pritchard is the only school I've ever been to.

"Our school used to be a parking garage," Jordan explains. "The gym is so small half the students have to get waivers from PE, otherwise you'd barely be able to run a lap."

The realization of the uniqueness of my circumstances floods me, but I want my cousins to understand that behind the glitzy exterior, my school life is still mostly terrible.

"Look, Pritchard is shiny and sparkly, sure, but everyone sucks. There's this tradition at the pep rally where the team captains announce all the football players by a nickname chosen by the team. This year, the quarterback is this kid Shannon—he's mixed, like me . . ."

I put on my sports announcer voice and cup my hands around my mouth to make a megaphone.

". . . Up next, Shannon: Quarter-Black the Quarrrrterrrrback!"

Jordan jumps back with her fists balled together so tight they shake on the tabletop.

"Are you serious? Who said that? What did you do? How was this not all over the news?"

I shrug, then pick up two handfuls of baggies and walk over to drop them in the crate at the bottom of the stairs. "The BSU held voluntary sensitivity training last year. Honestly, if I called people out every time they said something stupid and offensive, I wouldn't have time to breathe. They don't know any better."

Jordan's face is heavy with disappointment as she turns to me, "How do you think that's ever going to change if you keep your mouth shut, Nevaeh? How long is it going to take you to learn that staying silent means you're part of the problem?"

Embarrassment creeps up my throat. The rationalizations I have made to myself over and over when I ignore a bad joke or an off-color comment flood my brain. The truth is, I didn't want to put myself in the position of being scrutinized and targeted, so I stepped away, because I can.

"Hey! I can't tell you how happy everyone is to be getting these party favors! Y'all are the unsung heroes up there!" Darnell says, interrupting us as he comes downstairs. "Nevaeh, how are you doing? I hope you'll be at this month's open mic. You've really got something to say."

Jordan snorts. As kind as Darnell's words are, they couldn't be coming at a worse time. And then I remember something that gives me hope—a chance to turn this all around.

"Actually, Darnell? There's an anti–police brutality fund-raiser in a few months being organized by the Black Student Union at my school. I'm going to read something." I feel Jordan's eyes zero in on me from across the table. "Would you perform? They'd love to have you."

"I'd be honored," he says with a smile, and grabs the crate to take back upstairs.

In his absence, my cousins and I get back to work and let Janae's playlist, in all its chill pop-soul glory, usurp the conversation.

Stevie is waiting for me on the stoop when I return from volunteering. After weighing their options for the evening, my cousins decided to get an early start on the festivities. They have four parties to hit, and getting to all of them is going to be a trek, especially considering the unreliable holiday subway schedule.

Jesus invited me to a party at his friend's house weeks ago. If I went, I'd get to experience my first-ever real-life, midnight New Year's kiss, but Stevie and I always spend NYE together, and I can't risk having another fight with him; one every ten years is enough for me.

"Happy New Year, B!" Stevie waves with his free arm; the other clasps an overfilled bag of Chinese takeout for us to devour.

The house is buzzing as we enter.

Jerry marches down the stairs, dressed head to toe in black spandex and carrying a handmade papier-mâché panther mask with pride. He and Zeke are going to a special showing of *Black Panther* at the Harlem Children's Zone a few avenues away, a father-son date to ring in the new year surrounded by young Brown and Black men confident that they too can grow up to save the world—after they eat their weight in pizza, of course.

"Are you sure you don't want to hang out with us?" my mom asks from the doorway of the dining room, where we have set up our spread.

A look of terror flashes across Anita's face. They have their whole evening planned: a sister date with their favorite movies and a bottle of fancy wine my mom swiped in a moment of spontaneous spite from the house in White Plains on the day we moved out.

"Can't. Gotta stick with tradition," I say, much to Anita's relief.

My mom puts on a happy face through her disappointment.

"All right, honey." She leans over to give my shoulder a squeeze and kisses my forehead, a gesture of affection that feels forced and foreign, so I wriggle away and pile more wontons in chili oil onto my plate.

"She looks good," Stevie observes once she has left the room.

I shrug.

My phone buzzes in my bag, but I resist the urge to look at it. I know it's Jesus; the only other person who texts me is Stevie, and I don't need my FOMO to intensify.

"I'm grabbing seltzers. Let's see what movies are playing at the Magic Johnson theater," I say, and walk out of the room.

When I return with our drinks, Stevie growls, "B, what the fuck?" under his breath, careful not to let Anita hear his foul language for fear of retribution.

What could I have possibly done now?

He lifts my phone for me to see.

A handful of texts from Jesus are displayed on the screen: a bunch of kissy-face emojis and a selfie of him, Jordan, and Janae, all making duck-lipped kissy faces.

"A New Year's Eve party? With Jordan? Why do I have to keep finding out about these parties on your phone?"

"I thought you wanted to continue our tradition of ringing in the new year alone . . . together," I say, in disbelief that I misjudged the situation so poorly.

"Have you lost your mind?! And miss a chance for a midnight kiss? Do you want us to be virgins for the rest of our days?" he shouts.

I clamp my hand over his mouth before Anita comes in here to read us to hell and then help him pile the leftovers into the fridge so we can get moving.

We pull up to a house on Carpenter Avenue in the Bronx with a small front yard surrounded by a chain-link fence. Janae walks out with a bag of trash. Her face is barely visible, but it's hard to miss her in her floor-length neon green down jacket.

I roll down the window.

"Hey, ma!" I shout.

She looks up, irritated that anyone would have the audacity to catcall in this frigid temperature.

"What're you hoodlums doing here?" she says playfully. "I thought you weren't coming out tonight, Nevaeh."

The walls pulse along to Kendrick through the subwoofer inside the house, and the power of the music seeps into our cores— synced beat to heartbeat.

"We gon' be all right."

We weave in and around dancing couples to the liquor table, where Janae grabs a forty from a bucket of ice and passes it to me.

I open it and take a sip, unwilling to come off as a prude even though the skunky smell gives me pause. I place it back on the table the second she walks away. It tastes like filtered piss.

"NEVAEH!"

Jordan comes out of nowhere and hugs me with a genuine joy I have never had the pleasure to be on the receiving end of. She is followed by a posse of ladies, all of whom seem giddy and intoxicated, enveloped by the smell of Coca-Cola and whiskey.

"This is my cousin," she explains to her crew.

"I'm Breana, but everyone calls me Breezy." A pretty white girl with light green eyes and a mane of bright red curls so thick and full it's almost impossible to believe it's real introduces herself with a wave.

"Paulina," the girl behind her, equally as pretty, but with jet-black hair and a golden-brown complexion closer to my mother's, says with a nod. "And this is my sister, Dania."

"You are so right, J. She totally looks Dominican," Dania says, grabbing the messy bun on her head and pulling the hair tie out to let her curly locks fall onto her shoulders and outline her heart-shaped face like a custom frame.

"Like, for real, though," Paulina says to me. "You should do 23andMe. I swear I saw someone who looked just like you last time we were in Santiago visiting Abuelita."

Jordan hands a Solo cup of brown liquid to Stevie while she checks her phone. He holds it for her, thrilled to be acknowledged in any capacity, even if it means acting as her personal assistant.

"Where's Jesus?" I ask, anxious to find him.

Jordan points toward the kitchen without looking up.

"You good?" I ask Stevie, careful not to abandon him, but he waves me away, uninterested in anything other than his proximity to Jordan.

Jesus sits on a stool by the kitchen counter, heavily engrossed in a game of Heads Up! His phone is pressed against his forehead, displaying a word: *Aardvark*.

"Yo, that's the one that's got like, a long nose!"

"Nah, it's the hard one with a shell."

One of his friends jumps to the ground and begins to slither around, but Jesus's eyes remain wide and confused.

"It rhymes with—"

"You can't rhyme! That's cheating!" I yell.

Jesus stands when he sees me, shocked, and glad, I hope. I try my hardest not to reveal my eagerness, so rather than run, I speed-walk through the people huddled around a makeshift bong. He picks me up and spins me around the moment I reach him. I wrap myself around his neck, so the smell of the product in his hair gets into my sweater, and we breathe each other in, a simple comfort that makes all the difference in the world.

"You're here!" he says.

His boys greet me one by one, once I've been returned to the ground: Bobby, Kevin, Jeff ("El Jefe"), Brian, Big Ben, Tomas, and Malcom.

"You want some?" Jeff asks, handing me a plastic takeout-soup container filled with a terrifyingly pink liquid.

I look to Jesus for guidance, and he takes a sip before he passes it to me.

"Take it slow. It'll knock you on your ass otherwise," he says.

He's not joking. The drink is equal parts sweet and strong, and each of its elements accosts my senses.

"What is this?" I gasp.

"That's a nutcracker, baby girl," Brian says with a grin and a wink, swiping it from me and taking a large gulp.

"You're light as hell. What are you?" Tomas asks, looking at me with one squinted eye.

"She's Black and white," Jesus says, coming to my aid.

"Oh, you got you a zebra," Tomas says with a chuckle.

I shield my eyes with my hand, in search of something in the immediate space that I seem to have suddenly misplaced.

"Whatchu lookin' for?"

"My bad—I didn't realize this was the entrance to the zoo," I snap back. "I was trying to get to this house party to see my man."

"YOU JUST GOT SONNED!" Jeff bellows in Tomas's face.

The guys crack up and start the game over, this time with the accent category. They hand me the soup tub again, and I relish the strength and courage the nutcracker gives me each time it touches my tongue.

"You all better come on. We're 'bout to blow the roof off this place!" Janae calls into the kitchen from the doorway.

I look at the clock: 11:57. Damn, alcohol really does make the time fly.

Someone lowers the music, and the large TV screen focuses on the huge ball attached to the top of a building in Times Square. The living room is stuffy with sweat and booze, but no one cares. It's about to be a new year, which at our age actually feels like a chance for a new beginning.

I look around. Janae is on a chair at the front of the room, positioning her phone to take a 360 shot at midnight. Stevie stands surrounded by Jordan and her girls, one arm shaking under the weight of all four of their purses and the other raised before him, accentuating his thoughts whenever he can get a word in edgewise.

I remind myself not to let him live this shameful performance down. As another die-hard Potterhead, Stevie's Hufflepuff card is practically in jeopardy of being revoked with his muggle behavior.

Jesus comes up behind me and slips his arm around my waist.

"You ready?"

I nod, afraid that if I open my mouth now I won't be able to stop myself from kissing him, and you only get your first New Year's Eve kiss once, so I don't want to ruin it.

"*Ten . . . nine . . . eight . . . ,*" the room shouts along with the announcer on-screen. "*Seven . . . six . . . five . . .*"

I turn to face Jesus and put my arms around his neck.

"*Four . . . three . . . two . . .*"

He dips down and bumps my nose with his, and hot, sweet breath streams into my nostrils, alleviating my need to remember to breathe.

"*One . . .*"

He kisses me, and in the midst of the cheers and whoops and Janae's laughter and Jordan's chest bumps with her girls and Stevie's hope that his eyes might meet Jordan's, we stop being anything but one.

When we finally break apart, the world is different.

The change is subtle, but it feels as real as Jesus's lips on mine and makes me believe that maybe we all are really going to be all right.

Chapter 29

As the date of the audition has neared, Stevie has relocated our daily lunches to the rehearsal room he's reserved for the foreseeable future.

"Just watch it one more time, okay?" he pleads, and takes a bite of the Korean bulgogi burrito he got from the food truck of the week. I opted for the Korean fried chicken tacos, which were tasty but tiny, so I snatch some of his kimchee nachos as payment for attending this final dress rehearsal.

Broken Pieces, the title of his performance, is set to a compilation of pop hits that all tell the same story: young love lost. Stevie choreographed the whole thing and knows it front to back, but he's convinced he can do more.

"You're being ridiculous," I tell him, distracted by the unlikely pairing of fermented cabbage and cheese and wondering if it's truly delicious or if I am stress eating, anxious about my impending poetry performance.

The date of the BSU event was finally announced, and it turns out it's the same day as Stevie's audition.

"Can't you skip it?" he whines, irritated that I have my note-book out rather than focusing all my attention on him.

"What?! No! This is my first real performance, like an official one people buy tickets to see!"

"It's a fund-raiser, Nevaeh. They're buying tickets to support the cause," he reminds me with an eyebrow raised in judgment.

"Look, I'm just saying, you're not the only one here with a looming deadline, Stevie. LaShawn stopped me yesterday. I'm going to be the headliner."

It's sort of the truth. She appeared out of nowhere in the bathroom doorway to tell me that their initial headliner, an underground rapper called Royce II, dropped out to perform at Afropunk and asked if I could introduce Darnell as the final per-former of the night, which means, by association, I'm kind of the runner-up. (Plus, it's not like I'm sitting here complaining about Stevie not being there to support me.)

The Lena Zahira audition is being held at our rival school, Fort Hilten, which used to be an armory and was converted to a school in the seventies. Our schools compete against each other in everything, but there are clear lines drawn between us: they have the stronger arts program, and we're better at sports. Stevie paces the room, no doubt imagining the huge auditorium filled with kids from Fort Hilten, who will heckle and try to psych him out during his performance.

Stevie's anxiety makes me want to remind him that if he's selected, he won't be at Pritchard with me next year, which means I'll be alone, so asking me to help him is cruel. I want to remind him that once word of my belated bat mitzvah is an-nounced instead of a fancy sweet sixteen, I'll be the laughing-stock of the school. Sometimes I feel like he forgets that he's not the only one with talent or a dream, even if mine blossomed only recently.

"B?" Stevie stands before me with eyes that beg me to see how important this is to him. They remind me that without his mom, there is no one else to cheer for him, since he can never count on his dad.

"I'll be there. I promise. There's more than enough time between the two events," I reassure him, and push my work aside to give him the attention he so desperately needs.

"Go on, one more time."

The last chip on the plate is the perfect nacho, with an equal ratio of chip, kimchi, and cheese, so I pop it into my mouth to enjoy the crunchy, vinegary gooeyness and hit play on his phone yet again to watch him soar.

A member of Rabbi Sarah's synagogue, Mrs. Rosenstein, passed away years ago and left her belongings to the temple. Rabbi Sarah claimed the task of organizing the stash in exchange for the small office (an upgrade from her former closet) where it has been stored.

The furniture is overused and lopsided, but that doesn't seem to bother Rabbi Sarah—the untold story behind the couches and chairs makes her appear to have an origin, which I think is all she has ever wanted.

The door to her new office bursts open, and Mordechai, dressed in a tweed jacket, and six other nine-year-olds swarm in. After a few seconds, a tall girl in a head-to-toe flannel ensemble screams and waves a flat package covered in gold wrapping paper above her head, and the others disperse as quickly as they came.

"What was that?" I ask.

"Seder," Rabbi Sarah says, and walks past me with a smirk.

The classroom is dimly lit, and we peek in, careful not to disturb the lesson. Chaya, the teacher I met the first time Rabbi Sarah dragged me down here, stands in front of a long, banquet-style table made up of the smaller tables that are usually positioned in clumps around the room. Beaming, the tall girl carefully places the golden-wrapped rectangle in her teacher's hands in exchange for a small package.

"How is this night different from all other nights?" Chaya calls out, reclaiming the attention of her class.

She is answered by the strong voice beside me as Rabbi Sarah sings the first response in Hebrew.

"On all nights we need not dip even once, and on this night we dip twice!" the kids read along with conviction.

Chaya tilts her head, glad to see us, as she and Rabbi Sarah harmonize in Hebrew. Mordechai, unable to control himself around a perfect duet, jumps up to conduct his classmates in the accompanying answers in English.

"On all nights we eat chametz or matzah, and on this night only matzo."

"On all nights we eat any kind of vegetables, and on this night maror!"

"On all nights we eat sitting upright or reclining, and on this night we all recline!"

The group hangs on Chaya's every word as she launches into the story of Passover. They gasp when she describes Moses raising his staff to the Red Sea as Pharaoh's army closes in, channeling God's power to part the water as easily as a fine-toothed comb through some down hair like mine.

Mordechai and the rest of the class cheer once they're sure all the Jewish people make it to the other side before the sea crashes back to its rightful bed of sand, killing some of their former enslavers and marooning the rest on the other side. The kids dig into the plates before them, dollops of different foods around the circumference. A sliver of boiled egg, a stick of celery next to a thimble-sized cup of water, a piece of matzah, and a pinch of fresh herbs next to a clumpy tan spread that looks like the organic chunky almond butter Ashleigh eats for her cheat meal.

"Thanks for blessing us with that gorgeous voice," Chaya says flirtatiously to Rabbi Sarah as she hands me a plastic cup of sweet grape juice. "Maybe I can repay you with a drink later?"

Rabbi Sarah's face is overcome with terror. "Um . . . maybe. Gotta run." True to her word, Rabbi Sarah bolts up the stairs two at a time. I follow, barely able to keep up as she heads right out of the front door and onto the street.

"What is going on?" I hiss at her as she barrels down the sidewalk with no regard for the innocent bodies unknowingly in her way.

She tries to catch her breath.

"Chaya seems nice," I prod, trying to gauge whether she has any interest. "It's just a drink." I've never heard her talk about friends or partners; I don't even know whether she's straight or gay or if she falls somewhere else on the spectrum of sexual preference.

"It's got nothing to do with her. Relationships and me don't work. I like it better alone. So just drop it, okay?" she says out of the corner of her mouth.

I almost push back to try to get her to explain, but I've never seen her so distraught. So I drop it . . . for now.

Our power walk brings us from the East Village to the north end of Union Square, the big cement area by the park where the city holds a large farmer's market four days a week. Rabbi Sarah saunters over to a jam stand and begins tasting the samples systematically. Behind the counter, the white hipster lady in a Biggie Smalls T-shirt under a pale pink cardigan ignores her, as if customers do this all the time.

"OMG, go for the truffle honey next. It's everything!" she tells me with a wink.

A young Black girl walks over, maybe a year or two older than me, and reaches to pick up a jar of jam in front of her, but the lady behind the counter coughs right before the girl's hand closes over the top.

"Can I help you?" the lady asks, though her words sound more like an accusation.

"Just looking," the girl says, but not before she quickly pulls her hand back to her side. Burning with shame, she walks to the far end of the tent, and the white lady repositions herself so she can still watch her out of the corner of her eye.

How do you think that's ever going to change if you keep your mouth shut? Jordan's voice challenges me from my memory.

"I don't see a sign that says *No Touching Without Assistance*," I say. "Did I miss that?"

I lean over the counter, dramatizing my search for a notice I know does not exist, at least not for all of us. The woman behind the counter glares, incredulous that I, someone she mistook for a member of her home team, am not siding with her.

"We should get back and get at least one run-through in," Rabbi Sarah says to me. "But thanks for the walk. I just get overwhelmed sometimes."

I try to decode her language. After months of sessions, I can still count on one hand the personal details Rabbi Sarah has shared with me, but I feel closer to her than to either of my parents. She has become my safe place.

"No worries," I say. "Just one sec."

We wait to make sure that the girl moves on to her next stop at the market unscathed and then walk back to the temple.

Chapter 30

The BSU fund-raiser is being held in one of those hidden New York gems that from the outside look like dingy, decrepit buildings but inside are completely renovated. This facade masks a spacious loft with colonial columns and walls of endless windows. The ceiling glimmers with hundreds of hanging tea lights, and the wall behind the stage is adorned with a huge sign that reads *Black Lives Matter.*

LaShawn scurries around, lining up chairs and shouting orders to her minions, all of whom look like they haven't slept in forty-eight hours. When she sees me, she marches over.

"LaShawn, meet Jordan and Janae, my cousins," I tell her, making introductions.

I got Janae a gig recording the event, and Jordan tagged along because she wants to support the cause, but I get the feeling she also wants to be here in case I fall on my face.

"Is Darnell with you?" LaShawn asks. "We offered a last-minute digital ticket for people to get exclusive access to his reading, like a private performance live streamed directly into your living room. Which one of you is the videographer?"

Janae raises her hand.

"Come with me. There's a tripod holding an iPad that's set to start recording automatically at five-thirty on the dot. I just need you to position it so you have enough room to film the entire event with your setup."

Despite the fact that this is a Pritchard Black Student Union–hosted event, the school did not offer any financial assistance—claimed it was too political.

My phone rings, and I step away from Jordan to answer it.

"B, when the hell are you getting here? This place is packed, and it's all Hilten heads. Abe came, but I made him sit in the back so his breath wouldn't knock the judges out."

Stevie's dad promised him he would be at the audition today, but at the last minute, he backed out. Mr. McConnell claimed it was a work trip he couldn't miss, but I think he just couldn't bear the idea of watching Stevie do the one thing he and his wife could never agree on.

"I'll be there, I promise. I'm only reading one poem and doing the intro for Darnell; then I'm there," I tell him. "Just listen to 'Bodak Yellow' to hype yourself up."

The place has already begun to fill with guests. They swarm to the food and drink stations before taking a seat. For a student-planned event, the place looks fantastic, clean and classy with a touch of urban chic that Janelle Monáe would approve of.

Darnell strides into the space just before the live auction begins and pats my shoulder.

"How you doing?" he asks, all calm, cool, and collected in a stunning bright green V-neck dashiki.

I am freaking out and I can't believe I agreed to go through with this! the voice in my head screams.

245

"Whenever I'm about to go onstage, I get really nervous, but then I remember that there might be someone listening who needs to hear what I have to say more than I'm afraid to speak," Darnell tells me, reading my mind.

"But what if everyone thinks what I have to say is meaningless?" I ask, desperate for his wisdom. Darnell holds his chin with his forefinger and thumb, considering his answer judiciously.

"That's the beautiful thing about being a writer—all words have meaning," he says, and walks away to pick at what's left of the snacks just as Jesus enters the room.

"What is it about him?" he asks, eyeing Darnell with jealous curiosity. "All y'all women look at him like he's the goddamned messiah."

I hate myself for the butterflies I feel in my chest when he gets jealous—it's so pedestrian and antifeminist—but I can't help it.

"I dunno, but whatever it is, it's working," I tease, unwilling to feed into his insecurity.

LaShawn begins the auction onstage, so Jesus kisses me good luck before he takes a seat.

An unexpected bidding war over a set of photos pushes the whole program back, so by the time LaShawn calls me up, I only have five minutes to get through my performance and intro Darnell before the automatic live stream begins.

"Break a leg," Darnell whispers.

Rabbi Sarah crashes through the door and walks straight into a garbage can just as I reach the microphone. I see Jesus turn and look at her. I can't believe she's here. Ever since I announced the performance at Hannukah, she has been on my case for details, but I deflected her questions. She must have taken it upon herself to find the information online.

Her presence throws me off, and I feel my throat go dry. I look back over at Darnell, who waits in the wings. He pounds his chest lightly with his fist in solidarity. The room is huge, but the bright lights they positioned directly in front of the microphone stand are blinding, so I look into them until they burn my eyes and I can't see anything but the words in my head.

FAKE NEWS

The headline reads:
Maggots that crawl underfoot never expose the truth.
Evenly browned by solar-powered convectors,
a camouflage of soil rather than homicide.

But it is true.

There's a murdered man
who lies in an unmarked grave,
dissolving into his surroundings.
Nourishment for the orange trees
that feed young boys.

A cycle which later supports the media's claims of cannibalism in
  Africa.

Two-hundred-degree mists of body odor hang low,
not unlike the bum on the subway wearing old jeans and
  throwback Adidas.
And when the heat wave does not subside,
the trickle of juice falling down his chin

as he runs on top of his father and uncles
makes it all seem worthwhile for a time.

A young girl who runs on the cement
that covers layers of skin
and drinks her Tropicana (which is said to be pulled right off a
  tree)
on the corner of Rosa Drive,
tapping the beat to a song she can't remember with her toe . . .
the definition of carefree,
which is sometimes a synonym for careless.

Unaware she is capitalizing on the anguish
from the coup d'état and the heat wave.
But her house is brick.
Her walls are covered in imitation da Vinci in fake-gold frames,
and her water flows through stainless steel;
each flush does not send a quiver down her back.
And

It's only when the door locks behind her
that she grasps what was lying in the balance.

The applause rushes toward me, a tornado of recognition.

See, your words mean something, the little voice inside me says, convincing me of my worth and my right to exist as I am.

My phone buzzes: the alarm I set to make sure I intro Darnell in time. But the crowd hasn't stopped clapping, and their support sends a jolt of courage through my veins. Jesus stands in the center of the cheering crowd.

"Woo woo woo!" he shouts.

With each moment that passes, the attention nourishes me with a power so addicting I can't rip myself away. LaShawn waves her arm wildly and points at the iPad, but I don't move.

Darnell doesn't know about the live stream. Read another one; get your words out there. You've stayed silent long enough, the voice inside me urges. *He won't know the difference. He'd be proud of me for being so open with my work,* she says, and I agree.

I look over at Darnell where he stands ready for his introduction, but I face forward again, open my notebook, and begin to read a second poem.

When my creative output has reached its maximum, I introduce Darnell. He smiles at me as he walks onto the stage, oblivious to my deception.

Jordan is waiting for me behind the curtain. I must have impressed her.

She takes me by the collar and slams me against the wall.

"What is wrong with you? How could you do that to Darnell? He's the only one who believed in you in the first place."

How can she still be mad at me? For once I'm doing what she wants, declaring my public support for our community, and it's still not enough.

"Jordan, you told me to say something. You said I had to do the work and use my voice."

She rolls her eyes so far back in her head she looks possessed.

"Sometimes the best way for you to do that is to shut up and make space for someone else—uplift those around you whose voices are silenced."

"What are you talking about? Darnell's famous already! He can barely make it a few feet in Harlem without someone stopping him for a selfie."

"In *Harlem,* Nevaeh. He usually doesn't get access to this sort of audience, and you took that away from him. These are your people. You can perform for them whenever you want. This was a space for *us* to try to be heard."

"IT ISN'T MY FAULT I WAS BORN LIKE THIS!" I shriek.

"Yeah? Me either, and yet I'm the one who always has to defend my right to be alive."

Jesus comes around the corner.

"Yo, chill! Y'all are making so much noise," he says, looking from Jordan to me. "That was great, baby!" he adds.

"All right, break it up."

Rabbi Sarah pulls us apart.

"Who are you? Get your hands off her!" Jesus yells, pulling me from the other side.

"I'm her—"

"My teacher! My homeroom teacher!" I shout to protect my lies. He can't find out who I really am, not today.

The screech of metal chairs shifting in the next room fills the air as the audience peers over in our direction. Darnell looks at me from the stage, hurt by the disruption of his performance.

"I have to go. I'll call you later," I tell Jesus, and run out the back door.

"Need a ride?" Rabbi Sarah asks between huffs as she chases me onto the street.

It's six-thirty. I need to get going if I'm going to catch Stevie's audition.

"I have to get back to Riverdale," I say with a shake of my head.

Rabbi Sarah ushers me into a Subaru filled with potato-chip bags and soda cans and begins driving west toward the highway. After a while she breaks the silence.

"No offense, but Jordan has a point."

"What?"

"I think you spend a lot of time complaining about what's out of your control instead of considering and appreciating what you've got," she says.

Fury burns just under my skin, sweeping over my whole body.

"Do you think I chose to live as the brand ambassador for the Ambiguous Verging on Barely Perceptible Half-Black Club?" I shout. "It takes me fifteen minutes to fill out official forms because I never know which box to check under 'race,' so I eventually settle for 'other.' She wants me to just 'be white'? I don't know how to do that either. I don't know how to be me."

"I'm not saying everything is easy for you. I'm just saying you've got a family. You've got cultures, two of them! A surplus! You've got a history. If I had any of that . . ." She shakes her head in longing.

"I can't believe you're taking her side."

"I'm not taking anyone's side, but, Nevaeh, you have to learn to be wrong."

I take a deep breath and hold it to calm my nerves.

"Ya know, Rabbi, you've got a lot to say about my life considering you never talk about your own. But that's not what this is about. It's because I was born Jewish, isn't it? You think you get extra points for helping the confused biracial girl find herself or something? You think that changes the truth?"

251

She slams on the brakes and skids to the curb. A cab honks as it swerves and barely misses her side-view mirror.

"You want to know about my life?" she growls, paralyzing me with fear.

SARAH EDWARD HAS A STORY
BUT IT'S HERS TO TELL, ALL RIGHT?

I. The Beginning
Two things have remained the same:
Each day, when she woke up, she hid under the covers and stayed
In the world projected from the backs of her eyes into her brain,
Where her feet felt like a trampoline
And the treetops looked like ice cream,
And also,
She has always had two first names.

She stayed when the light from the hall spread across makeshift
  walls.
When the screams from punches softened
And the sound of rusty water streamed from the shower,
That's when he opened her door, that slippery sour.
A dad-faced demon, a gin-soaked creep.
She stayed and she stayed,
Because when the door closed behind him, it remained closed for
  hours.

II. The First Half of the Middle
There isn't much to say
Except

Winter in New York City
Is hard.
Especially if you are living on the street.

Especially,

Alone.

III. The Second Half of the Middle
Why is it that men can torment us,
But also get to be the superheroes who save our lives?

His smile was the first she had seen in a while.
As was the warm food.
But he didn't push.
Her life was a fight
(He could tell).
So he would just visit
Before day turned to night.
When her guard wall shattered onto the pavement through
    crooked tooth cackles,
When her shoulders relaxed from rock tight.
There wasn't much, but he did what he could.
He gave her a book that read from right to left, not left to right.

IV. The End of the Middle
Trust began to exist like an equator, measured in the tufts of his
    sparse white hair.
From existence sprouted possibility,
A word that always seemed fake or cruel or just out of reach.

And then she was a woman.

But when she found him again he was so old he was barely a
    whisper,
Which she trapped in her ears to keep
As he gave her what he had:
His smile,
A prayer,
And another first name,
Ariel.

V. Now
In Hebrew
Ariel means "God's lion."
And lions do more than rule.
They roar.

When she finishes her story, I get out of the car. There are no
words left to say, and the acrid taste of shame on my tongue makes
me worry I might get sick if I try to speak. Rabbi Sarah drives away
as soon as I shut the door behind me. On the sidewalk, I breathe in
and out, gulping up the remnants of hate and fear and sorrow she
left behind. I try my best to hold on to them for her, to give her
momentary peace before they break free and follow her, unrelenting and self-serving, the way hate and fear and sorrow always are.

By the time I get a car that's willing to go to the Bronx, it is peak
rush hour traffic, which is further delayed by a car accident. It's
not until 8:15 that I run into the fortress that is Fort Hilten. De-

termined not to let my disastrous evening ruin Stevie's, I decide to play it like I made it in time, because people are only now beginning to stream out of the building and into the night. I must have just missed the end.

I make my way through the exiting crowd and those milling around in groups until I find Stevie holding a giant gold disc attached to a ribbon in one hand and a bouquet in the other.

He did it. He won.

"CONGRATS!" I jump on him and scream and cheer and make a scene, but he remains still in my arms. "Let's celebrate! Are you hungry? My treat."

I grab his hand to drag him away, but it falls limply back to his side. Some jocks from our school, probably basketball or soccer players, pat Stevie on the back.

"Yo, you killed it, bro! There's a free crib in one of these Hilten herbs spots. They've got booze and we've got a blunt."

Stevie moves toward them, brushing past me without a second thought.

"Stevie?"

I run after him. Stevie stops, blank and motionless. I take him by the shoulders and stare directly into his empty eyes.

"I know your mom would have been proud of you. She *is* proud of you."

Stevie smacks my hands with the flowers.

"Don't you dare talk about her," he growls. "You are a liar. You didn't leave in time to see me dance." He holds his phone up. The video of my live stream plays.

"Stevie—" I say, but he walks away.

He heads in the same direction as the jocks, or maybe home, just anywhere away from me.

Chapter 31

Stevie hasn't spoken to me in weeks. Not even a glance.

No one has. Rabbi Sarah stopped scheduling our meetings, and Jordan gives me nothing but death glares. Janae smiles or nods whenever her sister can't see her, but otherwise, I'm on my own.

Last week, I walked into the library and found Stevie working. Instinctively, my body moved toward his table, but he looked up from his book and stared right through me. Now invisible to the one person who has never let me feel small, I have begun to tiptoe around the school, digging my nails into my sore and bloodied palms to convince myself that I haven't really disappeared.

Today, I decide to do something about it, so I sneak out of history class and post up in front his last class. I position myself to stuff my last hope for forgiveness into his hand when he walks out. In my letter, I beg Stevie to give me a chance to explain and apologize in person. I tell him I'm proud of him and that I miss him. I tell him I'll be in our spot outside for lunch tomorrow, waiting and hoping he'll be there too.

Then I run home and count the hours until midnight, when I officially turn sixteen.

Jesus shows up at my doorstep in the morning with roses and takes me to get doughnuts at the new spot, Fill-er-Up, that opened on 125th and 5th Avenue. They only make three flavors a day, and you get to choose your filling, fruit or cream, as you see fit. It's the type of artisanal place that would normally have a two-hour wait, but one of Jesus's boys, Brian, works the early shift before his classes at City College and he lets us in before they open.

Jesus changes into the official uniform and hairnet in the staff room in the back to give me the full experience. Brian supervises as he makes me six doughnuts: two chocolate with matcha cream filling, two banana with chocolate ganache filling, and two almond with blackberry filling. After the pastries are made, Jesus sneaks us into the staff room so we can drink each other up like water after a drought.

> *Did you know,*
> *when Jesus licks chocolate off your fingers,*
> *you can feel it in your toes?*

Brian eventually knocked on the door and told us we needed to bounce because he had to open the shop, so Jesus changed back into his clothes quickly before we snuck out the side door and slipped past the Columbia students whining about how long the line was out front.

"Have a great birthday day," Jesus tells me.

His fingers, sticky with sugar and my ChapStick, run up and down my lower back under my shirt and give me the chills, distracting me from the anxiety that Stevie won't show today.

"He'll be there, baby. No te preocupes." Jesus opens the door for me as a car pulls up, and I wonder if my psychic abilities have been transferred to him. "Call me later, boo."

"You live here?" my driver asks me when I get into the car. I wiggle my toes, unsure if the tingling will ever go away or if this a permanent side effect of having Jesus as my boyfriend.

"Hmm? . . . Oh, yeah," I respond.

"How can that be? You're too pretty to live in Harlem," he says, in a playful tone that makes me clutch my keys and put one between each knuckle, the way Janae showed me when some guys followed us home after this month's open mic.

I put my headphones on to drown him and the whole world out on the ride to school. First period is almost over when I arrive, so I decide to skip the rest of my classes until lunch as a birthday present to myself.

Today is one of those perfect days you always hope your birthday will fall on. Everyone sits outside at lunch, and even our spot, as far away from the main campus as it is, is overcrowded. I weave through the clusters of people lounging in the sun, searching for Stevie, and finally spot him lying on the grass, propped up on his elbows with his face to the sun.

He showed up.

I move faster, ready to make amends and enjoy my birthday with my best friend. But Abe cuts me off and plops himself down right where I was about to sit. Stevie looks up, his hand blocking the sun, but it's Abe who speaks.

"Hey, Nevaeh! Wanna join? I grabbed extra fries because the Steve machine is always hungry," he says, his rank breath hitting me in the face like a military tank.

"Stevie, can I talk to you . . . over here?" I ask, pointing to a patch of grass just a few feet away.

"Whatever you have to say, you can say in front of Abe," Stevie responds, popping a fry into his mouth.

His words slash me like a million simultaneous paper cuts, all small, superficial wounds but surprisingly painful.

My pride is hurt, but so is his, so I suck it up and plead with everything I have.

"Stevie, I'm sorry I missed your performance. I tried to be there. I really did. But some stuff went down, and there was traffic. You can't hate me forever. You're my best friend. I need you."

A vein I have never seen before protrudes from his forehead, pulsating and red, warning me to move with caution and care. He stands and moves toward me, propelled by fury.

"It's always about what *you* need and what *you* want, B. You've got your boyfriend and your new life and your newfound voice. You think *I* didn't need *you* all these months? I had one shot to get into that program and you couldn't even support me. *I needed you,* and you're so full of yourself you couldn't see it."

A flock of pigeons flies overhead, masking the sun as they swoop around like a giant dark cloud, mimicking the mood between Stevie and me. One bird lands on a branch directly above my head, a small, brittle stick that sags under its weight as it puffs out its feathers and takes a giant shit on my forehead.

"Oh my God!" I shriek as the hot goop dribbles into my eye.

I can feel people move around me, closing in to get the best angle for photos. The only way to free myself is to launch my Cobb salad in front of me, narrowly missing Abe and a few other spectators, before running into the building cupping my eye so as not to draw more attention. The nearest bathroom is off the cafeteria, but there's a line, so I run to the second floor and splash water on my face, nauseous from the smell of bird shit.

No amount of soap can remove the grime, so after three rounds of washing, I crumple to the ground, temporarily blinded by the peppermint soap, and scream into my sweatshirt. I scream because I still can't cry, and after all these months, the pressure from the tears that have been building inside me is almost unbearable.

The door to the bathroom opens and closes, and someone I can't see stops at my feet.

"Come with me," a voice says, and I feel a hand reach out to help me up.

Her heels click down a secret stairway I never knew existed, but I follow close behind because all I want right now is for someone else to make decisions for me, even if that person is Abby Jackson.

Outside, I'm ushered into a black SUV before anyone can witness my escape. The older woman behind the wheel gets us back to Abby's house in four minutes, displeased to be an accessory to hooky. Abby leads me inside her house and takes me to a bathroom on the first floor, where she hands me a towel and a bathrobe before closing the door.

The room is marble top to bottom, which makes it feel like the doorway is a vortex to a different world. I stand in the shower for so long that the steam starts to dehydrate me and I get dizzy, so I have to step out to let the cold air bring me back to life.

My dad stays at fancy five-star hotels when he travels. He took us with him on a handful of his trips to England and Paris and Tokyo, and I lived in the big fluffy hotel robes the entire time. Those upscale franchises must all use the same manufacturer, because the robe Abby left me has "The St. Regis" embroidered on its lapel and feels exactly how I remember: like a warm, weightless comforter with pockets.

My shirt and pants need to dry after I finish doing my best to rinse the bird crap off them, so I hang them on the shower-curtain rod and put my underwear on under the robe before heading upstairs.

Music streams from under Abby's door and drowns out my knocks, but eventually she swings it open.

"Finally!" she says, waving a half-empty bottle of prosecco.

She has a whole spread from Dean & Deluca set up: fancy salami, cheeses, olive pastes, and a nice sourdough baguette she's ripped apart. I take a seat on the ground, awkwardly positioning myself so as not to flash her with my polka-dot boy shorts.

"Look, I know I'm a raging bitch, but *that* shit today, that was cold-blooded."

Abby hands me a plastic cup filled to the brim and the bubbles explode under my nose, tickling me with the oddly appealing scent of honey and gasoline. The cool liquid coats my tongue with a forbidden effervescence that tastes sweeter than it smells, but it's not sugary—more like refreshing and bright and dangerous.

"Happy birthday to me," I say, holding the empty cup in front of me.

"It's your birthday?" she asks, embarrassed, as though she should have known.

I nod and she refills my cup and taps it with the top of hers.

"Happy birthday, Nevaeh." She toasts me with such sincerity that I chug my second cup in disbelief.

Abby turns the music up and starts to dance around her room. Unbothered by how we look, we focus on how good it feels to get lost in a melody, especially once the prosecco starts to take effect. My entire body buzzes, and gradually a lightness spreads through me that makes me feel invincible.

Abby takes my hand and we sing along to pop music from a time when boy bands were required to wear head-to-toe denim. I jump up and down so hard that every fear and worry falls off me, and with the deadweight removed, I'm so light that I begin to float up toward the ceiling.

In gratitude for her kindness, I bring Abby with me. We circle the room, giggling and spinning one another around, until eventually we flutter apart, relishing the last moments of calming unrestraint.

"It must be hard—your parents separating," she says, opening another bottle. "My mom threatened to split a few times, but she'll never leave him, can't give all this up."

The cork flies out of the bottle and lands on the platter of food between us.

"Woo-hoo!" she yells, and passes the bottle to me after taking a sip.

This bottle is heavier than the last one, and I lift it to find a label that reads *Dom Perignon*.

"Abby! This is like a two-hundred-dollar bottle of champagne!"

Over the years, my dad has received expensive champagnes as tokens of appreciation from clients. He looks up the cost and then saves them for his next dinner party.

Abby shrugs and pours at least sixty dollars' worth of booze into my plastic cup. She begins to take selfies in front of a tripod that has a bright ring of lights and a slot to hold her iPhone. She bends her body toward the camera, squeezing her cleavage between her forearms, and pursing her lips, reduced to nothing more than breasts and a blue verified check next to her name. She shifts her head so the light hits her hair at the right angle to fake natural highlights. Abby is the type of girl who has never looked bad in a photo. She may not make it to the toilet to vomit if she's wasted, but she will still do her full face routine before bed every night, no questions asked.

Abby catches me watching her. She beckons me.

"Come over here."

She walks to her vanity and spins the chair around. It looks like the ones at the hair salons, with a round metal bottom and black leather seat.

"What look do you want?" she asks, gathering supplies.

"Umm . . ." The champagne bubbles dance in my brain, making it impossible to hold on to a thought long enough to answer. "Whatever you think," I say, still unsure how I ended up here and why I'm having so much fun.

Abby begins to work, but not before filling my cup one more time.

"All right!" she says after what feels like an eternity. Abby un-clamps the eyelash torture device from my right eye and spins me toward the mirror.

My eyebrows are slightly darker than usual and dramatically arched, my lips are a nude peach, and my cluster of freckles is gone, covered by whatever skin-colored paste made of toxic ox-ides and whale fat Abby has smeared all over me. She drags me and the chair over to the other side of the room and positions me in front of the tripod.

This isn't real. It's all a game of dress-up, I think, and I loosen the top of the bathrobe so one side falls down to reveal my shoulder.

I want to escape. I want to lean into this new persona she has created and disappear. What have I got to lose? The only person waiting for the real me on the other side is Jesus, and that won't last long. Not when he finds out the truth.

I kick my foot back to spin myself around and the other side of my robe falls down, revealing my small breasts to the fresh air. Drunk and free behind this made-up facade, I pose, mimicking Abby from moments ago.

"Whoa, your nipples are like . . . *brown, brown*," Abby observes with excited curiosity.

Suddenly cold and self-conscious, I stop my chair from spinning and pull the robe up.

"Wait, wait, let me do a ponytail." Her fingers slither through my hair like snakes in the grass. "Oh . . . it's like . . . normal hair . . . like mine." She sounds disappointed.

Between the moving chair and the buzzing in my head, standing up has never been so difficult, but I smack her hand away and pull my body up all the same.

"What's your problem?" she snaps.

"Just . . . don't do that—don't touch my hair."

"Okay, Solange." She rolls her eyes.

"I should go," I say.

"Oh my God, get over yourself! People like you just search for reasons to be a victim. Newsflash: you're barely even Black, Nevaeh." She takes a swig from the champagne bottle. "I can't believe for one second I thought we could be friends again."

Anita's voice rings in my ears: *But get ready, because when you find your magic, everyone around you is going to try to snatch it away.*

Abby takes a step back, revealing my reflection to me again. For the first time in my life, I miss my freckles. The foundation she covered me with smears off the center of my face with a single swipe, freeing my own unique war paint from its short-lived hiding place. My freckles now hold new meaning in their reemergence, a reminder of who I am and what I will never wish I didn't have.

Abby stands, waiting for some explanation for my behavior or words of gratitude, but I don't owe her anything, so I go downstairs, throw on my damp, stained clothes, and walk to the subway.

Chapter 32

He usually waits till after dark,
Which is why I thought it safe to cross the park.
But of course, today would be the one
When the Ogre decided to step out for some sun.
He stopped and sniffed my head hungrily,
Then plopped down right in front of me.
"How do you do?" he asked with a yawn.
"I've been asleep for a year. What's been going on?"
He smiled a goofy and crusted grin
And waited patiently for me to begin.
My grandmother's warning ran through my head:
"Never trust an Ogre. Run or you're dead."
But this one seemed friendly and curious and bored.
I thought: Maybe they are kind creatures at their core.
Why should I believe that none can be good?
What if she was wrong and they're misunderstood?
So I told him about the weather and Ms. Brenda's choir.
I showed him a card trick and my new bicycle tires.

He learned quite a bit by the time the sun set,
But by then I was tired, and in need of some rest.
My shirt was wrinkled and sweaty, my pants covered in soot.
The ground shook beneath me as he stood back on his foot.
"Come with me; I have a safe place you can lie."
"Why, thank you." I accepted his gracious reply.
The bed was soft and huge and round,
My head barely laid before my sleep was sound.
The next thing I heard was the crunch of my bones.
The horrible, gut-wrenching gargle of moans.
The stench of his teeth, rotten and sour,
Is the last odor I smelled in my final hour.
But at the end, what I saw—I'll never unsee:
The piles of corpses that came before me.

I stop on the corner for a moment and meditate, willing my body and mind to function long enough to not expose my afternoon of drunken depravity.

My cousins are out on the stoop, enjoying the brisk spring evening.

"*Ooooooo,* you're in trouble! Your daddy called and told your mom you missed school. I could hear him even though he wasn't on speakerphone, and he sounded like the devil," Jerry divulges in a single breath. "But Auntie yelled back. She told him not to call and shout, just to email her from now on, and she hung up on him while he was still screaming on the other end."

I drop to the step directly in front of Janae, who greets me by opening my hand and dropping a packet of mints into it.

"Happy birthday, cuz," Janae says. "You reek," she says with a grin.

"Must be nice, doing whatever you want without a care in the world," Jordan says, disgusted.

"Chill, Jordan, it's her birthday." Janae calls her out. "Don't act like you never had a drink before."

Their twin-sister bond is supernatural. I have witnessed one of them stub her toe and the other grab her own foot. Of everything wrong that I represent, Janae's fondness for me might be my worst offense: her soft spot has acted as a shield from the full force of Jordan's disdain. But she's not holding back anymore.

"All you have to do is show up, and you can't even do that," she says, bitter.

"Yeah? Well, I'd gladly trade places with you."

"What? Regular? Princess Wanna Try Being Average?" Jordan sneers, and turns on her heel to take Jerry inside with her.

"You set yourself up for that one," Janae says, clapping me on the back, more amused than empathetic. "The dumb part is if you just got over yourselves for a second and listened, you would see you both want the same thing."

"What's that?" I ask, skeptical that Jordan and I could ever have anything in common.

"Recognition."

Anita pops her head out a window.

"Oh, Nevaeh, thank the Lord you decided to grace us with your presence. Let me ask you a question: What is the point of you all carrying around mini-computers in your pockets if you can't even use them for the basic function of a phone call?"

She holds her hands up before we can respond, then slams the window so hard that a corner panel cracks. Janae and I rocket up the stairs toward the yeasty, egglike scent lingering by the entrance to the house.

"Where's Stevie?" my mom asks from the living room, where she's tidying up.

"He couldn't make it. He got that dance fellowship he's been competing for a few weeks ago, and his dad is finally taking him out to celebrate."

My mom buys my story, but I track the look of skepticism from Janae's face to Jordan's.

"I am giving you a pass for tonight only, but there will be consequences for skipping school, young lady," my mom says, doing her best stern voice, which is barely convincing and not even remotely intimidating. She peers at me more closely and lifts her nose to the air like a drug-sniffing dog.

I run to the bathroom in the hallway and scrub the remaining bird poop off my chest, then spray myself with air freshener since there's no perfume handy.

"You might want to gargle that Listerine a little longer. You smell stronger than Deacon Willis after choir practice on Tuesday nights," Miss Clarisse says. She's waiting for me outside the bathroom and follows me back into the room.

"Oh!" I jump, startled by a sharp pinch to my left butt cheek.

"My ScRUMPptious Gurl tights would add at least two inches to that pancake booty," she announces.

Anita's top lip quivers in anger at Miss Clarisse and her inappropriate absurdity.

"You, you, and you." She points to me and the twins. "Go set the table."

"Yo, Pa must be into some freaky shit. Miss Clarisse is next level," Janae declares as she pulls containers from the takeout bags.

"Ew, Janae, what's wrong witchu?" Jordan huffs, grabbing some plates.

"So are you going to explain the real reason Stevie isn't here?" Jordan asks nonchalantly, as though interest in my life is normal for her.

"And save that tired story you told your mom for Iyanla," Janae adds. "We're not here to save your life, we just want the tea."

My head is pounding, and the alcohol sloshes around in my belly. All I want to do is lie down and forget this day ever happened, but that isn't an option.

"Okay, fine, so after the open mic . . ."

After dinner, my mom brings out a cake she baked. It looks normal, verging on tasty, but when we cut into it, we find a pudding-like texture in the center, surrounded by a dark crust. Jerry and I pass on it, too stuffed to even think about taking a bite. Miss Clarisse and Pa both plead high blood sugar, and Anita and the girls straight up refuse. Only Zeke finishes his slice, and then one more to compensate for the rest of us.

An hour later, Anita lets out a piercing scream, and we all rush to the second-floor bathroom, where we find Zeke collapsed on the tiled floor, conscious but clearly not well.

"We need to go to the hospital. NOW!" Anita says.

"But it's a birthday party!" my mom whines.

"Think about that the next time you try to make me a widow—or are you gonna take care of all of us, selling those lopsided shirts on the street corner?" Anita fumes.

My mom hesitates, but Zeke cries out in pain.

"I'm sorry, baby," my mom says to me, forlorn to have disappointed me again.

"It's okay, Mom, really. This was the perfect birthday. Take care of Uncle Zeke," I say, grateful that I'll actually be getting to sleep soon.

The door shuts behind my mom and Anita as they rush Zeke to the ER, and my cousins and I scramble to grab the plates and clear the table, trying to ignore the loud kissing noises coming from the living room, where Miss Clarisse and Pa relocated for some after-dinner delight.

"Go on," Janae says, releasing me from dish duty once we've brought everything into the kitchen.

"And take an Advil with a cup of water before bed. You'll thank me in the morning," Jordan calls after me, sounding exactly like her mother.

Chapter 33

When I wake up, my head feels like a shattered mirror, slicing me from the inside with every thought and movement. A full cup of water and an unopened bottle of Advil sit next to my phone on the night table. The phone screen is filled with text messages.

Whatchu up to? 10:01 P.M.
You good? 11:37 P.M.
Are you ok? I need to talk to you. 12:01 A.M.

It's two p.m. I slept half the day away. I peek my head out into the hallway and hear Zeke narrating the play-by-play to a vintage Knicks game. I'm relieved to know he is back from the hospital, but I can't go downstairs and interact with anyone in my state. Back in my room, I chug the water and some Advil and dial Jesus's number, but he doesn't answer. Instead, the ellipsis in our text chain blinks and he sends a new text.

Meet me at the rings in 45

The unopened restaurant that sits at the top of the stairs in River-side Park overlooks a jungle gym next to the highway and the water. Jesus swings himself furiously from one ring to the next, gaining momentum as he moves down the metal bar. I watch from the stairs so as not to disturb his focus. He makes it to the end and flips his body around, then drops and lands firmly on the sand beneath him when he sees me.

"You couldn't call all night?"

He walks over to me, sneakers pounding the ground.

"I had a crazy day and passed out," I tell him.

I go to hug him, but he pulls away.

"You weren't answering. I got worried," he says, hurt.

"I'm sorry," I say. "I'm here now."

Beyoncé rings out of my butt pocket—my ringtone, "Run the World." But I ignore it.

"How was your birthday, baby? What happened, with lil' man? Did he show?" he whispers, less annoyed, and kisses me.

My phone rings again.

"Sorry," I say, distracted by the smell of him. I pull my phone out to turn it off.

The word "DAD" fills the screen and I try to shield it from him, but it's too late. Jesus's eyes lock on the display. My body is lead. Immobile due to the weight of my dishonesty.

"I . . . I can explain," I say.

"What the fuck? How can he be calling you?" He jumps back, sickened. "How could you lie to me about something like that?" he asks with teary eyes.

Still barely able to move, I try to defend myself. "You don't know what I've been dealing with."

"Don't bother! How can I ever believe anything you tell me now?" he asks, and storms off, leaving me utterly alone.

The last thing I want to deal with is Ashleigh, but she's in the dining room waiting when I walk through the door to my dad's house. The table before her is covered with photos of flowers and tiny plates of sample cakes and cloth napkins in every color imaginable.

"I need you to pick a cake."

She takes me by the shoulders and slides the samples in front of me one by one. The pound cake with lemon glaze is my favorite: not too sweet, tastes mostly like butter. I point and rise from my chair to escape, but she stops me.

"Uh, uh, uh." Her finger sweeps in front of my face like a windshield wiper. "Sit down. We aren't finished yet. Sammy!"

My father shuffles into the room looking like he's aged fifteen years in the past few weeks. The daunting bags under his eyes sink deep into his saggy skin, and his hair has begun to thin, revealing his stark white scalp.

"You haven't given me your guest list. I need to get the order out for the adult invitations," Ashleigh says, holding up a large beige card made of thick, expensive-looking paper, which opens to an intricate three-dimensional Star of David.

I snort. It looks like a trick by a bad Vegas magician.

Ashleigh closes her eyes and waves her hand around in front of her face. "Excuse me! Multiple members of the Housewives franchise used this exact brand for their wedding, including the Countess. Ugh, I don't know why I spend the energy trying to include you, as if you could find one ounce of gratitude, you spoiled—" she rants, then stops and closes her eyes. My father and I watch, perplexed, as she centers herself with some colonizer chakra purification mantra she probably picked up on Goop.

"It doesn't matter," she says, eyes open, looking eerily refreshed. "Your invitations have already been sent out. The kids at Pritchard are all going to hire me after this party. It'll only be a matter of time before Bravo comes calling."

"What do you mean the invites were sent out?" I ask, alarmed. I wasn't planning on inviting anyone other than Stevie, and it's not like he's going to show up now.

"How many people did you invite exactly?" My father follows up my concerns, his voice returned to full strength. "Nevaeh has over a hundred fifty kids in her grade."

"I've worked so hard," she whines. "I won't tolerate this type of disrespect." She runs out of the room.

My father collapses into a chair. What he traded in was old and worn, but reliable; his replacement, newer and shinier but more stubborn and entitled.

"You skip school, you lie, you date some . . . menace. . . . I don't even know who you are anymore," he says, unwilling to consider that he might be to blame. "You don't know how much it hurts to see that you haven't learned anything."

This could be the rest of our lives: acrimony and disappointment; avoiding eye contact and memories that remind us we will never be the same. Or we could end it peacefully.

"I've learned something, Daddy. Rabbi Sarah gave me this book of stories—or more like fables. My favorite is Parashat Korach. God told Moses to separate the Jewish people into groups, like class systems. One guy, Korach, was convinced he was meant to be a kohen gadol, a title bestowed upon members of the community with the highest honor and influence. But he had no proof that he deserved that title; he just felt like he was better than everyone else. He rallied two hundred and fifty people to support his protests against what he claimed was Moses's divisiveness. Moses advised Korach and his brainwashed followers to build a fire and make an offering to God in apology, but they refused and revolted. Helpless, Moses reached out to God and asked what to do. God told him to go back and warn anyone who had forsaken his word in the name of Korach that they would be punished severely."

I pause to take the last bite of the pound cake in front of me.

"That's the end of the story?" my father asks.

"Of course not. Moses went back and relayed the message. He reiterated how dangerous it would be to argue with God, and some of Korach's followers repented, but a few moments later, the ground opened up and swallowed everyone who had remained faithful to Korach, never to be seen again."

My father stands up with a wild look in his eyes.

"Why should he be held back from his potential? If he thought he deserved more, he had every right to do what he thought was best for himself, even if he had to hurt people along the way!" He shouts so loud I can't tell if he's trying to convince me or himself.

"That's exactly what Korach thought," I say. "But after all this time, I wonder what he would say now if you pulled him out of the ground."

My father's gaze drifts to his feet to ensure their solid placement on the floor.

I walk away, and with each step I take, I feel a freedom from the burden of his betrayal.

Upstairs, I grab my backpack and open my mother's journal, determined to finish it, so the past can be wiped clean.

December 9, 2001

You know how people say always trust your gut? Well,
mine has been throbbing. Twisting and turning, begging
me to listen to my instinct that something wasn't right.
Turns out it was correct.

After months of grueling interrogation, Samuel finally
admitted that he lied. He had been with Becky that night I
passed out in his room, and he had slept with her.

"I'm sorry," he cried, but I couldn't forgive him. I was
too disgusted to even look at him.

He was unrelenting. First he begged me for a second
chance; then he got angry and said it was just a slip-up, a
one-time thing. He wrote me letters and made love song
playlists and sent flowers and chocolates for a while, but
eventually he stopped and I moved on with my life.

I decided to take an extra class, sign language, and my
teacher, Ms. Binder, chose me to teach first-grade ASL
classes with her at a local rec center for a small stipend
twice a week. We've only worked on the basics, but each
week the kids move through the letters of the alphabet
with pride. Now that I don't have Samuel, nothing makes
me happier than when they scoot closer to suck up new
information like adorable parasites. I like it so much that I
decided a few weeks in to get a head start on applications
for master's programs in teaching. (I can't apply until next
year when I'm a senior, but no harm in being prepared!)

I made more friends! Well, Jolie introduced me to her
friends, a group of girls who work hard and play harder.

They're nice—all white girls who I have to roll my eyes at at least once a meal, but nice. Before winter break, they crashed into my room and claimed that "enough was enough," that I had to go to at least one party in my college career. Normally, I'd have put up a fight, but I figured they were right, so I let them stuff me into a tiny black dress and take me out.

The party was in a house that reeked of damp laundry. Jolie and the girls made the rounds, delegating a shifting guard to ensure I didn't bolt when no one was looking.

"Here, take this." Jolie hands me a shot glass and a lime.

"I don't think I can—" I said, nauseated from the way the liquid sloshed around the glass.

"Oh my God, Corinne, you cannot be like this all night. You need to loosen up. Plus, it's like a third of the calories when there's no mixer."

"Fine!"

It tasted like death, but the burn went away pretty fast, so I took two more right away to get the drinking part over with.

The girls didn't have an ounce of rhythm between them, but once I got going on the dance floor, the whole party swarmed over. I started dancing with this guy who was nice and a really good dancer. Our hips moved together perfectly, as if choreographed. We improvised to the beat in sync.

The music slowed and he spun me to face him. He hoisted me up just enough that our mouths could reach each other. I was shocked at how good I still was at kissing. There hadn't been anyone since Samuel, and I'd figured I might never enjoy making out again, but this was fun.

My girls cheered behind me and he pulled me closer, like he couldn't bear to have even one inch between us, and I let him.

Then I felt his erection on my leg, and the same fear from so many years ago in that auditorium came back. I tried to pull away, but he wouldn't let go. All of a sudden, his slimy tongue lapping at the inside of my cheek made me want to throw up, and I began to wave my arms around to try to get away.

"*Hey!* Leave her alone!" Samuel came out of nowhere and wrenched the guy off me and I ran away.

"Corinne! Are you okay?"

Samuel caught up to me around the back of the house, where I stood, shivering.

"No!" I cried and collapsed into his arms. I never wanted to tell anyone, especially him, but the words fell out about Raymond and how sometimes, like tonight, the disgrace comes back and fills me with contempt until I feel bloated, like Violet Beauregard after the three-course gum.

Samuel listened to me, and when I was done, he rocked me back and forth and kissed my forehead.

"Corinne?" Jolie ran over and stopped short when she saw Samuel. She's never forgiven him for cheating on me, and I can smell her disappointment that I've let him back in.

"Hey . . . I'm actually not feeling great. I think I'm going to head home."

My eyes begged her not to make a scene, and eventually, she walked back inside to find her friends.

"Can I walk you home?" Samuel asked.

"You hurt me."

"I know I did, but I won't ever do that again."

He ran his fingers through the messy waves of his thick brown hair, which was a little too long and in dire need of a shape-up. I missed his smell. I missed his hair. I missed him. I needed him.

"Just to the door," I said, and never looked back.

The pages of my mother's journal flutter like sad confetti as I rip them out one by one until her pain covers the floor of this space I used to call mine. Over time, I've brought all my beloved possessions over to Pa's, and now my bedroom is just four walls with a skylight.

I descend the stairs to find my father, who has been temporarily relocated to the living room. Ashleigh is renovating his office—claims it looks like a place where her dad would hang out. He takes vigorous notes with his cell phone balanced on his shoulder, reaching for the various papers spread out all over the love seat.

"Mitch—Mitch, hold on one sec— Nevaeh, yoo-hoo!" he calls as I pass.

The rubber on the bottom of my dirty Converse squeaks against the freshly waxed floor.

"Yes, Daddy?"

"Where exactly do you think you are going?"

He gestures to the space between us with heightened irritation, but I make him wait, relishing how good it's going to feel to say the word, because it's true.

"Home."

Chapter 34

Jesus's phone rings, but he still doesn't pick up. I activate the Find My Person app, which we linked to each other's clouds, and wait in line for a Yellow Cab from the Metro North stop on 125th. A group of young Black women wave to a taxi as it drives past them and pulls up next to me. The driver rolls down the passenger window.

"Hello? We were waiting!" one of them yells from behind me, knocking on the trunk of the car.

"You get in. They always run without paying," the driver says to me.

All I want is to get to Jesus, but I won't let myself.

"Nah, I'm good," I say.

He speeds off, and the women whoop and cheer as he leaves empty-handed. Another Yellow Cab pulls up just seconds later and the group of women climb in, but one of them pokes her head out the window.

"Where you headed?" she asks.

"One Thirty-Fourth and Lenox," I say.

"Get in, we'll drop you." She opens the door for me and scoots in next to her friends in the backseat. They tell the driver to bump the music so we can dance on the way to my stop.

"Have a good night, sis!" they yell to me when we arrive a few moments later, and I watch them drive off toward their next adventure.

I march up the stairs and ring the doorbell to Jesus's brownstone before I can make a plan for what to do if his parents answer the door. Of course, that's just what happens.

"You must be Nevaeh," says a woman I assume is Jesus's mother. She has the same huge brown eyes and high cheekbones that act as altars to the heavens. "I'm Zoila."

She steps back to open the door wider and let me in. The smell of garlic and meat and tomatoes dances into my nostrils.

"Mamí, is dinner ready?" Jesus hops down the stairs dripping in sweat after a workout. He looks up, startled to see me.

"Hi," I say softly.

Zoila shakes her head. "You didn't tell me Nevaeh was coming over," she accuses Jesus.

"She's full of surprises," he says through pinched lips.

"Jesus!" His mother smacks the back of his head and turns to me with apologetic eyes. "He's just hungry. He turns into a monster when he hasn't eaten; all the men in this family do."

I lag behind Zoila to keep up the impression that it is my first time in the house.

"Who have we here?" Jesus's father says as he gets up from the table, a fresh bottle of Presidente in one hand.

"This is *Nevaeh*," Zoila says, accentuating my name with an excited wiggle of her whole body.

"Welcome! I'm Denis Junior, but everyone calls me Junior. Venga! Sit!" He pulls out a chair for me. "My Zoila made pastelón."

"Mmm, smells delicious," I say sincerely.

A metal cooking tray sits in the center of the table, filled with a dish that sort of looks like shepherd's pie meets lasagna.

"My Zoila makes the best pastelón, after my mamí, of course."

Junior looks like he has more to say but clamps his lips together at Zoila's massive eye roll.

"Ay dios, I hope you are hungry," she says to me under her breath, passing me a plate. "Go on, Junior. Tell your story."

He twists his neck and fingers to remove any tension that might affect his storytelling abilities.

"My father, Denis DeSantos, grew up with his seven siblings on a farm called Ranchito de lo Peralta in Puerto Plata, Dominican Republic. They all lived on the land next to one another, like their own village. On days when they completed their tasks early, they were loaned to neighboring farms to fulfill their hours in exchange for room and board and a few coins here and there. When he was old enough, my father left and found a job selling gas to local colmados for a company owned by my Tito Fernando, my mother Iluminada's oldest brother. One day, Iluminada came to the warehouse where they kept the gas to bring Fernando his lunch, but he wasn't there, and Denis refused to let her leave.

"'You are too beautiful and that food smells too delicious. You will be kidnapped for sure,' he said.

"Mamí was wary of him but agreed to wait. He wasn't much bigger than she was, and she had two pounds of pastelón in a metal container, so she had the upper hand if he tried anything. Two hours later, she'd fed him half of Fernando's lunch and eaten the other half herself. It was the perfect balance of mashed platanos to meat and so much caramelized garlic in each bite that the only way you could kiss someone after eating it is if you'd both just finished some so you couldn't tell the difference. He knew right then she was the one. They stayed in Puerto Plata until they could move here to New York, where some of his other siblings had come once they left the farm for the rest of their lives, and then they stayed right here. They never went below One Hundred and Tenth Street.

"My father never learned to write or read. He was a building super, and I had to go with him on jobs toward the end in case the device being installed was modern and required reading the instructions rather than building it on instinct and experience— that's how I came to be so handy." He winks at me and Zoila snorts with perfect timing, like we're on a multicamera sitcom.

"He didn't need much to be happy: just pastelón, beisball, and Iluminada." Junior holds his beer up in honor of his late parents. "To we DeSantos men, we know what we want."

Zoila rolls her eyes again, but this time with love.

Once most of the food has been devoured and we all sit in our post-pastelón daze, she rises to clear the plates. I stand to join her, but Zoila snaps and points down to my seat.

"No! You are a guest."

I get the impression that Zoila is the Anita of this house, which means what she says goes and there's no point in arguing.

"Okay." Junior hoists himself from his seat, his eyes laden and glassy. "Why don't you take Nevaeh out to the backyard," he tells Jesus before kissing his head and walking to the living room.

Jesus's lips are pursed. I brace myself for the truth to fly out of him and his parents to kick me out of their home, but he stands and walks to the back without a word.

The backyard looks so much larger without the buckets of booze and drunk kids hanging off the railing and around the grass. The flowers have also bloomed, filling the manicured bushes with bursts of wonder.

"Did you know I'm the captain of the Ultimate Frisbee team at school?" he says to me, looking out onto the yard.

I shake my head. "No."

"Or that I got the perfect test score to get into Stuyvesant, but I chose to go to Bronx Science because they have a more diverse student body? Or that I applied early decision to Fordham University and I want to be a lawyer like my dad, so I can represent immigrants and dreamers? My father worked his whole life to make sure Abuelo's sacrifices weren't for nothing. He met my mom at Columbia. She worked the desk where students went to replace lost keys on Friday nights, when everyone else on campus was out partying. She was goofy and sarcastic and a little scary if you tried to steal a sip of her cherry cola. One night over pizza slices and lukewarm rum, he asked her what she wanted to do in life. She said she wanted to help her community. She wanted a brownstone and a kid and not a day to go by when she wasn't grateful.

"Papi says he had never believed the story Abuelo told about how he knew he was going to marry Abuela the first day they met, until that night. He knew right then that my mom was the one, and he spent the next two years waiting for her to figure it out."

He turns to me.

"I want to be exceptional. I want to go to college and get a job and be great, not great *despite where I'm from*. I want to make a person feel so loved that they aren't afraid to share everything, even the ugly, dirty parts of life that no one wants to admit. I want that moment when I know that I have found the one to be how it was for Abuelo and Papi, without any doubts or hesitation."

The wells of my collected tears expand as he reveals his own wet eyes. This whole time I have kept him at arm's length, afraid that if I let him any closer he would leave. But by doing that, I missed out on really getting to know him. All he wanted was for me to let him in. I was so wrapped up in myself that I couldn't see that he wanted the real me all along.

"You saw me," I explain, "when all I was, was a shell of a person, hiding in the shade. With my parents' separation, I've had to redefine what love is, unsure that everything around me isn't just another illusion. You've been good and kind and honest and I told myself that if you knew the truth, you wouldn't want me. I am so sorry I lied. I understand if you can't trust me." I take his hand. "But if you asked me what I want right now, I would say that I want to tell you everything."

Jesus pulls his hand out of mine and walks down the stairs to the gazebo, turning his back to me and my apology. I should have known it was too late. The sadness is all-encompassing. I have to make it out of the house before I break down, so I shuffle toward the door. It opens with a creak, rusty from the spring rain we received earlier today. My foot barely crosses over the threshold inside when I hear him whisper. The words fall off the tip of his tongue, so soft and light they could have just as easily been a daydream.

"Nevaeh?" he says. "Then tell me."

Chapter 35

Remnants of a recently finished egg salad sandwich crust the corners of Mr. Bowels's mouth. It's Monday, and his cheeks are already shaking with exhaustion from holding up his big fake smile.

Abby sits at our table with her things spread out, leaving me barely enough room to take out my laptop.

"Sit down, sit down. We've got a fun day planned that will really put us in a good place for our final projects," Mr. Bowels announces with rehearsed enthusiasm.

The chalkboard is covered with a tarp, which he pulls off dramatically to reveal *Biology Jeopardy!*

Just then the door slams open and plastic Mardi Gras necklaces fly into the room, sliding across the floor with a hollow crash that jolts everyone from their seats. A slender young man carrying a sousaphone enters, playing a single note repeatedly to set the tempo. He is followed by a marching band consisting of kids with two trombones, a saxophone, a trumpet, a snare drum, and someone on the tail end shaking a maraca. Four bikini-clad women with huge feather headdresses walk in next, each with armfuls of the same beaded necklaces. The beads vary from blue to green to purple, but they all have a large pendant that looks like a gold coin with a giant Jewish star engraved in it.

I sink into my chair as the band forms a line in the front of the classroom, and with each moment that passes, I die a little more inside.

The women shimmy, rattling the beads on their barely covered chests, and begin to pull the necklaces off to throw at my classmates. They urge us to cheer and make noise as the band gets louder. One necklace falls into my lap.

Join Samuel Levitz as his daughter,
NEVAEH LEVITZ,
is called to the Torah
as a bat mitzvah,
Saturday, June 9, 2018
The Village Temple, 12 p.m.
#BettaLateThanNevah

"BETTA LATE THAN NEVAH! BETTA LATE THAN NEVAH!" the dancers chant as the band winds its way around the room and continues to play on its way out and down the corridor.

Abby immediately jumps out of her seat. "You are pathetic," she tells me. "Using my exact same invitation service. And a bat mitzvah instead of a sweet sixteen? You think that's going to make people want to come? You can't even get your best friend to hang out with you."

When I look at Abby now, I see the early signs of despondence in her bright green eyes.

"Oh, just shut up, Abby. You want to believe that we're all

jealous of you. The truth is, you're the one who's jealous. You're a fraud, just like your mother."

Shame floods her perfectly painted face with pink. No one heard me. Everyone around us is dancing to the music and taking Snapchats, but I know immediately I went too far.

"*Big* mistake," she hisses, and then she storms out.

Chapter 36

Every class I walk into for the rest of the day greets me with a loud "Mazel tov!"

The never-ending chorus is helmed by Abby, who makes sure to place herself front and center each time to enjoy my discomfort and embarrassment. Which means come lunchtime, I eat in the nurse's office, where it's safe. I wonder if Stevie thinks the invitations were my idea and that I've turned into Abby, but I don't text him; I need to get used to being in this place alone.

"Party's over, kiddo." The nurse finally evicts me when some kindergartners from the lower school are brought in. The kids shuffle past me, cranky and blotchy from the first signs of chicken pox.

"She's the old one having a bat mitzvah." A little redhead points me out to her companion as the nurse shuts the door behind me.

By the time the last bell rings, I'm ready to bust out of this place, steal a car, rob a bank, and never come back. I'll settle for as far away from here as possible that has pizza readily available.

"Nevaeh!"

Jesus makes his way from the street to the front steps of Pritchard. I watch my classmates stare as he passes them, half because he's gorgeous and half because they're uncomfortable with an unknown young Black man on their territory. His perfect white teeth catch the sunlight and cast a halo around him as he walks by some seniors who up until this very moment thought they were hot shit.

"What are you doing here?" I ask, running over to him with joy.

Jesus grabs me around the waist and kisses my neck, spinning me in circles. Once he puts me back on the ground, he hands me a letter.

Dear Mr. DeSantos,

Congratulations on your acceptance to Fordham University, class of 2022! In addition to your undergraduate admission, you have also been awarded the prestigious Presidential Scholarship, comprised of financial assistance for full tuition and room and board. The Presidential Scholarship is offered to only the top percentage of our applicants as a reward for outstanding academic achievement and demonstration of personal excellence. Enclosed please find more detailed information on guidelines for the scholarship as well as a welcome packet.

We look forward to seeing you in the fall.

Sincerely,
Steven Hillard
President, Fordham University

"You got in!" I scream.

Jesus sweeps me up in his arms one more time and I whisper in his ear over and over, *"You deserve this."*

My bag crashes at our feet from the step I abandoned it on, spilling its contents everywhere and ruining the moment.

"Aw! Is this hoodrat Romeo come to save his wannabe ghetto Juliet?"

Abby and the Bomb Squad stand behind us, but when I turn to face her, I notice that her human shadows are keeping a bit more distance from her than usual. She must be terrorizing them as well these days.

"Damn, you weren't playing. They really do talk like outdated *Gossip Girl!*" Jesus whispers, unable to stop himself from laughing.

"What are you celebrating? Found out you are the father after all?"

Abby hops down the steps covering me with her shadow, so it feels like it is just me and her.

"Abby, don't," I caution, meeting her gaze.

Her eyes are determined as she takes her cell phone out and pushes a button, grinning at something on her screen.

Every phone in our vicinity beeps, and people start to point in my direction and laugh. My phone buzzes in my pocket and I take it out to see what's going on. One of the topless photos I let Abby take while we were drunk has been posted on Instagram. To add insult to injury, little Star of David emojis cover my nipples, and every person in my grade has been tagged. I hide the screen from Jesus.

"Babe, let's just go. Don't listen to this noise," Jesus urges, carrying my refilled bag in one hand and holding out the other like Aladdin offering Jasmine that first magic carpet ride.

I want to be the bigger person and walk away toward our future and a snack and his lips, but my feet are weighed down with anger and shame and exhaustion. It's not just the day that I've had or the fact that I practically disavowed my father over the weekend or that his mistress has bulldozed my social life into the ground or that my only friend is moving to Europe or that it seems like I'm always going to be at war with myself; she has to take this moment away too.

The rage I've felt for so long bubbles over, and the avalanche of emotion is almost impossible to withstand. I want her to know that her words don't disappear when they leave her lips; they create tiny invisible lacerations, reminders that the sum of my parts will never be sufficient. I want to stop being expected to give people the benefit of the doubt as I take a seat at the table I would never have been invited to if I were three shades closer to my mom. I want to stop feeling like an imposter in my own skin, undeserving of my rich blended heritage.

I want to punch her in the face, so I do.

Hitting people is not as easy as it looks. You need to make sure you're at the right distance and swing at the right angle. You have to make sure your feet are steady, and that you put your weight behind your elbow and that you protect your wrist. Having never hit anyone before, I do exactly none of these things. My unimpressive jab is all Abby needs to go on the attack, and she uses every inch of her power to swing and claw and pull at me. People stand around us filming on their phones, and Jesus pushes through the crowd that has surrounded us to pull me away, but Abby and I are locked together, me holding two bunches of her loose hair and her punching my gut.

"EVERYONE, HANDS UP!" a voice roars.

Abby drops her fists and my eyes trace upward from the large waxy black shoes in front of me, past the dark gray uniform, to the white security guard who stands before us.

"What's going on here?" he demands as his eyes swoop past Abby and me to Jesus, his gaze landing on my purse in his hands.

I almost grab the bag from Jesus, but something tells me not to move.

"Hands. Eye contact. Listen. Be calm," I say under my breath over and over, and hope Jesus can hear me.

This guard is new and a bit older than the ones Pritchard has hired in the past, and he seems a little out of his element. He keeps looking around at our audience, uncomfortable without backup. The security guard focuses his attention on Abby, who is massaging the back of her head and whimpering.

"Miss, are you okay? Did he jump you?" he asks, taking a step in her direction. Abby looks up at him with tears in her eyes, scared.

"Things just got a little out of hand, but we're fine," I say, filling the silence.

"YOU NEED TO SHUT UP!" he yells back so loud that I jump.

"I didn't touch her, man, this is bullshit!" Jesus shouts, furious at his assumed guilt and unfair disadvantage. "Don't listen to this punk rent-a-cop. Let's—"

Before the last word comes out of Jesus's mouth, the guy has him by the back of his neck. A sharp inhalation ripples through the crowd like at a movie theater when a major plot twist is revealed, except this is real and happening to my boyfriend and no one is doing anything.

"Get off him!" I scream, and pull at the guard's arms, but he knocks me to the ground.

"Is that your bag, miss?" he asks Abby, dragging Jesus with him.

Abby's whole body is rigid except for her chest, which is heaving so quickly that she might pass out.

"Please, Abby, please tell him everything is okay." I find her eyes and beg with mine, but she shakes her head, unable to speak.

"It's my bag, sir," I tell the guard. "This is my boyfriend. He's not involved. I did it, I hit her."

His fingers are red up against Jesus's neck, his dirty fingernails digging into his skin.

"You let your girlfriend fight your battles?" he says mockingly to Jesus. "Who's the punk now?" His eyes bounce between the two of us as he tightens his grip. "Were they attacking you?" he probes Abby further, in a way that implies he already knows we were.

Abby opens her mouth, but nothing comes out, or maybe something does but we don't hear it because someone shouts, "STOP!"

And everything goes black.

The Mourner's Kaddish is a Jewish prayer that is recited to honor those we have lost. The reading of the prayer is somber as each syllable drops to the ground, laden with despair. Together a group of individuals recite these words in unison, missing their loved ones and acknowledging their continued grief. The prayer was the first thing I learned during my lessons. I don't know why, but for some reason it just stuck. I never understood the point of saying something that sounds so sad when that is already the way you feel, but it makes sense to me now—the words offer a momentary distraction, something to focus on other than the loss I have suffered. With my eyes clenched shut, I begin to say the prayer under my breath. The words echo inside my head, and I let myself escape into them until Jesus grabs my hand.

"Baby, open your eyes." His voice shakes as I slowly unclench my eyelids.

Mr. Bowels stands in front of us with his arms out to make sure we're protected.

"WHAT ARE YOU DOING?" he shouts at the security guard with more authority and power than I have ever heard come out of him in front of the classroom.

"This guy was attacking them. I had to step in," the guard lies. "I've seen his type before."

The guard's eyes burn through Mr. Bowels's frame and onto us.

"Leave: Get off this campus and never come back," Mr. Bowels says firmly. He points to the sidewalk just a few yards away.

"You'll be hearing from my union rep," the guard shouts.

"Everyone, go home. NOW!" Mr. Bowels bellows, and the crowd disperses like water bugs scurrying from the bathroom after the light switches on.

The moment everyone is gone, Jesus's knees buckle and I hug him tight until his breathing calms and he is able to hold his body weight up on his own.

"We're okay, we're okay, we're okay, we're okay, we're okay," I say in his ear as he clutches my back, shaking.

I wait inside the school until my parents can come pick me up—school policy after a physical altercation. They could expel me right now and I wouldn't care, I just want to go home. My worry for Jesus feels like a cement block on my heart. Pulling my soul to the depths of despair. He could barely get himself into a cab. I told him he could wait, we would drop him off, but he didn't want to be here, and I don't blame him.

"NEVAEH!" my mom screams as she runs down the school hall like a lunatic, passing me accidentally.

Principal Lackey runs out of her office, bumping my mother with the door.

"Whoops! Mrs. Levitz." She greets us as though we are being welcomed to a holiday party. "How lovely to see you!"

"It's Ms. Paire now," my mother snaps, cradling me in her arms.

"I'm sorry, of course. Will, um, Mr. Levitz be joining us?"

My mom steps forward and assumes the stance of a racehorse before the starting shot. "What is being done about this?" she demands. "There are videos all over the internet. That man should have never been an employee here!"

"Mr. Miller was a temporary replacement, and I assure you, he has been let go," Mrs. Lackey says, regaining her composure. "Since you have seen the videos, you also know that this all started with Nevaeh initiating a physical altercation. As I have just informed the Jacksons, Nevaeh has been formally suspended while we decide how to handle this. We will have copies of homework assignments sent home every day, and . . . I think it best that you have a lawyer present when we reconvene." Mrs. Lackey waits for a moment and then turns and closes the door to her office behind her.

"I'm so sorry that happened."

We turn to find Mr. Bowels sitting in a chair in the hallway. He looks up at me, still in disbelief, and asks, "Are you okay?"

My lip quivers as fear and pain and horror and humiliation rush through my body after an hour of numbness. This is the first time anyone has asked me that question since everything went down. My nerve endings feel like they have been exposed and set on fire, and the room closes in. I can't breathe or see or do anything but fall into an unknown inferno.

Strong arms with the softest skin I've ever felt catch me.

"I've got you," my mom says. "I've got you now."

Chapter 37

There was a flower
Who grew on the edge of a hill
That overlooked a city filled with buses and children and
ice cream,
And five golden retriever puppies who trotted behind their
owners wherever they went.

There was a man as well.

He chattered about dreams and wept for loss.
Translated through petals and soil,
What the flower heard was wind and bees,

And the spray of grass across his forehead,
And his breath adorned with scotch and caramels.

He was hers,
As was the city.

The new buildings sprouted from the center below, a challenge.
Or a bull's-eye.
Or a monument.
Or a tombstone.

She watched locusts sheathed in slim-fit jeans and vapor.
Marching, small as ants from her vantage point,
Spilling waste and terror.

The man came on his final day.
When grass molded to fit his body, a God-made Tempur-Pedic
*   pad,*
She reached her petals up to try to speak,
To beg him to fight,
To not give in,
But it was too late.
And he fell back onto her, pulling her from her place.

Only four puppies returned in the sun,
Panting and glad and unaware that everything was over.

The clouds cried when his body was removed,
Carrying the flower over what was left of the city,

Ashes scattered onto those she had so carefully protected for the
*   longest time*
and failed.

Jordan and Janae and Anita receive me on the stoop steps with blankets and bowls of ice cream and announce that *Sister Act 2* has been cued up on the TV. Their wet eyes scan my person for damage before ushering me into the house like a guarded treasure.

The force of Jerry's body when he barrels toward me sends us both slamming against a wall. My arms barely fit around his chubby frame, so I rub the spot on his back between his shoulder blades until his breathing calms.

"Hey." I pull his face up to mine. "I'm okay, okay?"

"You almost weren't," he blubbers, and pushes his head back into my chest to squeeze me a little longer.

"All right, that's enough." Anita sniffles and peels Jerry off me, passing him back to Zeke. "Come on." She takes my hand and leads me and my mom deeper into the house.

Everyone keeps checking in, asking if I need anything. I know they're trying to help and process what happened and be grateful that no one was too badly injured and let their anger out and make sure everyone gets fed. They want to keep living, because tonight, at the end of this story, we all did—I get it, but I just want to shut everything out.

I am fine; I always was. That guard didn't consider for a second that Abby or I could have been the ones at fault, even when I told him so. I confessed, and it didn't matter. How could I have allowed myself to be so ignorant? Why did it take someone I love being assaulted to make me really listen?

The doorbell rings and Anita goes to see who it is because my mom refuses to move from my side.

"Nevaeh?"

The sound of his voice makes my stomach turn.

My mother and I march into the hallway, where my father stands behind my aunt, who is seething. My father looks at me, then hardens when he meets my mom's eyes for the first time since they split.

"I called your office a hundred times, Samuel. I told them it was an emergency!" she shouts. "This is your daughter!"

"My daughter, who has never been in trouble in her life and is now dating some thug who almost got her killed and possibly got her stuck with a criminal record? My daughter, who has become reckless, cutting school and acting out, ever since she came to live here with you?" my father spits back.

"Don't you dare try to put this one on me," my mom says. "Nevaeh was defending herself—or do you only assume innocence when the case comes with a hundred-thousand-dollar check and late nights in the office with your secretary?"

They go tit for tat, unleashing the depths of their hate for one another.

"If you loathe me so much, why won't you sign the divorce papers?" my dad demands.

"I'd love to, but I can't! Because every good lawyer I call refuses to take me on as a client. You've made sure of that. So we're going to be married for the rest of our lives!" My mom stands on her toes and rises to his eye level.

"Stop it!" I screech.

"Honey, come here." My father reaches for me, but I dodge him.

"You don't know anything about Jesus," I tell him. "You don't know anything about love or trust. I thought I knew you, but it was an act, wasn't it?"

My father's mouth hangs open. For a moment, the three of us are still as statues as the truth sinks in.

Anita speaks up. "You need to get out of this house." Zeke has joined us in the foyer and placed one of his giant hands on her shoulder like an anchor, but Anita breaks free of his grip and lunges at my father. "Now! And don't come back here again."

My father runs his hands through his thinning hair. His hesitation stings like a rubber band pulled and released against my skin, until finally, he leaves.

At some point, dinner is delivered or picked up—rotisserie chicken, rice and beans, and maduros with extra green sauce. The smell makes my mouth water, but I have to spit the first bite into a napkin because it tastes like mud and grit.

We move back into the living room, where everyone continues to pretend to be fine and force out laughs. They are so committed to the act that no one notices when I get up and walk out of the room.

"I found her!" my mom shouts, jolting me awake in the morning.

"Well, this is some impressive architecture," she says, joining me on the floor.

I upgraded my attic nook last night by building a proper sheet tent; they have this magic power to transport you back to a time when your imagination was at its peak and all you needed to do was step inside to leave the real world. It's been years since I made one, but last night, it was the only place that made sense to sleep, because in here, I knew I could turn off my thoughts.

"I'm sor—"

Mom puts her fingers over my mouth to stop me from finishing the apology. "You have nothing to be sorry for, Nevaeh."

When she kisses me, her lips leave a sticky print on my forehead that I rub in like moisturizer.

"There's someone downstairs I think you might want to see," she says after a while.

❀

Jesus is in the living room. His arms are crossed over his chest, and his hands grip his shoulders with white fingertips from the force of pushing down. He sees me and stands as I enter the room, and his parents follow suit.

I rush over to them. "It was all my fault. This girl at school, she got under my skin and I shouldn't have let her. I am so sorry."

Mrs. DeSantos stands and takes my wringing hands in hers.

"You listen to me, mija," she says. "I watched that tape. That man was bigoted before you were even born. This wasn't your fault."

Mr. DeSantos turns to my mom. "Mrs. . . ."

"Paire," my mom says firmly. "Corinne Paire."

"Ms. Paire, I wanted to tell you in person that we are filing a lawsuit against the security guard, as well as the school."

His words are measured, but there is passion in his voice.

"What can I do?" I jump in.

"Well, it would increase our odds enormously if you could be a character witness, Nevaeh, as well as walking us through the events of the day."

Mr. DeSantos is a good lawyer. I can tell because he reminds me of my dad, but with a heart.

"I will. Of course I will."

"Nevaeh—"

"Mom, I might already be expelled," I remind her, and nod at Mr. DeSantos as a go-ahead to bring it home; he catches my drift and sticks the landing.

"What if I walk you through what we have so far, Ms. Paire? I understand you want to protect your baby. That's what we're try-ing to do for our baby, too."

While my mother listens to Mr. DeSantos, Jesus and I go out

to the front stoop. The steps are damp from the rain that I couldn't hear last night because I was protected in my tent. He rubs his neck in discomfort when he bends down to kiss me. I make him move his hands so I can see the tiny purple dents in his skin.

"I tried to make my parents just go after the guard, but they said they have to sue Pritchard because the school didn't do a thorough background check on him," he explains apologetically.

"I want you to sue them for everything they've got."

He tries to protest, but I won't let him.

"Why are you worried about me? I'm the diversity in that place. They can't expel me. They'd be crucified in the news."

I don't know if that last part is true, but it seems likely enough. Jesus's gaze relaxes a tiny bit, which is all that matters to me right now. I hug him, sick that after what he has been through, he still feels like I'm the one who needs protection.

"For a second, I thought you were gone, and I couldn't see anything clearly," I say. "The world around me melted like a candle, and all that was left were blurry patches of colors that made no sense."

Jesus kisses the tip of my nose and then my lips and then my neck. He holds my earlobe and rubs it between his thumb and pointer finger and leans down so only I can hear him.

"Hey," he says. "I love you too."

Chapter 38

Pritchard called yesterday. After two weeks, they're ready to have us back in tomorrow.

Pa shouts for me at the bottom of the stairs, dragging me from my bed and thoughts.

"Take these," he commands, handing me a kerchief and goggles. "And follow me."

My eyes and throat burn the moment I walk into the kitchen. I open my mouth to ask what's going on, but I can't speak through the pain, and Pa pulls the goggles over my eyes and ties the bandana over my nose in the style of a fugitive bandit.

"You'll be fine now," he yells, as if the goggles and kerchief impede my hearing.

Pa moves to the counter, which is covered in ingredients: allspice and ginger and browning sauce and thyme and pimento sauce and garlic and some already-homemade jerk sauce (a secret that I suppose is getting taken to the grave). Chicken sits in a metal bowl, clean and pink, and a pile of orange peppers—scotch bonnets, Pa says—float in boiling water on the stove, igniting the air with fire-kissed steam.

Grandma's secret jerk chicken recipe.

He works next to me, performing a demo of a task once before handing it over to me. I try my best to replicate his skillful knife work, but after a while, I resign myself to a simpler technique and separate the chicken legs from the thighs in rough chops that send cold bits of pink flesh all over the place. He mixes the spices and my goggles don't hide his displeasure when he pulls a jagged drumstick out of the bowl, but he presses on, leading me through the remaining instructions.

1. Sift the spices into the bowl until the meat is lightly covered and the majority of the seasoning is at the bottom of the bowl.
2. Pick up each individual piece and smash it into the pile of spices on both sides.
3. Massage chicken to spread seasoning into every slimy crease and pocket of skin, tenderizing until it slips out of your fingers and back into the bowl again and again and again.

Pa dons protective gloves as he moves to the concoction on the stove and carefully separates the heavily reduced liquid, a home-made hot sauce, from the pulp, which he throws into the chicken bowl in handfuls of orange slop.

"That's the secret even your mom and aunt don't know," he whispers into my ear before peeling off the gloves and covering the meat to marinate.

Pa makes ham and cheese sandwiches while we wait for the hot sauce to cool so we can pour it into small glass jars, which he stores for gifts and the apocalypse. We eat out on the stoop, he on a small round folding chair on the landing, and me on the steps because we couldn't find another portable seat. Tourists walk down our street to see the National Jazz Museum or the row of landmarked brownstones between 130th and 132nd on Lenox and stop to sniff the air in front of our house, unable to resist the signature blend of history and spice. Neighbors triggered by the familiar smell come out of their homes to remind my grandfather they're due for a hot-pepper refill.

My mom eventually comes up the block with rolls of fabric flopping in her arms. She found Grandma's sewing patterns and is determined to learn how to make a dress.

"Mmm! Daddy, it smells good." Mom kisses her father on the cheek. Her bright red lips leave a stain that spreads across his cheek when she tries to wipe it off.

Once the air makes me shiver, I get up to collect our plates, but he holds on to his tightly, not ready for me to leave.

"It feels good, doesn't it?" Pa asks me.

"What's that, Pa?"

He stares out at the brownstones on the street where he has built his life for the last fifty years.

"To move on."

It is Friday, judgment day at Pritchard. We stand seventy-five feet from my future on the corner, waiting for my father.

My father emailed last night, and my mother, for some reason unknown to me, acquiesced to his request that we enter the building together.

My father and a young woman pull up in an Audi, each in a perfectly tailored suit. The woman carries a small stack of manila envelopes in her arms and marches ahead of him, narrowly brushing his shoulder as she goes.

She is his type: trim and attractive. He's probably already sunk his teeth in. Poor Ashleigh.

"Let me do the talking," my father says with authority as he walks past us, shoulders back, head held high.

This is who he is. This is what makes him irresistible. This is how he carries on.

Pritchard feels bigger than usual as we enter its doors. The principal's office has been spruced up with flowers and a fresh coat of paint that makes the air taste acerbic.

Mr. and Mrs. Jackson, along with Abby, sit on the far side of the office with a few men in suits. Mrs. Lackey stands with a woman I don't recognize, probably the school's lawyer.

"Thank you so much for coming in." Mrs. Lackey welcomes us after the door is closed. "Normally, our policy on physical violence is clear—expulsion is within our right and to be expected. However, it has come to our attention that Nevaeh was reacting to a cyberbully attack initiated by Abby just moments before, which is also grounds for expulsion."

Mr. Jackson shifts in his seat and huffs at the idea that his child might face any real consequence for her actions.

"Because your families have been with Pritchard for so long, we want to offer a fair settlement. So, Abby, we thought you could join the anti-cyberbully alliance to educate students about the negative effects of social media. That leaves Nevaeh. You need to make a public apology on behalf of yourself and your"—she stops dramatically—"visitor for pushing the incident further than it needed to go. If you all agree, we can bring this unfortunate chapter to a close and move on like it never happened."

"But it did happen!" I say, unable to contain myself.

Mr. Jackson springs out of his chair.

"You are LUCKY my daughter has a warm Christian heart,

because she is the only reason we aren't pressing criminal charges!" he shouts, sounding like an alt-right troll on Twitter personified.

"Please, Mr. Jackson, you promised to remain civil," Mrs. Lackey begs, unwittingly exposing their alliance.

"My daughter is not publicly apologizing unless *she* is publicly apologizing," my father says, pointing to Abby.

"No!" I jump up.

"Nevaeh!" My dad tries to stop me, but I won't let him.

"I'm sorry, Abby. I shouldn't have touched you," I say before turning to face Principal Lackey. "I've gone to this school since I was four, and the whole time, it's as if I have been strapped to a buoy in the middle of the ocean. The waves keep crashing around me, and I'm not drowning, but I've barely kept my face above the surface. I've been fighting to stay afloat, because if I turn one way or the other, the salt water is going to rush down my throat so fast I won't even be able to take a dying breath."

The room is still, so I don't wait. I let my voice do what it has never done: I stand up for myself.

"I am not going to die on this buoy, Mrs. Lackey. I've held on too long for that. I take full responsibility for my actions, but you need to do the same. You are responsible for hiring that horrible, dangerous, racist man, who assaulted my boyfriend. So punish me however you want, but I won't clean this up for you."

My mom grabs my hand in hers, wet with her tears. She pulls herself together and winks as a show of support, which makes me breathe a little easier.

"*This is a load of horse manure!* You think you can hide behind your PC snowflake liberal nonsense?" Mr. Jackson yells. "Don't you pussyfoot around this. Your daughter is a predator." He leans forward and my father's arm flies across my chest, shielding me.

"You think I can't see it on you, but I can. Ya ain't fooling me," Mr. Jackson rants on. "Your daughter is obsessed with my Abby. I found a hundred of those topless photos on her laptop. She probably uploaded them to Abby's computer. That is sexual harassment, just like all you feminazis are always whining about."

He holds up copies of my topless photos, and even though my breasts have been covered with strips of tape, the humiliation sweeps through me all over again.

A few months ago, I would have expected Abby to say something to stop her father—a demonstration of that naive confidence instilled by our sheltered, affluent enclave and the willful ignorance that allows us to believe systems are fair and all people are good at their core. But I know what to expect now that my eyes have been opened: nothing. And that is exactly what she delivers.

Mr. Jackson's lawyers tap his shoulder and whisper behind their hands, conspiring.

"Nevaeh, I will have no choice but to expel you," Mrs. Lackey cautions.

"Take the deal, honey. You can get back to your life. Let me help you." My father's face is red, but his whisper is sad and sincere.

"That's not my life anymore, Daddy." I am firm, and he can tell there is no room for negotiation. "If you want to help me, then help me."

My father closes his eyes, replaying my words. When they open, he gives us a look to let us know the show hasn't even begun. He whispers something to his colleague that sends her digging through the papers in her lap. As soon as she hands him a thin red folder, he stands.

"I had hoped not to have to do this, but you have left me no choice, Mr. Jackson," my father says, and steps to the left to face Abby.

"Abby, the day that the photos in question were taken was my daughter's sixteenth birthday, is that correct?"

"Yeah."

"What does this have to do with anything?" Mr. Jackson shouts.

My father hands over photocopies of the Instagram post. The image itself has been blurred, but the time and date stamp is clear.

"Can you read me the date and time, please?" my father asks Abby.

"Umm, March thirtieth, five-fifteen p.m."

My dad paces the five feet of free space in the center of the room.

"Thank you. Just to reiterate, it was Nevaeh's birthday."

"All right, enough with the theatrics," one of the Jacksons' lawyers interjects, unprepared for proper litigation.

My father gives a wicked smile. "I'm getting there. I just need a little help from my wife."

The word "wife" slips out of him before he can stop it, and both of my parents jump a little, shocked by how foreign it sounds after everything that has gone on.

"Corinne, what time of day was Nevaeh born?" he asks, re-covering his cool before any of the other lawyers can pick up on the tension and use it against him.

"Eight-twenty p.m.," she says.

My father savors the moment as the Jacksons' lawyers stir and he moves in for the kill.

"That is correct. Which means when the photos were taken,

my daughter was not yet sixteen, which is the legal age of consent. She was still fifteen, which means that if you so much as mispronounce her name, I will slap your daughter with a distributing child pornography charge and she will spend the rest of her life on the sex offender registry."

Mr. Jackson's face turns purple, but he clamps his mouth shut and listens.

"Nevaeh will finish the rest of her sophomore year as a remote student. She will receive all she needs to complete assignments and exams. Anything that cannot be completed at home will be revised to accommodate her situation. She will receive references from teachers and from you, Mrs. Lackey, for whatever schools might require them, and all of you will sign agreements to never slander her name."

Energized by the flawless performance of her mentor, the young lawyer jumps up and hugs my dad in celebration. He allows her to linger pressed up against him for just a second and then shrugs her off. The other attorneys ask us to wait in the outer office while they confer. They call my father back a few moments later. When he emerges, he looks tired and disappointed.

"They didn't sign?" my mom asks, shocked.

"No, they did." He gives us a handwritten paper with the terms outlined. We won, but for some reason he seems upset.

"Cynthia," he snaps to his colleague as she organizes the files they brought. "Draft the formal contract and have the office send a final copy to my wi—" He stops himself and nods in my mom's direction. "To Corinne."

"Thank you," I say to my father.

"Nevaeh—"

"I'll see you at the bat mitzvah," I interrupt him—whatever is bothering him is not my problem, not anymore. We both know we can never go back to how it was between us. Even the way it's been this past year feels like a distant memory.

His face drops.

"With everything going on . . ." His eyes start brimming with tears. "I cancelled it. I thought that's what you wanted."

The words I've been wanting to hear now deafen and cripple me. I fall into a nearby chair.

"What do you mean 'with everything going on'?" my mom asks, decoding the language of Samuel Levitz in a way I never could.

"We have to move the divorce proceedings forward," he says in the type of quiet voice you use when you don't want to admit that the words you are saying are true. "Here is a settlement offer." He hands her a folder.

"What's the rush, Samuel? You knock her up?" she goads him.

He plays with the empty space on his wedding finger, avoiding eye contact, as if his dramatic shame is supposed to make us feel better—or worse, earn him pity.

"It wasn't planned," he admits, as if that makes a difference.

My mom starts shouting, but her words fade behind me as I run out of the building, past the steps and the corner, all the way to the subway.

Chapter 39

I unfold the piece of paper with Rabbi Sarah's phone number. It's been carefully tucked into my wallet for months.

"Hello?" Rabbi Sarah's voice cracks on the other end of the phone.

"It's Nevaeh," I say. "I need to see you."

The trip to Queens is long, and by the time I make it to her apartment and buzz the door, I can barely wait to push it open and get inside. Her satin leopard-print robe flutters behind her as she clunks down the stairs eating a bag of cheddar popcorn.

"What is it, Nevaeh?"

"My dad is having another baby and cancelled the bat mitzvah and my boyfriend has PTSD from being attacked and Stevie hates me and is leaving for England and I'll probably never see him again and my mom can't find a lawyer because no one will go against my dad and we're stuck—"

I stop, unable to speak through the heavy stream of huge, mutant tears that have been building behind the now-broken levee inside me. Each drop drains from my person after bearing down on every inch of my body for the past nine months. I cry for so long that when I finish, I can't tell if the floor beneath me is stained with tears or coffee, and my body shakes, wrecked from the emotional purge.

The cold fabric of her robe chills my shoulders as she wraps her arm around me. "Come," she says, leading me up the narrow hallway once I have calmed down.

The air gets hotter and thicker the higher we climb, making it impossible not to wheeze.

"I didn't know you were comin', so, uh, I didn't have time to clean the place up," she cautions, turning the knob to her apartment.

The studio has a small kitchenette with a white mini-fridge and toaster oven next to a stand-alone sink and a tiny room with a toilet inside. At the far end of the room, a bed peeks out of an alcove with a screen half unfolded in front of it. Rabbi Sarah runs around picking up socks and random shoes strewn about. It smells like cinnamon from one of those holiday-scented candles, and the walls are bare except for a framed crocheted Christian proverb that I'm assuming was left here by the prior tenant:

AS FOR ME AND MY HOUSE, WE WILL SERVE THE LORD.

"I liked the colors," she says behind me. "This is just temporary, you know. Still getting settled."

The couch, it turns out, is a frame with overused, deflated cushions that sink like quicksand with the slightest impact. I smile and engage my core to keep myself partially upright, doing my best to appear comfortable so as not to embarrass her.

"I don't have much but, uh . . . water? Do you want some water? Or did you want to keep talking?" She sits down beside me, sinking us farther into the couch.

The reminder makes the hurricane inside me gear up again, and before I can stop it, the tears are so thick I lose the ability to see, which makes me cry harder.

"I hate him. I hate everyone!" I shout.

"Get up," Rabbi Sarah says.

She pulls me off the couch and drags me out of her apartment, into the musty hallway.

"What the hell are you doing?" I shriek as a door opens in front of me and wind hits my face.

She pushes me out onto a roof deck you would never know existed from the street below. The brick railing blends in with the exterior brick structure and wraps around half the building—a secluded maze in the sky.

"You're angry, Nevaeh, and you have a right to be angry, but what you aren't going to do is be bitter and mean. You need to get it out of your system or it's gonna eat you alive."

"He could have let her go. Before I was born, she left him, and he pulled her back."

"Close your eyes," she says.

"No!" I shout.

In seconds, she flies over to me and covers my eyes with the tie from her robe, blindfolding me. She stands in front of me, her fingers locked with mine, and stretches my arms out as far as they can go.

"My parents were selfish assholes!" she yells into my face. "And what your dad has done to you and your mom is terrible. What that security guard did, that was terrible. But they win if you end up miserable too. You've gotta release it."

Her hands clench mine as she lets out a primordial yell. A yell so intense that the brick walls around us turn her voice into a wind tunnel, burrowing into my skull like a drill until I can't take it anymore.

"STOP IT!" I shout, but she doesn't. She takes another breath and yells again, and the sound drills deeper until I have no choice but to scream back.

Our voices cut through the air, discharging regret for us and our parents. We release the pain we've been forced to carry because of their mistakes. We spew anger for the selfishness of our fathers and the painful truth that one day, they will stop being people we wished had loved us more and instead will become distant memories.

When our throats are raw, we walk back to the apartment and I gather my things.

"So that's the trick? That's what you've been doing your whole life? You just . . . yell?" I ask, shocked at how much better I feel.

"Sweet Lord, no. That's just so you don't go around decking everyone and end up on *Dr. Phil.*"

"I am so sorry for what I said to you the other night," I say. "I know how bad it feels when someone tells you that you aren't who you are. What I said, it wasn't true. That was my own stuff. I've been sitting in this undefined box for so long, I wouldn't know what else to be if I tried, but that's no excuse, and I shouldn't have put that on you."

She wants to forgive me, I can tell, but it's not that simple when someone chips a tiny piece of you away.

"I just want you to know that this hasn't been a waste," I say, swallowing the realization that my lessons with her really are coming to an end.

"Let's make sure it isn't," she says.

Rabbi Sarah and I find my mom on the stoop, looking nervously back and forth.

"Honey!" She grabs me and hugs me. "You can't run off like that. I've been looking for you everywhere, I was so worried. Are you all right?"

"I'm fine," I tell her, and gesture with my eyes to Rabbi Sarah.

"Oh, Rabbi Sarah." My mom holds her hand out, a little confused.

"You're lookin' good," Rabbi Sarah says. They shake hands as though this is the first time they are meeting, which, given the state Mom was in the last time they met, isn't entirely inaccurate.

The house is dark and quiet, and we stumble over each other to find the light.

"Yo." Janae's voice comes out of nowhere, scaring us.

"What are you doing?" I ask once I've caught my breath and flipped the light switch to find her. Janae is lying on the living room couch.

"Just chillin' with my thoughts. What's good, Rabbi?"

Rabbi Sarah strides in, less unnerved than we are, and nods hello.

"No one was up for cooking, so they went out a while ago."

"Why didn't you go with them?" my mom asks.

"I wasn't hungry yet."

"Well, I guess I could go see what I can whip up," my mom offers.

"NO!" Janae and I both yell, and turn to Rabbi Sarah for adult intervention.

"Hmm . . . well, I can make a week's worth of meals out of a can of beans, some celery, and Ritz crackers," she says. "Let's see what we've got to work with."

She marches in the direction of the kitchen and we follow, leaving my mom with the task of sitting still and touching nothing even remotely edible.

"Rice, beans, ground turkey, broccoli, and a fried egg on top," Rabbi Sarah announces the dish she created. It smells delicious.

"Rabbi Sarah, would you bless the food for us?" my mom asks.

"I'd be honored, Corinne, thanks."

"BA-RUCH A-TAH A-DO-NOI
ELO-HAI-NU ME-LECH HA-O-LAM
HA-MO-TZI LE-CHEM MIN HA-A-RETZ.

"Ahhh–meinnn."

"Amein," we agree.

"That's pretty. What's it mean?" Janae asks, digging in.

" 'Blessed are you, Lord our God, king of the universe, for the sustenance and for the universe. For the produce of the field and for the precious, good and spacious land, which you have graciously given as heritage to our ancestors,'" I say.

"Very good." Rabbi Sarah beams. "You know, Corinne, Nevaeh told me that Samuel has cancelled the bat mitzvah, but I think it would be an awful waste to not hold some sort of celebration for all the work Nevaeh has done."

My mom perks up, intrigued.

"It's okay if you'd rather not," I say.

"No," my mom says. "I agree with Rabbi Sarah. You have to finish what you started."

I am torn. I had begun to feel an unexpected excitement

about the bat mitzvah. It was going to be my moment to declare to the world that I am me, in all my ambiguous glory. But now, with everything going on, it feels unnecessary. Do I really need another day to be all about Nevaeh?

"We can do it our way," Rabbi Sarah says while she and my mother begin to conspire with their eyes.

"Dope. I'm down," Janae says, making my mind up for me. "I'll film it, but you gotta pay me. My time is money."

The rest of the family returns right as we're finishing the dishes. Anita puts out the sliced red velvet cake they brought home from Amy Ruth's.

"All right, who wants to guess who the best Knick of all time was?" Zeke says, taking the stage.

Moans sound from every corner of the house as the entire family rejects his preferred activity after years of listening to the same question.

"You call yourselves New Yorkers?" he shouts. "All right, Rabbi Sarah, you're a native. Tell me, who do you think is the greatest Knick of all time?"

"You don't have to answer that," Anita tells her.

Rabbi Sarah looks overwhelmed with seven sets of eyes focused on her.

"I wanna hear who you say first," she counters, willing to play his game on her terms and buying herself time to strategize.

He sits up and rubs his hands together, ready to take on a new kill.

"The all-time leader in points, blocks, rebounds, steals, free throws, field goals, and minutes: Patrick Ewing. His only downfall was that he had the great misfortune of playing during the same time as Michael Jordan, so he never got a championship title."

Zeke rests back on the couch, cocksure that he's already won, and hands the floor over to Rabbi Sarah, who sits patient and unafraid.

"Ewing is for sure one of the greats, but he's obvious, ya know?"

The room quiets. This is proving to be a real matchup.

"I'm going to go with Bernard King. In the '84–'85 season he was dropping thirty-three a game, which is more than any other Knick, but then, come March of '85, halfway through the season, he blew his ACL, so after fifty-five games he never played for them again. But with those stats, he would've been the greatest."

"Let me get this straight: you are arguing that Bernard King wasn't the greatest, but he could have been if he didn't get injured?"

Rabbi Sarah thinks for a moment to make sure she agrees with his assessment.

"Mmm-hmm, sure am."

Zeke sits back and considers her response, but before he can announce his decision, Anita steps into the center of the room.

"Zeke, baby—you just got, got."

Jordan and Janae howl, and Jerry charges at him with all his might and lands on his lap. Zeke crumples for a moment, overpowered by the weight of his son and the defeat by Rabbi Sarah, but then he springs off the couch and swings Jerry around. Never too tired to joke with his kids.

In the midst of the commotion, Rabbi Sarah vanishes. I walk out to the hallway to find her gathering her things.

Jerry's high-pitched giggles waft out of the other room—an anthem of love and family.

"You don't have to leave," I tell her.

"I do," she says with a sniff and a forced smile, and walks out onto the street.

Chapter 40

Meet us at Signal. 12:30.

I am surprised to wake up to a text from Jordan.

Now that I'm a remote student for the remainder of the year, my days are quiet and boring, filled with research for my final projects and wishing Stevie would call me. After the incident at Pritchard, I tried to call and text him again, but nothing. There were a few times when the little ellipsis started to blink as if he was going to respond, but he never did, and after a while, the whole exercise was depressing me, so I gave up.

The imprint of my mom's body fills the space next to me. She's been gone for hours. These days, she gets up before everyone else to have coffee and work on her latest piece of clothing before heading into Midtown and pounding the pavement to try to convince a lawyer to represent her in this divorce.

It's amazing how easy it is not to shower or change your clothes when you have nowhere to be. I've been in the same outfit for four days, and I'm beginning to look like the version of my mother that I hated earlier this year, so I drag myself to the shower.

Signal High is Jordan and Janae's school. It's this progressive program that rebukes traditional tests as a viable way to gauge learning and somehow convinced the New York public school system to have standardized testing requirements waived so they could create their own curriculum. Because Signal is specialized and has its own application process, the student population is wildly diverse, or maybe just normal in comparison to what I'm used to at Pritchard. I'm so accustomed to the self-segregation at my school that seeing people my age of different backgrounds socializing with ease is enough to make me do a double take. I watch one teacher snatch a newly lit cigarette from between a kid's lips and stomp it out before turning on his heels to go inside. *This is nothing like Pritchard,* the little voice inside of me says, *in all the best ways possible.*

"Nevaeh!" Janae waves from the entrance as she and Jordan walk out of the building, followed by a cluster of friends.

We walk a few blocks to a corner store and load up plastic containers with the random assortment of food at the hot bars: lo mein, blackened chicken, a few vegetables for good measure, an egg roll, a quesadilla, and potato salad. Then we head to their usual lunch spot.

We stop in front of what is supposed to be a private park attached to a luxury apartment building, but the gate is wide open and there seems to be no security guard, so we walk right in. We pass a jungle gym and a fountain area, on the way to some benches positioned around the perimeter, which are completely covered with high school students eating lunch in small groups.

"Welcome to the smoke park!" Janae says as Jordan speeds ahead of us to meet Breezy and Dania and Paulina, her friends from the New Year's Eve party.

As Janae and I make our way to Jordan's bench, I notice the scent of marijuana lingering in certain areas, no doubt the inspiration for the park's nickname.

A white kid eating a folded slice of pizza walks past us. A sign hangs off his neck and flaps in the wind behind him. It reads *If I'm asleep, wake me at 59th Street.*

"Yo, Geoff," Janae calls out to him. "Your sign is still on."

Geoff's spindly, nearly translucent arm moves behind him with a freakishly long reach and confirms that what she says is true.

"Good lookin' out, J!" he says, taking the hemp string and sign off his neck and folding it neatly to put in his backpack.

"How often does that thing work for you?" she asks in an oddly flirtatious manner.

He shrugs. "Someone woke me up at Seventy-Second today," he says, not disappointed with the result. "I can't help it—that subway rockin' puts me right to sleep."

Janae lets out an unnatural giggle that sends my eyes along with Jordan's onto her in shock. Geoff heads over to a group of guys passing a blunt and a hacky sack around a circle.

"Really? Geoff?" Jordan asks.

"He's sweet and goofy and I don't wanna hear anything about it." Janae tries to sound harsh, but she can't stop the smile that breaks onto her face. I pretend not to see it and settle down on the bench to soak this place in.

I watch my cousins as they joke and laugh with their friends, easily navigating the masses of social groups who come and go from our spot. It's as if everyone else here is a planet with one job: to revolve around them—the sun. Jordan reads us the first draft of her final essay, which she has to defend to a panel of teachers at the end of the school year, a commentary on the Eurocentric standards of beauty in American mainstream media. As she reads, she is luminous, not just in her natural beauty, but in her brilliance. The paper sounds like it was written by a professional published author, not a high school student.

When she finishes reading, her friends hoot and yell. "Tell them, sis!" "Let them know!"

"You're a really good writer," I tell her once the commotion has died down.

"What, you thought you're the only person in this family who can put a sentence together?" Jordan snaps.

I shudder and scoot back on the bench, embarrassed to have implied anything of that nature.

"Thanks," she says, and playfully elbows me in the ribs with a wink and half a smile, which is almost as good as winning the Mega Millions jackpot, as far as I'm concerned.

"So whatchu gonna do now, Ney? Go to Fort Hilten or Fieldston? Another one of those bougie schools?" Janae asks as we begin to clean up our lunch so they can head back to class.

I honestly haven't thought about it, but for the first time, an untapped possibility reveals itself to me. I look around at my cousins and their classmates and breathe in the laughter and joy and comfort here. A place where everyone fits in because they are encouraged to be an individual and not just part of a quota or a stereotype.

"I don't know," I say with my eyebrows raised. "Does Signal accept transfer students?"

Home is sixty blocks away and it will take a couple hours to get there, but the busy streets of the city are calming, even soothing. As I walk I consider my future. I'd have a chance to learn and grow at a school like Signal. A chance to make new friends, to become a new, better me. . . .

> When your face is just one of many
> And scowls can't be differentiated from dehydration or hope or
>   fear,
> It means you are a part of something,
> Even if no one knows your name.

My mom is behind her sewing machine when I get back.

"Did you have a nice time?" she asks.

I nod and discard my shoes by the door per the house rules.

"You better get to that homework," she says, her head cocked in the direction of our room. I feel her eyes follow me as the stairs creak under my bare feet.

All it takes is a tiny push of my finger for the bedroom door to swing open, and when it does, I lose my breath. Stevie stands under the most perfect, magical tent ever. It covers the whole room and is carefully constructed from my mom's lopsided T-shirts and dresses. With the sunlight streaming in, the bright colors make the room glow.

"B—don't talk, I'm talking." He holds his hand out for me to take, but I don't move.

"I freaked out because I thought I was losing you, and then I did. I am so mad at you. You turned into this . . . self-absorbed, attention-seeking, out-of-touch monster. But I need you, B, even if it's not the same. I just . . . I don't know how to be. Not without you. Not without us."

The pain that my mom felt this year, the one that I condemned her for and categorized as a weakness, suddenly makes sense. When you spend your life with someone, they become a part of you. That's what my dad was for her; it's what Stevie has been for me.

"I'm sorry I wasn't there when everything went down with Abby. I should have been." He goes on. "I was already home when it hit the news, and I raced back to Pritchard, but you had already left. I came out here three different times, but I couldn't bring myself to knock on the door. I just miss you. Ever since I got the fellowship, everything has been so . . . quiet."

"I was a total herb," I admit. "I ruined everything. You didn't do anything wrong."

He looks into my eyes to make sure I'm not lying and I telepathize the words into his brain before I speak them.

"I'm so sorry, Stevie."

He immediately looks relieved.

"I'm sorry we didn't get to celebrate your birthday," he says.

"It's okay. I got drunk with Abby and then my mom almost killed my uncle with food poisoning."

"What? I can't believe I missed that!" he shrieks.

"How did you do this? How did you know I'd be out?" I ask.

Stevie gives me a devilish grin.

"Told my dad I had a migraine to get out of school and then called in a favor." He winks.

"Jordan?" I ask, shocked that she would ever assist in anything special for me.

Just the sound of her name turns Stevie's face red with lust. He stretches his hand out once more, and this time I take it. Stevie pulls me close, placing my other hand on his shoulder and his arm gently around my waist. He hums music into my ear, our song—"The Only Exception" by Paramore—and begins to rock ever so slightly back and forth.

In all these years, we've never danced, not together, not like this. I let him guide me with his feet, nothing difficult, and I give myself over to lean into his muscular frame.

Ours isn't a love that fits within the confines of romance; it exceeds that of friendship as well. Our deep love flashes through my mind like déjà vu, triggered by the smell of his shampoo, and I am reminded of all the ways we are intertwined and always will be.

"I'm going to miss you next year, but I'm so proud of you," I say into his shoulder.

"Thanks, B." His voice echoes in my brain before he spins me out and brings me back and holds me tight.

Chapter 41

My mom and I lie in bed relishing the final Saturday of the spring-to-summer crossover, when there is a soft knock on the door just before Jerry pokes his head into our room. He still hasn't grasped the concept that the point is to wait for the person in the room to answer before entering. He jumps onto the bed, slithering between my mom and me.

"Was there something you needed?" I pinch his chubby face and pull it toward me to kiss. Even when he drives you insane, his cheeks make him irresistible.

"There's a guy downstairs to see Auntie," he says. His mouth opens and closes, debating whether he should say more. Then he adds, "He's white."

"We're not selling this house!" Anita shouts at the bottom of the stairs. "You developers have no souls, coming out here on a Saturday and disturbing people."

The man cowers at the umbrella Anita has raised above her head.

"I'm Marty Goldberg—a lawyer friend of Sarah Edward. She

told me Corinne Paire needs representation," he says, protecting his face from Anita's wrath.

"Anita! Stop!" My mom rushes down the last stairs and stands between them. "Mr. Goldberg, I'm Corinne. What was it you were saying?"

My mom shoos Anita away and gently ushers Mr. Goldberg into the living room. He wipes his brow with a handkerchief and takes a seat. I step into the room to get a better look at him. He is huge, at least six foot eight, and has light brown curly hair that mushrooms out of the top of his head. Up close, the wrinkles in his forehead betray his age, but his eyes are young and the lightest shade of gray-green I have ever seen.

"Nevaeh?" he asks, and rises from the couch to hold out a hand that is so large I want to double check that it's real before placing mine inside it.

"How do you know Rabbi Sarah?" I ask.

My mom looks at me with a raised eyebrow and cocks her head to the door, implying I should let them talk about grown-up stuff. But considering she was on parental hiatus until a few months ago, I think I've earned the right to keep my butt where it is.

Mr. Goldberg moves his giant head back and forth between us, unsure who is in charge.

"Rabbi Sarah counseled me through a hard time recently, and I owe her a favor. I'm a divorce lawyer, and a good one."

"Would you look at the Lord work?" Anita cries as she reappears, sounding more like Miss Clarisse than she would ever accept. "Sorry about earlier."

She hands Mr. Goldberg a glass of water and invites herself to the conversation, squeezing onto the couch next to me.

"You were saying, Mr. Goldberg," my mom says, giving him back the floor.

"Samuel Levitz has quite the reputation. I've actually been hoping to have a chance to go up against him." Mr. Goldberg smirks. "So if we want to win, I need to know everything, because I don't like to lose."

My mom and Anita both give me a look.

"I'm not leaving," I say stubbornly.

My mom's chest rises and falls as she closes her eyes.

"He cheated," my mom says. "A lot."

She clasps Anita's hand for support as Mr. Goldberg takes notes on a yellow legal notepad. She talks for a while about the late nights and the lonely mornings.

"I don't mean to sound insensitive, but in these hostile divorce cases, it's rare that the marriage doesn't endure some sort of infidelity," Mr. Goldberg explains.

We all sit for a while as my mom's hopeful face goes sullen and pale.

"Mr. Goldberg, he made me a settlement offer. I have the paperwork upstairs. Do you think you could help me with the legalese? I want to make sure I understand before I sign." She stands to get the documents, resigned to give up the fight.

"Not so fast," Mr. Goldberg tells her. "If I can prove his dependency on you at any point in his career, you'd be eligible for at least half of his assets."

"Samuel Levitz has not been dependent upon anyone since he learned how good it felt to win on his own," my mom says on the way to the stairs.

"There has to be something!" I shout, unwilling to concede.

Mom turns to face me. "Nevaeh, the man gave me a beautiful

house. He paid for my clothing and my jewelry. He took me all over the world. The money in the settlement is enough to get us on our feet. Maybe this is God's way of telling me to be grateful and leave the past in the past."

"JUST BECAUSE HE DIDN'T HURT YOU THE WAY RAYMOND DID DOESN'T MEAN HE DIDN'T HURT YOU!" The words fly out of me and stop her in her tracks.

"How do you . . ." She trails off, confused as to how I know her deepest, darkest secret.

"Raymond? What's she mean, 'hurt you'? What is she talking about, Corinne?" Anita asks, rapid-fire.

"It's okay, Mom. It's okay to fight for yourself. You deserved more."

She looks from me to Anita to Mr. Goldberg.

"When Samuel was in law school," she whispers, "I paid for the apartment we lived in with money I'd saved up during college. I was going to use it to go to school, and then . . ."

She trails off, looking at me, the real reason we are in this predicament.

Mr. Goldberg stands and, in only a few strides, blocks my mom from leaving the room.

"Sit down, please, and tell me more about this apartment."

My mom takes a seat next to Anita.

"Nevaeh," she pleads. "Go."

This time, I listen.

I sit in bed, hoping to receive an update on what is happening in the living room, but the house remains quiet. So I wait and listen to the ticking of the clock.

"Nevaeh," my mom says as she enters the room with puffy eyes and dry lips.

I shoot up and into her arms.

"How did you know?" she asks when I finally let go.

I pull the journal from my backpack and put it into her hands. I wrap her fingers around it with mine, releasing her private thoughts and memories and mistakes back to her, freeing the truth between us. She opens the cover. All that's left are jagged stubs of paper that bloom from the spine.

"I'm sorry. I didn't even finish reading it. I got too upset," I say.

She puts her arm around my shoulders and closes the book.

"You should know the whole story," she says, and begins to recount what I destroyed in my tantrum of rage.

"Your father applied to a bunch of law schools senior year, but the only one he wanted to go to was Yale. The day he found out he was wait-listed was the day I found out I had been accepted into Teachers College at Columbia.

"Things had been good since we got back together. Samuel was attentive and kind and playful. You know how your father can make you feel like you're the only person in the room? Like the fact that he sees you is the only thing you need to make it through the day?"

It's been so long, but I remember. I would wait for the knob on the front door to turn and for him to walk into the house and give me a kiss before tickling me to the ground until I couldn't even breathe from so much love. I nod.

"I was afraid to tell him about Columbia. I told myself it was because I didn't want to throw it in his face with the news from Yale, but deep down, I knew he would never be happy for me to succeed if it wasn't on his terms. I waited as long as I could to tell him, but finally, the deadline to enroll was coming up and I couldn't wait any longer. We went to the Cuban sandwich shop, and then we went to the quad to eat. He was quiet the whole time, which was offputting. We sat there for a while, listening to the conversations around us, and right before I decided I was going to tell him, he interrupted. . . .

" 'Do you love me?' he shouted at me.

" 'You know I do,' I whispered, and prayed for him not to break my heart as he held me with both hands, rooting us to the ground.

" 'Will you move to Connecticut with me?' he asked, smiling so big that he almost split his face in two. 'Yale called this morning. I'm in.'

"He was so excited that he talked on and on, making plans for us, telling me it would just be a few years in New Haven; then we'd move to New York.

"I reasoned with myself in my head. Columbia was only an hour and a half from New Haven. I had saved almost twenty thousand dollars over four years of jobs on campus and other part-time work I had picked up along the way. I could use that to travel back and forth, maybe even stay with him on the weekends. We could make long-distance work for a year until I transferred to Yale or another school nearby. But I couldn't say the words.

" 'Please,' he begged, and kissed me deeply. 'I need you.'

"He needed me. He wasn't perfect, but he needed me. So I decided to defer a year.

"I told myself, *We'll get settled and then I'll go get my degree. Love is about compromise; it was just my turn first.* So I said yes to him and he kissed me and together we drank my salty tears and dreams away."

❋

I know how the story ends. She didn't go to Columbia; she stayed home to take care of me after she got pregnant just a few months after graduating; my birth is what stopped her from having a life of her own.

"Why didn't you leave him?" I ask her.

She closes her eyes.

"Sometimes, if something bad happens to you, you blame yourself. I thought no one was ever going to love me after what Raymond did, but then I met Samuel and he loved me and it felt so good. It got to the point where I couldn't function without him. Him loving me was the only way I could love myself, so I stopped seeing the bad stuff. I ignored it. I told myself it could be worse. I took a teacher's assistant role in Connecticut while I was pregnant, to pass the time while he was away, to keep myself motivated for the future. Then you came along, and the only thing that mattered was you and giving you the best life possible, and I couldn't do that without him. I was stuck because I believed that I could never amount to anything or give you what you deserved on my own."

"It's all my fault," I say through my tears.

"No, baby," she says. "You gave me purpose again. You are what saved me."

Chapter 42

SAMUEL LEVITZ, 39, RENOWNED PRIVATE ATTORNEY, AND ASHLEIGH HADDOCK, 27, AN ENTREPRENEUR, WILL BE WED AT THE SUPER-EXCLUSIVE WEBSTER HOTEL IN RYE, NEW HAMPSHIRE, ON LABOR DAY WEEKEND.

"I've always gotten what I wanted. It's a skill I've crafted over many years," Ms. Haddock said proudly, rubbing her pregnant belly. Her left hand is almost completely obstructed by a four-and-a-half-karat princess-cut-diamond engagement ring, which catches the sun from the skylight above and casts rainbows on the nursery walls around us.

"I think our story is really culturally relevant at the moment because we're such a blended family," Haddock states.

Levitz is Jewish, whereas Haddock is of Scottish descent.

"And four percent Iberian Peninsula!" Haddock adds with a wink.

Stay up to date on the festivities with I!Online, where we'll be following the newlyweds through the whole journey this fall on *Love, Marriage, and a Baby Carriage.*

"GET OUT!" Jordan shouts once she has finished reading the press release and scrolls down to a photo of my father and his bride-to-be.

In it, Ashleigh sits on a throne, her naked belly protruding from her two-piece spandex crop top and skirt, with my father positioned behind her, only half visible.

"How's Auntie handling it?" Janae asks, shivering like she caught cooties just from looking at Ashleigh's face.

"Better than expected," I say. "She's taking him to court—this public embarrassment is just the icing on the cake."

Jordan stands. "We've got to get going. You don't want to keep Lucia waiting."

My cousins surprised me with a hair appointment for the big day. Jordan hops down from the counter and unplugs the white fan she positioned in front of her. Janae and I do the same with ours, and we stack them neatly against the wall before heading out to the living room, where my mom sits sewing furiously in her corner.

"It's almost ready!" she calls.

With Janae and Anita's help, we talked her out of the ambitious goal of making my bat mitzvah dress and settled on the tallit that will be presented to me during the ceremony.

Until this week, the weather has been tame and lovely, with days that beg to be spent rolling around the grass in Central Park or exploring random streets with a cherry-mango flavored ice in hand. But on Monday, the heat arrived and is making up for lost time with record highs and the unrelenting aroma of hot ass across the city.

We pass the new coffee shop that replaced the bodega a few

blocks away. This place sells eight-dollar pour-over coffee with no seating available because they claim the artisanal beverage tastes best standing up. One more storefront furthering the gentrification of Harlem. Miss Clarisse's store, however, is still open, and business is booming. Once she debuted her ScRUMPtious Gurl Pantyhose, some underground fashion blog featured them, and now she's got a media influencer campaign on Instagram that's selling her out of stock every week.

"Hey, ladies!" she calls, and shimmies in our direction to a chorus of laughter from her customers.

We wave back but don't stop. Miss Clarisse can talk for days, and we're already running behind.

"Isn't that product a little bit problematic?" I say. "Like . . . how many centuries have the voluptuous bodies of Brown and Black women been objectified? And what, now that butts are back in style, she's selling them for $14.99 so every Becky, Susan, and Taylor can pad their behinds when they feel like it?"

Jordan and Janae stare at me, mouths open so wide a fly almost lands on Jordan's tongue.

"Bish, when'd you get woke?" Janae cries.

"But for real, though, if Miss Clarisse didn't do it, it woulda been a Becky, Susan, or Taylor. At least she's the one selling it," Jordan says.

We stop in front of the hair salon. Condensation from the air-conditioner gathers on the window. I watch the drops slide down the glass, making the magazine cutouts of women with outdated hairstyles plastered to the inside cry.

"What are you waiting for?" Jordan asks me with irritation before opening the door.

We are sucked into a whirlwind of gum smacking, hand clapping, and laughter. The space is small, with salon chairs at each corner so everyone else can congregate in the center and make sure not to miss any of the action. Despite the air-conditioner blasting, the hair-dryer station on the far wall fills the room with a thick heat that smells like burnt hair product.

Lucia is short, barely five feet in her two-inch platform flip-flops, and has a look of slight annoyance plastered across her face at all times.

"You're late," she states, pointing a comb in our direction.

Her words mute the room as every female in there stops mid-gossip to watch me. I march through a cluster of women in the center of the store who moments before were chattering a mile a minute, probably comparing the lack of space between their thighs.

"You want it up or you want it down?" she asks me in a tone so serious I have to work up the courage to answer.

My cousins talk over one another, throwing out suggestions, with additional commentary from the rest of the clientele. In this village, everyone has a say, but Lucia has the final word. She taps her toe on the laminate floor, maintaining a beat throughout the commotion until she claps her hands once. Silence falls over the room, as if she has grabbed all twenty sets of lips and stapled them shut with a single pinch.

"Umm." I look over to my cousins and try to read all their charades clues at once. "Half and half?"

Lucia squints and tilts, projecting a hairdo onto my head that only she can see. I hold my breath and stay as still as possible so as not to blur the vision.

"Okay!" she agrees, and shuffles to the cabinet to get the necessary supplies.

"Better not be tender-headed," she mutters as she comes toward me like a cowgirl in a western, each hand primed with a tool: in one, a large round brush, and in the other, a giant maroon blow-dryer with a missing switch.

Lucia turns the chair so my back faces my audience and pushes my neck down, flipping my hair forward and leaving a little in the back to rip at with her brush.

"Ah!" I cry.

She swats my hand away as it flies back to comfort my aching scalp.

"Mierda, blanquita!"

My cousins look on with sympathetic eyes as Lucia repositions my head to begin again, and I say a prayer to the powers that be that it's worth the pain.

Chapter 43

I Slept Sitting Up Last Night So As Not to Flatten My Twisty Hair Crown the Night Before My Belated Bat Mitzvah is the title of my future tell-all memoir. It's also the reason I cannot turn my neck this morning.

I carefully dress in the mirror. Ironically, the blue linen dress from Miss Clarisse is the most appropriate thing I own for this sort of affair. My mom peeks her head into the room. She wears a flowy yellow dress that makes her look like she's draped in sunflower petals.

"You are beautiful," she says, and stops to fan her watering eyes so as not to mess up her makeup.

"I love you, Mom." I hug her tight so she'll feel it in every inch of her person.

We walk down the stairs to the living room, and Jordan turns the corner into the hallway. The puffed sleeves on her purple top make her look like royalty.

"I know this is an emotional time and everything, but I need at *least* one hour if you want me to do my best work."

Peace and quiet is required while Jordan reconstructs my face in the makeshift beautician station she has set up in the living room, so I focus on Janae, who has been appointed both decorator and photographer of today's festivities. She works methodically, hanging the dozens of multicolored paper orbs she got at Party City from the ceiling. The final product provides this overwhelming sense that a huge multicolored meteor is headed straight for us.

"Masterpiece!" Jordan calls out, pleased with herself, after she places the last of the forty single lashes onto my eyelid. "Keep your eyes shut for five minutes so they can dry."

Anita rushes into the room just then.

"We have to get moving. Those old ladies are ruthless and only gave up the space for two hours."

Mom did everything she could to find a last-minute venue, but with only a couple months' notice, Mount Olivene Baptist Church ended up being the only place we could afford.

Anita drops us at the church and then goes off in search of parking. Zeke stayed behind to prepare the food for the party and put the final touches on the decorations.

The rest of the family races up the stairs of the church, but I move slowly, fighting the tremors of anxiety that rush through my body as I trudge to the top in my mom's four-inch stilettos.

"Oh, Jesus," I say to the portrait who greets me in the lobby, his arms outstretched in hospitality.

"Yeah?"

His voice comes from behind me, but I can't risk turning around and losing my balance after how long it took me to get up the stairs. Jesus kisses my neck, careful not to mess up Jordan's handiwork.

We walk into the main room, where a few people have already arrived. I see Dania and Paulina, Jordan's friends, milling around.

Mordechai from Hebrew school made it, dressed in his signature old-man attire: corduroy slacks, a bow tie, and a knit Yankees yarmulke. He sits next to Jerry, no doubt schooling him on bat mitzvah etiquette.

"My parents just got here," Jesus says. "I'm gonna sit with them, but you got this." He kisses my forehead before he goes.

"Whoa, B, you're lookin' fresh to death."

Stevie's voice bounces off the fifty-foot ceiling. He wears a slim-fit navy-blue suit with a mustard and white polka-dot top and a thin tie. Also some vintage gold sneakers. The whole look is very comfy couture, something Pharrell would throw on before grabbing a burger on the town.

He holds his hand halfway out and I meet it for three quick taps, each one coming between a word we say under our breath.

"Badgers. For. Lyfe."

Stevie joins Jordan and Janae, who have taken over the front row, reserving seats for our moms.

Rabbi Sarah searches under the podium for the microphone cord.

"Aha! Got it."

A high-pitched screech accosts us from the mic, brought to life with a jolt of electricity. Rabbi Sarah stands and brushes lint off her pants. In contrast to her usual jeans and wrinkled top, she wears a conservative but well-fitted black suit with a white tallit that hangs over her shoulders. A fancy gold silk kippah adorns her slightly frizzy dirty-blond mane, and her eyes are more frazzled and jumpy than usual.

My mom rushes into the room with two large flower arrangements that she must have assembled in the kitchen downstairs. She hurries down the aisle and almost trips when her heel catches on the carpeted floor. I hold my breath as she steadies herself.

"Look at God!" Anita and Miss Clarisse say at the exact same time from the entrance to the sanctuary, narrating the near disaster as if on cue.

The look of shock on my aunt's face as she turns to face Miss Clarisse, who is dressed like a firecracker in a pink crushed-velvet jumpsuit accented with white lace, already makes this whole experience worth it.

Darnell walks in. He tugs at the *Black Love* patch pinned to his freshly pressed shirt. A flood of shame replaces the nausea that's been coursing through me all morning, reminding me of the disappointment on his face at the BSU fund-raiser. He takes a seat behind Jordan, who sits up a little bit taller and elongates her neck for him to admire, much to Stevie's chagrin.

"All right, how you doin'?" Rabbi Sarah asks me.

I give her a hug. Her body feels small and stiff in my arms. I hope one day she'll allow herself to know what it feels like to be safe and loved. I hope that one day she finds arms she can crumble into, even if they are her own.

Rabbi Sarah squeezes my shoulders, unable to articulate her feelings, and walks to the small podium. I sit on the altar next to my grandfather, who is in his full Sunday robes. The space is huge—it could easily hold three hundred people—and until now, I've only ever seen it full. Today, about twenty-five people line the first few center rows, leaving the remainder to stand as the promise of a community I need to build for myself.

The door to the sanctuary creaks open, and Bubby, dressed in a powder blue skirt suit, enters the room. I can tell she is uncomfortable by the way she stands with her hands clutching her purse against her chest in caution. She slides into one of the farthest rows, nowhere near the rest of the makeshift congregation.

"In Jewish culture, every Friday at sundown until the following sunset, we greet each other by saying 'Shabbat shalom,' which means 'I wish you peace,'" Rabbi Sarah begins. She repeats the words.

"Shabbat shalom."

"Shabbat shalom," the small crowd replies with varying degrees of volume and enunciation.

"Well, I think it's safe to say that a bat mitzvah in a Baptist church is a first for everyone," Rabbi Sarah says, hamming up the New York accent to garner a few laughs. "But in some ways, a bat mitzvah is about firsts no matter where you are, because it is the moment that you become accountable for your own actions. As a bat mitzvah, you step into the role of a member of society who has impact. I don't know about you, but I don't think it's ever too late to realize your worth."

The crowd nods and "mmm-hmmms" the same way they do when Pa or another pastor speaks on Sunday.

"The first part of the ceremony is the aliyah."

Rabbi Sarah looks back at me with a quick wink and directs the tiny metal pointer, the yad, to the enlarged photos of Torah scripture, which have been laminated and placed in a binder for us to read from, since Jewish law dictates that the actual Torah cannot leave its sanctuary.

"Ba-ruch A-do-nai ha-m'vo-rach l'o-lahm va-ed!" Rabbi Sarah calls.

I peer at the stained-glass windows to make sure they haven't come to life at the majestic tone of her voice. Instead, the answer comes in the form of loud footsteps and a gorgeous cry that blasts out of the speakers.

"WE HEAR YOU CALLIN'!"

Shock catapults me from my chair. The Mount Olivene

Baptist choir march onto the altar in their black velvet robes wearing yarmulkes on their heads. With their magnificent voices, they welcome me to read from the sacred text of the Torah in Hebrew, along with Rabbi Sarah.

"Ba-ruch a-tah A-do-nai Eh-lo-hay-nu meh-lech ha-o-lahm, a-sher ba-char ba-nu mi-kol ha-a-meem, v'na-tahn la-nu et Torah-toh. Ba-ruch a-tah A-do-nai, no-tayn ha-Torah."

"AHHHH-MENNN!" Rabbi Sarah sings back, this time drawing Miss Clarisse out of her seat in ecclesiastical agreement.

Usually in a shul, congregants don't clap, as the sound can be interpreted as disrespect for the hallowed space. I see Mordechai squirm next to Jerry, allergic to this unconventional twist, but everyone else rises from their seats, drawn to the mashup of holy spirits and people, unable to resist the chance to bask in the joy of music and dance in this gorgeous space. The familiar church harmonies paired with the Hebrew language build a bridge between my two worlds.

"I would like to invite Nevaeh to stand for the presentation of the tallit," Rabbi Sarah says after everyone has settled down. She wipes her brow with her wrist, willing her face to drain itself of the redness brought on by the dancing and the jumping.

My mother rises in black heels sleeker and taller than the ones she lent me and is joined by Anita and Janae and Jordan.

They sprout from their seats like flowers, each one her own species, varying in style and grace and height and hue but equal in beauty. My mom slides her feet to the right like the hands of a clock and leads them all to me. Janae and Jordan unwrap a package of tissue paper. Then my mom and Anita each take an end of the shawl and hold it out.

The tallit covers my shoulders in fabric snow. It is off-white, the shimmery, satiny kind that looks like liquid metal, and so cold it could give you a chill on a lonely night. The corners are adorned with extra strips of lacy fabric that have been braided together and tied off so the ends hang in the air. I have often stared at this material in the attic from my corner, considering what it would feel like to wear something so beautiful.

My grandmother's wedding dress. From which my mother made the tallit.

The four of them stand around me, at once guards and flowers and women. Their call echoes within me, and I am overcome by the strength of these women—my family. I listen with every muscle and pore while I accept our collective magic from the inside out.

Rabbi Sarah walks over after they each give me a hug.

"Are you ready?" she whispers.

No, but who is ever ready to grow up? the little voice says in my head.

"I think I'm going to give my speech first, ya know, since we're winging it," I respond.

Rabbi Sarah shrugs, unbothered by the improvisation, and I shuffle toward the podium, barely able to feel my feet in the stilettos that I now regret ever setting eyes on in my mother's closet.

At the back of the church I hear a door open, and a shadow draws my attention. My father stands leaning against the frame, his arms crossed over his chest. He gives me a look that is neither impatient or excited. People shift in their seats, uncomfortable in the silence, so I pull my eyes away and open the last page of my notebook to the freshly dried ink.

"I first walked into this church over a decade ago for my older cousins' baptism. I was only five at the time, but I still remember it. Looking out at the congregation, I saw tiny pieces of me that I didn't know existed reflected in the eyes of everyone inside these four walls. Little glimmers of truth that I wanted to grab and hold on to and soak up. I didn't blink, because something inside told me that if I just kept looking, I would figure out what it was about this place that made me feel so alive. Eleven years later, I still walk into this church and hope to find the answer to the question I started asking myself that first day: Where do I belong?

"My Torah portion, Parashat Acharei Mot, is about how Yom Kippur, the Day of Atonement, came to be. Yom Kippur is the holiest day in the Hebrew calendar, and it couldn't be more appropriate for that to be my portion, because to truly commit to the promises that this ceremony represents, I have to be whole, and I cannot be whole until I atone.

"What is hard about apologizing is not admitting that you were wrong, but confronting what led you to make that wrong decision in the first place. I am so sorry that I failed for so long to see the boundless influence at my fingertips. I was so wrapped up in believing that I was owed some official validation that I ignored the truth: that I am a confluence of women and religions and races and leaders, which amounts to nothing short of a superpower. What I ask today is not for your forgiveness, which is something I need to earn, but a chance to show you how much better I can be.

"There are two people here today who deserve more than an apology from me, so I wanted to ask them to join me, if they would. Stevie? Darnell?"

They rise and walk forward. The room fills with sounds of shifting bodies on benches and toe taps and murmurs. Stevie positions himself behind me and Darnell bows his head to my left, as if he is here but his soul is somewhere else.

I begin.

"Here are the facts:
I live in an oppressor's skin, which isn't fun.
But also,
I can't complain because I am free of the constant degradation
  from their downturned thumbs
And the never-ending pressure of the worst assumptions,
Yet still not enough to be who, what, and where I am from.
Always left wondering: When will I be one?"

Stevie moves around the stage, translating with his body—
taking my words and making them beautiful.

"My neck breaks every time I turn it,
Searching for the answers everyone claims exist.
It's been sixteen years and I still haven't found even a gist
Or a clue,
And I started to believe that love wasn't true.
Then I started to believe that truth wasn't real and neither were
  you.
That the only thing that mattered was how I was made to feel.
I took for granted my power was more than strong; it is real.
What I know now is that privilege is a powerful drug,
Especially if you have the freedom to feel sorry for yourself.
What I know now is that sometimes, the best thing you can do
  with your voice is to listen."

Darnell's head rises, so I bow my head, to give him the floor
while Stevie continues to dance.

"Listen,
I know about pain.

But that's not what it's about, I'm not here to play games.
I'm here to make sure you put respect on my name.
And to ensure that the boy on the corner's laugh doesn't fade.
So we as people know that we are people, the same.
Here's what we are going to do:
We'll lift up from our roots,
With belief that we were each made in the most glorious hue.

"I want your eyelashes up so your vision is clear.
I want your spirits loud so the devil has no choice but to hear.
I want "future" to mean options, not a cloak of fear,
But courageous and unrelenting and undeniable.
And if you listen you might learn (because excuse the sacrilege)
But there's a bigger truth to this world than just what they put
*   in the Bible.*
And if you listen you might grow.
Because here's what I know:
If all you are worried about is what you don't own,
We will never convince them
That the life that you have and you hold
Matters."

The room explodes in cheers, and I step back so Stevie and Darnell can accept their applause. After they have returned to their seats, I walk back up to the podium.

Light streams through the empty doorway, where golden rays replace my father's image. He was never there. My mom argued that we should invite him for good karma; she claimed I might regret it if I didn't, but the people—my people—glow before me in his absence, and I know I made the right decision.

I open the binder behind my journal and point with the yad to the Hebrew words on the laminated pages to read my portion, terrified of how ugly my voice will sound. This morning, when I practiced in the mirror, the usual high-pitched dying-cat noise was accompanied by a strange gargle I had never heard before.

I close my eyes and listen in my head for the first note, and then, like divine intervention, Miss Eveline's voice echoes through the room.

"My feet are double the size they should be, burning like they got licked by the devil himself!"

The entire room turns to find the Gray Lady Gang in their relaxed Saturday clothes, which, despite the heat wave, include a silk scarf wrapped around each of their necks and sheer dress socks under their basket-weaved flats. They've arrived early, ready to begin their Bible study.

"I, uh, think we've done what we came here to do, don't you?" Rabbi Sarah takes hold of the yad and pulls the cold metal from my sweaty palm. "Mazel tov!" she sings out, drawing everyone from their seats once more to yell, "Mazel tov!" and a few "Amens!" with help from the choir.

Chapter 44

Bubby waits by the door while people congratulate me and then disperse, ready to get their party on. I walk in her direction and my mom follows, protective and worried at what her mother-in-law might say or do.

"Hi, Bubby," I say.

"That was a very . . . interesting ceremony," she says, unsure whether to be offended or intrigued.

"Aviva," my mom says, greeting her former mother-in-law with a tight-lipped, no-nonsense look.

"Corinne. You look very nice," Bubby states in an attempt to soften the mood. She rummages through her purse, unearthing an envelope, which she hands to me. *"Mazel tov."*

"Thank you." I take the card and hold it close to my chest.

"Open it," she urges.

Inside I find a thin gold chain with a small Star of David pendant.

"It was mine when I was young."

"It's beautiful, Bubby. Thank you." I grasp the cold metal tight, pushing the shape into my palm so it creates an imprint.

Bubby turns to my mom and I brace myself for a firestorm.

"Well, Corinne, it seems to me you've raised a very audacious young woman."

"Amen to that," my mom says.

Bubby looks like she has more to say. She stares at us in search of a sign or a clue as to how we proceed with any real relationship, then gives my chin a light pinch. As she turns to go, my mom stops her.

"Aviva, you are welcome to come to the party."

Bubby smiles at us, a rare thing.

"Maybe next time," she says, and leaves.

Jesus carries me to the car so I can release my toes from the torturous hell heels.

"I'm not gonna compliment you, because you hate compliments, but what I will say is you just won the House Cup and the Quidditch game, and everybody is buggin' out in the Great Hall because you also got a Nimbus 2000. You. Killed. It."

He started the Harry Potter series three weeks ago. I gave him a set to take to college, but he got an early start.

"Book three?" I ask, impressed at how quickly he's getting through it, though not surprised. J.K. is a genius, fight me.

"I don't care what anyone says, Hermione is Black," he says.

I fall more in love with him by the millisecond as he bends down to bring his lips to mine. Anita slams the door to the driver's side and we snap apart.

"I can hear what you're saying with your eyes. You all don't have to keep that act up for me," she says.

We sit in awkward silence until my mom and Jerry run toward the car, carrying what flowers and decorations they could grab before the GLG claimed everything for themselves.

A small woman with silver-gray hair in a polka-dot getup stands at the top of the church stairs, waving her cane in fury and yelling something in our direction that I can't quite make out.

"Something's not right with that short one!" my mom shouts, protecting the bouquets she worked so hard to assemble as Jerry swan-dives into the seat next to me and Anita drives off before any of the GLG can hobble over and attack.

The smell of grilled meat greets us as we walk out to the back-yard. Mrs. DeSantos hooked us up with her brother's landscaping company, and he came last week to hack through the overgrown weed forest behind the house. It took him eight hours, but he uncovered a simple ten-by-twelve-foot backyard and transformed the formerly brown patch into a serene paradise with freshly laid and cut sod and small bunches of flowers peeking out along the perimeter. Zeke decided to add a small herb and vegetable garden that he tends in the evenings after dinner, watering each plant with care and whispering his stories to his newfound rapt audience.

Geoff from Signal stands behind a table with a laptop and his phone, a last-minute DJ for the festivities.

"Oh my G—"

Janae clamps her hand over my mouth. "Not a word," she cautions.

"Nevaeh!"

Zeke walks over from the grill, freeing Janae to join her boo. He carries a platter of sausages and cheeseburgers.

"Take that second cheeseburger in the front. It's the best one."

I take a bite and salty meat juice trails down my chin and wrists, narrowly missing my dress as it drips to the ground.

"Mmm, thank you for cooking."

"Of course, lil' one. I'm so proud of you. Sorry to miss your service, but you know I'm always here for you."

He hustles back to the grill, where sausage grease pops and sizzles and makes the air taste like fennel and crushed red pepper.

"Thriller" comes on, and Geoff's Beatles-style mop-top bounces over his forehead as he whips his body around to Janae's delight.

"They've been sneaking around for weeks," Jordan says. "She had me cover for her last Thursday so she could go to some basement rave."

I jump. She settled so perfectly into Janae's absence that I didn't even realize she was there.

I follow her gaze to the other side of the backyard, where Stevie has Dania and Paulina captivated with a story. Jordan tenses up as she watches them, unaccustomed to seeing Stevie's attention directed elsewhere.

"I've got to get more water," she says to me as she walks to a cooler conveniently located past Stevie.

My mom sits on a small bench we found in the attic and brought down for extra seating. She watches the balloons and people sway in an attempt to inspire a breeze.

"You were right," I say, taking a seat next to her. "This is great."

Her lips are pinched together and she squints, nodding in agreement and holding in her thoughts so as not to ruin this happy day.

It isn't all happy—new beginnings never are—so I take my hand and put it on top of hers and let her feel the weight of my body to tell her she isn't alone.

After a while, Rabbi Sarah marches up to us.

"All right, you might've rewritten the book on bat mitzvah ceremonies, but you're not gettin' out of the hora!" She tugs me off the bench as the familiar sound of "Hava Nagila" streams out of the speaker.

I look back at my mom, worried to leave her in her fragile state.

"You go," she assures me with a less-than-convincing smile.

"Come with me," I beg, and hold out my hand, until she reluctantly gets up and takes it.

Rabbi Sarah grabs a chair and marches us to the center of the yard, where Mordechai is enthusiastically arranging people in a circle. She plops a chair next to the wooden one already waiting for me.

"All right, we're doing double duty here. Spread out the strength," she commands as my mom takes a seat.

Zeke, Jesus, and Darnell and Mr. DeSantos, Stevie, and Geoff break into two teams and bend to lift the chairs' legs and thrust us into the air. Mordechai demonstrates the dance to the people on the ground, and after some test runs, Rabbi Sarah tells everyone to grab hands and follow her. They circle us, weaving in and out and raising their arms up and down like a human carousel. My mom sits still on her chair with her eyes squeezed shut and her breath held.

She's missing it. We're flying, and she's missing it, the voice inside me says.

If there is one thing I've learned, it is that you only receive what you are open to, and you are only open to what you believe you deserve.

After everything she's been through, my mother deserves to fly.

"Mom!"

I lean toward her, accidentally throwing my chair off balance, and begin to slip. Anita's shriek makes my mom's eyes pop open to see me next to her, falling. She reaches out to clasp my arm, but before I'm halfway off the seat, Zeke catches me and slides me back into place.

With one arm gripping the chair and the other holding on to each other, my mother and I fly up one more time, together, with our eyes open, to catch a glimpse of the magnitude of what awaits.

Chapter 45

When the last piece of garbage has been picked up and the last dish has been cleaned and the final colorful orb has been pulled from the living room ceiling and crushed into a tiny ball of tissue paper, we sit.

My mom went to bed hours ago. She tried to allow herself to enjoy the party, but the hours ticked on, and as each one passed, the permanence of our new life settled in, so she left to lie down and think and cry a little and sleep and wake up, new.

Rabbi Sarah left early too. It was right in the middle of all the commotion, when Stevie was performing his best Britney Spears imitation. She waved at me across the crowd, but by the time I made it through the people and the hugs, she was gone.

All she has ever known is people coming and going, so I guess it's easier to skip the goodbye. This way, if we ever run into each other, we can just pick up where we left off. When we do, I'll tell her that in my story, it was a woman who was the superhero who saved my life.

Anita walks into the living room in her bathrobe.

"I'm going to my room to put on a Korean face mask and watch *Rocky*. I don't wanna hear from any of you until the morning." She turns to Stevie. "You are sleeping down here. I know every creak, every sound. I know every trick in this house. Do you understand me?" she asks in a way that isn't a question at all.

"Y-yes," he stutters, shifting nervously on his butt.

"The air mattress is somewhere in that closet at the top of the stairs. Take a flashlight," she says with a flip of her wrist before she disappears up the steps with her robe fluttering behind her.

"I'll go," I say.

"I think I know where it is." Janae follows me.

"I need to grab a hammer to fix my desk drawer," Jordan announces.

"Bet. I'll help you carry it all down," Jesus says.

Stevie stays on the couch, unsure where he fits in all of this.

"You better come on," I say. "Someone has to hold the flashlight."

We climb up the stairs to the very top and open the closet door. It is one of those closets that is filled with the loose ends and random items that end up in a house after a lifetime.

Stevie squeezes his skinny frame inside and begins to hand us items one by one.

"Damn, B, what's this ladder? Whoa! You didn't tell me you have roof access!"

"What?" my cousins and I ask, peering in with the light.

"Most of these old brownstones do. You've never been up there?" Jesus asks.

"Shine the light higher," Stevie calls from some secret universe we didn't know existed.

He climbs up the ladder and opens the rusty hatch.

"Come on!" he shouts.

The evening is warm and sticky, but the silver paint covering the rubber roof membrane is cool on our feet, and we each take a seat to watch the sunset.

I pat the twists on my head to relieve the strain from the restricted blood flow. They itch like crazy but have shown zero signs of loosening. Lucia really doesn't play when it comes to hair. Jesus pulls me toward him and begins to take the bobby pins out, one by one, undoing my hair crown. When the twists are freed from their structure, he carefully removes the tiny black rubber bands that secure them to my scalp and releases my hair.

"When we moved here a year ago, I really thought I knew what the rest of my life was going to look like," I say. The thought comes out of my mouth as quickly as it pops into my head.

"And you wish you could go back to that?" Jordan challenges.

The sunset turns from pink to orange, shifting colors on colors like scales on a mermaid's tail catching the light.

"Of course not!" I sit up and look her right in the eye.

Jordan's eyebrow remains raised, and her arms are crossed over her chest like she's a Wakandan warrior—always a little skeptical of me, but I don't blame her.

Jesus frees the last twist from my scalp and runs his fingers through the brittle gel that clings to my curls.

"I just have no clue what's going to happen now," I say, pushing past my instinct to keep my thoughts to myself.

"None of us do," Jesus says as he grabs at the spot on his neck where he was assaulted several months ago. "How can I be worried about the future? There's no guarantee I'm going to make it long enough to see what that is."

Cars and block parties and a train pulling out of the Metro

North station just a couple avenues away fight to silence the truth that he and my cousins face every day. The deflection is no match for our reality, and it hits us all with a gut punch, because in this moment, right now, there is nothing we can do about it. The hopelessness burns more than anything else.

Just a year ago, I was hiding. Hidden. Convinced I wasn't a real person, just a mashup of thoughts and truths I didn't believe I deserved to own. Now there is so much more for me to learn and grow into and feel, and to be honest, I've barely brought myself up to speed, but it is there: a world, a life, most importantly, a voice. A challenge to try and fail and fight. A challenge that I accept.

I look at my family and I see the strength and the hope and the joy that they represent. We make the world turn, and I don't know how I ever lived at all before I knew that to be true from the tips of my fingers deep down to my soul.

"Everyone stand up," I command, and rise to my feet, wiping the layer of soot from my hands to face reluctant stares.

"Nuh-uh, we're not doing that kumbaya group-hug mess," Janae protests. "It's corny and makes me uncomfortable."

I roll my eyes.

"No physical contact required."

Stevie is the first to stand, then Jesus, then finally Janae and Jordan (though I'm sure Jordan would claim that she stood first and left Janae no choice but to follow suit).

I spread everyone out, forming a slightly staggered line.

"Okay, this is going to feel dumb, and maybe it is, but it will make you feel better, and that has to count for something," I say. "Just do what I do: one, two, three!"

I go first and then, as a human chain, they follow.

Our arms stretch out and we open our mouths to release the

negative toxins into the abyss in a shrill, unified roar. The hurt flies out of our bodies and disintegrates into the air: a momentary relief. A gift.

We scream until there is no air left in our lungs and we have to stop and regenerate by sucking in the power from the plump orange sky.

As if summoned by sorcery, the clouds crack open and send sheets of rain that soak us on contact, breaking the weeklong heat wave and drowning out our cries. Kids laugh on the sidewalk below thrilled to avoid a normal shower courtesy of the cosmos. Cars honk long and loud, as if their horns hold any influence against the heavens. On the rooftop, everyone runs around, gathering their phones and shoes and trying to cover their hair and bodies with their arms. The hatch to the attic opens and they get in line, eager to head inside.

"Nevaeh? Come on!" Janae yells, her head barely visible from halfway down the ladder.

"I'll be right there," I call back.

Jordan and Stevie follow, hopping from one foot to the next as if the movement might trick the rain and keep them from getting soaked.

"Babe?"

Jesus stands at the opening, torn between the shelter that calls to him and the concern that he shouldn't leave me alone on a roof in a downpour.

"I'm good, go on." I nod, but he hesitates, unsure if this is some unspoken girlfriend test. "I'll meet you down there in a minute," I assure him.

The rubber soles of his sneakers squeak against the metal ladder as he climbs down, watching me as he goes, until he can't anymore.

Alone, I look up to find that the orange expanse is undiluted despite the clouds. Instead, hues of fire and candy corn deepen with each second that passes, so I stay for one more moment in solidarity with the sky. Tears slide down my cheeks in mascara streams that I drink, salty and unavoidable and mine.

As small puddles begin to collect, I root my feet to the ground, solid and ready to start anew.

> *And I throw my arms out,*
> *And I scream so they can hear me,*
> *And I match the wind and the rain in their fervor,*
> *And I stand on the other side of the shadows,*
> *And I refuse to be washed away.*

Dear You,

Color Me In is the book of my heart. I based this novel on my real life, even though I have written the story as fiction, but these elements are totally true: I am a multiracial woman who inadvertently passes as white; I had a bat mitzvah—my heritage is Liberian and Brazilian as much as it is Jewish; I am from the New York City area; and I have a wonderful, loud, blended, multicultural family.

My parents separated when I was four years old. Judges in divorce cases usually gave custody to the mother back then, unless there was an obvious threat of danger to the child, so I lived with my mom. My father wanted to be involved in my upbringing, and as a result, my parents' divorce papers stated that I was legally required to be raised Jewish. My father is ethnically almost 100 percent Jewish, but he has never been religious, so when I got a little older and he told me that I had to start attending Hebrew school, I was furious. Not because I had anything against Judaism, but you see, I mostly grew up around my mom's Black Baptist family, where I was the different one because I looked white and had a different last name, and now I could not be baptized in my grandfather's church like everyone else.

All I wanted was to be more like my mom's family, but my father's attempt to be in my life made me even more different.

So I pushed back against my Jewishness every step of the way, barely engaging in Hebrew school and being even less cooperative when it came time for my bat mitzvah preparation with a rabbi. I went through with it, because I had no other option. But in terms of the engagement necessary to properly "come of age" and understand the true meaning of the Ten Commandments and the obligations of the mitzvahs, I definitely fell below the mark. The bat mitzvah itself ended up being fine (albeit unconventional, considering the majority of the audience were my mom's family members and therefore not Jewish), and then it was over. I actually blocked the whole experience and tucked it into some far corner of my brain where I genuinely forgot it ever happened, as if this monumental spiritual experience were just a blip or hiccup on my lifeline.

When I decided to write about the multiracial, white-passing perspective, I was flooded with memories of this time in my life when I was actively fighting against who I was. As strongly as I believe that individuals should be allowed to choose their religious practices, I wish I had taken advantage of the experience of being a bat mitzvah. It was an opportunity to immerse myself in a culture that comprises half of my DNA, and as such, it was an opportunity to find a connection to the Jewish community I hadn't felt was mine. Writing this book was my opportunity to engage with Judaism as not just a religion or lifestyle, but as my people. It was a chance to claim this part of my heritage as my own.

I have always had a deep connection to my Brazilian and my Black, Liberian heritage. Both are also aspects of my identity for which I have zero visual claim.

Like Nevaeh, I was young when I realized just how different I was: people at the playground continually asked my mom how long she had been my nanny, as I was a little white girl with a Black lady. When I was older, I was stopped and questioned by the police while walking down the street with my stepfather, a

Black man, because they wanted to be sure he wasn't hurting me. I have seen family members and friends who are darker-skinned harassed by cops on the street. And one time, the cops showed up at my grandmother's house and made my whole family watch surveillance footage of an armed robbery—they thought my uncle was involved because he was a Black kid in a "good" neighborhood in Westchester, even though he didn't look remotely like either of the perpetrators.

As I got older, I continued to find myself ever aware of active racism and prejudice, but it bypassed me because I was white. Instead, it was directed at the people around me. I quickly came to realize that my identity as a multiracial woman is inherently tied to my white privilege.

Now, as an adult, the shame and guilt I feel for unintentionally benefitting from my white appearance is what ultimately motivates me to never stop trying to dismantle the system of white supremacy that creates an unfair and illogical advantage.

I wrote this book because I wanted to talk about the uniquely complicated world of biracial and multiracial identity, but the only way for me to do so authentically was to also shine a light on the colorism that benefits those of us who are light-skinned or white-presenting. I wanted to talk about how these ingrained privileges negatively affect communities of color. I wanted to talk about how it is possible for someone who is a legitimate member of these communities to be willfully ignorant to the damage they are causing by remaining silent. If a person is not actively fighting against oppressive white supremacist systems that hurt and hinder communities of color, specifically Black communities, then he or she is complicit in them.

I can't change how I was born, just as much as my family

members can't change how they were born. I was born the way I am, and as such, I have the opportunity and the choice to speak out with more safety (and possibly more impact) because I look white.

My hope is that reading *Color Me In* encourages all readers to initiate or partake in difficult conversations. I hope you will be emboldened to shut down a joke about any group or stand up for a stranger being harassed. And if you are white-presenting, I hope you will make the choice to step out of the spotlight to make space for someone who may not otherwise have a chance to shine, because sometimes it's better to accept that you don't have the right to speak on everything, even if the opportunity to do so presents itself.

My deepest hope is that anyone who has felt confined to the "other" box feels empowered to take ownership of their identity in as many ways that feel necessary. I believe that you have every right to be who you are, and that no one can take that from you. No matter the color of your skin or your religious affiliations, be who you are. Our society needs you and your unique perspective, now more than ever.

I write this with love, admiration, and an unwavering hope that this world can be equitable and safe for us all.

Natasha Díaz

for reading through uncorrected drafts and giving me the most thoughtful and helpful feedback. You were the doulas to my book birth, and I can't properly articulate how useful and necessary your support was to this process.

To the Las Musas, muito obrigado eu agredeço mais do que você sabe.

Real talk: good teachers can change your life. I'd like to thank my teachers at the Beacon School. Specifically, Mr. Lehmann, Ms. Binder, Ms. Matthews, Ms. Radin, Lublin, Bay-bay, Mr. McKenna, Geoff, Mr. Streep, and Mr. Miller. My high school years remain the time in my life when I felt most comfortable in myself. Thank you for prioritizing an educational environment that allowed students to strive far beyond the confines of what the public education system dictates. Thank you for recognizing that the best way to educate young people is by putting an emphasis on their individual strengths and encouraging us to think outside the box.

To my husband, Matthew, who wakes me every morning with whispers of support and lulls me to sleep every night with the hum of unadulterated love, I thank you. Without your unwavering belief in me, I might have never had the courage to turn this book-shaped hole in my heart into *Color Me In*. Te amo mucho y siempre, mi amor.

And last, to Black and Brown women, the people who made me and raised me: thank you for your strength, your laughter, your sisterhood, your wisdom, your strength, your beauty, your tenacity, your resourcefulness, your power, your sense of self, your unyielding ability to press on with grace . . . aka your strength. I see you, and I will continue to fight for you.

With love and thanks,
Natasha

About the Author

NATASHA DÍAZ is a freelance writer and producer. As a screenwriter, Natasha was a quarterfinalist in the Austin Film Festival and a finalist for both the NALIP Diverse Women in Media Fellowship and the Sundance Episodic Story Lab. Her personal essays have been published on *The Establishment* and *HuffPost*. *Color Me In* is her debut young adult novel. Originally from New York City, Natasha now lives in Oakland, California.

© Christine Chambers

Acknowledgments

Welp, writing the book was hard, but WOW, this is where it gets real. Thanks for sticking with me up until this point . . . let's do this.

Get you some incredible managers like mines. Jermaine and Richard, from the moment we began to work together, you have been nothing but bright shining lights of support and enthusiasm for this loud, NYC broad, and I couldn't have made it here without you. BIG PROPS TO SOPHIE AND RACHEL FOR FIELDING MY MILLIONS OF EMAILS—y'all truly make the world go round.

Beverly, I will never be able to thank you enough for taking a chance on me. You simultaneously gave me the space and the encouragement necessary to dig deep and tell this story of my heart the way I was supposed to. I feel so blessed to have you as the conductor behind the symphony that is the mind of Nevaeh Levitz.

Huge thanks to Colleen, Trish, Shameiza, and Tamar for making *Color Me In* look and sound better than I imagined it in my head. Rebecca, you are an angel—thank you for being so patient with my constant questions and check-ins. I love you, Delacorte Press. I really, really do.

To Regina and Bijou, you turned this world into a piece of art. I cannot thank you enough for your talented mind's eye. This cover is a masterpiece, and I adore it with every inch of my being.

Mom, thanks for reading each iteration of this novel, including the dreadful first draft. I feel so proud to have created a book that I know you truly, deeply love and support. It is perhaps my biggest accomplishment.

Dad, thanks for injecting poetry into my bloodstream. Without your DNA, this book would be missing its heartbeat.

To my beautiful blended family, Blonnie, Naomi, Noah, Nia, Bonita, David, Simone, Kaylah, (Baby) David, Lourdes, Jonathan, Alistaire, and Jaspar, I am so proud to be related to you and to share the richness that is us through stories inspired by our lives.

As an only child, my friends are also my family, and I am fortunate enough to say that there are a lot of you. So many that I am not sure I have the space to thank you each individually, but special shout-outs to my ILC loves, my Beacon '05 high school loves, and my Wesleyan loves. Your friendships are what keep me going. Thanks for sticking around as long as you have. Please don't ever leave me.

To Iluminada, Denis, Lusmaia, Dania, and the whole Díaz family, thank you for trusting me with your history. Sharing the surname Díaz with you is an honor and a privilege.

To my sister-in-law, Carla, thanks for getting it and reminding me that the words would flow again, even when they felt gone forever.

To my in-laws, Karen and Armand, and stepmom, Uta, thanks for being such enthusiastic cheerleaders!

To Rabbi Lisa Rappaport, thank you so much for your input. Your insight and advice were my guiding lights as I wrote this book. (Thank you to my cousin Debbie for the connection!)

To my generous and kind beta readers, I owe you the world. Satya, I cannot wait to offer you and your words the same support you gave to me and mine. Your writing is a gift, and the world ain't ready for you! Sacha and Nicki and Julie, thank you so much